Clara's Story

Clara's Story

A Holocaust Biography

by Gill James

Chapeltown Books

British Library Cataloguing in Publication Data

A Record of this Publication is available from the British Library

ISBN 978-1-910542-33-0

This edition published 2018 by Chapeltown Books
Manchester, England

All Chapeltown books are published on paper derived
from sustainable resources.

Contents

8 October 1918, Berlin: The end of a phase

Clara shuddered. It was one of those strange uncontrollable little movements. Her mother used to say it meant someone was walking over your grave. What did that mean, actually though? They were walking over where you were going to be buried? How would you know now? It was nonsense really but she had no better or even any other explanation for it. It wasn't as if it was cold in the kitchen: the Kackelofen was lit and the sun was streaming through the window.

She put the rest of yesterday's birthday cake away. Ernst had insisted she should celebrate her birthday despite his illness. She'd baked one of her special cheesecakes but nobody had had much appetite for it. It would keep a few days, she guessed. Perhaps when he was feeling better they would all appreciate it more.

She looked at the clock. He should have called for his tea by now. It was half an hour past the normal time. She'd looked in on him earlier. He'd been sound asleep. Doctor Friedrich had said it was good to let him sleep. Perhaps she should go and look in on him again.

The doctor hadn't really given a clear diagnosis. "It's a combination of things, Frau Lehrs," he'd said. "His worry about this war has weakened him. The rickets has got worse. And now this chest infection…"

"That shouldn't kill a man, though, should it, Herr Doctor? He will recover won't he?"

"I'm afraid I can't say. He's still quite young but you know this terrible war has taken its toll. It's made men even younger than him want to give up. I'm sorry I can't give you any better news."

Damn men and their wars. Clara made her way towards her husband's room. So many men killed on both sides and so many left with half-lives. And now they were all so poor. It wasn't so bad for them as for some of the people who worked in Ernst's factory. But they had had to cut Imelda's hours in order to pay for the nurse.

The door to Ernst's room was flung open. Schwester Adelberg rushed out. "Frau Lehrs, you must come quickly," she cried.

Clara hurried into the bedroom.

Ernst's breathing was laboured. His chest was rattling.

"Should we send for the doctor?" said Clara. But she could tell from the look on the nurse's face that it was too late.

"You must say your goodbyes," Schwester Adelberg whispered guiding her gently towards the bed.

Clara knelt down beside her husband and put her face next to his. She took his hand. He was trying to speak but she couldn't make out what he was saying. Yellow bile streamed from his nose and seeped from the corners of his mouth and his eyes. He tried to push the sheets and blankets away.

"Does he have a fever?"

"It's the blood rushing to his vital organs, trying to save them. His lungs are filling. That sound you hear is them working to expel the fluid but it has gone too far now."

"Is – is he in pain?"

"He's probably not comfortable and he's very likely afraid and lonely. Talk to him."

"Ernst – Ernst, my love. Don't leave me yet. It's too soon."

Schwester Adelberg touched her shoulder. "There's nothing more we can do," she whispered. "Try to comfort him."

Clara stroked his arm. "I'm here my darling. It will be all right. Sleep gently. You'll soon have no more pain."

He looked at once like a child and a man forty years older. Her father had not looked this frail when he'd died. Ernst's poor body was a twisted wreck. But it had been like that all of his life and he'd done so much despite his disability. She stroked his hair.

He relaxed a little. He took one final breath and the rattle in his chest stopped. His faced changed and he looked peaceful. Yet at the same time he looked like a piece of paper. His lips and cheeks were grey. Yes, the life had gone out of him. That wasn't her Ernst anymore. Even so she leant over and kissed his forehead. "Goodbye, sweetheart," she whispered.

She knelt for a few more minutes holding his hand and then she stood up. "We'd better get the doctor here to sign a death certificate," she said.

"I'm happy to stay and lay him out properly after the doctor's visit," said Schwester Adelberg.

"Thank you."

"And would you like me to help with the arrangements?"

"That would be very kind. Now, I'd better go and let the children know."

As Clara made her way down the stairs she realised that another phase of her life had ended.

15 July 1883, Mecklenburg: Sunday best

Clara looked out of the drawing-room window to the street below. They were there again, the same as every Sunday. The three little girls looked so pretty in their summer dresses. The older girl – Clara guessed she must be the same age as herself – and the two boys who looked like her own older brothers, Wilhelm and Rupert, were walking behind them, making sure that the little ones kept up with the rest. There were three younger boys who walked right behind the parents.

"They're exactly like us," said Clara.

"Except that they're not," said Wilhelm. "They're Christians and we're Jews."

"What difference does that make?" asked Clara.

Rupert sighed. "A lot, Clarachen."

"Don't call me that. I'm nearly twelve and then I shall be a grown-up."

Rupert tutted. "Well grow up then. They're on their way home from church. They go to church on Sunday and we go to the synagogue on Saturday. They have a day of rest on Sunday and we have ours on Saturday."

"But they dress like us and I expect they eat the same food. I expect their mama is as nice as ours. And there are nine of them, like there are nine of us. We could each have a friend."

Mama put down her sewing. "They might not want to be friends with us."

"Why ever not?"

Mama and Papa exchanged a glance. Papa nodded. "She's right. She will be grown-up soon."

"All right. Come with me, you big girl, you." Mama stood up and slipped her arm around Clara's waist. "You can help me make some tea and I'll explain it all to you."

As they set off down the stairs Mama whispered, "I didn't want the little ones to hear this yet."

They heard a scream from outside and then a child howling.

Clara knew it was one of the little girls. She ran down the stairs and opened the front door.

Yes, there was one of them lying on the ground, screaming. Blood was streaming from cuts on her head and her leg. The mother and an older girl, about the same age as Clara, were bending down trying to comfort her. The others were looking on helplessly.

"Oh, Mama, we must help her," said Clara. She rushed over to the family. "Will you come inside? We can bathe her leg and her head."

The two mamas exchanged a look.

"Please," said Clara. "She can't walk home like that."

The Christian lady looked at her husband.

"It's true," he said. "Perhaps you should stay here with her. I'll take the others home and come back with the carriage." He turned to Mama and Clara. "This is so very kind of you," he said.

"I am Frau Hellerman," said the lady, "and this is my daughter, Lotte, and her sister, Melissa."

"Frau Loewenthal. Clara." Mama was already helping Frau Hellerman to get Lotte on to her feet. "Come on young lady. We'll soon get you sorted out."

Lotte managed to limp into the kitchen and Mama lifted her up on to a stool. She filled a bowl with warm water. She gently dabbed the wounds on the little girl's knee and forehead. "I hope it's not stinging too much."

Lotte shook her head. "I've spoilt my dress, though."

"She should put some salt on it, shouldn't she?" said Clara. "Won't it stop it staining?"

Mama nodded. Clara fetched the krug and sprinkled salt on the stains.

"You see," whispered Frau Hellerman. "Frau Loewenthal and Clara are taking good care of you."

A few moments later Lotte was completely cleaned up.

"Would you like some tea?" said Mama. "Clara and I were about to make some. And Lotte, I think we might find some lemonade for you."

Lotte smiled.

The door opened. Papa walked in. "There you are. And I see we have some visitors."

Mama did the introductions.

"You have all been so kind," said Frau Hellerman.

Clara helped Lotte hobble up into the lounge. Käthe brought one of her dolls for her to play with while they waited for Herr Hellerman.

"This really is kind of you," said Frau Hellerman. "I'm sure my husband won't be long. I'm so glad – well I'm so glad the law is on your side now."

"Yes, it is easier these days," said Mama.

Clara wished she understood. Lotte and Käthe looked so similar and were obviously enjoying playing together.

"Ah. It looks as if your husband has arrived," said Papa. "I'll go and greet him."

"Can Käthe and I be friends?" Lotte kissed the doll and handed it back to Käthe.

Mama and Frau Herllerman exchanged a glance. Mama nodded. "You are welcome in our home any time, my dear."

"Come, let us find Papa," said Frau Hellerman. She smiled at Clara and Mama. "I'm so glad you've found a new friend."

"What did Frau Hellerman mean about the law being on our side now?" Clara asked Wilhelm later.

"It's not always been easy for Jews," her brother replied. "A lot of people don't like us. But now the law says we have to be treated like any other citizen."

This was so difficult to understand. They were like everybody else, weren't they? So why did they need a law to make them the same as everyone else?

"Is it because we don't believe Jesus of Nazareth was the Messiah? Is that why people don't like us?"

Wilhelm laughed. "It's not that simple, actually. You'll understand one day. Listen. You're in the first stage of your life. Enjoy it and don't worry so much." He turned and left the room.

It was so annoying. Why did they all treat her like a child? She was almost twelve and would have to pin her hair up soon.

Hanukah 1891, Mecklenburg: a phase begins

"My, that all looks fine," said Mama. "You girls have done well. I'm sure Papa's associates will be impressed."

Clara smiled to herself. Yes, they had worked hard and the drawing-room sparkled. The candlelight reflected backwards and forwards in the mirrors. It was getting dark outside and the warm glow defied the winter gloom.

Käthe giggled. "Do you think Clara will find a beau?"

Clara glowered at her younger sister. "Enough, young lady. Any more of that and I won't pin your hair up for you, nor lend you the peach silk."

"Really, Käthe, you mustn't tease you sister like that." Lotte spoke quietly as usual. Her fine blonde hair was already neatly pinned up and she looked much older than her fourteen years. Thank goodness, though, there was a smile in her deep blue eyes.

"I'm glad you've got a friend who is sensible," said Clara.

"Well, it's about time," said Käthe.

"Clara will find someone to love when she is good and ready," said Mama. It was obvious she was trying not to laugh.

The doorbell rang.

"Ah, that's the first of them here. Girls, go and get ready. Then you'll be in time to greet them all at supper after they've finished their business meeting.

"How do you manage to get your hair to stay so neat all of the time?" Clara asked Lotte. "It's so fine. Our hair is much sturdier. Yet we can't get it to stay put."

"I guess it's because I keep practising," Lotte replied. "I pin it up every day now."

Clara hugged the younger girl. "Don't be in too much of a hurry to grow up. Enjoy being young."

She moved back to her sister whose hair was only half done. "I do wish I could get your hair to behave," she said as she tried to brush the knots out. "What do you do to it?"

The doorbell rang again. Käthe jumped up from her seat and ran over to the window. She peered through the drapes. "Goodness, look at that funny man," she said. "He's all bent."

"Käthe!" said Clara. "It's rude to stare at people less fortunate than ourselves." She couldn't help looking herself, though. Four more young men had arrived. One of them was walking up the path with a limp. She could see that although he was quite young he had a huge hump on his back and his legs were bowed. It made him look much shorter than the others.

"Come on, then," said Käthe, rushing back to her seat. "Let's finish getting ready and get downstairs to meet them. Some of them look quite handsome."

Lotte sighed and raised her eyebrows.

One hour later they were downstairs. The noise of people talking came from the drawing-room. Clara opened the door and could see straight away that all her other brothers and sisters were there already as well as about ten of her father's business associates. Papa was talking to the young man with the deformed back. He signalled to Clara that they should join him.

"Doctor Lehrs," he said. May I present my daughters, Clara and Käthe, and their friend, Lotte. Ladies, this is my very good associate, Ernst Lehrs."

Two smiling brown eyes looked into Clara's and she knew that the second phase of her life had begun.

22 July 1899, The Black Forest: crucifix

Clara took a deep breath. She didn't think she would be sick but she couldn't be sure. She'd felt like this before – with both Leo and Käthe and all the miscarriages. She'd never actually been sick. There was this constant nausea. She needed to have some taste in her mouth all of the time.

She was fairly certain she was expecting another child. She'd missed her monthly bleeding twice and her breasts had become tender. And yet again, she couldn't drink tea or coffee.

She hadn't said anything to Ernst. She didn't want him to get his hopes up. She would wait another couple of months at least. And she ought to get out of this heat. If there was a baby it surely wouldn't be good for him or her.

Where, though? It was too far to walk back to the hotel. The sun would be beating down upon them all the way. All the cafés looked full.

There was a church on the opposite side of the square. It looked quite pretty from the outside and she could see that the front door was open.

"Come on," she said. "Let's go and have a look inside." She took Leo's hand.

"I thought we didn't go to church," said Leo. "I thought we only went to the synagogue."

"We're not going to pray. We're only going to have a look at the fine building and the lovely pictures and stained glass windows. It's a Saturday so there won't be a service going on."

"So why don't we go to the synagogue?"

"Because we're on holiday."

Ernst had thought about going but then had thought better of it. The nearest one was in the next town, some fifteen kilometres away. He'd decided to stay at the hotel and read. Then he would be there when Käthe woke up from her nap and maybe he and the nanny would set out to meet Clara and Leo.

It was gloomy inside the church. The colours on the windows

were quite dark and the sunshine had been so bright outside. But Clara's eyes soon adjusted and she became aware of the way the light streamed through the windows and created interesting patterns on the floor and the walls. "Isn't it lovely?" she whispered. One or two people were praying. They'd better not speak too loudly.

Leo nodded. "They're like fairy-angels," he said.

She couldn't think where he'd got the idea of fairies or angels from, but she knew what he meant.

He gripped her hand more tightly, screamed loudly and buried his head in her dress. He sobbed uncontrollably.

"What is it? What's the matter?" She tried to push him away from her so that she could look at him. People were beginning to stare. But he clung on to her all the more tightly. She held him close until the sobbing stopped. Fortunately he had his head buried so deeply into her clothing that he probably couldn't be heard. Then she felt him relax. "What's the matter?" she asked.

He turned away from her and pointed at the huge wooden cross with a life-size representation of Jesus Christ on it. The figure was well-carved, though the face was ugly. Blood appeared to trickle from beneath the crown of thorns and four huge nails pierced the man's hands and feet.

"Come on. Let's go," said Clara. "Perhaps we can find an ice-cream on the way back. As long as you promise you'll eat all of your lunch." What were these Christians thinking of, making such a display as that?

As they left the church she held his hand tightly and she could feel that he was still trembling. He hiccoughed every now and then as if he was still crying but didn't want to show it.

As soon as they were out in the sunshine a fresh wave of nausea hit her. She felt dizzy. "I think I'm going to be sick," she whispered to Leo. "I'm sorry darling." She quickly walked to the side of the church and found a convenient bush behind which she vomited.

"Mutti," whimpered Leo, holding on to her skirts.

A kind lady and gentleman fetched her a glass of water and offered to take her back to the hotel in their carriage. She nodded her agreement.

17

"Mutti, what's the matter? Are you poorly?"

"No, I'm fine, sweetheart. I think you're going to have a new brother or sister soon. This happens to ladies sometimes when they're going to have a baby."

Leo smiled through his tears. At least he seemed to have forgotten the horror of the crucifix. That was something.

"You should have told me," said Ernst later after the excitements of the day were over, the children were in bed and the nanny was off duty.

"I didn't want to get your hopes up again."

Ernst tutted. "But if it's making you unwell I need to know. And if you do have another miscarriage I want to be there to help you through it." He kissed her softly on the head.

She remembered the incident with the carving. "There's something else as well. Leo was so frightened inside the church."

"Oh?"

She told Ernst all about how he had reacted to the representation of the crucifixion.

"If it was that life-like he probably thought he was looking at a real body. Or a person still alive who was being horribly tortured. I shouldn't worry. He'll get over it. He's pleased anyway about the baby. And so – he's hoping for a brother."

They both laughed when they remembered what he'd said. "I hope it's a boy. Käthe's no good for playing with."

Clara had a feeling that this baby might be all right after all.

14 March 1900, Berlin: trams

"We've been learning about Berlin today at school," said Leo. "Our teacher said there are lots of interesting buildings in Berlin."

"She did, did she?" said Clara. "And do you think she's right?"

Leo shrugged. "Berlin is Berlin," he said.

"Oh it is, is it?" Clara could not believe that her son was so blinkered. This big vibrant city still fascinated her. Mecklenburg was big by some standards but Berlin. Berlin was Berlin. Leo was right there. But Berlin was a miracle and he couldn't see that?

Clara looked at the clock. It was not quite four. It would be light for a while yet. Imelda was busy in the kitchen. Käthe was still asleep. She could ask the maid to keep an eye on the child. They could be back in time for supper.

"Go to the lavatory and don't forget to wash your hands," she said to her son. "I'm just going to have a word with Imelda. Get your coat on. We're going out."

"Mutti?"

"Go on. Do as I say," said Clara.

"Frau Lehrs, I'm very busy today," said Imelda. "I don't know that I'll have time."

"Look, we won't be long. Fräulein Lehrs is still asleep. Rudi's out with Nanny. Just look on her now and then. And if she wakes up, she'll probably come and find you anyway."

"Yes, ma'am. It's just that…"

"Yes. I know. She can be difficult. Look, we'll give you a bonus this week. And you can have an extra hour off on Sunday. Will that do?"

"Yes, ma'am. Very well, ma'am."

It was clear that the young woman would do anything for more cash. Well, good. Käthe would be fine. She liked Imelda. And so what if supper was a bit late. Ernst wouldn't mind. Not if his son was being educated properly.

"Why are we going out?" asked Leo.

"We're going on an adventure," said Clara. "And how would you like to go on one of the new electric trams? We're going to ride the tram. We are from another planet and we've just arrived on Earth. And we're going to see this beautiful city called Berlin."

Leo clapped his hands. He had never been on a tram before. He walked to school. They walked to most places in fact but if they ever needed to go further afield Ernst would hire a carriage. Clara felt as excited as their little boy looked. She pulled her cloak over her shoulders and they were off.

It was a short walk to the Kurfürstendamm and there was already a tram at the nearest stop.

"Here we go then," said Clara, holding Leo's hand as they both climbed on.

"We want to go to the terminus," said Clara as the conductor came for the fare. "Return, please."

The young man nodded and gave Clara two tickets. A middle-aged man gave her his seat and Clara sat down, pulling Leo on to her lap.

The first thing she noticed was the smell. Unwashed bodies, she suspected.

"Mutti, what's that funny sm—?" Leo began to say.

"Look," said Clara, distracting him. She pointed to a tram going the other way. "Isn't it amazing that these carriages go on their own with no horse to pull them? And do you know what makes them work?"

"Lectricy," said Leo.

"And what is that, young man?" asked Clara.

Leo shrugged.

She wasn't sure either. They'd just have to ask Ernst that evening.

"Oh and look," said Clara. She pointed up at the building they were passing. "Aren't they tall? And look at how the glass shines in the windows. Oh, and all those elegant ladies and gentlemen walking along the streets. Look we're going faster than the carriages pulled by horses."

"How old is he?" said a young woman who had sat down next to them.

"Six. He's just six."

"Well he is so interested in everything, bless him. I wish my young'uns would appreciate half as much in the world. You've got a good'un there missus. What's your name, young man?"

Leo shied away from the woman.

"Leo. His name's Leo," said Clara.

"Well, Master Leo," said the woman. "I hope you enjoy the rest of your tram ride. I'll have to love you and leave you. This is my stop coming up. Good evening to you."

"Say goodbye to the lady," whispered Clara, kissing Leo's head.

Leo half smiled and waved shyly at the woman. She winked back.

Gradually more and more people left the tram. Finally they were the only passengers. The tram made a last stop.

"We have to get off here," said Clara.

"Why?" said Leo.

"It's the terminus."

"What's that?"

"Where the rails end. Look. Watch what happens."

The driver got out of the tram and moved to the other end. The conductor made his way along tilting the backs of the seats so that they faced the other way.

"Oh," said Leo. "He's changed them round."

"Yes. So that people can see where they're going. We'll get back on in a minute and go all the way back home."

Ten minutes later the tram was taking them back towards their home. There weren't so many people on now and Leo had a seat all to himself. He pressed his nose up against the window. It was beginning to get dark and the windows in the buildings that lined the wide street were lit up but the shutters had not yet been put into place. They could see right into the apartments and offices.

"Can't you see what a beautiful city we live in?" said Clara.

Leo nodded.

"Good," said Clara. "You can tell your teacher all about that tomorrow."

Ernst had already arrived home when they got back.

"Vati, we've been on a tram," said Leo. "All along the Ku'damm."

"A tram?" said Ernst. "All along the Ku'damm. My goodness we do have some style these days." He raised his eyebrows and looked at Clara. But there was a twinkle in his eyes.

Clara shrugged. "He needed to get to know the city. It was the quickest way."

"I should think so too. A truly splendid idea. You should make a habit of it."

"Why can't I go on a tram?" Käthe was scowling at them.

Clara laughed and bent down to kiss her little daughter on the head. "You shall, my love. Once you are six as well and you don't need your afternoon nap."

"It's not fair. Leo gets all the fun."

"Oh Käthe, you must be patient," said Ernst. He bent down and picked her up. "You'll grow up soon enough."

14 November 1901, Berlin: night watch

Clara couldn't understand why she felt so agitated. It had been the same routine as normal. She, Leo and Käthe had been out on the trams while Imelda looked after Rudi. The two older children had enjoyed the trip even more than normal this time. They'd come home bursting with ideas. Ernst had been in a particularly good mood and had told them all some jokes during supper. Then Leo and Käthe had gone to bed willingly – they were exhausted.

Rudi had been very good. He'd still been drowsy after his afternoon nap. He'd not fed very well that evening. He'd dropped off to sleep again before the others had gone to their bedrooms. She expected that would mean he would wake in the night. But so far he hadn't. That was what was worrying her. There was something wrong, she knew it.

A distant clock chimed two. Gosh, she was going to be tired in the morning. Ernst was sound asleep and snoring gently. She slipped out of bed as quietly as she could. She didn't want to disturb him. His health wasn't the best and he really needed his sleep.

She tiptoed past the children's rooms. Their doors were a few centimetres open. They liked to see a little light from the hallway and she liked to think she would hear them if they called out in the night. She made her way to the kitchen and got herself a glass of water. She stopped outside Rudi's room on the way back to her own. He was making strange rasping noises in his sleep. She pushed the door open a little.

The baby woke up and was struggling to breathe. Then when he could get his breath he screamed. There was a twinge of blue to his face and he felt warm. This child was ill. Possibly very ill.

All her efforts of keeping quiet were wasted. Ernst was beside her now, his arm around her shoulders. Her other two children were also standing in the hallway, pale, bleary-eyed and looking bewildered.

"What's the matter with Rudi?" asked Käthe. "Is he frightened?"

If only it were that simple.

"I'm going to go and find a doctor," said Ernst.

Clara shook her head. Ernst would take too long and Leo was too little to be sent out at night. "I'll go." She handed Rudi over to Ernst. It was killing her to leave her child while he was suffering so much, but this was the best solution.

"You can't go out on your own at this time of night." Ernst was frowning.

"It's only five minutes away. Nothing can happen to me in that time. Leo, stand by the window and you can see me go along the street and you can tell Vati that I'm all right."

Clara grabbed her coat and hat and pulled on her boots. Doctor Lamm's house was in the next street. It wouldn't matter at all that she still had her nightclothes on underneath. But she must hurry. She really must hurry.

She ran as fast as she could. The air was cold and it hurt her chest to breathe but that didn't matter. Her precious little Rudi must be helped. This was nothing compared with what he was suffering.

She turned the corner. Half way along this street was the doctor's house. She would soon be there. She hoped he wouldn't be cross at being woken. But the child was going blue for goodness sake. He was going blue.

There it was. Number 52. And the brass plaque. Dr Z J Lamm. There was a light shining from a downstairs window. Was the good doctor awake? Please God let him be there. Please God let him think it's serious enough to come and visit.

She rang the bell. Almost immediately she heard footsteps coming along the corridor. Another light went on in the hallway. Dr Lamm opened the door. He too was in his nightclothes and a dressing-gown.

"My dear Frau Lehrs, what is it?"

"Rudi," Clara managed to say, despite being breathless. "He can't breathe. He's gone blue."

"I'm coming right away." The doctor pulled his coat on over

his night clothes. "It's a good job I'm an insomniac or you would have had to wake me first. I can probably run faster than you. I'll hurry ahead."

Doctor Lamm set off, his coat flapping behind him. Clara knew she could trust him. Thank goodness he was so kind. Rudi would be all right, she was sure.

Gosh. It was a good job there was no one around. What would they think? A lady and a gentleman running through the streets together in their night clothes? She felt inclined to titter. How could she? Rudi was ill.

She walked as fast as she could but by the time she had turned the corner there was no sign of the doctor. Was he already with Rudi then? Was he already making Rudi better? She had a stitch in her side. It was taking forever to get back home but as she walked through the door she saw that it was not quite twenty-five past two. It was barely twenty minutes since she'd gone to get her glass of water.

And there was steam coming from under the bathroom door. Steam? There were voices, too, coming from the room. What was going on?

The door opened and out came Ernst with a kettle.

"Ah, Frau Lehrs," said Doctor Lamm. He was holding Rudi who appeared to be calming down. "You have one clever little boy." He pointed to Leo.

"I remembered about the steam," said Leo. He grinned.

The steam? What was that?

"He is so right. It is really effective at clearing lungs," said Doctor Lamm.

Of course. The steam exhibition they'd been to the other week. They'd read that as well as being able to drive powerful engines, steam was good for people with breathing difficulties. Why hadn't she had the presence of mind to think of that?

"Is he pink enough yet?" asked Käthe.

"He's getting there," said Doctor Lamm. He looked up at Clara. "We should keep up the steam treatment for another hour."

Ernst came back with the kettle.

Clara bit her lip. "I should have thought," she said.

"My dear," said Doctor Lamm. "When a mother sees her baby go blue there isn't a lot of space left for thinking. You were right to fetch me. And the steam has solved the immediate problem. But we do need to find the underlying cause."

Leo yawned.

"Oh, time you young people went back to bed, I think," said the doctor. "Maybe a day off school tomorrow so that they can keep an eye on their little brother, don't you think, Mutti?"

Clara nodded and watched as her two sleepy children made their way back to their beds. She felt so useless.

"He should be fine now," said Doctor Lamm an hour later. "I'll be here straight after breakfast but if you're concerned at all do come and fetch me again. And soon we'll get him properly looked at at the hospital. Try to get some rest yourself."

"I'll stay in his room for the rest of the night," said Clara.

"There's probably no need but if it makes you feel better, then do that. I'll see you tomorrow."

The doctor put on his coat and left.

Thank goodness her baby was all right. Thank goodness.

By the time Clara had seen the doctor out and had made herself a bed in Rudi's room, the baby was sleeping peacefully. His cheeks were properly pink and he was breathing easily. She longed to touch him, to stroke his cheek or even take him up in her arms. She didn't dare, though. She couldn't risk waking him.

She arranged the trundle bed so that her face was quite close to his and lay staring at him. "Sleep my little one," she murmured.

She felt too agitated to sleep herself. But lying there was relaxing, hearing her little son's gentle snoring. Then, though, she remembered what the doctor had said about him having to go to the hospital. It made her shudder. Was there really something badly wrong with this little boy?

She heard the church clock chime four. No, she would never sleep tonight.

She was surprised, then, that when Rudi's gurgling woke her, the sun was streaming in through his window.

"So, then, sweetheart," she said. "Are you feeling better today?"

Rudi smiled at her. He looked like any other baby. Clara pulled her shawl round her shoulders and went over to his cot. He stretched out his arms for her to pick him up.

At that precise moment the doorbell rang.

"Ah," said Clara. "It seems the good doctor is here and I think he will be pleased with you, young man."

25 March 1905, Berlin: changing faith

"So, my dear," said Ernst. "This is exceptionally cosy. How lucky I am to have such a family."

Clara laughed. "That sounds very philosophical. That's not like you."

"Well. You know. It's nice being at home with you and the children. It's madness at the factory."

Clara smiled.

Rudi, who had been sitting on the floor playing with a clockwork train, pulled himself up and rushed over to Clara. "Mutti, it's broken."

"Oh dear," said Clara. She hated these new mechanical toys. They broke so easily and then the children were disappointed. She liked it more when they used their imagination like she and Käthe had when they were younger, making up all sorts of stories about their dolls.

"Give it to me. I think I might be able to mend it," said Leo.

"I don't suppose you can," said Käthe. "As usual it will probably be me who fixes it."

"Let's hope one of you can," said Clara. She smiled to herself at how alike her daughter Käthe and her sister with the same name were. She was always doing things that were more like jobs for the boys. Was that because she had two brothers? Well, Clara herself had plenty of brothers. She had sisters as well, though. Käthe was the only girl in their little family. At nine years of age she had already decided that she was going to be a scientist when she grew up. An unusual ambition for a girl, but why not? Clara wished her well with that.

"I tell you what," said Ernst. "Why don't the three of you go down to the workshop in the cellar and see what you can do? Mind, only Leo should handle the tools."

"I can use them as well!" Käthe blushed bright red.

"I know you're deft," said Ernst. "But only Leo has big enough hands to hold them properly."

Käthe frowned and mumbled something under her breath. Clara couldn't make out what she was saying but guessed it would be the usual theme about boys having all the chances. She did, however, Clara noted, take Rudi's hand and was at least being kind to the little boy, like big sisters should.

"I've been thinking," said Ernst as soon as the children had left the room. "We should give up the Jewish faith and become Christians."

"You mean Catholics? But why?"

"It... it might be in our interest. You know that Jews are never welcome. And anyway, I meant we should join the Evangelical Church. The Catholic Church is so full of complicated rituals – all in Latin. The children won't understand."

"But... but all of our friends are Jewish. And a lot of our relations." Clara couldn't imagine what it would be like not meeting Frau Mattis for coffee. Nor no longer attending the Women's Sabbath Group.

"We'll not lose our friends," said Ernst. "We can still see them until..."

"Until what?"

"Well, as long as the hatred doesn't begin again."

"The hatred?" Clara felt sick. What did he mean, the hatred?

Ernst looked away from her. "Anyway, all this business about the Torah, all the rituals – they're so out of date. It all goes back to when we lived in the desert. I think we should be more modern."

"You mean you think that Jesus of Nazareth was the Messiah after all?"

Ernst smiled, shook his head and shrugged. "I don't know what I believe," he said. "I'm not sure I believe any of it at all. But what he's reported to have said and done seem fine to me. I just think it would be better for us to belong to a modern religious organisation. What do you think?"

"Well, I guess you're right. And I suppose it means we'll get to know some new people." Clara felt a little skip of delight in her chest. She didn't need to drop her Jewish friends. And now she could more easily be friends with people like the Frau Hellermann.

"Good. I'll get in touch with someone I know who will tell us how to go about it. And I think I should go and see what's going on in the cellar."

Clara smiled to herself as she looked down to the street. The sun was shining brightly. There were signs of spring everywhere. Once they'd mended the broken toy she would take the children out for some fresh air. Never mind that it was the Sabbath. That soon wouldn't matter anymore. And think of all of those new friends she'd make.

13 September 1910, Berlin: women

"My goodness, what have you been doing?" asked Clara. Leo was covered in dust and there was a tear in his right trouser leg. The other leg was covered in oil stains. His hair was sticking up.

"It's been fantastic, Mutti," said Leo. "We've been on a long tour round. Herman lent me his brother's bicycle. Bicycles are the best way to go."

"Even if they leave you looking filthy like that?" asked Clara. It would be difficult to repair the trousers or even clean them or the jacket. She may as well throw the whole lot away.

"Oh, it wasn't from riding the bike. We had to stop to repair it. I hit a stone, the tyre punctured and the wheel came loose. We managed to put it back together again."

"But why did you want to go around on a bicycle? What's wrong with the trams?"

"Mutti, they're so slow and full. You get more freedom this way."

Clara shuddered when she thought of the crowded streets. The carriages, the omnibuses, the automobiles. It wasn't safe anymore.

"It so exciting," Leo carried on. "The plans for creating green spaces in Berlin. We saw them doing some of the work. Berlin is going to be the greenest city on the whole of the continent. We'll all be able to breathe fresh air."

"Yes, I've heard about that," said Clara. "You say you were with Herman. Was Klaus not with you?"

"No. He was busy."

"Busy? Too busy to go out with you and Herman?"

"Yes. Yes… he was trying to see Ebba." Leo blushed bright red.

"Ebba? Ebba Karre? He has a girlfriend?"

"Not yet. He wishes he did. He wants Ebba to be his girlfriend." Leo's blush deepened.

"So, Klaus has a flame," said Clara. Gosh, these boys were growing up quickly. "And what does Ebba think?"

Leo shrugged. "I don't know."

"How does he know Ebba? How did they meet?"

"I think their mothers know each other. Perhaps she visited with her mother." Leo was looking away from her and staring at the floor. He was embarrassed, obviously.

But she couldn't leave it there. "What about you? Do you have a flame? Is there a girl you like enough to visit instead of going out with your friends?"

Leo looked at her and shook his head. "No. Not at all. The only woman I'd care to be seen with is you, Mother."

"Me?"

"I don't think there's another woman like you in the whole world."

"Not even your dear sister?"

"Especially not my terrible sister."

Clara couldn't help smiling at that. The two of them were always quarrelling and frankly she could usually understand Leo's side of the argument better. Käthe argued for the sake of it.

Leo, though, was shuffling awkwardly from foot to foot. The poor boy. He was so embarrassed. She should let him off. "Oh well," she said. "I suppose it's for the best. You have your studies to worry about. And right now I think you need to get cleaned up."

"Yes, I guess," said Leo looking down at his filthy clothes.

"Go on then," said Clara.

As Leo made his way towards his room Clara bit her lip and frowned. What was she going to do with the boy? She was glad he was getting a bit of exercise, fresh air and sunshine and having some fun with his friends. He wasn't as shy of sunlight as his father and there was no sign of the crippling rickets Ernst suffered from in him – not in any of the children thank goodness. But she wished he didn't dote so much on her. It was natural for young men of about his age to start taking some interest in young women. It wasn't natural for him to put her on a pedestal like that, though.

Clara sighed. Oh, she should stop worrying. It was good that she and her elder son got on so well. They were normally so easy-going with each other. Today had been an exception. She should enjoy it. Goodness, wasn't there so much else to worry about with her awkward daughter and her ailing younger son?

18 April 1913, Berlin: hospital

Rudi and the doctor had been gone a long time. She looked at the clock. It had actually only been twenty minutes. They would x-ray his lungs, test his breathing and take a blood sample. Then they would ask him all sorts of questions. Maybe they would ask her a few as well. She hoped they weren't poking and prodding him too much. Why wouldn't they let her stay with him? He was still only twelve. Twelve. Ah. If they were still Jewish he'd be almost ready for his Bar Mitzvah and he'd be regarded as a young man.

Another woman was in the waiting room. She was pale and kept getting up from her seat and pacing up and down the room.

"Are you waiting for a child, too?" asked Clara.

"My daughter," said the woman. "She's had TB. She's still not well. They're talking of sending her away. And you?"

"My son. He keeps getting breathing difficulties but they're not sure why."

"I suppose the x-ray machines help."

"Yes, it's fantastic what they can find out now."

The woman's mouth smiled but Clara could still see the worry in her eyes. "I'm sure your little girl will soon get better once she's away from Berlin. Where will you take her?"

"Bavaria, perhaps."

"Oh, yes, the mountains."

The double doors into the waiting room swung open and a nurse came through holding a little girl by the hand. As soon as the girl saw her mother she wriggled away from the nurse and ran over to her. "Mutti, Doctor Merten says I'm to go to the Chiemsee," she cried.

"There," said Clara. "That sounds a splendid idea."

"Doctor Merten will see you now, Frau Perschke," said the nurse. She turned towards Clara. "You have about another thirty minutes to wait, Frau Lehrs. But Rudi is doing well. Don't worry."

Good. Well, she wasn't surprised. He was a good child. And he was well at the moment. He hadn't had any night-time attacks for a few months. He wasn't as active as some of the other boys. He didn't like sports and he avoided the rough and tumble that Clara remembered her brothers used to enjoy. But he could get around all right. He walked to and from school every day. He argued with his brother and sister. And he ate well. Perhaps it wasn't so bad, then.

The nurse came out of the doctor's room. "Frau Lehrs, why don't you go and have a walk around our courtyard? The flowers are all coming out and it's lovely and sheltered. You'll only feel the sun, and not the wind. Go back down to the entrance hall and go out of the back door instead of going on to the street. Come back in twenty minutes. It'll be less boring for you."

"Thank you. That's a lovely idea."

Clara found the little garden without any difficulty. It was hard to believe it was really here. Who would have thought the shrubs and flowers would have been able to grow in such a small space and with only a little sunlight? They obviously had though. Someone must be taking care of it all. The garden was thriving.

She sat down on a stone bench near a small pond. A tiny fountain tinkled and caught a rainbow where the sun shone on it. I wonder whether the patients ever come here, she thought. It would give them hope.

She closed her eyes and enjoyed the sun warming her face. A bird started chirping, helping the fountain to blot out the sounds of Berlin. *This is peace. This is calmness.* How could Rudi not be all right after this?

She opened her eyes, got up from the bench and strolled round the garden one more time, occasionally stooping down to touch the flowers and look at them more closely.

Then it was time to go. She took a deep breath and made her way back up the stairs.

"Good timing," said the nurse as Clara arrived back at the waiting room. She was propelling Rudi towards the doctor's consulting room. "Doctor Merten is ready for you now."

The young women showed them in. Dr Merten, a tall man with shiny black hair and the most piercing blue eyes Clara had ever seen, smiled at them. He nodded that they should sit down. "Well, young man," he said looking at Rudi. "You're doing well." The doctor looked up at Clara. "We've found some scarring on his lungs, but he did well in his breathing test. We'll have to wait a while for the results of his blood test but he appears disease-free at the moment."

"So what's caused this scarring?"

"We can't be sure. Probably some virus that took hold."

"So, will he get better? Or could he get worse?"

"The scarring could always cause some breathing difficulties but only in certain circumstances, I believe."

Which circumstances would they be? What could she do to protect him? "What should we do?"

"It's best to keep him away from any irritants. Keep his home as dust-free as possible. Not too much clutter and make sure his bedroom is aired at all times. No strenuous exercise. And at all costs don't allow him to catch TB. Get him plenty of fresh air."

"How can we avoid TB?"

"Keep him away from crowded places. It would be good if you could get him away from Berlin."

Take him away from Berlin? How would that be possible? For a holiday, yes, but permanently? What about Ernst's work?

Rudi tapped her arm. "It's all right, Mutti. You always keep the dust out of the house and I don't like running anyway. I like being on my own." He turned to Doctor Merten. "Berlin has got a lot of fresh air," he said.

The doctor laughed. "Well you are a fighter," he said. "You are a really strong young man." He looked at Clara. "I don't think he's going to let a few scars on his lungs hold him back."

"He insisted on going to the Tiergarten on the way back," Clara told Ernst later that evening. "He told me it was full of fresh air."

"Well, it is, isn't it?"

"And animal dung and pollenating flowers."

36

"You get that in the countryside too."

Clara sighed. "Yes, but the doctor did suggest we take him away from Berlin."

"Well why don't you and the children go to your parents? Mecklenburg is a smaller town and the air is definitely fresher."

"It would mean breaking up the family."

Ernst kissed her head. "But it would keep our little boy safe."

The door to the drawing-room opened. Rudi stood there in his nightclothes.

"Are you all right?" said Clara. Her heart began to pound. Was he feeling ill again? Had he caught something at the hospital?

"Mutti, Vati, I don't want us to move from Berlin. I'll train my lungs to breathe more deeply. I'll keep my room clean. I'll leave the window open. You can't take Käthe and Ernst away from their friends. I'm happy to keep away from the other boys."

Clara could hardly see her son because of the tears in her eyes. She pulled Rudi into a big hug. "You're such a kind boy," she said.

Rudi pushed her away. "Don't be so silly, Mutti. I'm almost a man. I can make my own mind up about what I do. Now, I'm going to back to bed. Sleeping is good."

He turned smartly and Clara was sure that he would have clicked his heels if he'd been wearing shoes.

Ernst threw back his head and laughed out loud. "Well, that's told you."

"It has, hasn't it?" She began to titter.

28 September 1914, Berlin: going to be a soldier

Clara knew. She just knew. She had seen it coming.

She'd hoped the summer might have been promising something else. Leo was relaxing before going to take up his place at the university. They'd all hoped that this war would be over by Christmas.

Then in the last couple of weeks he'd become very quiet and now he'd asked to talk to her and Ernst. "Quite formally," he'd said.

Ernst stood with his hand on the mantelpiece. Clara sat on the chaise longue. She didn't dare stand. She was sure she would faint when he said what she dreaded but knew he meant to say.

Käthe and Rudi had been despatched to their rooms. Leo's dark eyes looked into hers.

"Well," said Ernst gently. "What did you want to tell us?"

"I've decided to volunteer. I want to go to the front."

Ernst put his hands over his eyes and nodded.

For a split second Clara almost felt relief. At last it was out in the open. Then all the wild thoughts came in. The panic. Goodness, he wasn't even an adult yet. He'd only just finished school. There had been causalities already.

"Mutti, don't look so concerned. Most of my friends have already gone to fight."

"And that's a reason, is it? You do what your friends do? If they jumped off a cliff you'd follow them, would you?"

"Mutti, I'd be doing it for Germany."

"Can't you wait a while? Let the professional soldiers do most of the work first?"

"If I wait until then it may be more dangerous. The more people we have out there the better. The sooner this can all be over."

Clara turned to Ernst. He said nothing but simply raised his eyebrows.

"Don't go. Just don't go," whispered Clara.

"I have to, Mutti. I have to."

She thought of her brothers. They would be too old wouldn't they? Ernst was perhaps young enough but surely his general health would count against him. And Rudi? Ironic that she'd been relieved that he'd been pronounced fit. Perhaps the residual breathing problems would be enough.

Clara sighed and nodded. "I understand. I do understand."

Ernst put his hand on Leo's shoulder. "It is good of you and brave. I wish I could do my bit."

"Ernst, you will. Your work at the factory. They'll need engineers. Surely." Clara shook her head. What was he thinking? Of course he would be useful.

"Yes, but it won't be the same as going to the front."

"I will be going for everyone. My uncles can't go. Neither can Vati. And Rudi probably won't be able to go later. I'm young and I'm strong. Please give me your blessing."

"He is so right, Clara. He really is."

No one spoke for the next few minutes. Clara stared at her son. His dark serious eyes looked into hers. He lifted his eyebrows. She stood up and reached out towards him. She placed her hands on his arms. She could feel the determination in him. It was clear that there was no turning back.

Ernst clapped his back. "Take care, my son. I'm proud of you."

"Will you give me your blessing, Mutti?"

Clara nodded. She couldn't bring herself to speak.

"Thank you." Leo bowed his head at a small angle and then turned to his father and nodded. He turned and left the room abruptly. Did he click his heels? Clara wasn't sure.

Clara looked out of the window at the clear night sky. The busyness of Berlin and all the electric lights hadn't stopped the stars shining. She heard the church clock chime two. It reminded her of staying up with Rudi when he struggled for breath. Only this time it was her elder son who was keeping her awake. And she was the one struggling. Struggling to understand why so many young men were offering to sacrifice themselves for their country. Not only here, in Germany, but in the other countries too.

And yet she felt incredibly proud of him. He was being brave. Was he scared really? How could any soldier not be scared? How could any soldier be brave if they weren't scared? Was it just because of all of his friends?

No. Never. Leo knew his own mind.

Ernst got out of bed and came over to her.

"I'm sorry if I woke you," she said.

Ernst slid his arms around her waist. "I couldn't sleep either. I shall worry too. All of the time. Of course I shall."

"You think he's right, don't you?"

"I think he has to do this thing. He has to find out for himself whether he's right or wrong."

Clara sighed. "I wish there could be an end to all wars. I wish we could all live in peace."

"Maybe that will happen one day. Maybe one of our children will find the way."

"I hope so. I really do." Clara shivered.

Ernst kissed the top of her head. "Come back to bed. You need to rest. I'll take care of you."

It was good to know he was there, to let him look after her. She felt safe in his arms. But who, she wondered, would keep her boy safe.

14 February 1917, Berlin: missing

Clara wasn't sure how she'd managed to see the officer out and then get back to the drawing-room. Her legs felt as if they would give way any moment. But somehow she did it. She stared at the box on the low table next to the sofa.

Thankfully Imelda was also out. She was completely alone. She howled, screamed, beat her fists on the cushions, bit her lip and then eventually, tears in her eyes, she decided she ought to open the box.

Her hands were trembling so much she had difficulty taking the lid off.

"Missing, presumed dead," the young officer had said.

She'd known it all along. Something like this was bound to happen. Men and their wars! In the box was all that they supposed remained of her dear first-born.

The lid gave way, and there they were; a few of his personal belongings that they'd found in his trench. It wasn't much left after a life.

A peculiar musty smell came from the box. Clara had a brief vision of Leo, cold and wet, his boots covered with mud. It must have been terrible in those trenches. No wonder he never said much about it in his letters.

She stared at the contents of the box, not daring to touch anything. Right on top was what looked like a small Bible. Though her hands were shaking even more, she somehow found herself holding the little book. Had he taken some comfort from that?

She lifted it to her lips and kissed it gently. "Leo," she whispered. Then she noticed that the cover was swollen. Perhaps it had got damp? But no, something was wedged inside it. It intrigued her and she lifted up the lining page which was loose.

There was a notebook hidden between the cover and the lining. She prised it away. It looked like a diary. Leo had been keeping a diary. Well, that was a surprise. He hated writing.

She couldn't bring herself to open it straight away. She should, though, she knew she should. She felt sick.

Come on. You owe it to Leo.

She took a deep breath and opened the first page. "Well, then, Leo, what have you got to tell me?" she whispered.

29 November 1914

So this has become my home. It is cold and damp, but occasionally you're able to get warm at night. We sleep with our clothes on, of course. The trenches are well constructed, but even so, it's impossible to keep the water out. We squelch around in the mud. Some of the men complain of sore feet. Others are covered in lice. I'm not too badly off yet. Well, I've not been here all that long.

I've not seen any of the others here. They may be further along. We've not heard of many casualties even.

There are a few small comforts. The odd bottle of beer or whisky. A cigarette. Yes, I've started smoking. Mother will be astounded but I think she'll understand. And sleep. Sleep is good. You get used to the noise after a while. I never thought I would. Gunfire. Explosions. Officers shouting orders. I now wonder whether I'd be able to sleep without it in fact.

We don't do a lot really. We just wait. One day we'll have to go over the top. I'm not looking forward to that. Could I kill an Englishman? Any man for that matter? I know that's what I came for. But they're all just people in the end.

The next page was smudged, so Clara flicked forward.

3 January 1915

I've heard the most extraordinary thing. Some of our men have been playing football with the English soldiers. Apparently, they got out of their trenches on Christmas Day, shook hands, exchanged schnapps and whisky, and cigarettes, and kicked a ball around for a bit. I don't know who won. It was a proper football game, I'm told. Shame we can't settle this war with a football game.

There was a bit of a truce generally. It was good to get parcels from home and we decorated our trenches with candles and extra lights. We sang some Christmas carols and then they sang some back. They knew 'Stille Nacht' and sang it in English.

We did get out of the trench and they did too. We kept our distance. But there was an understanding that we wouldn't shoot each other. It was good to be able to remove our dead though – fortunately nobody I knew personally.

Now we're back in the thick of it. There have been orders from on high that we're not to do that again. Madness!

Goodness. That must have been quite a sight. Surely it must have been cold in that terrible place in the winter?

The next few entries didn't really say a lot. At last, though, she came to one that was longer.

14 February 1916

This war is relentless. No Christmas truce this year. It still feels like winter. It's the damp rather than the cold. We've lost quite a few men this winter. There is one thing, though. They don't want to kill us and we don't want to kill them. So, every morning one of our men and one of theirs puts a board up from the trench. This means that it is breakfast time. We draw our water and collect our rations. I imagine they do the same. It remains silent as long as either board is in place. We can't drag it out or our commanders would be on to us. I wonder whether they actually know. And, of course, as soon as both boards are down any man who ventures out of his trench will be shot at.

They're only sixty metres away. We could shout to them, almost, and get to know their names. They're brothers, sons, husbands and fiancés, just like us. They're not really born to kill. Not deep down.

Several pages were stuck together and the next few after that had become damp. The ink had run so badly that she couldn't read the words. At last, though, she came to another part that she could read.

17 October 1916

Herman died today. We've lost other men and looking at corpses has become an everyday ritual. I wouldn't exactly say I was used to it, though. You can't get used to that look, that lifelessness. And sometimes they've been pretty messed up. Plus if it takes us a while to get to them, they stink. No, you don't get used to it. But you do begin to accept it as normal.

We went over the top yesterday. That's the fourth time we've been asked to do that. I always pray before we go. I still don't know whether I believe in God. But I pray anyway. I think they try not to hit us. I know we deliberately miss sometimes when they're up there. I even think Herman was shot accidentally. Because they're not very good at it. We're not either.

The noise was unbelievable this time. So many men screaming – ours and theirs. And the barbed wire. You've got to be careful of the barbed wire. You can get tangled up in it so easily. Or get a nasty cut. I did cut myself the first time we went over the top. It took six weeks to heal up. It went septic, the medic said. So I'm careful now.

Herman didn't die out there. We managed to get him back into the trench. But there was a gas attack early this morning. We did succeed in getting a gas mask on to him but when we checked him again later, after we'd taken ours off, he'd gone. We don't know whether it was the gas or his wound. He'd lost a lot of blood and the bullet may have been quite close to his heart. It went in through his back at about heart level. Or maybe moving him so much caused something else to happen. We had to be quite rough with him to get the mask on. The gas attack held the stretcher-

guys up. When they did get here, it was to take away his body.

At least he looked peaceful when he died. I don't think he knew anything about being shot or bleeding so much. He never came round. Just as well, I suppose. He'd have been in agony if he'd been awake.

Poor Herman! I don't know what I'm going to say to his parents and his sisters when I see them again.

All the killings are bad enough, but when it's somebody you know, it's terrible.

It's awful. It's really awful.

Yes, he was right. This was terrible. Poor Herman. Poor Leo. No one should have to face that.

She turned the page, eager to see whether he recovered from this shock. Oh, how could anyone? But did he cope? Could he still function?

19 October 1916

The general came to see us yesterday. Well, not in person. He spoke to our commanding officers and then the Feldwebel came and told us. Apparently, we are all to have the Iron Cross medal. Our work in the trenches has been exemplary, they tell us. Every soldier has been brave. No one has given in to cowardice. We have all worked together for the greater German good, he said.

We haven't. Not really. We've just done what they've told us to do.

There was schnapps for us all. And beer.

There were no deserters in our regiment. Only brave men. Brave? We're all scared senseless most of the time.

"How much longer do you think it will go on, sir?" I asked.

"Only a few more weeks," he replied. "That's why all leave is cancelled. So that we can push on through and then we can all go on permanent leave."

At least I won't have to face Herman's family for a while.

Today we all have sore heads. That will teach us to drink so much schnapps. The sniping and the shells sound louder than ever. It's getting even colder and wetter again. Let's hope it can all end before we have to go through another winter.

Clara put the diary back into the box. She couldn't bear to read any more. Those few extracts had been enough. Goodness knows why the censors hadn't found that. They'd never have let it through if they'd known about it. Leo had hidden it so carefully. Typical Leo. He'd wanted her to find out what it had really been like for the young men. It was gruesome. Horrible.

She was sure it was her he'd wanted to tell. Not Ernst, not Rudi, nor Käthe. Her alone. Of course she would share it all with the others later. Perhaps they'd give her the courage to read the rest. But how ironic as well, that she was also alone when that young man had come to tell her. Ernst had felt well enough for once to go to the factory. Käthe was at the university and Rudi was doing some voluntary work for the military.

She touched his Iron Cross. "Poor, brave Leo," she whispered.

Missing, presumed dead. It was worse, somehow, than knowing for sure that he was dead.

Oh, that poor young man who'd come to tell her. He looked hardly any older than Rudi. Considerably younger than Leo and he was – had been – was – still quite young. In the prime of his life.

He'd looked so vulnerable, Oberst Hoen. So pale. A commissioned officer no doubt. You only had to look at him to see that he came from the nobility. He carried himself in a certain way. But some mother's son, all the same. They were all just children, these young men sent away to fight.

He'd tried to insist on seeing Ernst.

"My husband is busy at work," Clara had said. "Also, he's not all that well himself. If you have some bad news you had better tell me and I can break it to him gently."

"But we have our commands, madam."

Clara had laid her hand softly on his arm. "What would your mother tell you to do?" she'd said quietly.

He hadn't answered. The two of them stared at each other for a few moments. Then Oberst Hoen had sighed. "You son's division was ordered to go over the top. There was a gas attack shortly afterwards. He didn't return to his trench. He hasn't turned up at any of the field hospitals. No corpse has been found." He hesitated. "Sometimes corpses are so mutilated that no one can recognise them."

Clara nodded. "And how many of those "missing presumed dead" ever turn up?" she managed to ask.

The young man looked away from her. "Very few," he mumbled to the floor.

Then he clicked his heels, saluted and looked at her directly. "We are sorry for your loss."

Clara nodded again and gestured that he should leave. She couldn't speak and she needed to be alone.

She shuddered thinking about it. And how was she going to tell Ernst, Käthe and Rudi? To think: a few days ago they had been enjoying the letter that had come from the front. He seemed to be safe and well and was obviously working hard and effectively or they wouldn't have made him an officer, would they?

Clara walked over to the bureau and took out the letter again. She tutted to herself as she looked at the date. It had taken two months to get there.

19 December 1916

Dear all,

Life continues in the trenches. We are wet and cold and sometimes scared but otherwise mainly quite well. We have been "over the top" several times and we have a better idea of what is expected of us there. We're getting good at fighting.

The big news is that I have been made into an officer. I am now an Oberleutnant and have several men under my command. I feel responsible for their well-being also.

We have all been awarded the Iron Cross, so if anything should happen to me you can be proud. I don't think anything will happen, though. It's almost as if we're being kept in a protective bubble.

Let's hope it can all be over soon and that I can come back to you. Oh to go riding on the trams in Berlin again. That is the peace we must fight for. Take care all of you,

Your loving son and brother,

Leo.

Well, your protective bubble stopped working, didn't it? And what do you mean, fighting for the peace so that Berlin can carry on being Berlin? Clara felt angry with him. She had not brought him up to think fighting was a good thing. Shouldn't peace be in every capital city – London and Paris as well as Berlin? Oh, she guessed he couldn't put what he really thought in a letter. Now it didn't matter anyway. He was most likely not coming back.

She heard the front door open and shut. "Imelda," she called.

"No, it's me," Ernst's voice called back.

She held her breath as his footsteps came towards the drawing-room.

"You're back early," she managed to whisper.

"What's wrong?" he asked.

She nodded towards the box on the table.

"Leo?"

She nodded.

"No! No! Not Leo."

She rushed over to him and they embraced. "He's missing, presumed dead. There is a little hope."

"A little. Just a little," Ernst whispered. He kissed the top of her head. "But you know it is just a little, don't you? It's rare…"

Clara nodded. "I know. I know."

"We know he was brave. We know they were pleased with him."

"They've brought some of his things. There's a diary."

Ernst let her go and walked over to the table. He opened the box and took out the battered note book. He frowned as he flicked though it.

"It's a bit gruesome. I've read a few pages. I will read it all eventually."

Ernst nodded. "The poor boy," he mumbled.

The front door opened again. Clare heard Rudi and Käthe giggling in the hall.

"I'll tell them," said Ernst. "You go and lie down for a while. You look exhausted."

Clara woke with a start. She was surprised she'd managed to sleep at all. It had been a gruelling evening. Käthe and Imelda had sobbed uncontrollably. Rudi had looked pale but had remained stoical. Ernst had been pragmatic.

"The worst is not knowing," he'd said. "Once they can tell us what's happened to him we can grieve properly."

"Will they bring him back here?" Rudi asked.

Ernst shrugged. "I've heard some plans to bury the dead of both sides up there."

"We don't know that he is dead," Clara whispered.

"No, that's true, but we must be prepared for the worst." Ernst had not looked directly at her as he'd said those words.

That had set Käthe off howling again.

Clara heard the church clock strike two. Another of those nights then. Always that church clock telling her she was missing her sleep. The rest of the house was quiet, though. Perhaps they were all managing to sleep their grief away.

There was a faint echo of a dream. She couldn't remember the details but it was something to do with Leo. It had left her feeling really calm and peaceful.

Then something inside her jumped. He was alive, she knew he was. It didn't make sense but she was convinced. She felt as if he was reaching out to her. They were so close and she could feel him there still. Surely that wouldn't happen if he'd died?

Ernst stirred. "Can't you sleep?" he asked.

"I'm sure he's still alive."

"Maybe. But you must get some rest. You'll need your strength over the next weeks. Try to sleep." He pulled her towards him and she lay snugly in his arms. His gentle snoring soothed her. She heard the church clock strike three and felt herself falling asleep. She hoped she would dream of Leo, alive and fit and well.

14 November 1917, Berlin: relatively speaking

Clara heard the front door slam. Ah. That would be Käthe. She always did slam the door like that when she came in. Only this time the footsteps didn't go towards her room but carried on towards the drawing-room.

"Mutti, you'll never guess what," she called as she opened the lounge door. "Professor Einstein came to talk to us today."

Käthe's face was flushed and her eyes gleamed. Her hair had come loose and she was wearing one of the shorter dresses that showed off her trim ankles. It looked more like the sort of thing you'd wear for a stroll in the countryside than for sophisticated Berlin city life but Clara guessed she was more comfortable that way and she needed to be comfortable while she was studying. Yes, her daughter looked wild but somehow all the prettier for being animated by her enthusiasm.

"Come on, then, tell me all about it," said Clara, ringing the bell to order some tea.

"He's leaving the university soon to go to Switzerland where he can have more peace and quiet to further develop his theories about relativity."

"Ah!" Clara herself had been to a public lecture by the famous Professor Einstein. He was a funny-looking man, with intense eyes and wild hair. But he had a sense of humour and she liked that, though some of his jokes were bold.

"If my theory of relativity is proven successful, Germany will claim me as a German and France will declare I am a citizen of the world. Should my theory prove untrue, France will say I am a German and Germany will declare I am a Jew," he'd said after explaining his ideas in terms so simple that she'd been able to understand.

Yes, even Ernst agreed with him even though what he was saying was throwing into disarray the solid science on which they built their engineering work.

A wave of sadness hit her as she wondered what Leo might

have made of it all. Maybe she could convince herself that he was relatively alive because no one had said that he was definitely dead.

"What's the matter?" said Käthe.

"I was wondering what Leo would think about it."

"Mutti, we have to carry on hoping." Käthe rubbed Clara's arm.

"I know. I know," said Clara. "Come on then. Tell me more about Professor Einstein."

"You see, he has a different attitude to experiments from most scientists. He looks at the findings of his experiments and assumes that they're true. Other scientists assume the theory was correct and that the experiment has failed if they don't get the results they want. He assumes that the experiments were correct and the theory has failed. Only, his theory isn't failing."

"Interesting. But why did he come to talk to you today?"

"He came to apologise because he won't be able to teach us anymore. He's quite ill and he's glad he won't be teaching large classes in the future. I was so looking forward to doing one of his courses next year. But he has said he will come back from time to time. And he may even be able to supervise some doctorates, though we'd probably have to travel to Switzerland to meet with him. But Mutti, I so want to work on relativity for my doctorate. Do you think it will be possible?"

"Well, we'll have to see what your father says but I'm sure he'll agree. Perhaps I could travel with you."

"Oh Mutti, that would be marvellous." She hugged her mother.

Clara smiled to herself as she hugged her back. It was rare for her daughter to show so much affection, but it was so exceptionally good when she did. Poor Käthe. She had such a hard time trying to assert herself in a man's world. There was only one other woman on her course and Käthe had not found her particularly friendly. She was the daughter of one of the faculty members and thought she knew everything about the university. Still, Käthe was holding her own as far as Clara could see.

Käthe pulled away. "I'd better go and do some more studying," she said.

"Don't you want some tea?" asked Clara.

"Can I have it in my room?"

"Of course. But get changed before dinner, will you? And let me help you pin your hair back up."

"Yes. All right. I shall."

It was getting dark now. But that had been a rare flicker of light from Käthe. Oh, there was much she should be proud of in her daughter.

The tea arrived. She poured a cup for Käthe and made her way to her room.

5 December 1917, Berlin: found

Clara couldn't settle. She'd tried sewing. She attempted to write some letters she wanted to get to friends before Christmas. She'd even tried to plan the Christmas party for the firm. But her heart wasn't in it. And it wasn't only because Leo wasn't going to be there. He'd not been there the last two Christmases, either. Everyone knew there was a war on.

No, it wasn't any of that at all. She had this incredible feeling that something was going to happen. Something spectacular. She wished it would hurry up though. The waiting was killing her.

She paced up and down the room. It was getting dark outside. She went over to the window to draw the curtains and pull the shutters across. She stopped to look to the street below first. The lights were reflecting off the damp pavements and up in the lamplight she could see snowflakes. Winter was here for sure.

Where was Leo? Was he cold? Was he suffering? She wished almost for a moment he had died. Then he couldn't suffer any more.

It happened again. That sudden lurch in her body. That certainty that he was still alive and that he was trying to tell her something.

She went to close the curtains but couldn't help noticing two young men in soldiers' uniforms walking briskly along the street. Could it be? Surely not? No, that was nonsense. It was wishful thinking. That could not be Leo. He had probably died. It was just another young man in uniform. One who was more fortunate than her Leo because he was here in Berlin.

She pulled the curtains to. She decided helping Imelda in the kitchen would be the best course of action. Chatting to the young woman would take her mind off things. Perhaps then whatever it was would happen and be done with itself.

As she stepped into the hallway she felt the lurch again and the doorbell rang at the same time.

This was it. It was happening. Her heart was beating fiercely. She rushed towards the front door. Her hand trembled as she tried to open it. The handle slipped out of her fingers a couple of times.

She managed at last. It was the two young men she'd seen on the street below. She thought she was going to faint.

"Imelda!" she called.

The maid ran out of the kitchen, a knife and a carrot still in her hands. She screamed and dropped them. "Master Leo, is that really you?"

"Mutti?" said Leo.

The young man with him clicked his heels. "I am pleased to meet you, Frau…"

"Lehrs," said Leo. "Our family name is Lehrs."

"Imelda, will you bring us some tea, into the drawing-room? I'll help you with the supper later."

The maid picked up the knife and the carrot and hurried back into the kitchen.

Clara took a deep breath and managed to get herself more in control. Her legs felt like jelly though and she couldn't stop trembling.

"Will you come this way please," she managed to say.

Clara returned to the drawing-room followed by Leo and the other young man.

"Please sit down," she said to the young soldier.

Both he and Leo remained standing.

"Oberst Konrath," said the stranger. "I have been looking after… Herr Lehrs."

"Oberleutnant Lehrs," said Clara. What was going on here? Why didn't the captain know her son's rank? Why was Leo here in Berlin and hadn't managed to come and see them, not let them know that he was still alive? Surely he must know how worried they'd been?

The captain went white. "You are Oberleutnant Leopold Lehrs? Really? I am honoured."

"What is going on?" said Clara.

"I think I should explain," said the captain. "But oh dear me. I am in good company."

"Yes, please do. And for goodness sake sit down. You too, Leo."

Oberst Konrath sat down awkwardly on the wingchair. Leo remained standing and was looking round the room, frowning faintly.

"Leo, tell me what has been going on."

Leo exchanged a glance with the captain. "It's all coming back," he said. "I used to live here." He pointed to Clara. "She's my mother."

Oberst Konrath nodded. "See, I told you something would trigger your memory eventually."

Clara put her hand in front of her mouth. "You've lost your memory?"

Leo stared back at her.

"Shell shock," said the captain. He turned to Leo. "Do you remember anything from the battle field now?"

Leo shook his head. "Just this house. This street. And the trams."

"What about…?" Clara started to say. She wanted to know whether he remembered his father or Käthe and Rudi but the captain gestured that she shouldn't ask him that question.

The door opened and Imelda came in with the tea.

"Oh, Master Leo," she said. "It's so good to see you again. And don't you look well and so fine in your uniform?"

Leo looked down at what he was wearing then back up at Imelda. A grin spread across his face. "It's Imelda isn't it? I hope your Zwiebelkuchen is as good as ever." He turned to face Clara. "Where are Käthe and Rudi? Will Vati be home soon?"

He remembered them.

Oberst Konrath was nodding. "Good, good," he mumbled. He turned to Clara. "Oberleutnant Lehrs was blasted by an exploding shell. He suffered a head injury. He had no identification on him. We think he may have given his jacket to a wounded soldier. He recovered quite quickly physically but has suffered complete memory loss ever since. He's been doing some light office duties and has been in my charge. We were out on a mission today when he stopped walking and said he thought he could remember something and insisted we took a tram. We got off round the corner and then he rushed up here."

"Oh, yes, I remember the trams," said Leo.

"How come no one made the connection that there was this soldier without identification and our son missing?" Why had they made them go through all of that misery?

"Madam, have you any idea how many men go missing? And how many men suffer from shellshock, including memory loss such as this?"

"I'm sorry. I didn't think." Clara felt her cheeks burning.

"Don't worry, Frau Lehrs. No one would expect you to know." He turned to Leo. "Come, we must get back to the barracks. And get you into a proper uniform."

"Will his memory come back completely?" said Clara.

"It's hard to tell. I'm no medic but I've had lots of experience of this sort of thing. Some men blot out their memories of the battle field completely."

"Doesn't that put them in danger of being accused of cowardice? Of malingering so that they don't get sent back to the front?"

The captain smiled drily. "Even if Oberleutnant Lehrs doesn't fully gain his memory there is no question of his ever being accused of cowardice. He is well-known for his bravery."

"Will he have to go back to the front?"

The captain shrugged. "I can't say. A lot will depend on how well and how quickly the rest of his memory comes back."

Clara thought of the diary and was glad that Leo couldn't remember what he'd written in it.

The two men stood up to leave. Oberst Konrath put his hand gently on Leo's back. "Come on then. We really must sort your uniform out."

Clara saw them into the hall. The smell of vegetables cooking for supper greeted them. Leo stopped and turned towards her. "They gave us a lot of pea soup," he said. "It wasn't bad, considering."

Oberst Konrath pursed his lips and raised his eyebrows.

Something sank inside Clara.

19 October 1918 Berlin: funeral plans

Leo didn't know what to say. His mother appeared calm and composed. Käthe was pale but her eyes were red and puffy so he guessed she had been crying. Rudi looked bewildered.

It was up to him now. As the oldest son he was the man in the family. He had to take charge. He kissed his mother's cheek, gave Käthe a hug and slapped Rudi's back.

"What needs to be done?"

"Nothing. It's all in hand," said his mother. "The shomer is with your father. The carriages come at three."

"I'll go and sit with him for a while."

His mother nodded.

Leo made his way into the drawing-room where his father's coffin rested on a trestle table. He was surprised to recognise the shomer as one of the men he'd seen in the trenches. He didn't know him all that well and it would have been disrespectful to start a discussion, but the two men couldn't help smiling at each other.

"Thank you," said Leo. "You may go and take some tea. I'm happy to stay here until it's time to go."

None of this could be real. He couldn't believe his father had gone. Yes, of course, he'd not been well enough to work for some time, but that was happening even to young men like him after all that they'd suffered in the Great War. And his father had never been all that strong anyway. But he couldn't believe he'd never see him again. He wished he'd been there when he'd died. What a shame he couldn't look at him as he lay in the coffin. Christians were allowed to do that, weren't they? Look at their relatives at peace. Make sure the right body was in the coffin. See one last image of the person they loved. Why didn't Jews? It was the same God, wasn't it, that they all believed in? Or that they were supposed to believe in. He didn't quite get it. It didn't quite make sense. He had a feeling there was something more there than his scientific training was telling him. But not all of this. They had to get his father's body into the earth as quickly as possible so that his spirit might be free, the Jewish law said. That made no sense. His father's soul, whatever that might be, had already gone.

Leo sighed. They had to do all of this, he supposed. His mother, he knew, would want to keep up appearances, for the sake of her Jewish friends, but not go overboard so as to offend the Christian ones. Everything should be done properly and without a lot of fuss. Even if he was having a Jewish ceremony at an Evangelical burial place. Why was his mother going back to the old ways?

The shomer returned. Leo nodded to him. He wondered whether he should after all strike up a conversation with him, but that still seemed callous. Nothing needed attention other than his father's burial.

Seeing that young man again took Leo back to the trenches. He could smell the mud and the smoke from the guns, he could feel the lice crawling over his skin and he could hear the men in his command, men a few months younger than himself, screaming in agony as they died. These images wouldn't go away. He'd done his best. He'd tried to be a good leader. He'd succeeded, he'd been told, and he'd been awarded the Iron Cross and had been made an officer, only it didn't feel to him like success. It was all useless anyway. It would all be over soon. They'd lost already, really. Everyone was poor. They all needed to rebuild only there wasn't anything to rebuild with. Nothing was settled.

He heard the horses and carriages draw up outside. He stood up and went to the window.

"It's time," whispered the shomer.

Leo nodded. He looked down at the hearse and the horses with their fine black plumes. He noticed that they had white fetlocks and noses. Why couldn't they have provided horses that were black all over? He turned to leave as the door opened and the shomer uttered a cry of surprise.

He could hardly contain his own surprise, too, when he saw what had disconcerted the young man. His mother was wearing a pale yellow blouse with her black skirt and jacket and her hat had yellow feathers attached.

"Well," she said. "What's the matter? Your father would have hated us to wear dark colours all the time. And look. I've torn my coat anyway."

She handed him a large pair of cloth-cutting scissors.

Leo took them and made a slit in his jacket and then tore it with his hands.

They were ready to bury his father.

9 October 1918, Berlin: ashes to ashes

Clara watched as they lowered the coffin into the ground. She was glad he was having an Evangelical burial. It was probably for the best. But she was also glad they'd done the wake the Jewish way: there was no way she would have wanted to look at Ernst's body. It wouldn't have been him.

"Are you sure you don't want to see him?" Frau Biel had asked. "It's wise to see that they have the right corpse in the coffin you know."

"Oh what a nonsense and a fuss," Clara had said. "That's the last thing I'd want. It wouldn't be Ernst."

"But Frau Lehrs," Frau Biel had continued, "didn't he look terrible as he died? You said so. All that bile. Didn't you want to see him at peace?"

"It wouldn't be him. Just an empty shell," Clara had whispered.

And now it was all over. The ceremony hadn't taken long at all in the end. Dust to dust. Ashes to ashes. Each of them – Clara, Leo, Käthe and Rudi – had thrown a handful of earth and a white rose into the grave. That was it. Over and done with. Gone.

The carriages set off back to the Lehrs home in Pariser Strasse and a few moments later Clara was welcoming the guests who had come for the small cold lunch.

"Mutti, I don't think they like your yellow blouse and the feather in your hat," said Leo.

"Well, they will have to put up with it," said Clara. She pointed to her son's torn jacket. "And if they're going to make comments, perhaps they'll have something to say about that. Oh it's so much nonsense. The Jewish way. The Christian way. How does anybody know what exactly is right? Tell me that."

Leo was staring at her. It was for a moment as if they both recognised something, though she couldn't put a name to it.

18 March 1921, Berlin: changing courses

Clara couldn't settle. Leo would be here soon. It was odd for him to visit on a Friday during the day. There must be something wrong. She had suspected for a long time that there was. But today, perhaps, he was going to tell her. She wasn't sure she was ready to hear it. Was he ill? Were his studies not going well? Or was it still the burden of that wretched war? So many young men, she'd heard, had been shaken by it. Some had even ended up in the asylums. Damn these stupid men and their wars.

She paced up and down the room. Leo wouldn't be here for another twenty minutes yet. And he was always on time, exactly on time. Never a minute early or late. But she wasn't going to sit and wait. She wasn't in the mood for reading or sewing.

She glanced out of the window. The daffodils in the window box of the apartment opposite were beginning to open. The warm sunshine was bringing them on. Her mood softened a little. Ernst always used to make sure their own window boxes were full of flowers and that their little balcony was adorned with plants and pots. Not all men were warriors after all.

But a nasty smear on her own window prevented her from properly seeing the display opposite.

That won't do. I'd better clear that up before Leo arrives.

She went to the kitchen to get a window leather.

"I can do that, Frau Lehrs," said Imelda.

"No, it's fine, Imelda. I'm happy to do it."

"But it's what you pay me for!"

Clara shook her head. "You do plenty. More than enough. I really wish I could give you more. And I can't be idle."

Before Imelda could reply Clara left the kitchen and hurried back to the drawing-room. Seconds later she was scrubbing furiously at the window. She relished the mild ache in her arm and felt her face growing warmer with the effort. A wisp of hair fell across her forehead and she pushed it back with her hand.

Just as she was satisfied that the smear had gone and the

window was sparkling and she was standing back to admire her work she heard the front door open. Good. He was here. They could get this over with.

Seconds later the door opened and there was Leo.

"Good morning, Mutti." He kissed her on the cheek. As he stepped back he frowned and stared at her. "What have you been doing?"

Clara turned to look at the mirror on the side wall. There was a big grey streak where she had touched it when she'd tried to push her hair back. It hadn't helped; her hair looked a mess. The window leather was still on the window-sill. She couldn't pick it up. And if she touched anything else she would make that dirty as well.

Leo followed her gaze. "Mutti, have you been cleaning windows?"

"Yes. That's the trouble with this sunny weather. It shows up all the smears."

"But shouldn't Imelda be doing that?"

"Imelda has enough to do. Goodness knows I pay her little enough."

"Ah." Leo looked away.

Was that it then? Did he have some sort of money troubles? Was he in debt?

"Well, then," said Clara. "I think you'd better tell me what this visit is all about. I presume it's not a social call."

"All right. But I can't talk seriously to you while you look like that."

Clara looked in the mirror again. Yes she did look a sight. She tittered. Leo chuckled as well. "I'll go and get cleaned up," she said. At least her unkempt appearance had broken the ice a little.

When she got back to the drawing-room Imelda had already brought in some tea and had removed the dirty window leather. Leo was looking a bit glum again. It had been good to see him laugh earlier, but there was obviously still something wrong.

"Well," said Clara. "Tell me then. What did you want to talk to me about?"

Leo sighed. "I wanted to borrow some money. I want to go to

a series of lectures. In Stuttgart. But I guess if you can't pay Imelda properly then you won't be able to lend me money for that."

"We might be able to take it out of the money your father put in trust for education. It's for all three of you, of course. But tell me, is this a supplement to your course? Why isn't it covered by the fees we've already paid?"

Leo flushed bright red. "It's not really part of my course, Mutti. It's a bit more – spiritual."

"Spiritual?"

"To do with the essence of things. The essence of everything."

"Isn't that what the new physics is about? Isn't that what you're studying at the university?"

"Well, yes. It's what Einstein and Planck are telling us. But I'm mainly stuck in laboratories, doing boring experiments and looking at boring data. But this man…"

"This man?"

"Rudolf Steiner."

The name sounded familiar. Clara wasn't sure why. But there was something that made her feel uneasy. What was it? Had she heard anything bad about him?

She looked at her son. His eyes were shining brightly and his face was still flushed. She'd not seen him look so animated and excited about anything since before the war. It reminded her of his enthusiasm when he was a little boy. Goodness, it would be good to get that back for him. And maybe it was spiritual education he needed. His soul, whatever that was, needed repairing.

"And this really will help you with your education?"

Leo nodded.

"Very well. I think we can use the trust fund."

"Thank you, Mutti. Thank you."

Imelda came into the room to collect the tea cups.

"Imelda, Master Leo is going on a course in Stuttgart. I can pay you a more if you will help him with his packing. We can take that out of the trust fund as well."

"Frau Lehrs, there is no need. I am happy to do that. You pay me as much as my friend gets. She works for Frau Bieber down the road and has to do nearly twice as many hours as I do. I'm grateful to be earning something and to work for such a nice family."

Leo smiled at his mother. The old Leo was coming back and Imelda thought they were a nice family. It was all looking good.

19 June 1921, Stuttgart: Rudolf Steiner

Leo stepped out into the bright summer sunshine. He hadn't realised how stuffy the room inside the school had become. The air outside was fresher. A gentle breeze made the leaves flutter. He was sure he would never forget the sight of this tree-lined street. There was something special about the place, he knew. It was as if he was seeing the world for the first time.

He'd heard them talking about colours during a coffee break. Goethe's theory of colour. Goethe. Da Vinci. Copernicus. The old guys. What they were saying was still true. But they'd never told the whole story. They couldn't have. They hadn't known it all then. Neither did Einstein or Planck. Yet. But this man. This man did, Leo was sure of that.

A cloud passed briefly in front of the sun. He remembered his laboratory where he'd normally be at this time on a working day. Where he'd measure, record and calculate, never finding any meaningful conclusion. He had to be accurate there. He must tell no lies. He mustn't guess. Yet there must be an explanation for everything. In fact, most of it we know. Deep down. We recognise it all.

The other day he'd heard Rudolf Steiner talk about what happens to adolescents during sleep. He'd described them processing the knowledge offered to them the day before by their teachers. It sounded so right and didn't contradict what the scientists were saying. Yes, the man used strange words like "astral" and "etheric" bodies, but all the same, what he said made sense.

Today he'd mentioned the scientists. He hadn't condemned them. He'd merely said that they didn't have the full picture yet and were only offering a partial explanation of how rather than why or for what purpose. Educating young minds – and souls – would be a good purpose for him; Leo was more and more convinced of that. Everyone was getting so excited these days about relativity and discovering how matter was formed but even if all of that was proved – and more – it didn't really answer some of the questions that were beginning to form in his head.

There was no unified theory of science yet. One truth contradicted another. The opposite of one truth was another truth. He knew that he was more than a bunch of nerves and reactions. Now he had some idea of what having a soul meant. But it wasn't like what they talked about in the synagogue or the church. Compared with what this man was saying all of that was just fairy tales. Though of course, some of those stories carried a message…

The others had all gone, making their way back to their lodgings and their supper. Leo guessed he should do the same. He heard the front door shut. He turned to see what had happened. And there he was, face to face with the man himself.

Steiner nodded briefly.

"Thank you for the lecture. I… er… I found it very… illuminating." Why was he so tongue-tied? Why couldn't he think of something intelligent to say?

Steiner nodded and his dark eyes looked straight into Leo's. Leo knew for certain that he had a soul and that Steiner was looking at it.

"We aim to please. Will you come to the series in September?"

"I hope to." Leo knew he absolutely would have to.

"Good." Steiner nodded again. "Good evening to you." He turned away from Leo and made his way along the street.

Leo thought he looked more like a forty-year-old. He knew Rudolf Steiner was over sixty but he had no grey hair at all nor hardly a wrinkle. His father had looked twice that age when he'd died and he's only been fifty-six.

24 September 1921 Berlin: like father, like son

Leo let himself into the apartment, hung up his coat and put his hat on the hat-stand. He was glad he'd got his own key. He wanted to have as much time as possible to himself before he took up this difficult conversation with his mother. She would ask him about his studies. He would tell her that they were going well. That wasn't a lie: they were. He would soon be finished and it looked as if he was going to get a distinction in his doctorate. It was what he wanted to do afterwards that would puzzle her. And perhaps annoy her. He wanted to be a teacher. He could think of nothing better than educating young minds. Now that he'd been to more of the Steiner lectures.

His sister would give him a hard time, he knew. She wouldn't be allowed to do anything with her degree once she got it. She wouldn't be allowed to work as a researcher or as a lecturer. She would be so cross with him for giving up the opportunity of doing something that was being denied her.

"Come to lunch on Sunday," his mother had said. "Käthe is keeping something from me. Maybe you can help me to get it out of her."

The front door opened again and in came Rudi. Where had he come from? Was there another mystery for their mother here?

"You're all heathens," said Rudi. "I'm the only one who has been to church today."

Perhaps that was one child their mother didn't need to worry about. Going to church meant they were keeping up appearances. That would please her.

"Are you coming through?" Rudi asked. "Does Mutti know you're here?"

Leo shook his head. "I'll be through in a moment," he said. "You go ahead. Don't tell them I'm here yet."

He looked in the mirror. He saw a man who looked much younger than the one he felt himself to be. "Who exactly are you?" he whispered. Was he an old soldier? A dutiful son? An engineer?

An academic? He knew that he was all of those things but that the real essence of him was something entirely different.

He felt dizzy. His reflection in the mirror changed. Then he was looking not at himself but at his father. Only it was his father without any deformity. He had a straight back now and straight legs and stood up tall. It was an image of his father as he would have been if illness and the Great War hadn't damaged him so much.

Leo shook his head again. The dizziness cleared. He was looking at himself.

What did that all mean? Why had he seen his father that way? He wanted to be more like him didn't he? Should he even name himself after him?

The door to the drawing-room opened. His mother came out. "There you are," she said. "I was wondering where you'd got to. Come in. Lunch will soon be ready. I've baked a cheesecake for dessert."

Leo tried his best to smile. Oh dear. There was so much to talk about. On top of everything else, he must discuss with his mother his desire to change his name to that of his father's. From now on he wanted to be known as Ernst Lehrs.

24 September 1921, Berlin: a mother's lot

"So, why do you want to change your name? I don't understand." Clara stared at Leo.

"Don't you think it's good that I want to take on father's name?"

It was a reasonable idea. But why? Why did he want to do that? "Well?"

"Well, yes. I suppose it's an honour for him. But I really don't understand. We named you Leopold Edgar for specific reasons and decided not to name you after your father. Why do you want to change?"

Leo looked away. "I think it would be a really good idea. It seems right."

She couldn't argue with that. She sighed. "I have no objection." She really didn't. She liked the idea in some ways. But she also knew there was something bizarre behind it. So, she had something else to worry about.

Was that a mother's lot, always to have to worry about her children, even when they were grown-up?

Rudi came in.

"Are you all right?" she asked Rudi. He looked less pale than usual. Perhaps the fresh air had done him good.

"Yes, fine, Mutti," he replied. "Please stop fussing."

Clara nodded. "Where's Käthe?"

"Sitting in her room," said Rudi. "She's taking the petals off some flowers. No company at all."

Clara was fairly certain she knew what that meant. Who had given her flowers? Who was he? Who was this man that was intriguing her so?

"Rudi, Ernst, I think your sister is in love, but she won't say with whom."

"Ernst? Mother, you're getting your names mixed up," said Rudi.

"She isn't, actually," said Leo. "I've decided to take on Vater's name. I want to be known as Ernst from now on."

"Why?" Käthe appeared in the doorway. She had woken up from her day-dreaming.

"Why not?" Clara was relieved that something had caught her daughter's attention. "Your father was a great man. It will be good if Ernst carries on his name."

Yes, he had been a great man and it still made her sad to remember him. But why, why, why was Leo doing this? Why did he want to do this strange thing?

26 February 1922, Berlin: a meeting in the Tiergarten

This had got to stop. She was going to get to the bottom of it. She had had enough of her daughter's mooning about and sulking. She was a grown woman but was behaving like a spoilt little girl. She'd been so rude at breakfast.

"I'm not going to church today," she'd declared. "I'm going for a walk."

"But it's so cold, Käthe and so slippery underfoot. It may snow again. I mean, we don't mind if you don't want to go to church. But for goodness sake, stay in and keep warm."

"No. I need some fresh air. I can't bear to stay in a moment longer." She got up from the dining table and left the room.

She could imagine what Ernst would have said. "Don't you remember what it was like? It's only natural at her age. It's about time she found herself a fine young man."

The front door hadn't slammed yet. More proof at least that she was off to meet a beau. She'd probably spent some time adjusting her hat and plumping up her cheeks. Not that she'd need to worry about that. The cold and the sunshine would soon give her a bright glow.

All at once Clara knew exactly what she must do. She waited for the door to slam. Then she quickly made her way to the hall, grabbed her cloak and she was ready.

As soon as she was through the door, she spotted her daughter at the end of the road, looking as if she was going towards the Kurfürstendamm. But then she turned into Lietzenburgerstrasse. She was walking pretty smartly, too. It was a job to keep up. Where was she going?

Käthe ducked into one of the side streets. She was going up towards the Kurfürstenstrasse. So, she probably was going to the Tiergarten. At least it would be easy enough to keep hidden from her, though if there were a lot of people there it would also be easy to lose her. Thank goodness it was so cold. Perhaps not so many people would be there after all.

Yes, Käthe made her way to the entrance of the Tiergarten. Clara followed her along the tree-lined alleys. She was heading towards the café near the lake. A few moments later she arrived at the entrance and made her way in.

What should she do? Clara decided to slip in the other entrance and sit down as far away as she could but near enough to be able to watch what Käthe was doing. She took one of the broadsheet newspapers off the rack and made her way to a table.

Ah. There he was. Käthe joined a youngish man sitting at one of the tables. He stood up and kissed her on the cheek. My, oh my, her daughter was growing up. A strange young man kissing her on the cheek in public – on a Sunday!

Clara looking out occasionally from behind her newspaper to see what they were doing. She tried to get a good look at the man but it was impossible without staring. But she could see that they were talking animatedly. Käthe's cheeks were getting rosier. Their heads were close together and they were holding hands across the table.

Who was he? Even though she was only able to take tiny glimpses of him she soon became aware that there was something familiar about him. She couldn't think how she might know him, though. He was clearly somewhat older than Käthe, but not enough that it really mattered. There was something that made her feel uneasy. She was not sure what. There was something not right about this relationship – why hadn't Käthe introduced them to him? Why didn't she want them to know?

They ordered more coffee. Should she do the same? Should she go over to them, perhaps, and introduce herself? But Käthe would really wonder what her mother was doing in the Tiergarten and would know that she'd been following her.

Clara decided she should order more coffee as well. As the waitress was about to pour it into Clara's cup her sleeve somehow caught on the side of the table and she dropped the coffee pot, breaking the cup and sending the hot liquid all over the white tablecloth. Clara jumped up from her seat and managed to avoid the coffee running on to her skirt.

"I am so sorry, madam," stammered the waitress. "Let me move you to another table and get you some more coffee."

Several of the other guests had turned round to stare. However, Käthe and her young man, Clara was pleased to notice, were still completely absorbed in each other.

"Don't worry at all," said Clara. "It was an accident and there is no damage except to your beautiful white tablecloth. That should boil so the stain should come out. You're not injured, are you?"

The young waitress shook her head. "If you'd follow me, madam."

She led Clara to a new table. They were going away from where Käthe was sitting. What a relief! But Clara looked up at the mirror that ran around the walls above the dado rail. Käthe was staring back at her.

"Mutti!" she called. "What are you doing here?"

Clara turned to face her daughter and then walked over to her. "I... er... I just wanted to see what you were up to." There was no point in lying.

"Mutti! Don't you trust me?" Käthe's eyes flashed.

The young man who had stood up at her side – who looked even more familiar now, though Clara still couldn't worked out why – cleared his throat.

"Well, aren't you going to introduce us?" Clara looked at her daughter.

"Mutti, this is Professor Hans Edler. Hans, this is my mother, Clara Lehrs."

"I'm pleased to meet you, Frau Lehrs," said Hans, offering his hand to Clara. "Why don't you join us?"

Clara took his hand and nodded. As she sat down at the table, the waitress appeared with another tray laden with a coffee pot and fresh cups.

"So, tell me how you two met," Clara said. She patted her daughter's arm. "Why have you been so secretive about this? I'm sure Professor Edler is a respectable young man."

"I am one of Käthe's lecturers," said Hans. "If our friendship comes into the open, she will have to give up her studies. We're hoping that attitudes will change in due course."

Ah. That was where she knew him from. And that was why they were being so secretive.

Käthe slammed the door as soon as they were through it. "I don't see why it matters. Why can't I walk out with Professor Edler and still carry on with my studies? It's barbaric. This is the twentieth century you know." She rushed off to her room.

Clara had spent the whole journey back agreeing with her daughter that it wasn't fair that she should have to give up her studies and that the age difference didn't matter. She'd even said that she found Hans Edler a charming man. As usual, though, Käthe argued with her even when she was agreeing. No one ever understood anything as well as Käthe did.

What would Ernst have done? Oh, how she missed him. He would have surely had something wise to say about the situation.

Should she ask her sons for advice?

No. It was all up to her.

Perhaps she should ask this Hans Edler to dinner. Yes. That would be a good idea. She should get to know him better.

2 March 1922, Berlin: a proposal

Clara felt inexplicably nervous. What was there to be afraid of? A respectable young man was coming to dinner. True, Käthe might be awkward, but she was used to that. It was just part of life. Was it because it was the first of their children to be involved in a romance? Ernst still showed no sign of any interest in the fairer sex. Rudi was too stuck in his books to bother much. And perhaps it was just as well. How would he cope with his illness and a courtship?

She remembered the early days with Ernst. She'd been absolutely sure he was the only man for her but at first she'd no idea how he really felt. So there had been for her too the day-dreaming, the anxiety – does he love me, will he visit, am I good enough for him? The butterflies in the tummy. The tingles of pleasure when they accidentally touched, especially when it had been a hand on a bare arm and the longing for more that couldn't come until after they'd married. All of that had been so wonderful. Did Käthe understand that side of the relationships between men and women? She dreaded trying to tell her but she supposed she ought to.

Poor Käthe. With all of this there was the desire to continue studying and become a scientist.

The door opened.

"What do you think?"

Käthe's dress was gold with floaty sleeves. The hem was jagged and at its highest showed half of her well-shaped calves. Its low waist flattered her figure. Goodness, if he didn't love her already he would fall in love with her tonight for sure.

"You look lovely, dear. Would you like to borrow my pearls?"

"May I? Oh thank you, Mutti." She embraced Clara and kissed her on the cheek. "I thought you were going to be terribly old-fashioned and tell me it was too short."

What was she like, this daughter of hers? Didn't she realise that her mother found the new fashions fun and liberating?

She fetched the pearls and gently fastened them around her

daughter's neck. "There. They go really well with your dress."

Käthe grinned. She really did look nice when she smiled, which actually wasn't often enough, Clara decided.

The doorbell chimed.

"Come on," said Clara. "Let's go and welcome him together."

The meal was pleasant. Clara had made the Apfelstrudel herself and Hans was appreciative. He was extremely good company. He chatted pleasantly about some of the topics of the day. His eyes shone when he looked at Käthe. Oh yes, he was in love with her all right. Clara could tell that he cared for her daughter very much. And Käthe behaved like the charming young woman she never usually managed to be.

"Thank you for such a lovely meal, Frau Lehrs. And now there is something I'd like to discuss with both of you."

"Oh?" said Käthe.

"I'm giving up my post at the university. I've been offered a position with Siemens. It will mean I need to move to Jena." He looked directly at Käthe. "Our relationship can come out into the open."

"But Jena…?"

"Please let me finish." He turned towards Clara. "Frau Lehrs, may I ask for your daughter's hand in marriage?"

"Of course," said Clara. Her heart was bumping into her rib cage. Please God don't let her refuse him.

Käthe went to say something but Hans put his fingers on her lips, stood up from the table and got down on his knees. He took her hand. "Käthe Lehrs, will you marry me? You can continue your studies in Jena. You may come back to Berlin if you wish. I am even happy for you to visit Professor Einstein in Switzerland. But please be my wife."

Clara held her breath. Käthe blushed. Hans looked pale. Then two tears made their way down Käthe's cheek. Was she going to refuse him?

"Yes," she whispered. "Of course. Yes."

Thank goodness.

"I think we should open a bottle of Sekt," said Clara, getting up from the table. "And welcome to the family, Hans."

As she left the room she couldn't help feeling glad that someone else would soon share in the responsibility for keeping her daughter happy. She would be able to concentrate more on her two sons. They needed her. One had been damaged by the Great War and the other was still physically weak.

It was late by the time Hans left. Clara had allowed Imelda to go off duty so she and Käthe were washing the dishes into the kitchen.

"You do understand, don't you, what happens when a man and his wife lie together?" said Clara, looking away from her daughter and feeling her cheeks going red.

"Oh you mean that he gets an erection when we touch and that then he puts his penis into my vagina and when he climaxes his sperm goes into me? And that's what makes babies? Mother what do you think? I'm a scientist. Of course I know these things. In fact, I've even noticed his erection when he's held me close a couple of times."

Clara turned her face away even further.

"I've even read that a woman can get a climax as well. An orgasm. Have you ever experienced that, Mutti? With Vati? Oh no. Don't tell me. It doesn't bear thinking about. You and Vati."

"Good, then. I suppose we'd better get our heads together about the wedding plans."

"Oh, yes please. The sooner the better. I can't wait for Hans to make love to me properly."

So, Käthe had simply been on her best behaviour tonight and hadn't changed at all. But there was one thing she wouldn't, couldn't tell her daughter: how glorious it had been making love with Ernst, even if it had led to seven miscarriages and three painful labours. Oh yes, she knew about female climaxes. But that must remain her secret. She couldn't bring herself to talk to her daughter about it.

15 October 1922, Berlin: career change

He looked pale again. Was he still troubled? Was he still remembering the war? They were all still suffering, to be sure. He sat staring at his tea.

"Are you going to drink that or just look at it?" Clara asked.

Ernst took a sip of the tea.

"So, what's the matter? Is there anything wrong with your studies?"

"No. It's not that."

"Well, what then?"

Was it some woman, perhaps? Goodness, she'd got the love life of one of her children sorted out. Had she got to start on another?

"I think I want to teach."

"Well, of course. I'm sure they will be happy to invite you in to give a few guest lectures. It's quite normal isn't it? Especially once you're established in your line of work?"

"That's not what I meant, Mutti."

Clara looked at her son. He became even paler now and began to sweat.

"So, what do you mean?"

"I want to be an ordinary school teacher."

Something collapsed inside Clara. There was a job waiting for him at his father's firm. He was supposed to become the chairman. It was what Ernst senior had worked towards, even after he became so ill. It was what his former colleagues were expecting.

"But what about the factory?"

Ernst shrugged. "Maybe Rudi can take my place."

Clara shook her head. It would be too much strain for Rudi. His health wouldn't permit him to take so much responsibility.

"Mother it will be fine. We'll still have shares in the company. So I'll still be able to make decisions at the shareholders' meetings. We can pay someone to manage it if Rudi doesn't want to."

"All right. But why do you want to be a teacher?"

"To give something back. To help young people avoid the stupidity we've seen recently."

"You mean the Great War and the hyperinflation?"

"Yes, that, and the lack of spirituality. The lack of soul. We've lost our way, Mutti."

Clara looked away from her son. Yes, she understood all of that. The Great War had been senseless. Nothing was resolved in the so-called peace. This ridiculous inflation was one of the terrible by-products. But Ernst completing his studies and taking the job in the firm his father had built up meant security of a sort. That aside, though, she understood exactly what he meant. Machines and science were all very well in their place. Mankind needed something else as well.

She turned back to face her son. "Promise me at least that you will finish your studies," she said.

"Yes, of course," said Ernst. "I'll be in a better position to teach anyway if I gain that qualification. They'll be pleased to see that I have the self-discipline to finish what I've started."

The sun came out from behind the clouds, flooding the room with light. The colour came back to Ernst's face. She could see him in a classroom surrounded by children. "Then you must do what you think right," she said.

15 March 1923, Berlin: a wedding dress

Clara removed the dress carefully from its tissue and hung it up on the stand in her daughter's bedroom. It was exquisite. So much like the one she had worn the day Hans had proposed: low-waisted, soft and floaty and quite short – coming a little way below the knee by the look of it. It had that same golden shimmer about it too.

"I don't want pure white," Käthe had insisted. "I'm not all innocent and virginal. I want something modern."

Clara had wondered how literally she'd meant that. Had they already slept together? Was Käthe already so used to making love to a man that she was no longer passive and had she already encountered that deep space within her body where there was that explosion of light and that intense feeling that there was nothing in the world but the pair of them? And if so, had they been careful? God forbid that any baby should arrive too early.

The dress was lovely, anyway, even if unconventional and not at all pure white. The train that would fall flow behind her and the veil that would drape over her head and shoulders at least made it like a wedding dress. Clara wondered how it would compare with what the bride of the young British prince would wear. Prince Albert was due to marry Lady Elizabeth Bowes-Lyon a few days before Käthe's and Hans's wedding.

The dressmaker, Frau Schachner, would bring the veil along when she came to fit the dress on Käthe later than evening. And then they must discuss the question of payment again.

Frau Schachner had been very kind.

"Don't worry," she said. "The government will have to do something soon. Once they have found a solution we can settle this."

It wasn't too bad for Clara herself. She received a pension from the firm. It wasn't fixed and followed the rate of inflation. But she never actually took the money in notes or coins – except for the exact amount needed for the house-keeping. She used most of her income as credit. Frau Schachner was relatively fortunate too. Her son was one of these rich young men who was playing the system and gaining a good dividends on his shares. He looked after his mother. She, in turn, was able to offer her clients credit.

Clara had suggested she might want to take one of the oil paintings or even Ernst's gold watch as payment.

"No," Frau Schachner had insisted. "We'll wait until there is real money again. This dress has been about a month's work. We'll decide at the time when they fix the new money exactly how much a month of my time is worth."

It was sensible, Clara knew. And she also knew that whatever her month's pension became, it would more than cover the dressmaker's bill. Frau Schachner was always reasonable.

Clara heard the front door close. Imelda was back. She hurried down to the kitchen to greet her. She found the maid looking flushed and triumphant. She was unpacking the big bags.

"I've managed to get fresh potatoes, onions and stewing beef for today. And a little cheese and fresh bread. And I've turned all the other cash into preserved fish, sausages, flour and tinned vegetables. I don't think we'll starve, Frau Lehrs."

Thank goodness Imelda always got the best out of the shopkeepers and that she was able to turn cash into goods so swiftly. Other families weren't so fortunate.

"You did well," said Clara. "Come, let me help you pack away. And as you have flour I shall make a few biscuits to celebrate. You must come and watch Käthe having her wedding dress fitted this evening."

"I should like that very much," said Imelda. "Thank you Frau Lehrs."

"No, thank you," said Clara. Imelda really was a godsend.

17 May 1923, Berlin: breathless

Clara heard the front door click shut. He was back. Typical Rudi. He made hardly any sound at all. Should she hurry out and meet him or wait for him to come and tell her? She heard him clear his throat. Was that meaningful? Was he telling her to come out and speak to him?

She rushed into the hallway. "Well? What did they say?"

Rudi grinned. He shook his head and raised his eyebrows. "Mutti, you are so impatient."

"Come on. Tell me what Doctor Merten said."

"That there is no more scarring. That my lung function is good. And." He bit his lip as if he was trying to stop himself from smiling but his eyes gave him away.

"Go on then," said Clara.

"And I don't need to go back unless there's actually a problem. He said it was like some sort of miracle."

"But the night attacks you still get sometimes? And when you wheeze when there is so much pollen?"

Rudi shrugged. "They'll probably go on forever. But he reckons I'm taking care of it all well enough. There may be some new drugs coming out soon and he'll recommend that Doctor Lamm prescribes them if he thinks they'll be helpful."

Clara nodded. Yes, Rudi knew how to get the right amount of steam into his room to help his breathing. But if there could be drugs that could help him to stop that happening at all, even better. "Look, I'm popping out for a few minutes. When I get back perhaps we can talk some more?"

Rudi shrugged again. "If you wish."

Clara was still out of breath as she sat in Doctor Lamm's consulting room. She had run all the way from Pariser Street.

"Take your time," said the doctor. "And tell me what the matter is."

"It's Rudi," she said. "I think he's lying to me."

"Lying to you? Oh, yes, he had his hospital visit today, didn't he? How did that go?"

"He says that they don't want to see him again."

"Well that's good news isn't it?"

"I don't believe him, though. Can you tell me if it's true? I'm sure he's only saying that so I'll let him go away to study."

"Frau Lehrs, he's a young man of twenty-two. Of course he can go away and study. Lung disease or not."

Damn this man. Why wouldn't he help her? She pulled herself up as straight as she could in her chair. "Doctor, Lamm, will you please tell me whether my son is cured?"

The doctor sighed. "Frau Lehrs, even if were allowed to tell you – and I'm not – Doctor Merten has hardly had time to write his notes and send them to me."

"Well, can't you phone him or something?"

"He would still be in clinic, I'd imagine."

"Please?"

The doctor hesitated. He looked as if he was going to reach for the phone but as he did so it rang anyway. He picked up the receiver.

"Good morning. Doctor Zelig Lamm."

Clara went to get up but the doctor indicated that she should stay in the room. She gripped the sides of her chair. She wished he would hurry up and finish his call and then phone the hospital to find out about Rudi.

"I see. Good. Thank you for letting me know."

Clara could hear the distorted voice of the person on the other end of the phone but couldn't make out what they were saying.

"Yes, yes. I'll do that. Good day to you."

"Doctor, please…"

"Well, Frau Lehrs, I shouldn't really tell you this but that was Doctor Merten. He wanted to let me know that he has discharged Rudi and also that the clinical trials on the new drug should be finished as early as next week. He wants me to prescribe them for Rudi. Are you happy now?"

Clara leapt out of her seat, rushed over to Doctor Lamm and kissed him. The doctor blushed.

"I'm sorry. Oh I'm so sorry. But thank you. Thank you." What was she thinking, embarrassing the doctor like that?

She ran out of the building and started making her way back to Pariser Street.

Rudi really was well. And with this new drug he could have a normal life. She couldn't wait to get back to the apartment. They could make plans. She ran. She ran as fast as she could. It probably wasn't dignified for a woman her age running like that but she didn't care. She ignored the people staring at her.

It was odd. She was running so fast yet she was taking in all of the details of her surroundings. Colours were more vibrant than ever. She noticed window boxes where she'd never seen them before. Each had its own particular arrangements of plants. She noticed doors and curtains in different colours. She could hear birds singing, babies crying and children playing. Voices, everywhere. This world was wonderful and she and Rudi were going to enjoy it for some time yet.

She was breathless again by the time she got home. She slammed the door behind her, Käthe-style, and leaned against it, trying to get her breath back.

Rudi appeared in the hallway.

"Mutti, where have you been? Are you all right?"

She nodded. "I went to see Doctor Lamm," she said when she could breathe again. "I wanted to find out if it really was true. That you are well enough not to have to bother with any more hospital visits."

Rudi rolled his eyes. "Mutti, I don't tell lies."

"I know. I know. It sounded too good to be true."

"Well, it is true. And now will you let me go and study mathematics?"

"Of course. Yes, study what you like. Come on. Let's go and talk about it."

2 June 1923, Berlin: preparations for a journey

He had to get away. He needed time to think. He knew he'd promised his mother that he would finish his doctorate. But he was being pressed to complete his training for teaching at the Waldorf School. He was so close to finishing, but the Steiner association said they needed him. Rudolf Steiner was insisting.

Rudi had suggested that they go on a short trip together. He had been less certain. Rudi shouldn't exert himself, really. And was going for a trip in the mountains advisable for someone with malfunctioning lungs?

"Ernst, it will be good for me. We won't do anything too strenuous. Some gentle strolls. The doctors say I need some exercise."

Yes, he was very persuasive. Okay, so they were going to do it.

They'd decided on the Black Forest. It wasn't quite so high up there. There were some quite easy walks, too.

Ernst stared at the rucksack in the shop window. If he and Rudi did do this trip he would need a new one. He knew that his old one had holes in it. The price of 1,000,000 marks wasn't bad for one that looked as sturdy as that. Maybe he should get Rudi one, too? Or perhaps not. 2,000,000 marks would be a lot of money to spend if they didn't go after all. They had yet to persuade their mother.

He set off back towards the Pariser Street apartment.

Rudi and his mother were in the drawing-room when he got there. Rudi was looking pleased with himself. "Well, big brother," he said. "We are going away. Our trip is on. The good doctor has given his permission."

His mother was grinning. Well, he guessed he couldn't argue with them anymore.

"Certainly the fresh air will do you both good. And I hope you can come back refreshed and complete the last few weeks of your work with new vigour, Ernst."

"Easy. It won't be a problem, Mutti. He'll manage it fine. Mind you, he'll have to watch out. I'm catching him up rapidly."

"You didn't have a war to contend with," said Clara quickly.

"No, just lungs that don't work properly."

"It's not a competition," said Ernst.

"So, when will you set off? Do you need anything? Can I help in any way?"

"We could do with new rucksacks," said Ernst.

"Good," said Clara. "I have some cash that needs using up." She handed Ernst 25,000,000 marks.

"Mother, that's far too much," said Ernst.

"Well, spend it anyway. It won't keep. You'll surely need some provisions as well for the journey."

Ernst took the money and set off back to the shop where he'd seen the rucksack.

There were two left when he got there.

"I'd like the two rucksacks in the window," he told the assistant.

"That will be 20,000,000 marks," said the young man.

What? They'd gone up that much in what – how long had he been – an hour?

"Very well," said Ernst. "And what could you sell me for 100,000 marks?"

"Nothing really. You could try the stationers next door. Maybe a note book?"

That might be an idea. He could record their journey in it or try and work out his thoughts on this new life he wanted to take on. He handed the money over to the assistant.

"I'll go next door while you wrap those up," he said. If he waited a moment longer the 100,000 mark wouldn't even buy a piece of paper.

23 June 1923, Berlin: Albrecht Strohschein

Clara sighed contentedly. All three children appeared to be happy. Ernst had decided exactly what he needed to do. He hadn't said anything but she could tell he was more content. And he'd certainly not mentioned giving up his studies. Rudi had come back from his trip looking extremely healthy and had started applying for a place to study. The doctors were still pleased with his progress. She'd heard nothing from Käthe, apart from a postcard from Geneva. They'd be back from honeymoon. Clara could only conclude that married life must suit her daughter. She guessed that if there had been any problem she would have heard about it.

Ernst would be here soon, for dinner. He was bringing a young man he wanted her to meet. She was glad at least that he had some friends. No sign of any young lady. This young man, though? Well, perhaps Ernst was a bit different. No, surely not. Hopefully not. He'd been keen for her to meet him. There must be some reason.

She smoothed the tablecloth over once more. Yes, it all looked good. There were flowers on the table and the wine glasses sparkled. It looked inviting. Any friend of any of her children was a friend of hers and she would always make them welcome.

Imelda came in with the plates of salad. She'd managed to put some colourful bits and pieces together. She was such an asset, this young woman.

"Will they be here, soon, Frau Lehrs? Only I don't want the vegetables to spoil."

"I'm sure they will. Any second now. And thank you for taking such care."

The front door opened and they heard the two young men's voices.

"Mutti, we're here," called Ernst.

Clara went into the hallway.

A tall, straight-backed, smartly dressed young man smiled at her. He was self-assured.

"Mutti, this is Albrecht Strohschein. Albrecht, meet my mother, Frau Clara Lehrs."

Clara took the young man's outstretched hand and shook it.

"I'm so pleased to meet you, Frau Lehrs. Ernst has told me so much about you. It is very kind of you to invite me this evening."

Goodness, thought Clara. He's so confident. And so charming.

He was younger than Ernst, but it looked as if he knew where he was going.

"The dinner won't be long," said Clara. "I'll go and tell Imelda you're here. She's already taken the salad through. Ernst, show your guest where he can freshen up and then take him into the dining room. I'll join you gentlemen in a few minutes."

"So, you're going to continue with this work in Jena." Clara wiped her mouth and put her serviette down on the table.

"Jena, just think, Mutti," said Ernst. "Around the corner from where Käthe lives."

What was her son talking about? She didn't need one of Albrecht Strohschein's cures. Neither did Käthe, she hoped.

"And why would that be so interesting?" She noticed Ernst and Albrecht exchange a glance.

"Mutti, they need a housekeeper at the institute that Albrecht's going to set up there. I – we – think you'd be ideal."

"What are you talking about, Ernst? Your friend has never met me before this evening. How would he know whether I would make him a good housekeeper or not? I'm over fifty for goodness sake. He should find someone younger and more energetic."

"You don't look a day over thirty-five, if you don't mind me saying so, Frau Lehrs," Albrecht said quickly.

Clara burst out laughing. "Oh, flattery will get you everywhere, young man."

Ernst and Albrecht exchanged another glance and then both of them grinned.

"Seriously, though, I don't want to leave Berlin. There are too many happy memories here and all of my friends. And I really do think you should look for someone younger and stronger."

"That's a shame, Frau Lehrs. From everything that Ernst has told me you would be ideal."

"What have you been saying, Ernst?"

Ernst shrugged and shook his head. "I can't think what he means."

"That you are extremely kind, that you have the most incredible sense of humour and that you always see the best in everyone. All fantastic qualities for anyone who comes to work at our institute. Oh, and of course that you are excellent at housework and cooking."

"Oh, Herr Strohschein, really. You try hard, I'll give you that. When would you need this housekeeper by?"

"June next year, perhaps."

"Well, I tell you what," said Clara. "Ask me again in a few months' time. I'm very impressed with this – what do you call it – 'healing pedagogy'. That you can do so much to reach out to those tortured souls. Especially the children."

She hadn't said no. She really didn't want to disappoint them. This wasn't for her. And surely in that time they would find someone else?

"Indeed. Especially the children." Albrecht glanced at Ernst, who nodded his head.

"Frau Lehrs," Albrecht continued, "would you come to Stuttgart in July? To the teachers' conference? Karl Schubert is organising a special class at the Waldorf School. You could see for yourself how this all works."

Clara wanted to say yes. She did find all of this interesting and she was glad that Ernst had found something to feel passionate about. Besides, a trip to Stuttgart couldn't hurt, could it? Yet she mustn't be seen to be encouraging Ernst too much. It may not be practical for him. It was essential that he gained his qualifications first. So that he had something to fall back on if all of this went wrong.

"Ernst, you made a promise to me. Please tell me that you are going to keep that."

"Absolutely, Mutti. My viva is set for 13 September."

"I assure you, Frau Lehrs, I will not let him fail. I keep giving him practice by playing Devil's advocate. He knows his material. He will pass. I'm sure."

"Good, good," said Clara. "An education can never be wasted even if you don't use what you studied ever again." I probably sound like a grumpy old woman, she thought.

"Mutti, I'm not threatening to give up my studies. I'm just asking you to take a look at something I'm interested in."

They probably had no idea how relieved she felt that Ernst had at last found something that set his soul on fire.

"All right. You've persuaded me. I'll come along with Ernst in July."

"Then I very much look forward to showing you how our special teaching methods work," said Albrecht.

"Your friend is a very clever young man," said Clara. "Did he catch the tram all right?"

"Yes. It wasn't a problem anyway. He could have walked if he'd been too late. It's a fine night."

"It was a fine evening as well."

"You liked him?"

"Yes I did. I really did." Why can't you be as confident and as content? thought Clara. But she knew that answer. Albrecht was that bit younger and had not known active service during the war. He'd not been damaged like Ernst.

"I'm so pleased that you've said you'll come to Stuttgart next month," said Ernst. His face was alight.

He looked as if he'd been talking to angels. Goodness, where had that thought come from? She didn't really believe in angels, did she?

"And I will finish my studies and pass my viva. I promised and I do keep promises."

"I know, I know," said Clara. "So Stuttgart, here we come." It was going to be a wrench. Yes, it was only for a few days, but she loved her little routines, here: the strolls in the parks, the meeting with other ladies, some of them also widows, for coffee and cakes and the visits she enjoyed making alone to all the wonderful museums and galleries here in Berlin. Yes, they were all suffering because of the Great War but there was still a lot to be thankful for.

Still, perhaps it was time she learnt something new.

21 July 1923, Stuttgart: Kurt

"Kurt!" she heard the woman cry.

She turned to see the boy – she guessed he was about eleven years old from his height but there was something about the way he moved that made him look younger. The boy had his hands in one of the bowls of fruit and was squashing the berries to make a messy juice. He looked up and grinned at Clara. He held out a red-stained hand towards her.

"Kurt, don't touch the lady. You'll spoil her clothes." The woman turned to Clara. "I'm so sorry," she said. "He does this. Any liquid or anything that can become liquid he has to put his hands in – and then paint everything in sight with it. We're getting him out of it gradually but he's a bit nervous today. He's going to be presented to Doctor Steiner later."

"Is he…?" Clara wasn't sure how to phrase the question.

"Yes, he's one of the special children but he's come on such a lot with all the help he's had here."

Kurt was laughing and waving his hands wildly.

"Look out for your dress!" the woman cried.

"Oh this old thing. It won't harm." Clara was having some difficulty keeping her face straight. She managed to step away from Kurt in time.

"I really am sorry about this," said the woman. "I'm Sister Greta by the way. I'd better go and get this young man tidied up. I won't shake hands – he's already touched me. I really am so sorry."

"Think nothing of it, my dear."

"Come on, you," said Sister Greta, leading Kurt towards the cloakroom. "Let's get you sorted."

It had been a welcome interlude – the conversation with Kurt and Sister Greta as much as the fruit and opportunity to stretch your legs. The delegates were well looked after at this conference. They never had to sit for more than two hours without some refreshment being offered. They'd just enjoyed bowls of fresh raspberries and strawberries. All grown by local families associated with the school, apparently.

She was impressed by the teachers, too. They were friendly, and it was clear that they cared a lot for their pupils.

It was almost time for another break. She was beginning to daydream a little.

She thought of all the places Ernst had shown her. They must have walked a good twenty kilometres over the past couple of days. The people were so friendly, too, though it was difficult to understand what some of them were saying – they sounded a bit as if they'd forgotten to put their false teeth in. But at least they persisted until you understood. Yes, she could see why Ernst would be happy to live and work here.

Now, though, she could do with another break. Not quite yet though apparently. Albrecht Strohschein and another man she thought must be Karl Schubert walked on to the small platform at the front of the hall. They were followed by Sister Greta and Kurt.

Everyone in the hall went quiet and Albrecht stood up and started talking. What he said made an awful lot of sense – even more so than what Doctor Steiner had said earlier.

"It is the task of a healing pedagogy to strengthen positivity and to bring all aspects of the spirit into harmony," he said. "It must help the formation of the personality and aid the child's total development, physically as well as intellectually. The Waldorf School aims to do this anyway with all normal children. A special pedagogy must be developed for those children with troubled spirits. It must also teach them moral responsibility."

There was nothing odd or disturbing about what Albrecht was saying. Of course everybody needed to be brought up in a rounded way. And if anyone could do something with these feebler minded youngsters, then that had to be good.

"We're privileged to have here today Kurt Hansch, his carer, Sister Greta, and his teacher, Karl Schubert," Albrecht continued. "Kurt is going to tell us a little of his experience of learning in a Waldorf School. So, Kurt, please."

The boy stood up. "I like – it in – the Waldorf School. – The – doors in the Waldorf School – all look – like – the – angels' hands – when – they – stretch – them out of the clouds." He looked round at Sister Greta and then turned back towards Albrecht.

"Twelve months ago he couldn't say a single word. He hadn't ever spoken." Albrecht looked out towards the delegates. "It's our mission to make life as normal as possible for these children."

Everyone clapped. Kurt joined in. Then he started wobbling Albrecht's arm. Sister Greta and Karl Schubert both tried to pull him away.

"I want to talk to the lady in the green dress," Kurt shouted. He pointed at Clara.

Clara felt her cheeks burn.

"We're going to have another break, Kurt," said Karl Schubert. "Perhaps you can speak to her then."

Kurt hurtled down from the platform and ran over to Clara, grabbed her hand and pulled her up from her seat.

Clara found herself being rushed through the other delegates.

"I want – to show – you the – flowers," said Kurt. "We planted – the – flow – ers. Do you – like flowers?" He dragged her through the French windows.

"I do. I like them very much," replied Clara.

"Slow down, Kurt. Let Frau Lehrs get her breath back." Sister Greta raised her eyebrows and shook her head.

"It's fine," said Clara. "Well, young man, why don't you show me which flowers you planted?"

Kurt pulled her over to a bed full of lobelia. "I did – the blue – ones. Hansi did – the –white ones and Maria made – the – yellow – flow-ers."

"Well you did a splendid job," said Clara. She pointed to a small garden bench that was in the shade. "Why don't we go and sit over there and you can tell me all about it?"

"Yes," said Kurt. He gripped Clara's hand even tighter.

They moved over to the bench. Sister Greta followed.

I would never have imagined, thought Clara as they sat down, that so much could be done with a child like this. If only more people could live in and be here all the time for children like him. She smiled at the boy.

23 July 1923, Schwäbisch Gmund: dreams

Clara relished the fresh air. It was glorious that she and Ernst could spend a few days here before they went back to Berlin. It was warm but not hot. And the air was so fresh. Just right for walking. For up here the land rolled away and they could see kilometres of woodland and open meadow, punctuated by small villages and divided by brooks and rivers. Berlin was all very well with its new green parks but it wasn't quite the same as being out here in the open countryside. Ernst would be so lucky. He could come here at weekends and maybe in the school holidays if he didn't come back home.

"Schwarzbrot and Käse?" said Ernst. He opened the rucksack and took out two sandwiches wrapped in paper. "There's fruit and some Sprudel as well."

"That's such a practical little bag," said Clara.

"Considering how much it cost."

"It was expensive?"

"That's why I bought us both one – me and Rudi – before they went up in price again."

It was madness, all this money. At least some of hers was safe and invested in her jewellery. "Just think," she said, "if I sold my pearls I could buy a house and set it up for the teachers of the Waldorf School. What do you think?"

"A nice idea, Mutti. But do you think it would really be practical? We need you at the Lauenstein."

"Mmm."

"What does 'mmm' mean?"

"I don't mind running a house I own but I'm not as sure about working as a paid housekeeper."

"We need you, though, Mutti."

"And I need some fruit. Pass me an apple."

Clara gave him one of her looks – and knew he would not broach the subject again until she gave him permission.

30 January 1924, Berlin: stale coffee

"What on earth is the matter, Clara?" Griselda held the coffee pot, ready to pour. "You've not touched your coffee. It'll be cold. Shall I get the waitress to bring you another cup?"

"Yes, you've been day-dreaming. Is there anything wrong?" Jarvia's eyes were kind, though both Griselda and Katrina were frowning.

"Not still worrying about those children of yours, are you?" said Katrina. "It's time you left well alone. They're old enough to look after themselves. Come on. Make the most of this. We're all luckier than many. We should be grateful."

"Oh, I'm not worried," said Clara. She wasn't telling any lies. She was thinking about them, that was all. Not worrying, just thinking. Though she was wondering whether she should be doing something more. Was Ernst right? Should she move to Jena to be nearer to him and Käthe?

And she was asking herself what she was doing here. It was the third Wednesday of the month and the four ladies had met at the Romanisches Café. It was busy as usual. It always was on a Wednesday afternoon. People would sit at their tables for hours, the four of them included. It wasn't really the sort of place they'd normally go to. It wasn't elegant enough and the food was rather simple. But the other people who went there were fascinating.

"Oh, look," said Katrina. "It's the poet again. He's muttering to himself, like he did last time."

"Do you think we should ask him what he's been writing? You never know, he might be famous one day." Griselda's eyes were sparkling.

"Go on. I dare you." Katrina nudged her.

They're behaving like teenagers, thought Clara.

"Leave the poor man in peace," said Jarvia. "What do you say, Clara?"

"I say it's none of our business. We shouldn't be spying on

these people like this. If they want to come and write poetry here it's up to them."

"Oh, Clara, really. Stop being such a killjoy. It was your idea to come here in the first place. You told us how fascinating it would be to rub shoulders with the next generation of literary greats. And it is interesting. Go on, admit it. You know it is." Griselda was looking straight at her. Her eyebrows were raised.

Clara wanted to look away.

"Well it was your idea, wasn't it?"

Clara sighed. "Yes, I suppose it was." It had been such fun when they'd first started coming here six months ago. All those serious young men, and one or two young women as well and all those long-haired professor-types, all bent over their manuscripts and writing away. But today it felt wrong – like a type of voyeurism, and intrusive.

"You know, I think Clara has a point."

Thank you Jarvia, thought Clara. The woman was younger than Griselda, Katrina and herself, and poorer as well. In fact she blended in better with the other people in the café than the rest of them did. Her grey felt hat perched modestly on the side of her head and her thin-rimmed spectacles made her look more serious than the other two women with their flamboyant flower-bedecked headwear. Clara felt self-conscious about her fur cape and her pearls. What were they thinking, showing off like this?

"So Clara, how are the children?" said Jarvia.

A waitress passed at that moment and Griselda stopped her. "Will you bring a fresh cup for this lady?" She pointed to Clara's cold coffee. The young woman looked flustered.

"It's all right my dear. Take your time," said Clara.

Katrina frowned. "It's not very good service here," she muttered.

Clara ignored her and turned back to Jarvia. "Ernst is settled in teaching. Rudi's enjoying his studies and Käthe is thriving on married life. And what about your two?"

"Magda's broken off her engagement to Thomas."

"Oh, I'm so sorry. Whatever happened?" Clara put her hand

gently on the younger woman's arm.

Katrina and Griselda looked at each other and shook their heads.

"She says she doesn't want to make life difficult for him. With us being Jewish, you know…"

"Oh, surely there's no need for that?"

"She thinks it's for the best."

"It might be. She might be right," said Katrina.

"You can't think that's right?" What was wrong with people? Race, religion – none of that was important. Personal happiness, following your dreams – that was all that mattered. Wasn't it? "But Georg? Is everything all right with him?"

Jarvia grinned. "He had the results of his exams last week. He has completed his studies and is a fully qualified doctor. He starts work at the clinic next week."

"I'm so pleased for you."

"I must say, I'm grateful we don't have any of these worries," said Katrina. "Our sons will simply go into the family business. No need for hours of study and certainly no question of religion interfering with anything."

Griselda was nodding vigorously.

Well, good for you, thought Clara.

"That waitress is taking a long time with that cup," said Griselda.

"Look. It doesn't matter. I've got a bit of a headache. I think I'm going to go home." Clara got up out of her seat.

Three pairs of eyes were looking at her. Katrina and Griselda looked almost offended. Only Jarvia was sympathetic.

"The coffee was stale, anyway," said Clara. "Do you mind if I settle up next time?"

She got up from the table and made her way out of the café before any of them could reply.

It wasn't only the coffee that was stale. It was the company as well. She used to enjoy these get-togethers so much. Now they had become a complete bore. What was the matter with her?

It was beginning to get dark already. The sun was quite far down and the sky was a deep pink. The pavements glistened with newly formed ice.

I shall have to be careful I don't fall, she thought, but then actually had the curious idea that at least falling and hurting herself might be rather interesting.

Yes, she was bored, and irritated by the other women's superior attitude. Not Jarvia though. Jarvia was sweet. Stale, that's what it all was. Really stale.

Her head began to clear. It hadn't really been a headache as such, rather a sort of foggy feeling. The brisk walk and the crisp air were helping to chase it all away.

She was soon back at the flat. Welcoming and familiar. But was it all too comfortable and was she ready for a change? Perhaps.

21 February 1924, Berlin: post

"Post for you, Frau Lehrs." Imelda had arrived back from shopping.

"Thank you," said Clara. The second post must be early today then. It didn't normally come until they were having their lunch.

"It looks as if something's come from Stuttgart." Imelda handed her a white envelope.

It did indeed. She wasn't sure, though, that she was glad to see it. Ernst's last letter had been a bit depressing. He'd been finding it harder than he'd thought it would be, teaching young people. Hopefully things were going better now.

"I'll leave you to read your letter in peace, Frau Lehrs. I'll go and start the lunch."

"Thank you. I'll come and give you a hand with the shopping in a few minutes."

Imelda left the room. Clara felt sick as she looked at the envelope. She didn't really want to open it, just in case. But she must. She knew.

She took a deep breath and tore it open.

She scanned the contents of the letter. She felt a weight lift from her chest as she saw no negative words and then she started to read it properly.

Stuttgart, 19 February 1924

Dear Mutti,

I'm sorry my last letter was so depressing. I hope I didn't alarm you too much. I'd just had a bad few days. All is progressing well now. I'm finding my feet as a teacher. They all tell me I'm doing well and that I shouldn't expect it to be easy at first. That it will be exhausting until I'm used to it and I am getting used to it. And I have a most extraordinary story to tell you.

I received a letter from Sister Greta – you remember the carer you met at the conference last summer. She explained that Kurt – the young boy in her care – had written a letter –

yes that's right, he had written a letter – to Rudolf Steiner. Could I pass it on to him? Sister Greta knew that Steiner was with us at the school at this time.

Anyway, Steiner was talking to us about these special children. He was making notes on the board. He used each child's initial. So in this case K for Kurt. Apparently the boy had asked Steiner to ask the angels to allow Sister Greta to go with him to the Sonnenhof in Arlesheim. Steiner was holding the letter in his hand and then looked straight at me.

"A letter from your boy," he said.

My boy? I'm scarcely old enough to be the boy's father. So, after the lecture I challenged him about it.

"Such remarks aren't made without them meaning something," he said. You know the way he looks at you sometimes? It was as if he was telling me more than what the words said. He was friendly, though. He said it in a kind way. As if there is some special connection between us and the boy.

It strikes me, Mutti, that the boy probably has more to do with you than he does with me. Anyway, sadly, he can't go to Arlesheim. But we do think we may be able to find enough sponsorship for him and Sister Greta to go to the Lauenstein institution.

Have you thought any more about it, Mutti? We do need you there. Do you have an answer for us?

I hope to come to Berlin for a weekend soon. Perhaps we can talk about it then.

Your loving son,
Ernst

Clara put the letter down in her lap and stared out of the window. She wasn't looking at anything, though. She needed to think. What to do? What to do?

She would miss Berlin if she moved away. But there would be other friends she guessed. What about her age? Nonsense. She was still energetic. She was still twelve years younger than most men were when they retired. And she had so much experience to offer.

She'd be nearer Käthe, of course. Käthe? No sign of a family yet though that was sure to happen sometime, wasn't it? Wouldn't it be good to be near the grandchildren? She'd probably see more of Ernst in Jena than she ever did in Berlin. What about Rudi, though? Oh, he'd probably relish the independence. He was always telling her off for making such a fuss. He was coping well these days. The doctors said his diseased lungs were doing the same work as normal healthy ones, if not more. He was twenty-three. He was a man. Perhaps it was time he learnt to look after himself.

She reread the letter. So this Kurt had been designated as their boy. It was like a sign. Right. So, good. Her mind was made up.

She went over to the small bureau and took out some writing paper and a pen and began to write.

Berlin, 24 February 1924

Dear Ernst,

Thank you for your letter of 19 February. I've read and reread it and I have some news to give you that I think you'll be pleased about. I have decided I will take up the offer of being the housekeeper at the institute in Jena. There are some conditions, however:

When your sister starts having children I shall be allowed to take time off to be present at the birth and time to visit when they are little.

Your sister and brother-in-law will be allowed to visit as often as they please.

If anything happens to Rudi I shall be given leave straightaway to return to Berlin or to go to wherever he is at the time.

You will visit me often there.

I shall be allowed to pay for young Kurt and Sister Greta to come to Jena.

I shall not be expected, yet, to take on the whole of Steiner's belief system. I admire what he does with young people, but I can't quite agree with him on other matters. I am quite willing to learn, however.

There. Now you may celebrate. It is almost as if this is

meant to be. That is one very special young man, and in the end, it is he who has persuaded me. Along with your friend Albrecht, of course.

I am so glad you are finding the teaching easier and I hope that you are not getting too exhausted.

I'll have plenty to do. I must rent out the apartment, get rid of a lot of personal belongings and inform all my friends and associates. I'll probably need different clothes for this type of work. Most importantly, I must try and find a new position for Imelda. I suppose she might come too, if there is a need for people with her skills, though she may not want to leave Berlin.

Will you come to Berlin soon so that we can make detailed plans? Or, if you prefer, I can come to you in Stuttgart.

I hope to hear from you soon.
Your loving mother.

Well, she'd done it. She'd committed herself. She reread what she'd written, folded the sheet of paper in half and put it into an envelope.

There was a knock at the door.

"Come in," called Clara.

"I've put all the shopping away, Frau Lehrs. Shall I start on the lunch? We could have the rest of the chicken broth from yesterday, perhaps."

"No. I tell you what Imelda. Let's put on our hats and coats. I'm taking you out to lunch. We can post this letter on the way. There is a lot I have to tell you and I hope you'll be able to see it as good news."

Imelda's eyes grew round and she stood perfectly still with her mouth open. She didn't seem to be able to find any words to say.

19 October 1924, Lauenstien: angel work

Clara sat in the sun room luxuriating in the late afternoon sunshine. The view from the window was splendid. Bright blue sky with a hint of pink, bringing out the yellows and reds of the leaves on the trees. There certainly were views to be seen here. She wondered what it would look like in winter and spring. She'd already seen the end of the summer and the autumn and they had been glorious. So different from Berlin, of course.

It was quiet today. The children were all out hiking in the nearby countryside. The staff who were not on duty had gone to spend Sunday afternoon with their families. It was rare that she had any time to herself so she was relishing her own company for a while. Did she ever really stop working, though? Here she was, repairing some of the children's clothes. She didn't have to. There were other people to do that. But she liked to make herself useful. *What's the point of embroidering little flowers on handkerchiefs? Who will see them?* She knew, though, that some of the teachers here would disagree with her. There was every point in making things pleasant and beautiful. The children were constantly encouraged to do so.

She could be reading, she supposed. She had to read up so much about this Steiner philosophy but she knew she would probably doze off. It was complex and she was tired. Not unpleasantly so, though. She was content and relaxed. Everything was running smoothly. And oh my, wasn't her life different from what it had been in Berlin?

There. She had finished replacing all of the missing buttons on the boys' shirts. She took them upstairs and put them in the clothes cupboard. Next she would tackle the girls' socks and stockings that had holes in them. Then she would treat herself to a little walk around the garden and afterwards a cup of tea.

She smiled to herself as she looked at the carefully ordered boys' clothes cupboard. It hadn't taken her long to see what needed to be done. It had taken longer to get the staff to work with her and trust her and she'd constantly forgotten that it wasn't up to her to do all of the work herself.

"You must remember to delegate, Mutti," Ernst had written to her. "It's your job to keep an eye on the bigger picture. You're made for this. All those years running our house and organising the social side of things at Vati's factory."

She'd found that being firm but fair was the answer. Everything must be done to a high standard but it was important to thank the staff for their hard work and give out praise where it was due. Be forgiving when people made mistakes. And above all, have a sense of humour and encourage others to develop one.

She liked the children, as well, though they could be difficult sometimes and most of them were hard work physically.

Ernst had been so right. She was made for this job and it was made for her. She almost wished that she had thought of it earlier. No, she thought. Ernst and the children needed you.

She picked up a stocking from the basket of items that needed darning. "What do you girls get up to?" she mumbled to herself as she looked at the large hole in the bottle-green stocking. Could she even repair this one? Well she'd have a jolly good try. Waste not, want not. That's what the Great War had taught them all.

She replaced the stocking in the basket, picked the basket up and made her way back to the sun room. She could hear voices as she approached. So, that was the end of her peace and quiet. Never mind. She enjoyed company anyway.

"Oh Frau Lehrs, we hope we won't disturb you."

It was Sister Greta with Kurt.

"Not at all. Didn't you go on the hike, Kurt?"

"He's got a bit of a cold," said Sister Greta. "We didn't want it to get on his chest."

No, of course they didn't. From what she'd heard Kurt's lungs were as delicate as Rudi's. If not more so.

"That's a shame. I hope you're feeling better soon."

"I feel better already." The boy looked at Clara with his deep serious eyes. "The angels sent me to find you. We should take you out into the garden."

Clara turned to Sister Greta. "Would it hurt him to go outside?"

"No. It should be fine." The nurse turned back towards the boy. "I think the fresh air will do us all good. But we must all wrap up warm. Will you go and get your coat and scarf and fetch mine and Frau Lehrs's?"

"He does talk about angels a lot," said Clara as they waited for Kurt to come back with the coats.

"Well they are an important part of what we believe in."

Clara shivered. "I take it we don't mean blond-haired beings with fluffy wings that spend all their time floating on clouds?"

Sister Greta laughed. "All the same, those pictures are the way they are for a reason."

Kurt arrived with the coats and a few minutes later the three of them were wandering around the small but naturally landscaped garden.

"It is so pretty," said Clara. She was always impressed with the care the staff and the children took of the gardens.

"The angels have been here too," said Kurt. He skipped along, every so often stopping to dead-head a flower or break off some dried-out stalks.

Well yes, she could buy that. Hadn't she always had the feeling that somebody or something was urging her to do her best and not to stop until everything worked perfectly and looked beautiful and harmonious at the same time? The tidy linen cupboard. The carefully laid table. The expertly repaired clothes. Was that voice that urged her on an angel voice?

"Just a few more minutes," said Sister Greta, "and then we must go back in and make a start on preparing the supper."

"Oh, I can help," said Clara.

"No, Frau Lehrs. It's your afternoon off. The others will be back soon."

Kurt ran round the garden making motor noises and calling, "The angels have been here. The angels have been here."

I suppose they have, thought Clara as they made their way back inside. Though I don't imagine angels have engines like that.

It was getting dark. It was true; she would only have a little time to herself. She must make the most of it.

"You go and get settled in the sun room," said Sister Greta, "and I'll organise a cup of tea for you."

"That is so kind. Thank you." Clara hung her coat up and walked along the corridor. She couldn't help but feel proud about the carefully waxed and polished floors. Yes, the young people would be back soon but they were so good about changing into house shoes and taking care to keep the place clean. She'd insisted on that. Not that they didn't have fun. This was such a happy place.

She has almost finished darning the green stocking when Kurt appeared, carefully carrying a tray laden with a teapot, cup and saucer and a small plate of biscuits. His tongue poked out as he concentrated.

"Look what the angels have sent you," he said as he carefully placed the tray on one of the low tables.

"You're an angel yourself," said Clara. "Thank you my dear."

"Ah, but it was the angels who helped me to carry the tray," said Kurt. Then he turned and skipped back towards the kitchen.

Clara darned another sock and then took a sip of her tea. It was lovely. The cup and teapot were well designed too. She looked at the walls of the sun room. Pictures the children had made were tastefully framed and arranged in an attractive way. They weren't naïve and simplistic pictures as you might have expected but ones that showed a good deal of skill and sound aesthetic judgement in the young people who had worked on them.

Angel work indeed, thought Clara. They have been busy. She still wasn't sure she believed in angels but there was certainly something that kept people going. Look at how hard the staff worked here. And look what these youngsters achieved despite their difficulties.

She darned a third sock and then finished her tea. As she took the final sip she heard voices outside. There was much laughing and shouting. They were back. She put down her cup and made her way to the back door. She needn't have worried. Wellingtons and boots were being peeled off and put on to the boot racks.

Goodness, they all had a healthy glow. And she could smell the fresh air on them.

"Good trip?" she asked Wilhelm, the young man who'd been in charge today.

"Yes. Fantastic. We walked a long way. And we didn't have to carry Beate once."

"No, I'm a big girl now," said Beate. She ran over to Clara and flung her arms round her. "But we missed you, Frau Lehrs. Why didn't you come with us?"

"Now, now, Beate. Give Frau Lehrs a bit of peace. It was her afternoon off and she needed a rest."

"But I am fully recovered and full of energy." Clara could smell the soup cooking. Chicken this evening, if she remembered correctly. "I expect you're all hungry. So hurry along, wash your hands and then into the dining room."

Several of the children cheered and there was a general exit in the direction of the bathrooms.

Clara smiled to herself as she looked at the neatly stacked boots and the coats lined up on the pegs. This move had been so right. Ernst had been clever to suggest it.

11 January 1925, Lauenstein: great expectations

Clara didn't want to pull the blind across the window. The sun was warming her shoulders nicely. But it was catching the side of her face and also making the white paper glare back at her so much that she was getting a headache. Besides which, she could not make these figures balance. It looked as if they were doing extraordinarily well but she guessed she was overlooking a payment or two somewhere. That didn't make sense either, though, because she was so careful with her bookkeeping.

Perhaps she should take a break. Come back to it later. But she did want to get this done by lunch time. She sighed and leaned back in her chair. She glanced out of the window. So, this was what the Lauenstein looked like in winter. So clear and crisp and fine on a day like today where the bright blue sky contrasted so sharply with the deep white snow that had softened the shape of the trees and plants.

She stretched, prepared herself to get back to work and reluctantly stood up to pull down the blind but before her hand touched it she heard footsteps running up the stairs.

"Frau Lehrs! Frau Lehrs! You have a visitor," called an excited voice.

The door was flung open and there stood Angelika, the new kitchen maid, cap askew and her apron all twisted.

I'll really have to teach that girl not to run everywhere. "A visitor? Who? Where is this visitor?" It looked as if she was going to get a break after all.

"Darn. I've forgotten the name."

"Language, Angelika."

"Sorry, Frau Lehrs. But it's a very glamorous young lady and she's in the small sitting room."

"Thank you. I'll be down in a few minutes. And tidy yourself up, please."

Angelika blushed and smoothed down her apron – then left the room at a gallop.

Clara sighed again and took out her small mirror to check her own appearance. A glamorous young lady? Perhaps it was someone offering sponsorship.

She looked in the mirror and patted her hair. Yes, she'd do.

Clara's heart was beating fast as she made her way down the stairs. It always worried her so much when she met potential sponsors. She would hate to lose them money because she was too undemanding or too hasty. You had to get the tone exactly right. She took a deep breath and walked into the sitting room.

The young woman was looking out of the window and had her back to the door. Yes, she certainly looked glamorous. She wore a well-cut coat with a fur collar and a smart hat. She turned to face Clara.

"Mutti!" cried the young woman and rushed over to kiss Clara.

Glamorous? Käthe? Oh, she supposed she could afford to dress nicely now that Hans was doing so well in his work. And goodness, didn't she look well? Clara had been worried about her when she'd seen her over Christmas and in the New Year. She'd been pale, her eyes had been quite dull and Clara thought she'd looked a bit thin. She'd noticed, as well, that she'd only been picking at her food. She hadn't much appetite.

Now, though, she looked much better. Her hair and her eyes were shining. Her cheeks were prettily pink and as they'd hugged Clara had thought she'd felt rounder, maybe had put on some weight. Of course, it could have been the bulk of the coat.

Käthe was grinning. "Mutti, I'm going to have a baby. You're going to be an Oma."

An Oma? She was going to be a grandmother. This was good news indeed. And perhaps becoming a mother would mellow this highly-strung daughter of hers. It was exciting. The thought of new life was always exciting.

"When?" Clara was already making plans. She had to know when this new person would come into the world.

"August 15th. That's what the doctor said."

"I was quite worried at Christmas. You looked…"

"Chronic morning sickness. Kept throwing up. Couldn't eat. But that's all over. I'm feeling good."

So that explained the bright eyes, the pink cheeks and the shiny hair.

"So, Mutti, what do you think about becoming an Oma. Doesn't that make you feel old?"

Clara shook her head. "Quite the opposite. It will make me young again. Having a little one in the family."

Käthe rolled her eyes. "I'd have thought you were quite used to having little ones around. You're surrounded by them." She gestured vaguely round the room.

"Yes, but my own flesh and blood. That's different. Is Hans pleased?"

Käthe nodded. "Yes. Yes, he's pleased. Of course, he's hoping for a boy."

"What about you?"

Käthe shrugged. "I don't mind. A son would be nice but it'll be more fun dressing up a girl."

Goodness, thought Clara. This isn't a game. Still, it allayed one fear. Everything must be all right on that level between her daughter and her husband. "So, you and Hans…"

"Mother! Not that it's any of your business, but since you're asking, yes, absolutely: we have a fantastic sex life, thank you very much."

Clara felt herself blush and looked away. *Come on, get a grip. Say something.* "So, you're taking good care of yourself?"

"Of course I am. Mother, you know I understand all about biology. I'm eating plenty of nutritious food, getting plenty of rest and keeping nice and calm. I know what's good for the baby."

"You need to be careful though. It's still quite early days." Clara shuddered as she remembered the miscarriages. They'd been uncomfortable enough but the worse was the feeling of loss afterwards. It wasn't even like when someone died. You didn't hold a funeral for the mass of blood and other matter that came away.

Goodness. The silly girl was still wearing high heels. She could so easily slip and fall, especially with the streets being so icy.

"Don't you think…?" Clara stared at her daughter's elegant court shoes.

"Of for goodness sake, Mutti. I'm not going to end up looking like a frump just because I'm pregnant. I'm being careful. I said so. And do you know what? I'm getting quite used to my afternoon nap. It's delicious. I'm going to carry on after the baby's born. I'll take a nap when he does. Will you stop staring at my ankles?"

Actually, her ankles did look all right. Clara looked up and smiled at her daughter. She was so proud of her. But did the girl realise that?

A car horn hooted.

"Oh, that's Hans. I'd better go. Love you, Mutti." She kissed her mother's cheek and rushed towards the door.

Don't run, thought Clara.

But Käthe did run. Clara was relieved to see that she got down the front steps, along the path and into Hans's waiting car without even tripping. The engine was still running. Hans stepped out. "Good morning, Clara. Sorry we can't stop. I have to get her to her appointment with Doctor Rippel."

Typical Käthe. Always cramming such a lot in that she was almost always running late. "Congratulations!"

Hans grinned. "It's wonderful isn't it?"

Clara was glad he was pleased about being a father.

Then they were off, Käthe waving frantically.

She supposed she had better get back to the more mundane task of balancing the books. When she got back to her office, the sun had moved enough that it wasn't going to dazzle her anymore. The earlier headache was forgotten.

As she sat down at her desk she noticed two pieces of paper sticking out from under her blotter.

I'll be blowed, she thought. Yes, they were the missing invoices. What a relief.

Goodness, everything was coming together. She smiled to herself. By this time next year she would be used to being a grandmother. She wondered for a moment whether Kurt's angels had been at work.

30 March 1925, the Lauenstein: life cycles

There was something strange about today though Clara couldn't decide quite what. It reminded her of the day Ernst had come home. She had that feeling again that something was going to happen. She was absolutely convinced of it. She had been right that day. Would she be again today?

It was a beautiful day. Now she was seeing the Lauenstein in the spring. The last of the snow had melted. The sun was higher in the sky now that the equinox had passed and there was some warmth in it. There were still frosts overnight but everything was waking up with a will in the garden.

She'd woken with a start during the night and it had been so black. No moonlight. Yet when she'd looked out of her window that sky had been dancing with stars. Yes, there was definitely something important about today.

All of her chores were complete. She'd inspected the children's rooms, sorted out the laundry, got the big wash underway and checked over the menus for the week. She was ahead for once.

She would work in the garden. It wasn't her area, but no one minded. In fact, usually people were glad of the extra help. And she'd begun to find it therapeutic, working with the living things and getting her hands in the soil.

She slipped on her old coat and found her gardening gloves and made her way outside.

Soon she was busily cutting back twigs and snapping off heads. A bird was chirping nearby. She couldn't spot where it was. It was probably keeping itself hidden. That was another sure sign of spring, though. It was most likely part of a courting ritual.

The soil, she noticed was soft. It had been broken up by the frost and then warmed by the sun. She removed her glove and took a handful and held it up to her nose. It was rich and moist – and no doubt fertile. It felt like a gift.

A low branch off one of the trees waved in front of her. On it, tiny buds were swelling ready to burst.

And all the time, this excited feeling in the pit of her stomach. Something was going to happen. She knew it. Could it be that she was getting excited about the spring? About the baby? Käthe was really swelling up. Surely, though, it was more than all of that?

"Frau Lehrs," called a familiar voice. "Are you collecting things for a bonfire?" Kurt was standing next to her. His dark eyes stared into hers, blinking occasionally.

"No, Kurt, I'm tidying up the garden a little."

"But what are you going to do with all of those twigs and dry flowers?"

"Well, I suppose we should burn them. You're right."

"Can I help?"

He was so enthusiastic she didn't want to refuse him but the thought of him and fire mixing? He'd probably try to put his hands into it. She shuddered.

"You'll have to make a fire."

Yes, he really was right. "You can help me put the debris into the brazier and you can watch it all burn as long as you promise to stand back."

"Come on then."

A few minutes later they had filled the brazier, the small pieces at the bottom and the bigger ones on the top. Clara opened the box of matches. "Stand well back, please," she commanded.

She struck the match and lit the kindling at the bottom. Soon smoke was curling into the sky. Then the flames started. The twigs and branches began to crackle and the smoke started going up in a straight line. Clara hoped it wouldn't spoil the sunshine for the neighbours. The wood smelt good as it burned.

"The flames cleanse the soul of the entrapments of the body," said Kurt, "and the smoke carries it up to the angels."

"Goodness, you make it sound as if someone has just died."

"There is always someone who has just died. And someone who has just been born. Thus the exchange of souls continues."

"Those are very grown-up thoughts for a young man."

"The child is father of the man."

The way he looked at her she knew she had to believe it. He obviously did.

Then the phone rang. Would somebody answer it? She went to walk towards the door into the house. It stopped ringing.

"The smoke carries the soul up to the angels," said Kurt. He was staring at the fire but his eyes weren't focussing on it.

I wish he wouldn't do that, thought Clara. "Come on. I think we'd better get inside. The fire will die down on its own. It's safe enough."

Kurt turned and started to skip ahead of her towards the house. That was that then. It would soon be lunch time. She supposed she should go and see what was going on. She knew something was up and that phone call had something to do with it.

When she got into the house she met Sister Greta. The poor young woman looked quite pale. "What on earth's the matter?" said Clara.

"We've had a phone call. Doctor Steiner has died."

"Died?" said Clara. "How? Why?"

"He's not been the same since the fire at the Goetheanum. We know he's been tired and cancelled several lectures… but this…" She looked as if she was going to cry.

Clara remembered the report about the fire. The Goetheanum at Dornach had been a beautiful if odd building. No one had even been sure exactly how the fire had started.

"It carries the soul up to the angels," Kurt whispered. He walked quietly into the sun room.

"My dear, I'm so sorry."

Sister Greta nodded. "I'd better go and see to Kurt."

What would happen now? Clara didn't feel as close to the great man as the people here. But she knew it was his teachings that held them all together. Oh dear. She supposed she'd better do something practical. She could see that lunch was organised properly. No one else would, most likely.

Clara sat in the chair in her room. She felt weary, oh so weary but couldn't move to get herself into bed. She longed for the comfort of the down bed roll but couldn't persuade her feet to move a centimetre.

Whilst the others had mourned Rudolf Steiner she had seen that the household ran as smoothly as ever. She'd made sure that the children had enough to eat and that everything was kept clean and tidy.

It had been three days.

The adults had been shocked and the children had been uneasy because they weren't used to the grown-ups being so vulnerable. On top of doing all of the housework she mopped up more tears from the children who'd cried more often because of the perplexity of it all and she'd endured almost total silence from the others.

No, she didn't feel the loss of him as keenly as they did. She didn't know him as well, nor did she really understand him. But she was beginning to respect him because if he meant so much to them – and she respected them – then there must be something in what he said.

A pity to realise that now when it was too late.

There was a gentle tap at her door.

"Yes," she managed to whisper. "Please come in."

It was Sister Greta.

"The vigil has ended," she said. "His soul is in flight and completely free of his body."

"I see." She didn't really but she was surprised to find she wanted to know more.

"We are so grateful, Frau Lehrs, that you have looked after us so well."

"Just doing my duty."

"Thank you so much." The younger woman walked over to her and kissed her lightly on the forehead.

"What will happen now?"

"We'll carry on following his teachings. It will work out."

Clara nodded. They were all so sincere. They really did believe all that he'd said. That she recognised.

"Rest, Frau Lehrs. You must."

Sister Greta closed the door quietly behind her.

Clara somehow managed to get into bed. She would step back tomorrow. Let the others take charge a little. See what happened.

Her head touched the pillow and she slept.

5 July 1925, Jena: stormy weather

It was the most spectacular storm yet this summer. Black clouds rolled across the sky. Fork lightning tore it in half, lighting up the whole of the sun room then disappearing and plunging it into darkness. Not for long, though, for then there would be another explosion of blinding light.

Clara was not surprised that the storm had come. It had been unbearably hot for the last three days and this afternoon particularly close and sticky. Many of the children had been bad-tempered. The garden and the streets had been startlingly quiet. No birds singing. No one out and about. It was almost as if a strange force had taken over the whole of nature, humans included. If only it would rain. They'd had one or two storms over the last few weeks, but no rain at all. The gardens were dry and thirsty.

There was another flash. Then what looked like a big ball of fire floated through the window into the sun room. It hovered in front of her and she had the curious feeling that it was trying to tell her something.

But that's nonsense, she told herself. Lightning doesn't talk. Even so, it had been decidedly uncanny.

"What was that?" asked Sister Greta who was standing right next to her. "I've never seen anything like it before."

"Neither have I," said Clara. "Though I dare say my sons or my daughter would have an explanation."

Then the rain started. Gently at first, then more strongly and finally torrential. A wind had sprung up and the air temperature dropped. Still, though, the flashes and the bangs continued with very little time between the lightning and the thunder. The storm wasn't moving.

The air had become quite cold.

"I'm going to fetch my shawl," said Clara.

Sister Greta nodded. "I'll go and see that the children are all right."

As the two women arrived in the hallway there came a frantic knocking on the door and a ringing of the doorbell.

"Some poor soul caught out in the storm," said Clara, hurrying to open the door.

"I'll go and get some towels," said Sister Greta.

Clara nodded as she opened the door. Then she gasped in surprise. Standing in front of her was her son-in-law, his hair plastered to his head and in the short walk up from the car, the engine of which was still running, his clothes had become soaked.

"The baby's coming. She's asking for you."

What was he saying? He must be mad. It was much too soon. "But it's almost a month early."

"If anything happens… she'll need you. We both will."

Clara thought he was going to cry. She didn't hesitate. She grabbed an umbrella from the stand near the front door.

"I have to go to my daughter," she called up the stairs to Sister Greta. "The baby's coming."

The nurse rushed down the stairs. "Let me come with you. Maybe I can help."

Hans nodded. "The midwife's already there but the more help the better, I guess."

They hurried down the path, Clara and Greta huddled under the umbrella and Greta still clutching the towels. As soon as they were in the car, Hans put it in gear and they were away.

The rain was driving so hard they could hardly see through the windows. Normally it would only take twenty minutes to get to the Johannisstrasse but today they had to drive more slowly and it took longer. Hans's face was contorted in concentration as he drove. The thunder and lightning persisted. The rain would not let up.

At last, though, they arrived. Clara jumped out of the car, not waiting for Sister Greta and the umbrella. The nurse and the worried son-in-law followed her a few seconds later.

Clara rushed into her daughter's room. The midwife, a woman almost as old as Clara herself, and Doctor Rippel were there. They both nodded to Clara and Sister Greta. Hans stayed out on the landing. Clara didn't like how pale her daughter looked.

"Again!" cried Käthe, her face screwing up in agony.

"Try not to push. Not yet," said the midwife. "You're not open enough."

"Damn those bloody men and their insatiable desires," shouted Käthe. "Castrate the devil. See how he'd like this much pain."

"Käthe!" said Clara. Then she remembered that she'd had similar feelings to that shortly before her three were born. She hadn't said anything, though. She'd merely thought it.

"Don't worry, madam," said the midwife. "I've heard a lot worse, believe me. She'll be fine once we have the little one out."

Greta, who had gone bright pink, was holding Käthe's hand. "It will be all right," she said. "The baby will be here soon."

The doctor leant over her with his stethoscope. He put it to her enormous belly. "Mm," he said. "The heart rate is strong, if a little slow. But I think we should get this baby into the world as soon as possible."

"Excuse me," said the midwife. "If you wouldn't mind looking away."

Clara and the doctor turned their backs on Käthe. Greta looked to the ground.

"Right. Fully crowned. With the next pain, push as hard as you can."

Silence followed. Everyone waited for the next pain. They seemed to have stopped. Then there was another flash outside and a clap of thunder. Käthe groaned.

"Push, push, push!" called the midwife.

Clara and Greta held her either side.

"Good," said Doctor Rippel. "You're doing really well, Frau Edler."

"One more push," said the midwife. "Push down, down, down. Don't strain your throat. Imagine you're constipated. That's it."

Käthe groaned once more.

"It's here," cried the midwife. "Frau Edler, you have a little girl. She's tiny, though." She took up the child and wrapped it in one of the towels and handed it to Sister Greta. "Could you...? I have to deliver the after-birth."

Why isn't she crying? The baby's face looked blue. *Wasn't she breathing? No. Please God don't let this happen.* The miscarriages were bad enough but she'd never had a still-birth. How would her over-sensitive daughter cope with that?

She watched feeling helpless as the doctor put his hand on Käthe's abdomen. He nodded.

"My baby. I want to see my baby," said Käthe.

"All in good time," said Doctor Rippel, moving over to the table where Sister Greta was bending over the baby. He put the stethoscope on the baby's chest. "Yes, a good heart beat and she's breathing but with some difficulty. Let's see if we clear this mucus from her."

Sister Greta worked away busily at her.

"Yes, that's right. Rub her tummy. Yes, she's pinking up nicely."

Thank goodness!

The baby yelled.

Hans burst through the door. "Are they all right?"

"Yes, Doctor Edler, for the moment yes. Your wife should make a full recovery. Your daughter is very small, however, and I fear somewhat underdeveloped."

"She has a soul, though," said Sister Greta. "And we must take care of that."

"If you are religious at all," said the doctor, "you might consider getting her christened. She seems quite strong but we don't know how well her vital organs will work at this degree of prematurity."

"I think we should," said Clara turning to Hans. "We've got to get her a birth certificate anyway."

Hans nodded. "I'll go and see if I can rouse someone at the rectory."

"Let me hold her," said Käthe as soon as Hans had left.

Sister Greta brought the baby over to the mother. The little girl immediately tried to put her mouth to Käthe's breast.

"That's a good sign," said the midwife. "Come on; let's see if we can get her to feed."

Sister Greta and the midwife helped Käthe to get the baby latched on to her nipple and soon she was feeding away greedily.

"Well, it doesn't look as if there's anything wrong with her," said Greta.

"Early days," said the midwife. "But it's a good sign at least."

Clara marvelled at how strongly the baby was sucking and how naturally Käthe took to breast-feeding. She'd really enjoyed feeding all of hers. It had made such a special bond between mother and child. But they had never taken to it that easily on the first day and they had been full-term babies. In fact all three of them had been a few days late.

"Have you thought about names?" she asked.

"Yes. Renata, spelt the Italian way. Then Clara, as her second name, after you and Oma Edler."

Clara felt her cheeks go pink. What a lovely idea.

As the baby finished feeding, they heard the front door shut. Footsteps came up the stairs.

"I've found him," cried Hans, flinging the bedroom door open. "Father Brandt."

The two men entered the bedroom. Father Brandt was a strange-looking little man. He had long grey hair, scraped to the back of his neck and tied with a piece of string. His cassock was faded and grubby.

"Where is the child?" he asked.

Clara screwed up her nose. His breath smelt of alcohol. He was unsteady on his feet too.

Sister Greta took the baby off Käthe and walked over to the priest with her. Father Brandt took out a bottle of water. He held his hand over it and mumbled something Clara found quite intelligible. Then he turned to Hans. "How is the child to be named?"

"Renata Clara," Käthe called from the bed. "Isn't that right, Hans?"

"Yes, Renata Clara."

"Very well. Klara Renate."

"Renata Clara," said Clara.

"Renata Clara," mumbled Father Brandt. He sprinkled some

of the water from the bottle onto his fingers and made the sign of the cross on the baby's forehead. "In the name of the Father and of the Son and of the Holy Ghost, I name thee Klara Renate."

"Renata Clara." Hans glared at the priest.

"Clara Renata," Father Brandt whispered, once more making the sign of the cross on Renata's head.

The baby started screeching. Sister Greta tried to soothe her. "Hush, hush, little one. It's all over. You can go back to your mama for a nice cuddle."

"I'll need to fill in the certificate," said Father Brandt.

"Come along to my study," said Hans.

"Remember, it's Clara with a 'C' and Renata spelt the Italian way," Käthe called after them.

"Yes, yes," answered Hans.

"I'll be on my way," said Doctor Rippel. "You should all try and get some rest."

"I'll be going too," said the midwife.

It occurred to Clara only then that she did not know the woman's name. How rude of her not to have asked. "Thank you so much for all of your help, Frau…" she stammered.

"Wildberger," said the midwife. "Look, here's my address and phone number. Do call if there are any problems." She handed Clara a card and started packing away her things.

"I shall call round tomorrow soon after breakfast," said the doctor. "The next twenty-four hours are crucial for the baby. Do send for me in the meantime if you feel the need to, though it looks as if she is doing well."

Renata was clearly enjoying another feed.

"Greedy little pup," Käthe whispered, looking down at her baby.

A few minutes later the baby stopped feeding and fell asleep.

"I'm so tired as well," said Käthe.

"Then rest," said Clara. "I'll sit here in the armchair until you're asleep."

"I'll leave you in peace," said Sister Greta. "But I'll stay overnight, if that's all right Frau Edler. Then I'm here if you need me."

Käthe nodded and yawned.

Sister Greta took the baby and put her into the cot they'd got ready. "Sleep little one," she whispered and then tiptoed out of the room.

Clara was soon comfortable in the overstuffed armchair. The rhythmic breathing of daughter and granddaughter was soothing. She felt her own eyelids closing. It wouldn't hurt to sleep here. That way she would be ready if either of them needed her.

Clara woke with a start. At first she couldn't remember where she was. There was a faint gurgling noise coming from the corner of the room. Then she remembered. The baby. The priest. The thunder-storm. Yes, and Renata and Käthe waking once in the night and the baby feeding again so beautifully. The storm had still been rumbling a little then but had been further away. It had been so cosy, mother, daughter and granddaughter all together in the still of the night.

Sun was streaming through the window. The grandfather clock in the hallway struck seven. Goodness the doctor would be here again soon.

She got out of the chair and tiptoed over to the cot. The child was wide awake and sucking her fist. "Hello, little one," she whispered.

There was a faint tap at the door and then it opened slowly. It was Sister Greta with a breakfast tray. She set it down on the small table near Käthe's bed and joined Clara next to Renata's cot. "Well she's doing well, isn't she?"

Clara nodded and smiled.

"Bring her over to me," mumbled Käthe, her voice still thick with sleep.

"Have your breakfast first, darling," said Clara.

"No, I want her now," said Käthe. "I'm her mother, after all."

Clara knew it would be useless arguing. She picked the baby up gently and carried her over to Käthe.

There was a loud bang as a door was slammed shut. Hans ran into the bedroom holding a piece of paper. The birth certificate by the looks of it.

"Damn the man. Damn the drunken old fool," he cried.

"What's the problem?" Clara hoped she would be able to calm him down but it didn't look likely.

"He's only gone and put Klara – with a 'K' and Renate spelt the German way. And he's put them the wrong way round. Klara Renate instead of Renata Clara."

Käthe's face crumpled and tears started to run down her cheeks. Klara Renate started howling. Something inside Clara sank. She hated it if people spelt her name with a 'K'.

13-25 February 1926, Lauenstein: trouble in Paradise

The meetings normally didn't bother Clara. In fact, she enjoyed them. She loved reporting on what they'd achieved, listening to other people's new ideas and offering her own. But today it felt different. She felt different. She felt old. And she would rather have been anywhere else than squeezed into the front lounge as they were now. The room was stuffy. It may have been cold outside and the fire was bright and warm here but there were too many people in a small space. She felt suffocated.

"What do you think, Frau Lehrs?" asked Carl Bauler. "Should we get the older girls involved in helping with weekly bed-changing? They would learn so much and it would be so good for their development?"

It would, she supposed. But it would also be a lot more effort. She and the other helper could do it in half the time and twice as effectively as the senior girls. She couldn't believe she was thinking that way. She would normally do anything that encouraged the children to learn. "I don't really have a strong opinion," she said. "I'll go along with what everyone else thinks."

Carl looked startled. One or two others raised their eyebrows too. Gosh, she hoped she hadn't offended anyone. "What I really mean," she continued, "is that you've heard enough of my opinions. Everything is working well but it's probably time for some new ideas, for some fresh blood."

"Clara, that is certainly not true," said Albrecht. "Good and new ideas are always welcome but we have you here because we value your wisdom and your opinions."

Clara nodded. "I know. I'm just a little tired tonight."

"Well," said Sister Greta. "You should get some rest. You go along and get to bed and I'll bring you a hot drink. We've more or less finished, haven't we?"

"Yes, yes, I think so. Thank you for your report, Clara. Will you agree, though, to letting the senior girls help with making up the beds?"

Albrecht was staring at her with that look. The one she found so hard to resist that said "Please stay with me on this one". Clara nodded. She dreaded the chaos it would cause actually. Maybe she would feel better after a good night's sleep. She would agree to anything to be allowed to get to her room and get her head on the pillow.

"Good, then sleep well. You do look tired, Clara. Take care. We need you." Albrecht then turned to speak to one of the other workers.

She couldn't hear what he was saying, nor did she care. She wanted to get into bed as quickly as possible.

As she walked back to her room she realised she was running a fever.

She opened the door and almost fell into the room. She swayed and her knees buckled. She had to crawl across the floor. Then she started shivering. She managed to undress and get into bed somehow and pulled the bed roll over her. For a few seconds she felt ashamed that she had dropped her clothes on the chair but then told herself that for once it didn't matter.

A few moments later Sister Greta arrived with some lime blossom tea. "My mother always swore by this," she said, "when anyone had an attack of influenza or a chill."

Clara nodded. She knew if could be effective. But when she came to take a sip she couldn't hold the cup and it felt as if her throat was swollen. She couldn't actually swallow. She shook her head.

"Oh dear," said Sister Greta. "I think we might have to get the doctor for you."

"No," said Clara. "I'm sure I'll be better after a good night's sleep."

She didn't hear Sister Greta's reply. She was still shivering but the featherbed gave her a bit of comfort and she drifted into a strange sleep.

She felt a pain in her chest even though she was asleep. Her throat was dry and swollen, even in her dreams. Were they dreams anyway? Or was it rather some sort of living hell?

Then time raced by. She was vaguely aware of people coming and going. She thought one of them was a doctor. Sometimes it was daylight and sometimes it was dark. People tried to make her eat and drink. She couldn't, though. All she wanted was more sleep. When she was awake she ached all over and felt as if she couldn't breathe. Was she going to die? Perhaps she was. Would she find Ernst again if she did? Would she go to a place filled with light?

Then one time she was aware of a voice reciting to her:

> *"I want to weave together*
> *Shining light*
> *With dulled darkness*
> *I want to intensify the life-tone*
> *It should ring out sparklingly*
> *It should shine out tonefully."*

The same words over and over. There was something she recognised about the voice. Where did she know that voice from?

Ernst. It was Ernst. Ernst junior, though. So she wasn't dying. As she listened to the words her breathing became easier. She fell into a calmer sleep.

When she woke what she knew was a few hours later Ernst was still there and still reciting the words. They were so familiar. She joined in. But she knew it wasn't only because Ernst had kept repeating them. She knew the whole of the play they came from. Rudolf Steiner had written it. Yet she'd never seen it or read it. How had that happened?

"Mutti, you're awake," said Ernst. "Do you feel better?"

Clara managed to nod. It still hurt when she breathed in and she still didn't want to talk.

"We want to try a special cure. It will be tiring and uncomfortable but it might work. Will you try it?"

Clara nodded again.

"Good. I'll go and make the arrangements."

Two hours later Clara was sitting in a bath of warm water. It had been strange getting out of the bed she hadn't left for ten days, except to use the commode or to have a bit of a wash. Sister Greta and one of the other nurses had helped her to get undressed and get into the bath. It was quite pleasant, actually, sitting in the warm water though she wasn't so sure she was that happy about Doctor Magerstädt seeing her naked.

The doctor had the promised jug of cold water ready. "This will be a bit of a shock, Frau Lehrs. You may find your heart speeds up – enough maybe to make your ears ring. You're sure you're happy for this to happen?"

"Yes. Please get on with it before this water gets cold or it won't work."

Doctor Magerstädt threw the cold water over her right side.

She gasped. He was right. Her heart started hammering. Sister Greta frowned as she handed the doctor the second jug of cold water.

It's all right. Don't worry, thought Clara as she braced herself for the second shock. I'm all right. It's working.

She gasped again as the second jug of water landed on the left side of her chest and felt herself take in a deep breath.

"Good, good," muttered the doctor. "Breathe as deeply as you can."

She could really feel the places in her lungs that had been so idle recently begin to fill with air.

The doctor looked at the two nurses. "Let's get Frau Lehrs warm and back into bed before she gets a chill. We don't want any complications."

Twenty minutes later she was sitting in bed feeling clean and warm and realising what if felt like to breathe properly again. The doctor was listening to her chest.

"Excellent," he said, nodding as he put away his stethoscope. "Frau Lehrs you have a really strong pulse. And your lungs are clear. Now you must get some rest."

"Haven't I been resting enough?"

"Not really. All of that sleep was your body's way of coping with not being well. It needs some good quality rest."

"Whatever you say, doctor."

"Good. I'll be along tomorrow."

Clara sighed as the doctor left the room. She felt wide awake and she wanted to be up and doing. But it was cosy here in bed, actually. She felt relaxed. Her eyes closed and she fell asleep.

She again drifted in and out of sleep but it was pleasant this time. She sat up and talked to Ernst for a while and then to Sister Greta while she enjoyed a bowl of chicken soup. She couldn't keep her eyes open for long, though, and dozed on and off all day.

It grew dark. The evening noises of the house gradually receded and it became night and then she fell into a deep, natural sleep.

When she awoke her room was full of light. She was aware that someone was there with her. But that didn't matter for the moment. She was aware of something else, too, though she couldn't quite define it. Everything was beginning to make sense. What Rudolf Steiner's lectures had all been about. What young Kurt said about the angels. And for some bizarre reason she remembered the conversation she'd had with Ernst about his rucksack when she'd told him about her idea of selling the pearls.

"Ah, you're awake," said Sister Greta. "And goodness, you do look better."

"I feel it, my dear. And I want to get up, get dressed and stay up long enough to have porridge for breakfast and some more of that excellent chicken soup for lunch. I want to have a good look around and then I want to talk to someone about Rudolf Steiner."

"Right, then. Good. I'll get it all arranged." Sister Greta grinned.

"What date is it?"

"The 25th of February."

She'd been ill that long! Yes, she really must get up.

25 March 1927, the Lauenstein: angel work

Albrecht Strohschein stared at Clara.

He's almost as bad as Rolf Steiner when he looks at you like that, thought Clara. Albrecht was reading her soul like Steiner used to, she was sure. But he wasn't quite the same. He was warmer and friendlier and what he said always made sense. Almost always, anyway. She wasn't so sure about what he was saying today.

"Clara, you are so good to the children. Too good. We need to make them do more for themselves."

"But I like to mother them."

"Yes, but you mustn't smother them."

Clara felt her cheeks burning. She turned away from Albrecht and started piling the freshly laundered towels into the airing cupboard.

"They make such a mess, though."

Albrecht's firm hands were on her shoulders and he was turning her round to face him. "And you are exactly the person to show them how to do it better."

Clara sighed. "They miss their parents. They need some homely love."

"And they need to grow up. Most of them will still outlive their parents. We must make them as independent as possible."

He was right, she supposed. But she was a home-maker not a teacher or trainer.

"Will you try, please, Clara?"

She nodded. "Yes, but you must let me get on, now."

"Good. I'll send someone along to help you. I'll set up a rota."

Clara carried on putting the linen away. It wasn't so much that she put it away really rather that she firmly placed every single towel and sheet exactly where it was meant to be and gave it the silent command that it was to stay there neatly folded and not move until it was required. She was a little out of breath by the time she'd finished and needed to sit down. She realised that her fists were firmly clenched and her face was set in a frown. It was her own fault. She shouldn't have let herself get into such a state. The linen didn't need that amount of energy to be used on it.

She tried to work out what was making her so angry. Was it perhaps because they didn't appreciate how well she did her work? Was it because she enjoyed everything being just so and the teenagers' "helping" would not get the results she liked? Was it because they were asking her to let go of her control?

Oh, whatever it was, she shouldn't be like this. These were good people here, at the Lauenstein, and the young people, despite all their difficulties, were warm-hearted and always willing to try their best.

She was weary. Was she still recovering from last year's chest infection? Yes, she was out of breath but was that down to her furious working? Anyway, it wasn't so much the physical symptoms as a weariness of the soul. Where was the joy she used to feel about her work? Was her time here drawing to a close? Did she need a holiday? It would be Easter soon. Perhaps she could go away for a few days with one of the children.

Clara closed her eyes. She gradually began to calm down and was pleased to hear the birds outside singing. But this peace and quiet didn't last long. The sound of someone clearing their throat made her open her eyes with a start.

"Frau Lehrs, Doctor Strohschein says I am to help you."

It was Liesel, the fourteen-year-old who looked and behaved like a seven-year-old.

"Oh, sweetheart, I've finished putting the linen away."

"Is there anything else I can help with? Doctor Strohschein says I've got to learn to help with the housework."

"Yes, let me think what I can get you to do." What would be simple enough?

Clara remembered that one of the towels in the second floor bathroom had looked grubby earlier. It wasn't the day she normally changed them but it wouldn't hurt to change any dirty ones, would it? Could Liesel manage that? Why not try?

"Right," said Clara, "I want you to go round all of the bathrooms and if there are any towels that are dirty or very wet, bring them here. Then we can sort out some nice clean dry ones for you to take back. When you've found all the dirty ones, put them in a pile in front of the linen cupboard and come and tell me. I'll be in my office."

The girl's eyes lit up. "Yes, Frau Lehrs. I can do that. I'll be as quick as I can."

"No need to hurry, dear. It's important to do the job properly."

Liesel grinned and scampered away.

Clara was soon absorbed in her paperwork. There was a lot she needed to do. Some new stock had come in from the company that provided their linen. They'd also begun to purchase clothes for the children. They grew so quickly their parents couldn't keep up. By buying centrally and in bulk through the institute they could get big discounts. Then there were the medical supplies. It meant, though, that she had a lot of bookkeeping to do each month. Just as well, perhaps, that she would be getting some extra help from the older children.

There was a crash on the stairs. Clara looked up at the clock. Goodness, Liesel had been gone an hour. What had the girl been doing?

Clara rushed towards the stairwell. There was Liesel, sitting at the bottom of the stairs, surrounded by an assortment of towels and two trays.

"Are you hurt, child? What happened?" said Clara as she made her way quickly down the stairs.

Liesel shook her head.

"But why the trays? And why all of these towels?"

The girl's eyes filled with tears.

"I couldn't decide whether they were dirty or not, so I decided to bring them all on two trays. One tray for the ones that were definitely wet or dirty and one tray for the ones I wasn't sure about."

"But these must be all of the towels. And what made you think you could carry two trays at once?" It had obviously been too much for her.

"I'm not very clever," said Liesel.

"Oh, I don't know," said Clara, putting her arm around the girl's shoulders. "Look, as these are all muddled up why don't we put fresh towels in all of the bathrooms? These can go in the laundry. We'll carry a pig pile around and you can choose which ones we use in each room. And we'll carry them in laundry bag, not on a tray."

Liesel nodded.

"Come on, then. Wipe your eyes and let's get on with it."

One hour later, all the towels were replaced.

"Thank you for letting me help," said Liesel.

"My pleasure," replied Clara. Except I could have done it myself in ten minutes, she thought. The girl had taken the greatest delight in routing through the laundry bag to find the best towel for every room. Even though they were all white. Except, Clara supposed, some were greyer than others.

In fact, Liesel herself said, "Let's put this old grey one in the little boys' bathroom. They will only make the fluffy white ones dirty. We should give those to the grown-up girls."

Clara smiled at her. She was a dear girl and she had really tried hard. "Thank you for all your help."

Liesel beamed at Clara, then waved and ran off out into the garden to join her friends.

Clara felt more tired than ever.

She wondered whether she might go and make herself a cup of tea and sit in the sun lounge to sip it. That would be so nice. But it was not to be.

"Frau Lehrs," called a familiar voice. "You have been doing the work of the angels."

Kurt was standing in front of her.

"What do you mean, young man? Liesel and I have simply been putting fresh towels in all of the bathrooms."

"That is most certainly angel work. We all feel better when everything is neat and tidy and clean and ready for us. You and Liesel are angels."

I wonder what the little boys will make of the grey towels, thought Clara. Hmm. I don't suppose they'll even notice.

"What are you smiling about, Frau Lehrs? You look like an angel when you smile."

"I was thinking that some of the towels are getting worn and they're turning grey."

Kurt stopped to think about this. Then he nodded. "Knowing when to discard because there is no more use in an item and knowing when to make do are also angelic acts. Our angels can guide us in this if we ask them."

"I'm glad to hear it." If only it were that simple.

Kurt was frowning. He took Clara's hand. "Sometimes the angels want us to do something new for them. We need to listen to them to find out what it is. Sometimes…" He cupped his hand over his mouth and whispered. "Sometimes the angels want us to shine out in the darkest of places and they will help us to do that. Remember that, Frau Lehrs. It's important."

Clara shivered.

Kurt pulled away from her and grinned. Then he shuffled off, muttering or singing softly to himself, Clara wasn't sure which.

Ten minutes later she was in the sun lounge with a cup of good hot tea steaming in front of her. She closed her eyes while she waited until it was cool enough to drink.

Her eyes couldn't stay closed for long, however. Another person cleared their throat. Oh, she must be very wicked for she had no peace today and didn't they say there was no peace for the wicked?

"Clara, you're looking exhausted." It was Albrecht. "You see, you do need some help."

Clara opened her eyes and smiled. But don't you realise it's more tiring when I get the so-called "help"? she thought.

"Liesel enjoyed working with you today. She won't stop talking about it. She says she wants to be a housekeeper when she grows up."

"She's a sweet girl."

"Indeed. But are you all right, Clara?"

"I'm fine, really I am. Perhaps I could do with a holiday."

"Yes, of course. Why don't you take a few days over Easter? Perhaps spend some time with your daughter and her family?"

Clara laughed. "You've met Käthe?" It was hardly restful being with her highly-strung daughter and her fast-living son-in-law though of course Renate was a delight.

Albrecht grinned. "Yes, I know what you mean."

"But I might go away for a few days. Maybe I could go and see Ernst instead of him coming here. Would it be all right if I phone him later?"

"Of course," said Albrecht. "I think this is a very good idea. Now, I'll leave you to your tea. You make that call as soon as you like."

As Clara finished her drink she began to form a plan. Yes, she must speak to Ernst soon. And Rudi and Käthe, of course. But Ernst first of all. What she had in mind was more important to him than to the others.

19 April 1927, Schwäbisch Gmund: a plan

It was so relaxing here, at the little inn with the shabby wooden tables. Who would have thought that it would be warm enough to sit out in the garden and that you would need a sunshade this early in the year?

"And you make all of the cakes yourself?" Clara asked the landlady.

She was a cheerful sort of woman and obviously quite fond of her own cooking. She was tall and broad and her elbows had dimples. But a careful worker. The place was spotless. The woman's apron was starched and bleached and reflected the bright sunshine.

"Oh yes," said the young woman. "My mother's recipes. We have to keep the hungry hikers fed. And we get supplies of milk and apples from my brother's farm, five kilometres from here. It's all part of the family business."

"You do very well," said Clara.

"I'll bring you some more coffee."

"Thank you!" *This is the life,* thought Clara as the woman went back into the kitchen. It would be so good to get back to this type of relaxed living. Of course, she should give the tenants in the flat two months' notice and she thought she should work another three months at the Lauenstein. She had to break it to Ernst, of course, and she hadn't found the courage yet. She would be travelling back to Jena tomorrow.

She glanced at her son who had his head in his book. He snapped it shut. "That's it. I know where we can walk before lunch."

"Actually…" Clara bit her lip. "I'd rather like to sit here and talk a little." This was it. It was now or never.

The landlady came out with a fresh pot of coffee. Clara nodded. *Please don't talk to me or I'll never do this.*

The woman smiled. "I am going to be busy in the kitchen," she said.

"Mutti, there's nothing wrong, is there?" Ernst looked really concerned. Gosh, she hadn't wanted to worry him.

"Not really." *Except I don't think you're going to like it.*

"So what is so serious, then?"

"I want to go back to Berlin."

Ernst stared at her as if he didn't believe her. He didn't say anything for several minutes. Then he shook his head. "You can't, Mutti. We need you at the Lauenstein."

"I'm getting so tired. They really need someone younger and stronger. And I can't really agree with them any more about the way they want things done. I want to create a home for those young people. I want to look after them. But no, they must learn to do everything on their own."

"You know they have to learn how to look after themselves."

"Yes, I do know that. But I think someone else should teach them. I don't have the patience."

"You? Not patient? You're the most patient person I know."

"You'd be surprised."

"Anyway, you can't turf the Kellermanns out of the flat."

"Oh, I know that. I wouldn't be going straight away. Maybe July."

"Your mind's made up?"

Clara nodded.

Ernst looked away. She could tell he was disappointed. She would have to give him time to let the news sink in.

Clara was aware of their hostess pottering about behind them. She turned to see that she was attending to the window boxes, setting out some new late spring flowers. "Those will look nice," said Clara. "I'm sure they'll flower really well."

"I hope so," said the young woman. "I like the place to look pretty for our visitors."

Oh, how I envy you, thought Clara. This woman was in charge of her own world and no one told her what to do.

The woman carried on working, singing softly to herself. Clara would have found it all so wonderful if she didn't feel that she was letting her son down so much.

"I know," said Ernst. It was clear he had thought of something, His eyes were shining. "Mutti, do you remember when you said you could sell your pearls and we could build a house in Stuttgart?"

Clara laughed. "That wouldn't work now, would it? The mark's settled down. I mean, yes, I'd still get a tidy sum but not enough to build a house."

"Wouldn't Uncle Wilhelm help? Didn't he keep offering to lend you money so that you can have a house with a garden instead of living in an apartment? And Doctor Kühn has wanted to invest in a project like this for some time."

"Well, yes, but…"

"Wouldn't you like to live in Stuttgart, near to me?"

Of course she would, if she was honest. She would really rather be near one of the children. Käthe, Hans and Renate would be still be here in Jena. Rudi had said that he wanted to go and study in Canada for a while and Ernst was still attached to the Waldorf School. The only advantages about Berlin had been that she still owned the apartment and she still had some friends there.

"Wouldn't you?"

"Of course I would but…"

Ernst sprang onto his feet. He came over to her and took her hands in his. "Mutti, we could build a really big house there. You can run it. Some of the teachers can live there. And also some of the students who want to come from other towns. And you can cook, and clean and organise as much as you like. And look after the garden and plant the window boxes. And mother everyone. You'd also learn so much more about what Rudolf Steiner was trying to teach us. Just think, Mutti!"

Ernst's eyes were bright with excitement. She couldn't help but catch some of his mood.

There was the delicious smell of bread baking coming from inside the house. Oh, to have the excuse like that to bake bread and cakes for other people. This woman had it so good. Was Ernst saying it could really be like that for her?

"What do you think, Mutti?"

"I think… I think… it's a… a good idea."

She thought of Kurt and his angels. What would the angels make of this? Would they want her to do it? Goodness, what was she thinking?

She closed her eyes for a few moments and tried to work out what it could be like. The oddest thing happened then. It was a type of vision. She could see the house in detail. It was big but still homely. All the bedroom windows were open and the bed-rolls were hanging out of them. There were flowers on the tables and the woodwork smelt of polish. No grey towels here. And there was bread baking in the kitchen. She would plant fruit trees in the garden… so that she could always make delicious desserts for her guests.

My, she really did believe Kurt's angels were urging her on.

"Well, Mutti, can we do this?"

Clara opened her eyes. "I do believe we can!"

"Really? You'll go for this?"

"Yes. I'll get the pearls valued as soon as I get back."

"Will you write to Uncle Wilhelm? And I'll talk to Doctor Kühn."

"Yes, I'll write to him. I think he'll be pleased, actually."

"I'll look for a plot of land. In fact, I've seen one on Schellberg Street – it's not far from the Waldorf School. I'll find out."

"Do that. Do that."

"Mutti, it's going to be glorious."

"One thing, though. I'm only borrowing the money from your uncle and from Doctor Kühn. It's important that I actually own the place."

"Are you sure?" said Ernst. "You'll have a lot of debt."

"Don't worry. It will always be your home. And I don't need much. Every pfennig I earn will go into paying off the debt."

Ernst grinned. "It's going to be fantastic, Mutti."

The landlady had come out of the house again. "You two do look cheerful. Can I get anything else for you?"

"Do you have some Sekt?" asked Ernst. "And bring a glass for yourself and join us."

"So what's the occasion?" asked the young woman when she

142

reappeared carrying a tray with three glasses and a dusty bottle of Sekt.

"I am going to become a landlady," said Clara. "My son and I are going to build a house together. You must give me a lot of advice."

"Wonderful, wonderful," said the woman as she opened the bottle and poured out the bubbling wine.

Yes, and the third phase of my life is really beginning, thought Clara as they clinked glasses. All that had happened since Ernst senior died had been a false start.

5 July 1927, Stuttgart: signed and sealed

The window to Doctor Nothstein's office was open a little and was allowing in some air. The birds were chirping outside and it all seemed normal. Thank goodness. This office was not normal, though. The furniture was ridiculous. All too elaborately carved and too big. The solicitor himself was frightening. He was a bit too big as well. Well-fed, Clara decided. And he was certainly well dressed. He probably made a lot of money from this sort of work.

But Ernst had said he was good and she trusted her son.

He cleared his throat. "Frau Lehrs, Doctor Lehrs," he said, handing them each a set of the papers. "The transactions you instructed us to do are complete. Perhaps you would care to look at these documents."

Clara felt the urge to giggle. She would be so glad when they could get all of this formality over with and get on with building the house.

Doctor Nothstein cleared his throat. "As you can see, we have acquired the land in Schellberg Street, Stuttgart, as instructed."

He shuffled through his papers. "Pages three and four outline the terms of the loan. Should your brother die before you, Frau Lehrs, the loan will be annulled and you will be required to make no further payments. Should your brother outlive you, the remainder of the loan should be paid by your estate or by the sale of the house. Alternatively, your children can agree to take on the loan. The agreement between yourself and Doctor Kühn is valid for five years, by which time you should have paid off the loan. Note, that Doctor Kühn is willing for you to renegotiate the terms at any time, if you should encounter difficulties in meeting payments or indeed if you find you can pay the loan off early."

The solicitor blew his nose and almost set Clara off wanting to giggle again. "Pages five and six show you how the monies have been raised and how much is left for the building. That is a good amount and you should be able to build to a high standard. Your pearls were of excellent quality, apparently."

"Good. Where do I sign?"

"Just here and here." The solicitor pointed to two places on the document and offered Clara a pen and ink stand.

She signed and returned the two copies to Doctor Nothstein. She watched as he signed the papers as well, blotted them and then sprinkled some powder over their signatures. "There. I suggest you allow us to keep your copy and you may keep the blank one, which I'm also happy to sign, for your own records. All you have to do now, Frau Lehrs, Doctor Lehrs, is build the house." He actually smiled.

So, she was to become a house-owner and would be in charge of her own household. It was really happening.

"We did it," said Ernst as they walked down the path from Doctor Nothstein's front door.

"We did," said Clara. "Let's go and have a look at the land that we own."

9 January 1928, Stuttgart: Dachfest

"I'm so pleased to see you've wrapped up warm, Frau Lehrs. I won't shake your hand. I'm still dusty."

Clara smiled at the little man. She thought once again how lucky they'd been to have Herr Raffel in charge of the whole project. He had been so reliable and helpful. She'd heard some terrible stories of people whose builders had let them down. But this short, blond-haired, determined little man had made sure everything had got done on time and to the highest possible standard.

"It'll still look a bit ugly," said Herr Raffel. "The insides need to be finished and we still have a lot of equipment stored inside. It'll actually seem quite small because it'll be difficult to imagine what it'll look like with furniture in it."

"But the roof's on? It looks as if it is."

"Almost. Almost. You yourself will put on the final tile – from the inside of course – we wouldn't want you climbing up any ladders."

Why not? That sounded like fun.

"So I'm pleased you're wearing your fur. It'll be cold up there."

"But it's such a sunny day."

"You'd be surprised. Shall we go on up?"

"Yes please."

Herr Raffel offered Clara his arm and they made their way up the stairs. The others chattered excitedly and clattered up the uncovered stairs. Some of the helpers from the Waldorf School were already there and had the bottles of Sekt and the glasses ready.

Herr Raffel handed Clara the tile. "Let me help you. It's heavier than it looks."

She took the tile and allowed Herr Raffel's hands to guide hers to place it into exactly the right spot.

"There. It slots in like that. Then—" He gave the tile a gentle tap. "That's perfect. May the Dachfest begin!"

Two Sekt corks popped out of their bottles.

"A toast!" called one of the helpers.

"Yes, indeed a toast to Haus Lehrs."

"We should call it the Little Goetheanum. It's going to be such a retreat for our hard-working teachers."

"Especially with Frau Lehrs in charge."

Clara felt her cheeks going red. The young woman who had made that outrageous remark – goodness she looked about eighteen and her dress was much too flimsy for standing on the roof in January in a house that wasn't quite finished yet – was carrying round a tray of pastries that Clara and a couple of the Waldorf women had spent all morning making.

"I do like the quality of your work," said Herr Molt to Herr Raffel. "When I need another house building I shall come and seek you out."

"Thank you, sir."

"It's splendid," said Doctor Kühn." Truly splendid. So, when will it be finished, Herr Raffel?"

"Frau Lehrs and Doctor Lehrs should be able to move in by the first day of spring," said Herr Raffel, "and you should be able to move your teachers and students in after the Easter holidays."

"Excellent!"

A thrill of excitement ran through Clara.

"Now, then everyone," called Herr Raffel, "are you ready for the grand tour? Do mind your step – there are still a lot of loose bits and pieces around."

There was a general murmur of agreement.

"So this is one of the bigger bedrooms," said Herr Raffel as he showed them all around the first floor. "Maybe some of the children will share in here – perhaps you will keep the smaller ones for the teachers."

"So how many beds will this hold?" someone asked. "It's difficult to visualise."

"It depends how close you want to put them," said Herr Raffel. "You could have bunk beds, I suppose. Goodness, you could get twenty people in here and they'd still have enough breathing-space."

Everyone laughed.

No, thought Clara. This was to be a room for four little girls a bit older than Renate. They would have four pretty little beds and plenty of space for playing and dancing. And she would tuck them up every night, and read to them so that they wouldn't miss their mummies too much.

In fact, as they carried on their viewing of the house she didn't join in the conversations at all. She concentrated on working out exactly how it was going to look.

It's angel work, she thought, remembering Kurt. She couldn't wait for the next phase of this project.

24 October 1928, Stuttgart: Mutti Lehrs

It was always so quiet after breakfast, when they all left to walk round to the school. It was a real routine. First they were reluctant to get out of bed. A little healthy chaos followed as they all struggled to get ready in time. Next came the chatter which got louder and louder until the panic set in as they grabbed books and bags and rushed off to school.

Then she would tidy up and enjoy the peace for a few moments. Not that there was too much to tidy. The children cleared the table before they left. She thought she was getting it right. Some discipline but a lot of love and care as well.

She smiled to herself as she watched them set off down the garden path. Young Walter was hurtling along at quite a speed, though. His bag was flying behind him. He'd better watch out or there'd be an accident. Clara held her breath.

Walter tumbled. There was a loud smack as his head collided with the stone path and the peace was shattered as he started yelling.

Goodness, I hope the child hasn't given himself concussion, thought Clara as she rushed out towards the boy. There was blood oozing from his head. Older sister, Zelda, was already bending down and trying to help her little brother.

Some of the other children had stopped to see what all the commotion was about.

"You go on ahead," Clara called to them. "Zelda and I will see to Walter. Adalbert, will you tell their teachers they're going to be late?"

Adalbert nodded and he and the others set off again.

Clara turned to the child. He'd stopped screeching at last. "Can you stand up?"

Walter nodded and got to his feet. Zelda helped to prop him up. "Ow! Ow!" he called as he stepped on his foot.

"Can you walk?" asked Clara.

"It hurts," said Walter.

"You can lean on us," said Clara, as the three of them struggled back towards the house. She really wanted to get him cleaned up so that she could see whether a trip to the hospital was necessary or whether they needed to send for the doctor. "Come on, Hopalong."

The little boy giggled.

As they made their way up the path Zelda didn't say a word. She just stared solemnly at her little brother. At last they arrived at the kitchen.

"Come on then let's see what's the matter," said Clara as she lifted Walter up on to the counter.

"Be good for Mutti Lehrs," said Zelda.

Mutti Lehrs?

"Be brave," said Zelda, patting her brother's arm.

Clara dampened a cloth and gently dabbed at the knee. There was really only a tiny cut. She got another cloth for his head. There was a lot of blood there but again the cut was tiny.

The little boy flinched as she bathed his wounds. She could tell he was trying to be brave.

"Now then, do you think you'll be able to walk to school?"

Walter shrugged.

"Let's see how well you go then." She lifted him off the counter and set him down on the floor.

He wobbled a little.

"I could give him a piggy-back," said Zelda.

"Mmm. I'm not sure that's a good idea. You'll get tired in no time." She ruffled Walter's hair. "Young master Walter can stay here with me until someone can wheel him round there or until he can walk a bit better. But maybe you should make your way there now?"

"Yes, Mutti Lehrs. Walter, remember to be good for Mutti Lehrs."

"I will!"

Well, that name's beginning to stick, thought Clara.

Zelda had only been gone a few seconds when Walter's eyes filled with tears.

"Oh dear," said Clara. "Now, is that knee or that head hurting? Or do you wish you were at school? Or are you missing that big sister of yours?"

Walter shook his head. "I miss my Mutti," he said. The tears rolled down his cheeks.

"Oh come here, you poor child." She pulled the little boy towards her and hugged him. "Can't I be your weekday Mutti? Can't I be Mutti Lehrs like Zelda suggested?"

"I'd like that," he said.

"Mutti Lehrs it is, then." She stroked his blond curls again. "Now, would you like some lemonade before I get Thomas to take you round in the cart?"

18 July 1929, Stuttgart: strange happenings

Clara was looking forward to Ernst's lecture. He was becoming so confident. She still didn't really get all of these spiritual matters that they talked about but she enjoyed listening to her son speaking. It was always so cool in the main hall. A nice breeze usually came through the open windows. Anyway it was such a pleasant walk on a warm summer evening like this one.

She should hurry, actually. The others had left over ten minutes ago. She hoped they wouldn't start without her. Surely they wouldn't?

Of course they wouldn't. The people who worked here were always so nice. So were the children. There must be something in what they said and what they believed – if it made them so good. But she didn't get it. She wished that she did but she didn't. Ernst, her husband Ernst, didn't exist anywhere but in her memories. There was no heaven. When you died, that was it. At least it must mean there was no hell either, surely? It didn't matter whether you were Jewish, Catholic, Protestant or even an anthroposophist. You had to try your best. That was what she was doing.

Good to be amongst such kind people, but that's all they were: kind people.

There was a scream from above. It sounded like a small child. Sure enough a child was tumbling through the air towards her. A boy or a girl? She couldn't be sure. She caught the little one in her arms. Had he fallen out of the sky? Or perhaps from a nearby tree? Except there weren't any trees growing above her.

The child was wearing a sort of long-sleeved and long-legged romper-suit in pale yellow. It was impossible to tell whether it was a boy or a girl. It wasn't a baby, though. It was older than that. Maybe two?

The child began to grizzle, then put its fist in its mouth and made loud sucking noises. The little one was hungry.

Perhaps she should take it back to the house and try to feed it.

The others would understand why she'd missed the lecture when they came back and found her with the child.

She hurried back towards the house.

Then she felt dizzy. The world started turning rapidly and she thought she was going to pass out. She didn't though. She was back on the street where the child had fallen from the sky. She was standing with her arms open as if to catch the child. A couple who were passing on the street stared at her and whispered something.

What had happened? Had she had some sort of fit? Had it looked as if she'd been talking to herself?

She must hurry. It was really getting late. How long had that all been? Ten minutes maybe? She walked as fast as she could.

She was surprised to find that everyone was still outside. A group of teachers, Ernst amongst them, were talking in whispers, their faces serious.

"I'm sorry I'm so late. Were you waiting for me?"

Ernst shook his head. "We thought you might be with Berndt's parents."

"Berndt's parents?"

Ernst exchanged a look with Karl Schubert. "You've not heard?" said Karl softly.

"Heard what?" Clara's heart was bouncing and her mouth was dry.

Karl put his hand on Clara's arm. "Berndt collapsed and died earlier this evening. Heat-stroke. We've sent for his parents. There will be a vigil after the lecture. We haven't told the other children yet." He looked over to where some of the bigger boys had begun a play fight. "Maybe we should get them in."

"So where have you been, Mutti, if you haven't been with Berndt's parents? We set off over an hour ago."

An hour? That strange incident had taken over an hour? "I'll tell you later," she whispered. "You'd better get your lecture started."

Clara couldn't concentrate on the lecture. What had happened earlier kept going round and round in her mind. She was certain that child dropping from the sky was something to do with Berndt's death. So, then, there were things beyond life as she understood it after all. It still didn't make sense. None of it did. She would have to accept it, though. She'd had the proof, hadn't she?

Later still, back at the house, she crept into the room where Ernst was keeping watch over Berndt's body. The boy looked pale and as if he was sleeping. There was still something of him left. Wasn't it supposed to take three days for the soul to leave the body? It looked to her as if Berndt's soul was still there. Yes, that was it. She gasped.

"So?" whispered Ernst.

"I think I caught his soul and brought it back to him." She told Ernst about what had happened earlier.

Ernst nodded and rubbed his mother's arm.

29 August 1929: a new friend

"My goodness, you are a good little walker," said Clara. "I'm going to have to sit down on this bench for a while. I can't keep up with you, young lady." The little girl never stopped surprising her. They must have already walked at least three kilometres and the child showed no sign of tiring. She really looked the part too, with her short dirndl skirt, her walking boots and thick socks, and the little knapsack she carried on her back. It was hard to believe she was only four years old.

They'd had great fun packing a picnic. Maybe now was the moment to enjoy it.

"May I have some lemonade? I'm thirsty."

"Of course you can. That's why we brought it along, isn't it? And the bags will be lighter when we've had our drinks and eaten our sandwiches."

"I want to put some leaves and stones in my bag. I want to make an arrangement for Mutti when I get back. May I?"

"Of course you may. But won't it make our bags heavy to carry?"

"I don't mind."

It was pleasant sitting in the shade. A breeze cooled them after their strenuous walk and made the leaves in the trees dance around. They could hear birds singing and other creatures moving in the undergrowth.

"Oma, aren't you and Uncle Ernst lucky having those woods so close to where you live? It's a shame Mutti didn't come."

It was indeed. Käthe had decided to get her hair done. Hans had been off to a business meeting. Had those two no idea what the word "holiday" meant?

Clara took the bottle of lemonade and two tin cups out of her own rucksack. She poured a cup for Renate and handed it to her. "And now for the rolls. There's cheese and salami. And do you remember what we put in your knapsack?"

"The tomatoes and the apples! I hope I didn't squash them."

Clara smiled to herself as the little girl unpacked the bag. Within seconds she had found the red apples and the juicy tomatoes, thankfully not squashed. And then she squealed with delight when she found the two biscuits with the broken pieces of chocolate inside. They'd only been tiny bits so there was no danger of them making a mess if it melted. "How did those get there?"

"I've no idea," said Clara. "It must have been the forest folk."

Renate tittered.

They enjoyed the picnic.

"It's nicer when you eat food outside." Renata grinned at Clara. "I'm sooo hungry."

"Well, eat as much as you can. What a good girl you are." Yes, indeed, it was quite a trick of hers on fine days to take the lunch outside to encourage the more reluctant eaters. Fortunately there appeared to be no problem with Renate.

Clara began picking up the paper from their sandwiches and putting away the empty bottle. "Well, shall we get going?"

But Renate was not looking and listening. She was busy collecting leaves, twigs and pebbles off the ground.

"No too many, or your knapsack will get too heavy."

Renate stopped what she was doing. She stared towards the pathway. Clara turned to see what she was looking at. There stood another little girl, also dressed in a dirndl and walking shoes and with a knapsack almost identical to Renate's on her back. Except that this little girl looked hot and bothered and worn out from her walk and she was rounder and plumper than Renate. And there was no sign of any Mutti or Oma with her.

"Goodness, look at you," said Clara. The little's girl's legs were covered in scratches.

She flopped down on the ground. "I'm thirsty. I've lost my Mutti." She started crying.

Renate was staring at Clara, her eyes and her mouth wide open.

"Now, now," said Clara, putting her arms around the little girl. "We'll help you find your Mutti." She took the other bottle and one of the tin cups out of her rucksack. "Would you like some water?"

The little girl nodded. Clara poured the water and the little girl took the cup.

"So, where did you lose your Mutti?"

"My ball rolled away and she went to get it. But she was a long time so I thought she must have got lost. So I came to look for her."

Oh dear. There was probably some equally frantic mother looking for her little daughter. "Never mind. I'm sure she's not far away. You finish your drink and we'll go back the way you came. I'm sure we'll find her in no time."

They didn't have to.

"Hani! Hani!" they heard a voice calling.

"Mutti!" Hani sprang to her feet and ran into the arms of the young woman who was standing in the opening.

"Thank goodness you're all right."

The young woman looked up at Clara. "Thank goodness you found her."

"I think she rather found us."

"It was so silly. Her ball rolled down the embankment. I told her to stand on the path while I fetched it but then I turned my ankle and I had to take a few minutes to get my breath. It hurt pretty badly at first. Then when I could walk again I got back up to the path and she'd gone."

"Well you're back together. So no more worries."

Hani had taken the ball from her mother and was throwing it to Renate.

"Look," said Clara pointing to the two little girls. "And how's your ankle?"

"Not too bad. I think I'll manage to limp to the tram stop then we can take the tram home."

"I think you can rest it for a while. Those two are happy enough. Let me wrap it in our picnic cloth. I can put some water on it. It might take the swelling down."

"Thank you. You are so kind."

Clara smiled.

The girls became absorbed in their game and when they became tired out from playing with the ball, Renate insisted on showing her new friend one of her "arrangements". Clara enjoyed chatting with this pleasant young woman. She liked her. Frau Gödde was her name. Helga Gödde.

"It's so nice to see her with a real friend. Some of the little girls who live near us are strange. She's not really enjoying Kindergarten."

Frau Gödde went quiet. She probably thought she'd said too much.

"Have you thought of the Waldorf School?" said Clara. Goddess, what was she doing – trying to be a saleswoman?

"Funny you should say that. My husband and I were only talking about it the other day. We've heard some good reports. We want to find out more about it."

"Well you're speaking to the right person."

"Is that where Renate goes?"

Clara was on the point of explaining that Renate was only visiting and that she really lived in Jena when Hani bounded across.

"Mutti, I'm hungry."

"When aren't you?" Frau Gödde shook her head and laughed. "I'm a terrible mother. I'm not organised like you, Frau Lehrs. I get so busy helping my husband with his work sometimes… I just don't think. How about if we go to the café by the tram stop? I can get both of you girls an ice-cream and Frau Lehrs and I can enjoy a nice cup of coffee?"

"Yes please!" The two little girls hugged each other.

"That sounds a really interesting way of life, Frau Lehrs. You are so brave, looking after other people's children."

"I really enjoy it."

"And it will really be fine if I come and talk to your son?"

"Of course." Clara looked through the window to where Renate and Hani were playing on the seesaw in the little garden next to the café. "And bring Hani too. I'm sure Renate will love to play with her again. She probably misses her friends from home when she's here."

"Well, I should be going," said Helga Gödde. She made her way to the door. Clara followed her.

"Come on. We must set off home."

"Oh." Hani's bottom lip wobbled and she looked as if she was about to cry.

"Your Mutti will bring you to see Renate," said Clara. "And you can play together again. Will you like that?"

Renate and Hani hugged each other. "Yes please!"

The tram was waiting at the stop. Hani and her mother climbed aboard and a few moments later it set off. Clara and Renate waved vigorously until Hani and her mother were out of sight.

"Are we going to go back by tram?" Renate asked.

"We could if you like. There'll be one that goes our way in a few minutes."

"Can we walk home instead?"

"You're not too tired?"

"No." She started skipping back towards the woods.

They were so different from each other these two little girls. But Clara knew they were going to be the best of friends.

19 June 1930 Stuttgart: helping the Hilfsklasse

The house was sparkling. The young guests had learnt to tidy up after themselves and this morning she'd managed to get all of the rugs beaten, wash the paintwork in the communal rooms and clean the windows inside. It was looking good. Yet she found herself frowning.

There was something not quite right, something was out of place. She couldn't quite see what. She looked carefully round the room. What could it be?

Then she saw it. There was a drawstring bag hanging off one of the chairs.

Clara shook her head and tutted to herself. Who had left what and why in the lounge of all places?

She took the bag off the chair and opened it. It was a costume. A dance costume. A green leotard with a chiffon skirt sewn on and small pieces of chiffon attached at the shoulders to look like wings. One of the girls in the upper school, then. Clara thought for a moment and looked at the size of the costume. A petite girl.

Dagmar! Of course. She'd been reattaching the wing last night. Oh, and goodness, she'd need it this afternoon. They were having a dress rehearsal of the summer show. Clara supposed she'd better take it round to the school.

Dagmar's classroom was empty when Clara got there. They hadn't already started their run through, had they? No, there were several bags like Dagmar's hanging off the back of chairs and out through the classroom window, she could see them all, looking up at one of the trees. The teacher was pointing and talking. A nature study lesson, no doubt.

Now, then, which was Dagmar's place? Obviously one where there was no bag hanging. There were one or two of those but of course they might belong to students who weren't taking part in the show. Perhaps she should leave the costume on the teacher's desk. Then she spotted an exercise book open on one of the desks.

That looked like Dagmar's. Tiny, neat handwriting and exquisite pictures. Biology, by the looks of it. And there they were. Outside, having a practical lesson on this lovely day. Wonderful!

Clara was always amazed at how well the children at this school could draw and paint, but Dagmar was exceptional, even amongst them. She looked at the name on the cover just to be sure but wasn't surprised to see that the book did in fact belong to Dagmar Müller. Dear Dagmar. Artistic, practical, neat and tidy – but forgetful. Clara carefully placed the forgotten costume on the desk so that Dagmar might see it when she returned. Job done, then.

As she made her way back towards the main entrance, a child came hurtling out of one of the other classrooms. He bumped into Clara, falling to the floor and dropping the pieces of paper he was carrying. The gentle breeze coming in through the open door at the end of the corridor caused the papers to dance and swirl all over the place.

"Oh my goodness," said Clara. "We'll have to be quick."

She hastily started gathering up papers and after a moment's hesitation the boy joined in.

"Wilhelm, how many times have I told you not to run?" said a voice.

A man made his way out of the classroom. Clara recognised Karl Schubert. Clara had had several conversations with him because the children he taught here in the special Hilfsklasse were so similar to the ones she'd known at the Lauenstein.

"It's all right," said Clara as she and Wilhelm continued to gather up the escaping papers. "We've almost got them all back." More lovely pictures she realised. These weren't as finely drawn as many she'd seen produced by the children here but they were certainly colourful.

"What do you say to Frau Lehrs, Wilhelm?"

Two serious eyes that were filling with tears looked back at her. "Thank you, Frau Lehrs."

"Oh sweetheart, that could have happened to anyone. Please don't be cross with him, Doctor Schubert. He only wanted to get these fine pictures to their destination as soon as possible."

"I know, I know." Karl Shubert bent down so that his head was level with the boy's. "Walk and concentrate, please, Wilhelm, then come straight back to class once you've taken them to the office."

Wilhelm nodded and set off briskly down the corridor. Karl Schubert shook his head and laughed.

"At least he's not running," said Clara.

"There is that. And at least their pictures will be seen. Of course their paintings aren't quite as good as the other children's but they deserve to have them displayed. They've really worked hard on them."

"I'm sure they have. I know how difficult it can be. The Lauenstein, you know."

"Of course. Of course you'd understand." Karl Schubert grinned. "Frau Lehrs, would you like see what we're doing?"

"I'd love that."

"Come on in, then." Karl Shubert led her into the classroom.

The children were all working quietly. One girl looked exhausted and had laid her head on her arm. She was still writing but looked as if she would rather be sleeping. A couple of the other children were concentrating so hard that their tongues were poking out.

"We're practising our handwriting today," said Karl Schubert. "We still have to associate the letters with the shapes of our body."

Clara nodded. Most of these children looked as if they were twelve years old or older. This sort or work was normally done by six and seven-year-olds. The children here were not as severely disabled as the ones she'd worked with in Jena, but they were certainly different from the rest of the children at the school.

"We'll be working for another half hour and then I'll read them a story before we finish for lunch. I'll need to go round and comment on their work. Would you like to look at some of them?"

"I can help you, if you like. And would you let me read the story? You look very tired."

"That would be wonderful. But don't you have to get back to the house for the lunches?"

Clara shrugged. "Most of them have brought a packed lunch because of the rehearsal. The rest are having an indoor picnic.

We'll have something warm this evening. If lunch is late they can start on their homework while they wait. Is that all right?"

Karl Shubert grinned.

An hour later Clara had helped seven children with their writing, shown another five a clever trick for making the letter S look more elegant, admired the work of those children who had made few mistakes, worked quite hard herself but watched Karl Shubert work even harder, read a story to the children and answered several questions about the house on Schellberg Street.

"But now," said Clara, "I do believe it is time for you to all go home, eat a splendid lunch, have a nice afternoon nap and then be ready for the rest of a wonderful afternoon and evening."

Karl Schubert was grinning at her again. "That was quite fantastic, Frau Lehrs. Boys and girls, please thank Frau Lehrs."

The children started clapping and cheering.

"Will you come again, Frau Lehrs?" asked one of the girls.

"Yes, I'd like to." Clara glanced up at Karl Schubert.

He shrugged and raised his eyebrows.

One or two of the children stopped to speak to her or their teacher as they made their way out of the classroom.

"Well," said Clara, after the last of the children had departed, "I could help you for a couple of hours Mondays, Wednesdays and Fridays. What do you think of that?"

"Are you sure?"

"Of course I'm sure. I wouldn't have said so, otherwise, would I?"

"Good. Then let's do it."

"Yes. Let's."

15 December 1930, Stuttgart: career change

"Look at the lights," whispered Clara. "Aren't they pretty?"

Renate nodded her head and clapped.

It certainly was a sight. All of the children, even the ones from the Hilfsklasse, were carrying a candle. It was getting dark. The sky had been streaked with pink as they arrived, promising that the next day would be fine but cold and that there would be no more snow overnight. There was enough on the ground for it to look clean and pretty but there would be no danger of them getting cut off.

And the hall was lit with nothing but the candles. It was magical.

Clara had worried at first about so many candles.

"It will be fine, Clara," Karl had said. "The children will be taught how to handle them safely. All of the adults are primed to keep a close watch on proceedings. They're safety candles, anyway."

He'd been right. He was also right about how magical it would be to live by more natural rhythms and really understand the darkness of these short days before Christmas. The candles represented the light that would return after the winter solstice in a few days' time.

That's one really intelligent little girl, thought Clara as she watched her granddaughter sitting very still, totally enchanted by the singing and acting of the Waldorf School students as they told their story of the returning light. Käthe on the other hand had fidgeted and sighed. She had little patience with stories like these.

"So, you enjoyed that, did you?" said Clara as at last the school conceded to 20th century life and put on the electric lights as the play came to a close.

Renate nodded.

"How would you like something to eat and drink?"

"Yes please."

Clara took her hand and led her to the classroom where the food was being served.

"How do you manage all of this?" asked Käthe. "These days?"

It was quite a spread. There were Wiener Kipferln, Stollen, Strudel and Christmas shapes made from Lebkuchen. There was tea and coffee and warmed apple juice flavoured with cinnamon. There was even some cream though if truth be told it was really Quark, thinned with milk and flavoured with a little vanilla.

"We can do a lot when we pull together as a community," said Clara. She was only too aware how hard the students, parents and teachers had worked to produce this feast. Everyone had found something in the store cupboard that could be used and had given their goods and their time generously. The kitchen at 20 Schellberg Street had been used to capacity over the previous two weeks. It had also been a warm and welcome retreat from the bitter cold.

"Oma, will you teach me how to make Lebkuchen?" said Renate.

"Hmm. Lebkuchen are a bit tricky but we certainly can have a go at some Strudel or a cheesecake if you like."

"Yes please, Oma," said the little girl; trying to wipe the sticky crumbs from her face but actually making it worse.

"Look at the mess you're making, will you?" said Käthe, spitting on her hanky and scrubbing at her daughter's face.

Time they were going.

It was completely dark when they got outside. Despite the lamps they could see a sky that looked like dark blue velvet covered in sequins. The snow glistened in the lamp light.

"Mutti, can I run to the end of the road then run back to you and Oma?" Renate was already skipping along and Clara couldn't work out how she managed to keep herself upright on the very slippery pavements. She and Käthe were walking gingerly.

"Go on then," said Käthe.

"Aren't you frightened she'll fall?"

"Not that one. She's more-sure footed than a mountain goat and even if she does fall – it doesn't happen very often, mind – she bounces back on to her feet."

Clara held her breath as she watched her granddaughter run backwards and forwards. She didn't slip once and Clara couldn't believe how fast she was for such a little girl. She was relieved, though, when they arrived at the house and there had been no accidents.

"She can run, can't she?" said Clara.

"Oh yes. Faster than anyone else in her Kindergarten group. No one else comes anywhere near her. Not even any of the boys."

By the time Clara had overseen the preparations for supper for the guests and laid up a table for Hans, Käthe, Renate and herself in her private sitting room, the little girl could hardly keep her eyes open. It was really past her bed-time.

As soon as supper was done, Renate laid her head in her mother's lap, stuck her thumb in her mouth and fell asleep.

"Goodness, she's worn out," said Clara. "I'm not surprised, though, with all that running backwards and forwards."

"And the play. She enjoyed that but it made her tired," said Käthe.

"She ought to go to bed," said Hans.

At the sound of her father's voice Renate awoke.

"Bed-time," whispered Käthe.

"Can Oma put me to bed? I want Oma to read me a story."

Käthe raised her eyebrows and looked at Clara.

"Yes. It's fine. Of course I'll read you a story. Come on and let's get you up those stairs."

After Renate had kissed her mother and father goodnight, Clara took her upstairs, supervised her washing and cleaning her teeth. She helped her to get undressed and then made sure she snuggled down into the bed in the little room off the one where her parents were going to sleep.

"What will you read me?" said Renate.

Clara thought for a moment.

"I know just the one. I won't be a moment. It's a story about a snowflake."

Renate nodded.

Clara fetched it from the younger girls' room along the

corridor. Klarissa wouldn't mind, she was sure.

As Clara read the story of the little snowflake's journey down to earth where it melted into a lovely sleep on the window of a house warm with a Christmas family gathering, the little girl's eyelids dropped again. Clara was sure she'd missed the end of the story.

But as Clara tucked the little girl in and whispered "Sleep well, little one," Renate's eyes opened.

"Oma, I liked it at your school and I like it at your house. Can I come and live here? And go to Uncle Ernst's school?"

"Oh, I don't know about that. What would Mutti and Vati do without you? But you can come as often as you like in the holidays. Would you like that?"

Renate nodded.

"Good. That's settled then. You know where to find Mutti and Vati if you need them in the night?"

She nodded again.

Clara pulled the door behind her and made her way downstairs.

"So you have managed to get everyone to call her Renate?" she said to Käthe and Hans when she got back down to her sitting room. "The Kindergarten people were all right about it?"

"Yes, though she's still Klara Renate on anything official. And we're resigned to spelling it the German way," said Käthe.

"I don't see why we should have to be," said Hans. "We should choose her name. Not some drunken priest."

"Well it's done now."

Clara couldn't help but notice the irritation in her daughter's voice.

"Anyway, we've got much more important things to discuss with Mutti. Shall I tell her or will you?"

Hans glared at her.

"Right. Listen, Mutti. We're moving to Nuremberg."

"Nuremberg?" A pretty enough old Bavarian town, as far as she could make out, but she'd also heard rumours of big parade grounds being built there. Why they were doing that she wasn't sure.

"I'm going to be working for Siemens," said Hans. "I'll be working on defence weapons."

Clara shuddered. "You don't think there's going to be another war, do you?"

Hans shrugged. "Every nation must have its defence."

"Mutti, it's a well-paid job. It will help to secure Renate's future."

Clara shivered again. Like on the day Ernst died.

"I do hope you're right," she whispered.

26 March 1931 Stuttgart: Herr Hitler

The shouting was coming from the dining room. That was two floors down and Clara could almost make out the words but not quite all of them. How many of them was it? Ten or so? The older ones. Boys and girls. She'd better get down there before they started pulling each other apart.

She rushed down the stairs and followed the noise. It wasn't even in the dining room, as she'd thought, but actually outside the back door. They were making that much noise, then? What was this all about?

"You can't say that!" screeched one of the girls. "What are you thinking?"

The rest noticed Clara arrive. There was immediate silence. One or two of them looked down to the ground.

"What's going on?" asked Clara. "What's all the shouting about?"

The silence continued. There were seven of them. Only seven.

"Well. It must have been important if you have to make so much noise."

Still no answer.

"So, I think you'd all better go in and get to your rooms. And don't even talk to each other if you can't talk in a civilised manner."

Most of them were looking at the ground and no one moved.

"All right, then," said Clara more gently, "does someone want to tell me what has been going on?"

One of the boys looked up. "We were arguing about Herr Hitler."

Ah. Him.

"And what couldn't you agree about Herr Hitler?" asked Clara.

"He's not even German," said one of the girls. "He's Austrian."

"No, he's not. He gave up being Austrian."

"But he didn't make himself German."

"And he's been in prison."

"Yes, but it wasn't really like being in prison. The guards were nice to him and they let him write a book."

"And he had some good ideas about what to do to get things right after October '29."

The voices were getting loud again.

"Enough!" Clara shouted. Goodness, how did these young people know so much? October '29? October '29? What happened then?"

"That was in America. Not here." Of course. The Wall Street crash.

"Yes but it affected things here. And after the inflation those other idiots aren't offering anything very good."

This was terrible. Terrible that they were falling out and terrible that they understood so much about so many things that should really be left to the grown-ups.

The sun burst through the clouds and illuminated the group of young people standing in the yard.

"Breathe deeply," said Clara. "Close your eyes, feel the sun and listen to the silence a while."

It wasn't silent of course, not quite. The branches of the trees rustled. Birds sang. People were going about their business in their gardens and on the streets.

Calmness descended all the same.

"All right," said Clara. "Open your eyes and in you go. And no more talk about Herr Hitler, thank you very much."

Just as the students were making their way up to their rooms, the front door opened and Ernst walked in.

"What's been going on here?" he asked.

Clara told him about the argument. "I'm amazed that they know so much about the man and all the political things. More than I do, I think."

Ernst shrugged. "Well, we do teach them to take responsibility for the world and to be aware of it."

Clara nodded. In some ways, she supposed, it was good that they were informing themselves. "He doesn't seem to be a very clear-cut person."

"He isn't," said Ernst. "But he was in the war, just like I was. He's passionate about Germany. And he has some ideas that at least sound good about how to build up our economy. He's giving some people hope."

"But do you actually like him?"

Ernst shrugged again. "Difficult to say. He's too far away for me to know whether I would actually like him or not."

Clara remembered seeing a photo of Herr Hitler. His eyes scared her, like Rudolf Steiner's had. Only Steiner's had only made him appear incredibly powerful. Hitler's eyes made him look evil and powerful at the same time.

"I think I need to find out more about him," she murmured. She fetched her hat and coat.

"Where are you going?" asked Ernst.

"To the library. I'll be back soon."

Four hours later Clara glanced up from the papers she'd been studying. The sky had clouded over again and it looked grey outside. Yes, that would be about right for the mood she was in.

The young people had been right in everything they'd said. And there was more. The man was a house-painter for goodness sake. How did someone like him become so grand?

She found another photo of him. Those eyes again. They gave her goose-pimples.

She could understand why there had been an argument. But she knew what she thought: she did not like him No, she did not.

She gathered up the papers and handed them back to the library assistant. She pulled on her hat and coat and set off. She must hurry. She had duties back at the house. She must also convince Ernst and all the other teachers along with the other people who worked at the house and the school that they should not vote for this man. No, they must certainly not.

As she turned into Schellberg Street it began to rain.

26 July 1932 Stuttgart: spots

The front door slammed. That would be Käthe then. Nothing changed. It was odd, though, that Renate wasn't awake yet. Yes, Käthe and Hans had wanted to set off early, before her getting up time but she wasn't the sort of little girl to lie in bed late. And it was late. Half an hour past her normal getting up time in fact. Should she go and wake her?

They'd got an exciting day planned. They hadn't done a lot for her birthday the day before – they'd all only travelled here yesterday morning – but today was going to be fun-packed. They were going to buy a new swimsuit, and then have some lunch in the Scholssgarten Café. Once lunch had gone down Ernst was taking her swimming in the afternoon. Later Hani and her mother were coming over for a day-late birthday tea. Yes, it was going to be fun but hectic.

So, they'd better get started.

Clara made her way upstairs and into Renate's room. She opened the curtains. It was a beautiful day. Good for swimming. Good for everything. "Wake up. Rise and shine. Time to start the day."

Renate sat up and rubbed her eyes. "Mutti?"

"Oma. Mutti and Vati are out for the day, remember. And Hani's coming later."

Renate started crying. "I want my Mutti."

Goodness, this was unusual. Normally the child hardly noticed whether her mother was there or not. Especially if Hani Gödde or swimming were on the agenda. Perhaps it was because her parents had left without saying goodbye?

"Oh, she and your Vati will back by tea-time and then Hani and Frau Gödde are coming too. That will be nice, won't it?"

Renate shrugged. Oh dear, she hoped she wasn't sickening for something. She felt her forehead. It was warm. And was that a little spot at the top of her eyebrow?

Renate pulled away. "Can I wear my blue dress today?"

"I don't see why not."

"Well, what about the blue one? It will go with your dress."

"It's too big girl. I want a pretty one."

"Well what about the ones with flowers on?"

"It's too pink."

"Well, I don't know, Renate. If we don't find you a swimsuit Uncle Ernst won't be able to take you swimming."

"I don't want to go swimming. I want to go home to find Mutti."

Oh no. There really was something not right. Clara looked desperately round the shop for something that might please her granddaughter.

Then she saw it. A really playful one covered in colourful butterflies. Renate loved butterflies. "We'll try that one," she said pointing to it. The tired shop assistant looked grateful.

"Come on Renate." She marched the little girl towards the changing room. For the moment at least the child was fascinated by the butterflies.

"Now then. Let's get this dress off."

Renate held her arms up so that Clara could slip the dress over her head.

"Ow! That hurts. My back."

Clara turned the child round. Goodness yes. It was covered in a rash. She recognised it but couldn't quite remember what it was. She felt her granddaughter's forehead again. It had become was even warmer.

"I think we'd better go home," said Clara.

"Can't I try the butterfly suit on first?"

"Well, yes. But I think we'll have to buy it if you try it on. Do you really like it?"

Renate nodded.

Perhaps it was some sort of allergy. Perhaps she would be fine again soon. Maybe even by this afternoon.

But getting the costume on and off wasn't easy. The spots must have been really sore and Renate ended up crying.

A smile did appear on her face, though, when Clara paid for the swimsuit and the lady serving said, "My goodness. I expect you're going to be the smartest young lady at the swimming pool in that."

"Is she sleeping?" asked Ernst.

Clara nodded. "At least the spots can't be hurting too much. And it'll do her good. Help bring down the fever."

"What did the doctor say?"

"He'll be round as soon as he can. He's had to go and see some other little children."

"It's a good job it's the holidays, I suppose. Or we might have an epidemic."

"Yes."

Ernst put his arms around his mother's shoulders. "Don't worry too much, Mutti. Children grow while they're ill. They may even be ill because they're growing."

"Oh Ernst, you do say some strange things sometimes."

"She's strong, Mutti. She'll be fine."

"I wish I could let Käthe know." Clara put her hand in front of her mouth. "And I must let Frau Gödde know."

She started making her way out to the hallway, towards the phone when it actually started ringing.

"Clara Lehrs," she answered.

"Frau Lehrs," said a breathless Frau Gödde. "We won't be able to come. Hani has chicken pox."

Chicken pox. Of course. That was it. That's what the spots were. She remembered when her three had had it. One after the other, exactly ten days apart. First Rudi, then Ernst and finally Käthe.

"Yes, you are quite right, Frau Lehrs. It is indeed chicken pox. Quite a few spots, but not too many. She'll feel better in a day or two. The spots can be a nuisance, though. They'll get itchy. She mustn't scratch them or they can make a nasty scar."

"Yes. I remember."

174

Renate pulled a face.

"I'll prescribe some lotion to help soothe the rash."

"Her little friend has come down with it too."

"Probably from the same source. It takes ten days to spread, usually."

"No, Renate only came from Nuremberg yesterday."

"Quite a coincidence then. Still the disease is everywhere at the moment."

Clara wanted to ask the doctor whether what Ernst had said was true. Did children grow whilst they were ill? Before she could, though, the front door slammed.

"We're back," called Käthe.

"Where's my day-late birthday girl?" said Hans.

"We're up here. We have chicken pox," Clara called.

The door burst open. Käthe rushed in. "Chicken pox? Oh, Hans you'd better not come up." She turned to Clara. "He's never had chicken pox."

"He should stay away," said the doctor. "It can be very nasty in adults."

"It's not very nice in children," said Renate. "Please go away and leave me and my spots in peace."

The doctor frowned. Clara tittered.

1 August 1932, Stuttgart: elections

They would know. Later today they would know. Everyone was uneasy. The students had continued to argue about him. Even the adults had started quarrelling. But Clara was getting the measure of him.

She thought about what had happened over the last few months.

On 25 February he had been given the citizenship of the free state of Brunswick. That allowed him to become German.

Creeping up on us, aren't you? thought Clara.

And there he was, the cheek of him, putting himself up for president. Thank God Hindenburg had held on. But there had to be two rounds of elections and Hitler had come out strongly in both. Besides, Hindenburg was getting quite old and frail-looking. Clara had the impression he didn't want to do the job anymore. If anything happened to Hindenburg would Hitler take over?

Now they were waiting for the results of the Federal elections. Hitler's party, the NSDAP was getting more popular.

The time was going slowly. Clara tried to keep occupied. There were the normal chores to do. Some she completed more quickly than usual. But then she found herself day-dreaming and forgetting what she was in the middle of doing.

It was quiet without the students. At least if there'd been more to do she wouldn't feel as if she was waiting all the time. Ernst was out and had promised to come back as soon as there was any news. She was totally alone.

She decided to make some bread. They didn't really need a new loaf as it was only the two of them at the moment. But kneading dough always made her feel better. Fresh bread was always good and she could use the other bread for dumplings. She had a big lunch to prepare for the meeting in two days' time. Soon she was pounding away at a lump of dough on a floured board. The only problem was she'd had to light the oven and it had become so hot in the kitchen.

Whilst the bread rose for the first time she decided to hang some rugs over the washing line and beat out the dust. Then it was back to pounding the dough. There was still no sign of Ernst by the time the loaves had risen for the second time. She put the dough into the tins and then the tins into the oven.

As she shut the oven door, the front door of the house opened.

"Mutti, where are you?" called Ernst.

"In the kitchen."

"My goodness, it's hot enough in here," said Ernst.

"Never mind hot. What are the results?"

"13,745,680 votes. That's 230 seats. 37.27% of the votes. The party with the most votes."

"Oh dear." Someone walked over Clara's grave again.

30 January 1933, Stuttgart: cautious neighbours

Breakfast was all cleared away. The bedrooms had been cleaned. All the preparations that could be made in advance for lunch had been completed. Clara had even swept the snow off the path. She put some stale bread out for the birds.

What else could she do? She couldn't think. Or maybe should go through the linen baskets, like she used to at the Lauenstein, and look for anything that needed mending. Perhaps that would keep her occupied until lunch time. Then she'd have the guests for company. And after lunch Ernst would bring her the newspaper to read. Then maybe she would find out what was making her so agitated.

She settled herself down near the window so she had the right light. After a short rummage through one of the baskets she came across a pair of socks that needed darning. She found the right coloured thread in her workbox and was soon working away.

At least there was still something satisfying about darning. Getting the tension even, making the stitches the right length and creating something that would have the strength of the original were real skills. And she could do it. It would give that pair of socks another few months' life.

As she finished her mending she glanced up and saw her next door neighbour nailing a piece of wood across the window to the cellar. How extraordinary. She always wanted to get more light into the basement so that they could use it as an extra living room. He was trying to make his darker.

She watched him working for a while. He was definitely hiding the window. Why? Oh, maybe he wanted to keep potatoes or something down there. It was his house. He could do what he liked.

She'd spoken to him a few times. He was a pleasant enough man. Herr Ehrlichmann. A good neighbour. He kept himself to himself most of the time, but helped out when there was a need. Earlier this week he had joined the other men to help to clear the snow from the road so that the supplies could get through for the guest-house. He was a widower, she thought. Perhaps he would like a cup of coffee and a chat. Or might he think she was trying to attract him? Oh, nonsense. They were both too old for that sort of thing. There was nothing wrong with being neighbourly.

She opened the window and called out. "Herr Ehrlichmann you're working so hard. Would you like me to make you a cup of coffee? Come into the house and warm up a little?"

"That would be grand, Frau Lehrs. Give me ten minutes."

Ten minutes later the coffee had brewed. Clara and Herr Ehrlichmann sat at the kitchen table. Clara had also put out some biscuits she had made. The coffee was too hot to drink yet so Herr Ehrlichmann was enjoying one of the biscuits.

"That is what I miss since my wife died," he said. "Home-baking. What you buy in the shops isn't nearly as good. And it's much too expensive."

"Well, you must come and enjoy some more often. Or I could make a little extra each time, just for you."

"You are too kind, Frau Lehrs. I couldn't put you to that amount of bother."

"It's no bother. No bother at all." It was no good. She had to ask him. "You were working so hard out there. But why were you covering up the window to the cellar?"

"I wanted to make it a bit more private. So I could hide things down there. If I'm away at any time then perhaps a would-be burglar wouldn't realise there was a cellar there."

"Ah. Are you intending to go away?"

"I haven't any plans at the moment. But with the way things are you never know."

"The way things are?"

"You've not heard the news?"

Clara shook her head.

"Adolf Hitler has become chancellor. He is being sworn in later today. There will be a coalition government between the NSADP and the DNVP."

"Isn't the DNVP Hindenburg's party?"

"Yes."

"But he's still the president?"

"Yes, for the time being, but he's getting frail. And the NSADP is getting more and more popular."

That was only too true. Clara knew that. But why did that mean Herr Ehrlichmann needed to go away?

He must have seen her puzzled face. "There may be another war. The NSADP are not at all happy with the Treaty of Versailles."

"That was all about the rules we were given after Great War, wasn't it?"

Herr Ehrlichmann nodded.

"But surely you're too old to be a soldier?"

Herr Ehrlichmann laughed. "Of course. But if we do end up in another war I'm not stopping in town. I would go to stay on my brother's farm in the country. Hiding the cellar might prevent looters."

"I see your point. And here's me trying to make my cellar lighter so that the children can play down there on rainy days."

"You're so right, Frau Lehrs. A much better idea. Don't take any notice of a grumpy old man like me." But Herr Ehrlichmann wasn't smiling. "I don't trust that man."

They finished their coffee.

"That was so kind of you, Frau Lehrs." Herr Ehrlichmann stood up and slipped his jacket and hat back on.

"Come again soon."

Clara washed up the coffee things then went back upstairs to continue with her mending. She watched as Herr Ehrlichmann continued to work. The cellar window had soon completely disappeared. He was in the process of piling earth up against the wooden board he had put in front of the window. That must be hard work with the garden frozen as it was. In no time, though, it looked as if there had always been a garden there.

I hope he'll make it look nice with some flowers in the spring and summer, thought Clara. He was really serious about this, then.

She didn't trust that man with the funny little moustache and the piercing eyes either. But perhaps you could get rid of evil by bringing in more good. Yes, she was determined to make her cellar a good place for the children. She would talk to Ernest about it when he got home.

18 May 1933, Stuttgart: closing in

Clara stared at the letter she had just read. She could not believe it. Not Frau Schonberger. The Schonbergers were exactly like them, weren't they? They'd given up the Jewish beliefs and become good Lutherans. So why had this happened to them? It didn't make any sense at all.

Clara read the letter again.

Berlin, 15 May 1933

Dear Frau Lehrs,

I'm writing to let you know that Klaus and I have decided to sell up and move the whole family to Holland. We think it will be safer for us there. We are all going to live on Heinrich's farm. (Heinrich is my cousin. His wife is Dutch and they have inherited her father's farm.) There is plenty of work there and there will even be enough for Jakob and Benjamin once they have finished their schooling. The farm is expanding.

It wasn't too bad when the boycott first came in. A lot of our regulars still came and some Jewish families who lived a little further away started coming as they couldn't get served in the German shops. But then the German customers started to get into trouble for shopping at our place and the Jewish customers stopped coming because they had no money; their jobs were being taken away too. It got to a point where we couldn't pay our bills.

So, we had no option but to sell the shop and the business – what was left of it. We had no difficulty finding a buyer but we did not get a good price. The German gentleman was only too pleased to get his hands on the property.

"A nicely-shaped little bakery," he said. "Very practical. Naturally I shall rent out the apartment above. To a nice Aryan family, of course. I won't be giving up my big house in the suburbs."

When Klaus argued about the price he replied, "But my good man, you have lost so much business because of your race that I am going to have to build it all up again. This is really the best you can hope for."

Well you know, Frau Lehrs, it was barely enough to cover our travel costs to Holland. Never mind. We're on our way tomorrow. And only too glad to get away from the Nazis.

We'll probably try and rent a flat or a small house for the family so that we're not too much under my cousin's feet. As soon as we have an address I'll write again and let you know. You do know, don't you Frau Lehrs, that you would be welcome to come and stay with us any time if things get too nasty in Germany.

All my good wishes. Do take care. My regards to the rest of your family.

Hilde Schonberger

This just wasn't believable. Surely there was no danger? She was a well-respected housekeeper, wasn't she? And a property-owner. A lot of her colleagues were members of the NSADP and they hadn't changed a bit. What had Frau Schonberger called them? Nazis. Then she'd used the word "nasty". Goodness wasn't the English word for "nasty" very similar to the word Nazi?

And they had had to leave that wonderful little bakery. She made bread that was quite good but it still didn't have the edge that a Schonberger loaf had. Not to mention the cakes. How the Berliners were being deprived!

"Come and let's go and tell Mutti Lehrs," she heard a voice cry from the hallway. What could this excitement be?

"I'm in the lounge," she cried.

The door burst open. Tilde and Johann. "Well, are you going to show us how to make pancakes? Doctor Schubert wants to come to Kaffetrinken this afternoon."

He did, did he? And these two wanted to make pancakes for him. She supposed they should make a start.

"Come on then. We'd better get into the kitchen. But mind you wash your hands."

She slipped Frau Schonberger's letter into her apron pocket. It was ridiculous. There was such a lot of love here. How could any German – Nazi or not – ever wish to hurt her?

13 July 1933, Stuttgart: the stupid man

The front door banged. Clara heard muttering and footsteps. It sounded like Ernst. What did he want at this time of day? He should be teaching, shouldn't he?

"Mutti! Mutti, where are you?"

He sounded angry. That didn't happen often but when it did… Well, she'd rather not be there. However, she rather suspected that this time she would have to listen. She wiped her hands on the towel and went out to meet him in the hallway.

"What on earth is the matter?"

"It's that stupid man. That stupid man again."

"Which man? Come on, let's go and sit down on the patio. There's a nice breeze and it's cool there. I'll bring us a cold drink."

She took her time finding a bottle of Sprudelwasser in the pantry. There was some raspberry juice left over from yesterday's dessert. She stirred some into the fizzy water and added a little sugar. She made sure that she took at least ten minutes.

It worked. By the time she got outside with the tray Ernst was looking considerably calmer. At least whatever he had to tell her would probably make some sort of sense.

"So what's happened?" She realised it was only eleven o' clock. "Shouldn't you be teaching?"

"That's the thing. I'm not allowed to anymore."

"Not allowed to?"

"Because I'm Jewish."

"But we're not Jewish. We're Christian."

"They're talking about race, Mutti, not religion."

"Oh, I thought the Waldorf people… They don't see you as Jewish, do they?"

"No, of course not. That's why they've let me carry on. But the authorities, you know. And a lot of the parent governors are members of the NSDAP. What was it they're saying? 'The state has the duty to distance these young people, even if it is against the will of their parents, from the atmosphere of the Jewish occult spirit.'"

"Jewish occult spirit? What do they mean by that?"

"Mutti, that's not all. We can't take on any new students next year. We're going to have to turn away the forty who are already registered. They even regard the Waldorf schools as a bit 'occult'."

"Oh my goodness." Clara put her hand in front of her mouth. "But what will you do?"

"It's all right, Mutti, they're still going to pay me. I'm not allowed to teach any more. I'm going to give some lectures and help write some materials. But I expect I'll have to go eventually."

"Go? Go where?"

"Holland, or perhaps England. They're opening new schools all the time."

"I don't understand, though. We are not Jewish. We're anthroposophist."

"The Nazis would probably consider that as being just as depraved as being Jewish anyway." Ernst would not look at his mother.

"Depraved?"

"Different. Not good and German." Ernst sighed. "You will probably have to leave at some point, too."

"I can't though. The boarders?"

"Mutti, there soon won't be any boarders. There will be no first class next year then no first or second class the year after and so on."

"But perhaps in a few years' time they'll change their minds?"

Ernst sighed again. "I don't think they will."

"Well, I'll carry on until they carry me out either in a coffin or kicking and screaming. While people still need accommodation – even if it's only one person – this house remains open. Besides, I've so nearly paid off the loan it doesn't really matter whether I have boarders or not."

"All right. But Mutti, please don't be too stubborn."

Clara decided to ignore the last remark. It was usually her stubbornness that saved her. "That man. You said something about that man?"

"Our lovely friend, Herr Hitler."

Ah. Him. Clara felt one of her shudders.

10 May 1934 Stuttgart: pastry going wrong

"I still don't understand," said Clara. "How can they think of you as anything but a loyal German. You were a soldier in the Great War weren't you? You even lost your memory and you were in the trenches. What more can they want?"

"Mutti, there were a lot of us like that. But they're saying there are too many people. And they don't want the children's education diluted by our weak beliefs."

"Nonsense! It's such nonsense." Clara banged the rolling pin down on the table. "Now look. I'm going to have to start again." The pastry she had been rolling had big holes in it. She gathered up the dough, rolled it into a ball and then started kneading it on the floured table."

Ernst touched her arm lightly. "Just stop a moment, Mutti, and let me read you the letter they sent to the school."

"Go on then." Clara wiped her floury hands on her apron and folded her arms across her chest.

"Whilst we appreciate the efforts of Doctor Ernst Lehrs during his time in the trenches, the fact remains that he is of a non-Aryan race and as such cannot be entrusted with the education of young German minds. For the time being work of a more manual nature is freely available to him in appreciation of his contribution to the defence of the Fatherland."

"The Fatherland. Non-Aryan race. What is this nonsense? When we lived in Mecklenburg and we were still Jewish, we were as German as the Christian people in the town."

"German is nationality, Mutti. They're talking about race."

"And what is race supposed to be? Are we monsters or something? Have we two heads?"

"Not quite. But it's a bit like that."

Clara sighed and returned to her pastry. "Well, I still wonder what they're thinking at the school. They should be standing up for you." She pummelled the ball of dough.

"They've been quite generous, actually, Mutti. Remember

they're still paying me. And they're even letting me write some of the materials for the lessons. They could get into a lot of trouble for that."

"At least that's something sensible they're doing."

"Bu they won't be able to keep on doing that. Especially as we can't take in any more students. The finances won't work."

Clara stopped working and looked at Ernst. She thought she knew what was coming next. "What will you do then?"

"I'm seriously thinking of going to the Netherlands. They would like me to work on setting up more schools there and helping to train the teachers. The Dutch think much more freely. But I want you to come with me, Mutti. I don't want you to stay here on your own."

"I'm not going anywhere. I have my lodgers. And I still have to help Karl with the Hilfsklasse."

"Mutti, I'm certain that class will have to close as well soon."

"Over my dead body," muttered Clara. She ran her rolling pin quickly over the pastry. "Anyway, Rudi, Käthe and Renate are still here."

Ernst shook his head. "Then I won't go yet. I'm not going without you. But I'll start preparing my lectures and talks and I'll be making a few trips there in the coming months."

"As you wish."

Ernst quietly left the kitchen.

"No way," muttered Clara. She looked at the hopeless pastry on her board. She shook her head, gathered up the grey mess and put it into the bin.

13 June 1934, Stuttgart: The Hilfsklasse

"That does look really special," said Clara admiring the picture that Viveka was waving in front of her. Even the children in the Hilfsklasse had a good sense of form and colour. She had really enjoyed helping them today with their paintings.

"I'd like you to have it Frau Lehrs," said the girl. Her eyes shone when she smiled.

"That is so kind, Viveka. But don't you want to give it to your Mutti? Or even to your Vati? Won't it look handsome in his study?"

"I want you to have this one." She held the painting out to Clara. Her lips were pursed.

Clara knew she would have to take it. "Very well then. Thank you so much." She had a growing collection of pictures completed by members of the Hilfsklasse. Soon there would be no more room on the walls in her study. She would have to find somewhere else to hang new ones.

Viveka's mother arrived a few moments later. "I'm so sorry I'm late."

The poor woman looked flustered. Clara knew though that she had three other children at home and two of them had problems similar to Viveka's. "It's not a problem, Frau Tremel. Viveka is always good company and such a good girl." She smiled. Really, she didn't need to worry. The girl was a delight. Clara did understand though.

The woman smiled weakly and nodded. "Come on then Viveka. Let's get home."

The little girl waved and seconds later Clara and Karl Schubert were alone.

"Another successful class," said Karl. "Thank you so much for your help again. It really makes a difference."

Clara sighed. "Yes, but how much longer will they let you go on with this? What'll happen when the school shuts down completely?"

"I don't think it's going to be a problem."

"Really?"

"We've already taken one precaution."

"Oh?"

"The Hilfsklasse is no longer part of the Waldorf School. It simply hires a classroom from the school. Therefore it may well be allowed to carry on after the whole school closes down."

"Goodness! I am surprised. What about this idea of teaching them NSDAP principles?"

Karl snorted. "Do you think children like this would ever be able to learn those ideas?"

"Hopefully not."

"They probably don't care that much about these students anyway."

Clara felt a lump form in her throat and couldn't swallow.

"There's something else as well."

"Oh?"

"Did you know that I'm actually partly Jewish as well?"

Clara spluttered.

"I'm sorry about Ernst. I really am. But let me show you something." He pulled a letter out of his briefcase and handed it to Clara.

She read it silently. She had to read it two or three times before she could take it in. "So it's because you fought as a soldier on the front that they don't expect you to leave the school? But so did Ernst."

"Yes, but read the paragraph underneath."

Clara read the paragraph again. "Does that mean they won't pay you as a teacher but if you can run the class as a business and the parents pay you enough they're willing for you to carry on?"

Karl nodded.

"Why?"

"I think perhaps they're rather hoping I will fail."

"Why should they think that?"

"They don't value these children. Just like they don't value Jews. The top people, I mean. In fact, if the decision hadn't been made by local officials, I'm sure I'd have had to go, like Ernst. And they wouldn't have given a moment's consideration to our young people."

"There are some good people in this town."

"There are. Thank God."

"So, the class is safe for a while?"

"For a while. As long as the money lasts. They realise, of course, that without the parents paying I'll not be able to carry on and who knows how long the parents will be able to pay?"

"We'll have to hope, won't we?"

Clara had so much to think about as she walked home. Slowly the school was being closed down. Yet the Hilfsklasse looked as if it would survive. It was a question of money in the end. Money, she knew, always had a way of turning up when it was needed. It did for her, anyway. It was also something to do with people's attitudes. And people always did the right thing in the end, didn't they? It would all come right, wouldn't it, surely?

Next, she was walking up the path to the front door of the house. Goodness, she couldn't work out how she'd got there. She could hear voices from one of the upstairs windows. Some of the older children had had a free period last lesson. One of the teachers was off sick and as these students were considered responsible enough they'd been allowed to go home early.

It would be a sad day when there were no more children's voices in this house. Well she for one would do her best to make sure that there always were.

Clara pushed open the door and made her way to the kitchen. There was the preparation of lunches to supervise.

16 September 1935, Stuttgart: Jewish or not?

"Look, Mutti, it shows that you clearly are a Jew. So am I, and Rudi and Käthe. Of course Hans isn't but it still all makes Renate a first-degree Mischling."

Clara stared at the paper Ernst was showing her. "What do all these circles mean? I don't understand."

"The black circles represent people with Jewish blood and the white ones those that have pure German blood. This example is exactly Renate." Ernst pointed to a diagram entitled 'Special Mischlinge' at the bottom of the page.

Yes, Clara could see it was indeed Renate. Two Jewish grandparents – if you absolutely had to define her and Ernst as Jewish – and two German ones. Why were they considered unusual? "So, are your father and I special because although we were brought up in the so-called Jewish faith we didn't practise it? Anyway – Renate only has one grandparent. Your father died, if you remember."

"Mutti, you know what they mean – it's all to do with the blood. That's why it's called the Blutschutz law. Protecting the blood."

"Hmm. Makes us sound like a pack of race horses."

"Yes, it's a bit like that I'm afraid. These people think in strange ways."

"But we're no different from other Germans. Cut us and we bleed. We die. We laugh. We cry. We make love. We give birth. And we even enjoy the same art and literature. We wear the same clothes. We eat the same food."

"Not all Jews do, though Mutti. The new government wants everyone here to have German ways."

"Well we do have. Which is why we are not Jews. We are anthroposophist. You can be German and anthroposophist at the same time, can't you? Or will they bring in a law about that soon as well?" There. She'd said it. Ernst ought to be pleased. He'd wanted her to have his faith, hadn't he?

For a few seconds he did look pleased. Then his features tensed up again. "But Mutti, they know Jewishness is in your blood and will eventually come out."

"Eventually? It had better get on with it, then. I'm almost sixty-four."

Ernst shook his head. "Please Mutti, don't be so obstinate. It's getting dangerous here."

"Dangerous?"

"Well, uncomfortable."

"What do you mean?"

"We can no longer be counted as German citizens."

"Not even Renate?"

"Not even Renate."

Clara frowned and pursued her lips. But what did that mean, not being a German citizen? "So what happens then? What changes?"

"You can't call yourself German, you can't fly the German flag and you can't employ a German female under thirty-five."

"That's annoying but it's not dangerous. If I need an extra cook I'll get the school to employ her instead. Or find a Jewish one. I never did believe in flying flags anyway. Too nationalistic."

"The school will be closing soon."

"We've a few years yet. I want to see this through."

"I was afraid you might say that." Ernst looked away. He took a deep breath and then looked back at his mother. "I'm definitely moving to the Netherlands. I can't expect them to go on paying me to do so little. Won't you consider coming with me, Mutti?"

Clara shook her head. She couldn't leave this house. They'd built it together and it had such a special purpose. But she did understand why he had to go. She stood up and walked over to him. She put her arm on his shoulder.

"The Netherlands is going to gain a fine teacher and some extraordinary schools. But I must stay behind and carry on looking after the Little Goetheanum. You understand, don't you?"

Ernst took his mother's hand and kissed it. "You'll come and visit me, won't you? And you promise you'll leave if the craziness gets worse?"

"I promise," said Clara. She didn't mention it to Ernst – he would only argue, she knew – but she was sure this silliness was going to end soon. Hopefully they would get rid of that horrible little man as well. People were bound to come to their senses sooner or later weren't they? Gosh, they'd had a lot to put up with but things must eventually get better mustn't they?

Ernst stood up and hugged his mother. "Good. And there's something else I need to tell you."

The doorbell rang. Ernst went to open it. "Too late. I hope this won't be too much of a shock. Hopefully it will partly be a pleasant surprise."

"What?"

"Wait there, Mutti. I'll get it."

What was he up to?

Seconds later, as she heard voices in the hallway, she knew. She'd know that voice anywhere. Ernst was talking to Rudi. How could that be anything other than a pleasant surprise? She did not see enough of her younger son.

"About time too," she said to Rudi after he had embraced her.

"You could always come and see me as well, you know, Mutti."

"True enough!" Though I'm not really actually sure that that is true, she thought. Rudi was so fiercely independent. Too many visits could make it look as if she was keeping a close eye on him. She'd always sensed that he'd wanted her to leave him alone.

She saw him and Ernst exchange a glance.

Ernst shook his head. "I've not told her yet."

Rudi nodded. "Mutti, I've really come to tell you that I'm going to be going further away."

"Oh?"

"Yes, after this semester ends I'll be going to continue my studies in London." He sighed. "They don't want Jewish scientists here."

Clara sighed and pursued her lips. "I wish they could get this right. We're not Jewish."

"Mutti, you know we are," said Ernst.

"Will you come to England with me if you won't go to the Netherlands with Ernst?"

"Like I told your brother, I will not be leaving here whilst I'm still needed. This nonsense must come to an end soon. I'll go and make some tea."

No way will I ever leave here. This is my home. She'd really made it a home, hadn't she? Why should she ever give that up?

16 July 1936, Stuttgart: schools

"So, did you enjoy the play?" Clara said to Renate as they made their way out to the school yard.

"It was lovely," said Renate. "I wish we did shows like that at our school."

"Don't you have end of term concerts, though?"

"Well, yes we do. But we're all girls and the school is much smaller. So they can't be as much fun."

"I suppose you might have a point."

Clara exchanged a glance with Käthe who rolled her eyes and shrugged. "Well, anyway, it's no good you going on about wanting to come to Oma's school because it is going to close soon. And you'll be going to a new school soon anyway."

"Will she get into the Gymnasium?"

"She's got good marks. She should do," said Hans.

"I mean…"

Käthe shook her head and put her fingers on her lips.

What did she mean? Clara couldn't ask though because everyone was lined up ready for the outdoor final assembly. Doctor Kühn was going to talk to them about the Steiner Foundation.

"Heil Hitler!" said Doctor Kühn.

Reluctantly Clara raised her arm. She hated this. Käthe and Hans raised their arms without hesitation. "Heil Hitler!" she heard them say. Although she could have sworn Hans had actually said, "Heil Edler!" Surely not?

She didn't have time to dwell on that for long though because she was too amazed that Renate stood there with her arms rigidly at her side. What a brave little girl! Clara wished she had the courage to do that.

Doctor Kühn kept his speech quite short. Everyone would be grateful, Clara was sure. It was tiring standing out here in the sun without any shade at all.

Then it was "Heil Hitler!" again. She heard it loud and clear that time. Hans definitely said "Heil Edler!" Good for him. She had to work hard not to giggle. At least "Edler" sort of rhymed with "Hitler". She couldn't very well say "Lehrs" and get away with that, could she?

Clara realised that Doctor Kühn was staring at her. Or rather at Renate who was standing there again with her arms at her side.

"You must do the salute," Clara whispered, grabbing Renate's arm.

Renate pulled away from her and scowled. There was nothing to be done. Clara knew she would have to go and apologise to Doctor Kühn.

"I'm so sorry about my granddaughter," she said to him a few moments later. "They must be more lenient in Nuremberg."

"In Nuremberg, of all places? Surely not."

Clara felt her cheeks burning. She didn't know what to say.

"I don't blame the girl," said Doctor Kühn. "Good for her, actually. And I know you don't like this ridiculous saluting either. Neither do I, if I'm honest. But we have to be seen to be doing it."

Clara nodded. "I know."

Doctor Kühn touched her arm gently. "I don't think anybody important was watching today. And I actually don't think any of our more – what shall we say? – enthusiastic parents noticed. Go on. Go and enjoy your time with your family."

Clara caught up with the others half way down the street. Renate was as usual running on ahead and then coming back to urge them all to be quicker.

"Was I hearing things?" said Clara to Hans. "Or did you really say 'Heil Edler'?"

"I did indeed," said Hans, grinning.

"Yes, and one day you'll get us all into trouble for it," said Käthe. "I wish you wouldn't."

"I think it's rather good, actually." Clara giggled.

"Well, you would, Mutti."

What was that supposed to mean? And if her daughter was so concerned about Hans's deliberate slip of the tongue, why wasn't she bothered by her daughter's refusal to raise her arm? "But Renate...?"

"She's not German is she? Her teachers think she shouldn't be made to join in these things."

Käthe was not making sense. Renate was more German that either of them. And what she was doing – or, rather, not doing – was far more dangerous than what Hans was doing.

Renate came skipping back towards them. Käthe gave her mother a look that said this conversation was over.

Later that evening Clara and Käthe washed up after supper whilst Hans and Renate went for a short walk before Renate's bed-time.

"I hope he's not 'Heil Edlering' all over the place," said Käthe.

"Oh, the neighbours don't bother too much," said Clara. *And if they did, the problem might be more to do with Renate.* "But how do you get on in Nuremberg?"

Käthe sighed. "We keep out of everybody's way."

"Do you see anything of the rallies?"

"We hear them! When they're on you can hear them marching through the streets to get there."

"That sounds horrible."

"It is. Even the children have to march."

"Renate?"

"Well she's not old enough to join the BDM, and she doesn't have to go to the younger girls' group. So her teachers keep her away."

"Don't the other children find that strange?"

"Not really." Käthe put her dish cloth down and turned to face her mother.

Clara noticed how tired she looked. There were dark rings round her eyes.

"We haven't told Renate she's Jewish. I don't think she would understand what that meant. Neither do the other girls in her class. We want to keep it that way as long as we can. Her teachers know, though, and they protect her."

Clara touched her daughter's arm but felt her pull away. She was always like that. She always resisted accepting any gesture of concern or affection. "And you? Do you consider yourself Jewish?"

Käthe closed her eyes. "No. Not at all. I'm German. Not even that. I'm just human. But you know, Mutti." She opened her eyes again. Clara could see that there were tears forming. "If we go out anywhere, I'm sure people know. I'm sure they can tell when they look at me."

"Surely you get a lot of respect because of Hans's job?"

"Oh yes, of course." Käthe took up her dish cloth again and started scrubbing furiously at an almost clean plate. "The important man designing his clever weapons that will defend the German people. Yes, we are so respected."

The front door opened and Clara could hear Hans and Renate chatting and laughing. She guessed this conversation also was over for a while.

13 September 1936, Stuttgart: England calling

Clara sighed. She could not get used to this. Yes, she still had a few boarders but not as many as before. There was no longer a first, second or third class. It wasn't just that, though, because in fact there were always fewer students from the lower forms. Such young children might not be expected to live away from home. As well, other parents had started taking their children away from the school. "If the school's going to close anyway we'd like to get them settled in their new one as soon as possible," they'd said. But Clara had seen the fear in their eyes.

This is madness, she'd thought. We have to resist this at all costs.

There were only a few breakfast plates to clear. The work for the whole day would take a no more than two hours and she didn't need any extra help anymore. She laughed to herself. Just as well, really, now that she was no longer allowed to employ any German young women under the age of thirty-five. If things improved she guessed she might have to put up with an older grumpier woman of at least thirty-six, or a man, or even – God forbid – a young Jewish woman. Who thought of these rules? They must be mad.

She started to stack up the dirty dishes.

Then she remembered again. Rudi would be setting off back for England tomorrow. He'd said quite firmly that he would not come back for Christmas. That, in fact, he would not be coming back to Germany at all until "some sort of sanity returned". She didn't mind that he was studying in England. He was following a good course, with all the best people. But turning his back on his home like that?

"Come and live with me, Mutti," he'd said. "I need a housekeeper."

"You'll never be able to afford one as good as me," she'd replied. "Besides, I'm needed here." And that had been the end of it.

She couldn't blame him for being obstinate. Look where he got it from. Well, she'd have to make the most of his last day here. When he'd finished tidying up that flower bed she would suggest that they go out for the day. It was exactly the right temperature for walking. Maybe they could take a picnic.

She went to tell Rudi of her plans but saw the postman arrive. Perhaps she should check the post first. She emptied the box. There were a couple of what were obviously bills and one on which she recognised Ernst's writing. All addressed to her.

She took them all up to the office, put the two bills into her in-tray and opened the letter from Ernst.

9 September 36

Dear Mutti,

You have probably spoken to Rudi by now and he has no doubt informed you that he has no intention of returning to Germany for the foreseeable future. I'm afraid to tell you that that is also my intention: we are regarded as Jewish, despite everything and the Jews are just not wanted in Germany.

Also: I too am going to England. An opportunity has come up to work with the Steiner schools there. My work in the Netherlands is done. Rudi and I intend to share some accommodation in London. We really do need a housekeeper, Mutti. Won't you consider coming to live with us?

Käthe and Renate should move, too. Hans as well if he can. We can look for work for them there and of course Renate will be able to go to one of the English Steiner schools. I actually fear, though, that Hans may not be allowed to leave because of his line of work.

Mutti, I really urge to give this some careful consideration. It is no longer safe or healthy for people like us in Germany. Please write soon, Mutti, and send me a positive reply.

If this reaches you before Rudi leaves, give him my regards and tell him I'll see him soon in London.

All my love,
Your devoted son,
Ernst Lehrs.

As Clara finished reading she heard footsteps running up the path. "Mutti Lehrs. Mutti Lehrs. I can't find my geography book," called a familiar voice. Claudia! That girl would forget her brains if she were able to keep them in a jar overnight.

"When did you last have it? Can you remember?" Clara met the girl on the landing.

Two brown eyes filling with tears looked back at Clara, and the girl shook her head, making her tight mousey plaits bob.

"Come on, then. Let's look. It must be somewhere."

A twenty minute search in the bedroom that Claudia shared with two other girls uncovered the book between the wall and Claudia's bed.

"What's it doing there?" said Clara.

"I was revising for our test," said Claudia.

"All right," said Clara, "but next time put it back in your bag as soon as you've finished with it."

"Yes, Mutti Lehrs," said the girl. She was smiling now.

"Go on then. Back to school."

Clara smiled to herself as she watched the girl skip up the path. Then she sat down and reread the letter.

She sighed. It was so nonsensical, all this business about them being Jewish. They really weren't. Surely people would realise that sooner or later, wouldn't they? People were much too sensible not to, weren't they?

And as Hans's job was so important, surely they would be respected for that? All three of them? Anyway, didn't Hans have that cousin who was important in the government? He would see that the family were all right, wouldn't he?

She heard Rudi come in. She went down and met him in the back vestibule. "I've had a letter from Ernst," she said.

Rudi was pulling off his dirty boots. "I suppose he's told you about his plans to go to England?"

Clara nodded.

"And will you consider coming with us?" He was washing his hands.

"No."

"Mutti…"

Clara handed him a towel. "That would be letting them win. Besides what will happen next time Claudia forgets her geography book if there is no Mutti Lehrs to look for it?"

Rudi shook his head and turned away from his her. Without saying another word he walked into the lounge.

She guessed there wouldn't be a picnic today after all.

22 April 1937, Stuttgart: school fate

Everyone chattered nervously. Doctor Kühn had called the meeting. He'd said he'd got something really important to tell them. There'd been speculation all day. It was surely going to be one of two things: either the school would be called to close down completely or it was being granted a reprieve and they could carry on as normal, perhaps reinstating the missing classes.

The hall was full: teachers, students, parents and other supporters of the school. It was a good turnout, despite the closed classes.

Doctor Kühn walked on to the stage and cleared his throat. Clara held her breath.

"Ladies and gentlemen, boys and girls, I have asked you here this evening because I want to give you some important information. You may remember that three years ago the chief inspector of schools paid us a visit and gave us a promising report even though we have subsequently had to close down classes. I have to tell you he has visited us again this month and I would like to read you the notes he passed to me."

Doctor Kühn hesitated and shuffled the papers in front of him. He looked up at his audience, took a deep breath and started reading.

"I believe in this detailed report I have given a quite full picture of the diverse work of the Waldorf School. I have taken a critical stance to this work but have also recognised the positive achievements of the school. It can't be the duty of this report to decide whether the Waldorf School should be considered, or even indeed to what extent it might be considered, a special school and whether because of the anthroposophist principles in its curriculum whether is stays in existence today or not. It is the interests of parents, students and teachers that a decision should be made as soon as possible.

"I believe, in relation to this, that I should once again give expression to my conviction that this experimental school that brings together varying abilities both at primary and secondary level and in whose curriculum emphasis is given to technical and artistic subjects, even today has a right to exist and can indeed point to new ways for the future. Three years ago I did indeed encourage the Waldorf School to work on a new basis and the change into a German secondary school, that would have a relationship with primary schools, and which could carry on giving room to technical and artistic matters, as the Waldorf School has up until now. I am still inclined to look for a similar solution and am at your disposal to help in this matter."

Doctor Kühn looked up at his audience again. "In many ways very positive – again. But he is not categorically saying that we can carry on. I believe they basically want us to give up our anthroposophist beliefs."

The audience started muttering. Then there were questions and comments. What would happen to the teachers? If Herr Bauer thought the school was as good as he said, why couldn't he be more supportive? If the school was doing such good things and it did have to close, where would the students be able to find as good an education elsewhere?

The discussion went on for over an hour.

"Well," said Doctor Kühn as the audience began to run out of things to say. "Perhaps we should vote. Those in favour of the school carrying on but without the anthroposophist input. Parents and teachers only please. Sorry, students, but do discuss this with your teachers over the next weeks."

Only a few people put up their hands.

"Well, then," said Doctor Kühn. "It looks as if we carry on as normal – even though that might mean that we have to close. Thank you for coming. Let's carry on the debate over tea."

Frau Schmitt, the mother of one of the day students was serving. "I don't know, Frau Lehrs," she said as she filled her pot from the big urn. "Whatever will we do if – or when this school closes. It won't be the same if our youngsters have to go to an ordinary school, will it?"

"Do you really think it will come to that? The man gave us

quite a good report didn't he?" Clara looked into Frau Schmitt's eyes, trying to read what she thought. It was impossible.

Frau Schmitt rubbed her forehead. "But they still want us to change, don't they?"

Clara sighed. "And I suppose we don't want to really, do we?"

The other woman shook her head.

Clara could see that the queue was building up behind her. She supposed she should move on.

At the table with the sugar, milk and biscuits she met Karl Schubert. "It's not looking good, is it?" he said.

"Well, it seems to me that that man wants our school to be successful."

"Oh yes, he can see that what we do is basically good. He's a decent man. But we have to realise that his hands are tied."

I must be so naïve, thought Clara. I can never understand what's going on in the background. She thought that Karl looked strained. "And there's something else worrying you, isn't there?"

"I really don't know what will happen to the Hilfsklasse when the school closes."

"Don't you mean if?"

Karl shrugged and grimaced.

"Something will turn up," said Clara. "Something always does."

20 December 1937, Nuremberg: bakers all

"They shouldn't be long – at least I hope not," said Käthe as she showed her mother the room where she'd be sleeping. "Hans got it into his head that he should get her passport sorted out before the holidays."

"And this is for her trip to Italy?"

"Yes, she has to have her own passport as we're not going with her."

"Well, maybe…"

"I hope it's not taking so long because there's any problem."

"Surely not… with Hans as her father…"

"You'd have thought so, wouldn't you?" Käthe's lips were pursed as she helped her mother to hang her clothes in the wardrobe.

The front door slammed. Clara could hear Renate's and Hans's voices. "Mutti! Oma! Are you here, Oma?"

"In the guest room," Käthe called.

Renate rushed up the stairs and into the bedroom. "Vati had such a row with the official but then we went to see Herr Müller – you know, he's Vati's friend – and he said I can have a grown-up passport and that next time I need one I'll be a proper young lady. It will be ready straight after Christmas."

"What's he been doing this time?" Käthe muttered almost to herself. Then more loudly to Renate she said, "Go and tell your father to arrange for some tea to be made and some of the biscuits we baked yesterday to be put out. Then he'll explain it all, I'm sure."

As soon as Renate had left the room Käthe flopped down on the bed. "He doesn't know when to keep his mouth shut. He'll get us into such trouble one day." There were tears in her eyes.

"Let's see what he has to say first." Clara rubbed her daughter's back. "I'm pretty well finished here. Tea and those biscuits sound good."

"He was an officious young man," said Hans, licking the crumbs off his fingers. "Goodness, Renate, you must take after your grandmother – these are pretty good. Your mother certainly can't bake like this."

"I can and I helped her," said Käthe. "Stop changing the subject. What exactly happened?"

"He wanted to put Klara Renate on the passport and I explained she was supposed to be Renata Clara. He wouldn't have it."

"And when he said 'Heil Hitler' Vati said 'Heil Edler!'"

"Oh for goodness sake, Hans. I wish you would stop that. One day, one day…"

"Calm down, woman. Even Klaus does that."

"Then he'll get into trouble as well. And that young man was only talking common sense. You know that the passport has to say exactly what it says on her birth certificate. The man was only doing his job." Käthe glared at Hans.

"He looked all of seventeen and he was far too sure of himself."

"Vati roared at him. You know how he does sometimes."

Clara thought how sad it was that such a young man could be so bureaucratic. She felt sorry for him, though, if Hans roared at him. She knew only too well that her son-in-law had a fierce temper. "But why did that mean she had to have an adult passport? I don't really understand."

"I think I did frighten him a little. And he was absolutely right: she is old enough to have an adult passport. She didn't have to, but she could. He wanted to get rid of us as quickly as possible. I think he was a bit afraid of me despite his bravado."

"And Herr Müller was ever so kind. How do you know him, Vati?"

"Oh we did some classes together in Berlin. When we were students."

"Well, it's a good job he was there and made you see sense. Renate, go and see if there are any more biscuits. It looks as if you and your father have finished the whole lot."

As soon as Renate had left the room, Käthe turned once more to Hans. "Do you think it might help her, having a full adult passport? Will there be anything on there that says she is Jewish? Will she be able to leave Germany more easily? Please tell me that

that's why you did this and you made the scene with the young man for Renate's sake? What does Klaus say?"

"No, it really all happened like we said. Klaus doesn't know anything about this. But I will ask him. I promise I will."

Clara was alarmed to see tears in her daughter's eyes again. She turned to Hans. "You don't think things are that bad, really, do you?"

Hans for once didn't look as if he was about to laugh. "All those rallies make it look serious enough. You should see them, Clara. They're terrifying. And you should see Herr Hitler sitting there at his window at the Deutscher Hof Hotel. As if he's some sort of god." Then he grinned. "But this can't go on forever. Sooner or later all we sensible Germans will realise he's a madman and do away with him and his cronies."

"I'm sure you're right, Hans." Clara was so relieved that her son-in-law thought the same way as she did.

"Mutti, we'll have to make some more. There's hardly any left. Oh no." She ran over to her mother. "You and Vati haven't been arguing again, have you?" She turned to her father. "Don't be rude about Mutti's baking. Her apple cake is excellent and she can make biscuits."

Much better to think about baking than madmen and their armies. "Tell you what. I'll make some more biscuits tomorrow." She smiled at Renate.

"Will I be allowed to help as well?"

23 February 1938, Stuttgart: a new classroom

They'd all got to get back into their boots today, and pull on their thick coats and woollen hats and scarves. The snow was deep and frozen as well. All of the parents had arrived before they'd even finished getting the children ready. Heidi wasn't expecting her mother or her father, though. Her mother was ill and in hospital and her father was working away from home. Clara had understood that he was in the same line of work as Hans. No question of him being allowed to take time off to look after his little girl. It had only seemed natural to Clara to invite the child to stay with her. There were so few children still living in the house on Schellberg Street and she was, after all, used to children like Heidi from her time at the Lauenstein.

"Cheer up," said Clara. "What about if when we get back, after lunch, we make a big snowman in the back garden? You'd like that, wouldn't you? Perhaps you can invite Maria and Hans to help?"

Hans's and Maria's mothers agreed to bring their children round that afternoon. "And you ladies are invited to tea and Apfelstrudel," Clara said.

"You really are so kind, Frau Lehrs," said Hans's mother.

"Can we bring anything?" asked Maria's.

Clara shook her head. "Just your good selves and your lovely children."

The last of the students left the building. Clara went back into the classroom to find Karl shaking his head and trying not to laugh. "You just don't give up, do you?"

"There's no point in doing that, is there? We have to keep on trying."

"But what about when there really is no solution?"

Clara noticed how pale he looked. He had aged a lot recently. Even though he'd almost been laughing a few seconds ago the light had gone from his eyes.

"Tell me then. To what is there no solution?"

"To the Hilfsklasse carrying on."

"But I thought you'd secured some grants for that?"

"Yes, but that will hardly keep me alive. It won't pay to hire another room to teach them in once the school is closed. And even if there were enough money I have a feeling that they'll make it as difficult as possible for us to find a suitable place."

"Then I think you had better come to lunch. Don't you agree, Heidi? I can add a few more potatoes and some more tomato juice and the stew will stretch to feed another mouth. Come, Doctor Schubert. Wrap up warm and let's hurry along. Young Heidi here is hungry."

"Right, both of you in the kitchen with me once you've pulled off your boots and hung up those coats, hats and scarves. Yes, Heidi, I want you to hear this as well. Doctor Schubert can help to peel and cut the potatoes and you can help me to persuade him that this is good idea." Clara was enjoying this, not least of all because of Heidi's and Karl's puzzled faces. She'd thought about this for some time and she had made her mind up.

"There you are," she said, handing Karl a sharp knife and a chopping board. "Cut them quite small, like this." She cut the potatoes she was holding into small cubes. "They'll cook more quickly that way. We need to be ready to build this snowman when Heidi's guests arrive."

"Well, what do you want to tell me?" Karl had got into a routine with cutting the potatoes as Clara had shown him.

"I would like to offer you this house for the Hilfsklasse."

Karl put down his knife. He shook his head.

"Clara we couldn't. It's your home, your way of making a living. We couldn't pay you."

"I don't need paying. Anyway, once the Waldorf School is shut I won't be taking any more paying guests. I own the house outright. I have a good pension still. More than enough to get by."

"But Clara, to make this suitable for teaching, we would have to make some alterations. We would have to spoil your lovely home."

212

"What could be lovelier than having the place full of children again? Tell him, Heidi. How wonderful it would be. Just think, you wouldn't have to go out to school on cold mornings."

"Doctor Schubert, it would be lovely. I could stay in bed longer in the mornings."

Clara and Karl laughed. Clara took the potatoes from him and added them with some tomato puree to the saucepan. "That will be ready in ten minutes. Now, help me to set the table and after we've eaten I'll show you what I have in mind."

"I've always wanted to make better use of this large room," said Clara. "I did think about turning it into an indoor playroom for the guests but I never got round to it. But do you think it could make a good classroom? You see, there is a window." Clara shuddered as she remembered Herr Ehrlichmann covering up his window in case he needed to make a hiding place. Hopefully they would never need that.

Karl was saying nothing but Clara could see some light had returned to his eyes. She looked at her little house guest. "Well, what do you think, Heidi? Would you like your lessons down here?"

"Oh yes," said Heidi. "I could pretend I was a rabbit living in a burrow."

"And of course, Karl, you are invited to take one of the rooms upstairs for yourself. You can even have one as a study as well. I shan't need them for boarders and it still leaves me room for my daughter and her family and for my two boys should they ever gain some common sense and come home again."

"I suppose we could ask for some classroom furniture from the Waldorf School," said Karl. "I'm sure they'd agree to that. But there might be a problem with the stairs for some of the children."

"I've thought of that too. We could employ a nice strong young man to help those who need helping. My pension will run to that as well, I believe."

"But Clara…"

"Enough. If the parents can pay some and your grants and

stipends go so far, fair enough, you can send some money my way or contribute to the house expenses. But until that happens you can live here as my guest. What do you say?"

"You should say 'yes' Doctor Schubert. Please." Heidi was shaking his arm.

The doorbell rang.

"Come, on Heidi, we need to let your guests in."

Clara held the girl's hand and they ran up the stairs together. Clara opened the front door. "Let's go straight round to the back garden," she said. "Heidi and I will quickly get our coats on. Will you come and help us build a snowman, Karl? And then when we're ready for tea, I have some most extraordinary news to give you."

The three other adults smiled at each other. *I'm looking forward to good news and tea,* thought Clara.

31 March 1938, Stuttgart: marking an ending

"Well, that's that, then," said Clara as the last of the children left. "It's hard to believe they won't be here together again. It's strange. It feels like any other day."

Karl shrugged. "Well, we thought it was best. Show them that we really think our school is good and reliable. Main lesson still rules."

"Oh, yes. Except they were tired. Not so much this class as the others. Some of them were involved in *Julius Caesar* as well as being at the memorial last night. Odd to have it on a night when they had to come to school the next day."

"Probably because it's exactly five years since he died."

Clara shuddered. Of course Rudolf Steiner had been an important man. Especially to the people here. But it was a bit creepy remembering his death day every year. Did they think he was some sort of saint or something?

"Did you find it tedious yesterday evening, then?"

Clara shook her head. Surprisingly she hadn't. It had been an evening full of warmth, love and celebration. Yes, celebration at a time like this. There was, after all, something sensible about that. Life should always be celebrated.

Emil Kühn's head appeared in the doorway. "Come along to the staff room," he said. "I want to show you all something."

"Better go," said Karl.

They abandoned their tidying up. Almost all of the teachers were there already, some of them sitting on the shabby but comfortable easy chairs, others perched on the edges of tables and a few of them sitting cross-legged on the floor.

One of the younger members of staff stood up to let Clara have a seat. She was about to refuse – she would have been perfectly happy sitting on the floor or resting her bottom on the edge of a table – but then thought better of it. It will please her to do me a favour, she thought. She smiled at the young woman and whispered "Thank you."

Emil Kühn cleared his throat. "I have all of the letters that you wrote to your classes. Before I put them into the archives I'll share them all with you. I'm not going to read them out loud. We can just pass them round. I think they will do us all good."

It was quiet in the room as everyone read. Not silent though. There was the odd chuckle and occasionally a stifled sob. As she read the letters she realised how right Doctor Kühn had been to suggest this. They certainly encouraged the children. They encouraged her. Had her contribution to Karl's letter to his class been adequate? Oh, nonsense. Why was she being so hard on herself? It had all come from the heart and that was what mattered. She was particular impressed by Emil Klimmich's letter to Class 10b, though. He wrote:

Dear students of Class 10b,

Now the school, where you have been able to learn and experience so much, must let you go. From this abundance I would just like to emphasize one thing today. Your teachers have shown you over and over again in recent years, how the great people concerned with the German spiritual life have indicated that your task in life is the education and the development of the higher human being, of the inner person. If you do want to make that your task, then know that you are connected to all of those you have lived and worked with in the school. If you do make that your task, know that that is the best thanks you can give the school.

Your teacher,
Emil Klimmich

Goodness.

And even the school doctor had written a long letter. One section brought tears to her eyes:

"Let's look inside with a winged soul: we learnt here how the human stands upright. And we look at the love between the children, between the teachers, the love of the children for the teachers – and of the teachers for their students: your love for this house."

Gradually all of the letters came back to Doctor Kühn and they all sat there for a few minutes in absolute silence.

"And so, ladies and gentlemen," said Doctor Kühn at last, "I expect you are all wondering what will happen to the buildings. Well, we plan to sell them to the town of Stuttgart. Some of the money raised will go to support the new schools opening in England and Holland, and some – and some will go towards the rebuilding fund." He paused to look round at his audience and to get individual eye contact with everyone in the room.

At least Ernst might benefit, then, thought Clara.

"Let me be clear: what is happening is absolute nonsense and sooner or later this madness will end. In the meantime we must take what we know out into the world and spread our good news amongst other people. As many of these letters have said. But sooner or later, sooner or later, my friends, we shall be allowed to bring our work back out into the open.

"There is still the celebration this evening. Let us use this as an occasion to honour the success of the school to date and let us not allow this to be a sad occasion. We shall be seen to be closing with dignity.

"Some activities will continue – eurhythmy classes and meetings in our homes. With some care and as inconspicuously as possible, of course. And it is indeed wonderful that the Hilfsklasse is able to carry on, thanks to the generosity of Clara Lehrs."

The others clapped enthusiastically at this and one or two turned to smile at Clara. She felt her cheeks go red.

"Indeed, indeed," said Emil Kühn as the applause subsided. "Well deserved."

"Now, I want to bring this meeting to a close as quickly as possible. Go home with gladness in your hearts. There are some difficult times ahead of us and there is work for you to do. But you have the spiritual strength to face that challenge. Your first task, of course, is to help the others in this community experience this evening's festivities as something positive. Go and find your finery. I shall see you all later."

There was some more applause, and then gradually they all

made their way out of the room, some people stopping to chat to colleagues as though they didn't yet want to lose sight of each other.

"At least it won't be too different for the Hilfsklasse," said Karl as they made their way back to finish tidying up the classroom. "Different classroom but the same teachers."

Clara stopped walking. "How easy would it be to get a message to all of the families?"

Karl shrugged. "Some are on the telephone. I could cycle round to the others. Why?"

"I'd like to invite them all over to a picnic in the garden tomorrow. We could take them for a walk in the woods afterwards."

"Why, Clara? Wouldn't it be better spending the time getting ready for the new term?"

Clara shrugged. "The room's ready and the furniture and supplies aren't arriving until Monday. Isn't this a good way to use the extra day's holiday?"

"I guess," said Karl.

"Good. Then let's get finished here as quickly as possible. You have to get some messages out and I have some baking to do. Ask the families to bring sandwiches and salads to share. I'll provide the dessert."

"Don't tire yourself out before this evening."

"I won't but you might."

Karl laughed.

22 September 1938, Stuttgart: good people

The Gödde's's house always took Clara's breath away. It was three storeys high, with dormer windows in the roof indicating that there were rooms in the attic as well. The house was half as wide again as her own and the gardens were clearly much bigger. She couldn't help but admire the front garden though where there were some shrubs still in flower and others whose leaves were turning red and golden. A German flag waved over the front door. Yes, they were a good German family, then.

Goodness, if 20 Schellberg Street were this big she would have been able to accommodate twice as many children as she used to have. Not that there were boarders at the moment. Still, she mustn't complain. The Hilfsklasse had been operating for over six months from her cellar and so far so good.

But what could Frau Gödde want? The letter had said that she should definitely come here this afternoon as the Göddes wanted to talk to her. They had a proposal to put to her. Could it be to do with Renate's visit at Christmas? Surely not. Surely that was a matter for Käthe and Hans to arrange directly with them.

She still felt hesitant about ringing the doorbell. Oh, come on, she said to herself. They invited you. It would really be rude of her to keep them waiting. She took a deep breath and rang the bell.

A few seconds later she heard footsteps and a tall, blond-haired young man opened the door. She'd not met him before. He must be new. The Göddes did like to take on new young staff now and then and train them up. "Ah, good afternoon," he said. "You must be Frau Lehrs. Herr and Frau Gödde are expecting you. Come in, come in. Here let me take your coat."

He smiled at her. He had lovely eyes. Clear blue, so kind and sincere.

As he hung up her coat he frowned. "Oh. I'm not sure where I'm to show you. Their last meeting has overrun a little." He turned to a staircase that led from the hallway. "Wilma! The visitor's here. They haven't finished yet, though."

"You're to take her straight in." Wilma, a woman Clara had always thought must be about the same age as herself, came up the stairs and was out of breath as she reached the hall. She nodded at Clara and fought to get her breath back. She stared at Clara for a few seconds as if she was trying to work out something about her.

Then she grinned. "We are so ill-mannered. Can we offer you a drink before you go in there?" She nodded to a curtain behind which Clara supposed there must be a door.

"No, perhaps I should go straight on in if they're expecting me."

Wilma nodded, drew the curtain back a little way and knocked on the door.

"Come in," called a male voice.

Wilma opened the door for her and gestured that she should go on in. Clara made her way into the partially darkened room and heard the door shut behind her. As her eyes grew used to the gloom she realised that the shutters were down but half open and that there were about twelve people in the room. She recognised one of them as Emil Kühn.

"Ladies and gentlemen, this is the lady I was telling you about," said a man that she guessed must be Herr Gödde. "My dear lady, I am not going to introduce you properly. We find it better not to know names. I have told these good people about the ideas I am going to suggest to you and they are in agreement. I hope you will find them acceptable too. Once they've all left, I'll explain it all to you."

The others in the room smiled and nodded at Clara. Frau Gödde, whom she knew quite well because of Renate's friendship with Hani, was particularly warm. But even so, what was all this? What was she getting into? Some sort of secret society?

Quite quickly, the others got up out of their seats and took their leave. A few moments later, it was just her and the Göddes left.

Herr Gödde had broad shoulders and a short beard. His hair was grey and he looked as if he must be at least ten years older than Frau Gödde. He stood up from his chair and Clara almost gasped when she saw how tall he was. She had to bend her head quite far back to get eye contact with him.

"My dear Frau Lehrs, do sit down." He pointed to a chair and sat down himself. "Helga has told me all that you and Karl Schubert are doing for the Hilfsklasse. And we would like to help."

"I'm sure Karl would be grateful. How would you like to help?"

"We'd like to donate some money."

"That would be extremely generous of you. Poor Karl has no wage and always puts the children's needs first in any case. The parents help a little but some of them are quite poor themselves. I do what I can."

"Of course, we'll have to pretend that Karl offers some sort of service to us. We'll have to think of some business he could be running."

"We can't say you're him paying to help run a school for some poor children less fortunate than the rest of us?"

Herr Gödde leaned across towards Clara. "You do understand, don't you, that children like these will soon be as resented as much as the Jews?"

Clara had never thought of that. How could that be so? These children couldn't help the way they were.

"We must be discreet," Herr Gödde said gently.

"Tell lies, you mean?" Clara whispered.

"Better a lie than a truth that will get us all killed."

"Killed?"

"I sincerely believe so," said Herr Gödde.

"Perhaps I could make cakes and you could order them for your meetings."

Herr Gödde threw back his head and roared with laughter. "Frau Lehrs, that certainly won't work. You are Jewish. I cannot be seen to be trading with you. And no way can any but those involved know about our meetings."

Frau Gödde put a hand on Clara's arm. "But maybe we could pretend Doctor Schubert made cakes and supplied flowers for the meetings of the good German wives and mothers."

Karl? Baking cakes? Clara could not supress a giggle. She began to titter. Then so did Herr Gödde and finally Frau Gödde.

"Maybe that will work," said Herr Gödde when they had at last stopped laughing.

"And I would actually like to be of more practical help," said Frau Gödde. "Helping to get materials ready and maybe meals. And I have some contacts – some in the group you saw here today – who may help supply stationery and that sort of thing."

"I think that would be splendid and I'm sure Karl will be pleased."

"Good. Then it's settled," said Herr Gödde.

"One thing, though," said Clara. "Could you call me Clara instead of Frau Lehrs?

"Certainly. Then I am Ralf."

"And I am Helga."

9 November 1938, Stuttgart: burning

Clara pulled her coat closer to her body. But it wasn't really the cold that was making her shiver. It was the sight of the fires still blazing and the smoke that was hanging in the air. They said it was the synagogue that had been set alight first but then they'd started on the shops and businesses. All Jewish ones. She had a good view of the city here, from the Obere Weinsteige and she could see pockets of smoke and flames though she couldn't see well enough to make out if some of the places she knew so well had been affected. More madness. The neighbours had reported that they'd seen people smashing shop windows and looting. They were vandals. Nothing but vandals. But who were they? She wished she knew.

A figure came out of the darkness and up the hill. A respectable enough gentleman from the way he was dressed but how could you really know? Her heart began to beat faster and her mouth went dry. Perhaps she should have listened to Karl who'd tried to persuade her not to go out.

"Oh it's you, Frau Lehrs," said a familiar voice. Herr Ehrlichmann. "What are you doing out? You shouldn't be watching this."

"But haven't you just come back from the town yourself?"

"You have me there. I had to see it for myself."

"That's what I wanted to do, too."

"Believe me, Frau Lehrs, you do not want to look closely at that horror. It is terrible. Terrible. So much senseless destruction. Our beautiful city. People's businesses. The synagogue. Come, let's turn our backs on it and go home."

"Why are they doing it?" said Clara as they made their way back to Schellberg Street.

"Who knows? It's the work of madmen. I'm so glad I covered up my cellar window. Who knows who might need a hiding place?"

"You're not…?" Clara regretted straightaway the questions she had almost asked.

"No, no, no. Evangelical Christian. German. But I have plenty of Jewish friends and I don't see them as any different from me. Yourself?"

"The same."

"Well, here we are. You take care and keep safe. Good evening to you."

"There you are," said Karl as Clara made her way back into the house. "Your daughter telephoned. She wanted to know whether you were safe, and whether it was as bad here as it is there."

"Oh, I must speak to her at once." Clara went towards the telephone.

"No, she said it's best not to. It's probably not safe. And you'd be lucky to get a connection, anyway."

"And it's bad there?"

"I'm afraid so. They're smashing windows and looting shops there as well. They've even ransacked ordinary family homes."

"Oh dear! But they're all right, because of Hans?"

"For the moment, yes."

Clara felt her legs turning to jelly and she was afraid she was going to fall.

"Come, Clara." Karl led her into the sitting room. He opened the large carved cupboard and took out a bottle of Asbach-Uralt and two glasses. He poured some of the brandy into the glasses. "Give me your coat and drink some of this."

Clara sipped the brandy. She didn't normally like alcohol apart from an occasional glass of wine but this was doing her good.

Seconds later Karl returned from hanging up her coat. "The other news I must give you is that she is thinking of trying to get to England and taking Renate with her. She thinks you should go too. Some relation of her husband's – Klaus? – can help."

Clara took another large mouthful of her brandy.

27 November 1938, Nuremberg: face to face

27 October Nuremberg

Dear Mutti,

We have secured a visa for me to leave Germany and I'm hoping that Rudi and Ernst will be able to find me work in London so that I can then get a visa and work permit to be able to live in England. Ernst is trying to get Renate a place at the Steiner School in London and we have her exit visa already. Klaus, Hans's cousin, has been able to help us with this. You know Hans was right: Renate having her own adult passport has been so useful. That, and having Klaus in the know has really helped. Perhaps it's as well that Hans argued with that young man after all.

I had to wait what seemed like a really long time. It was nerve-racking, I can tell you. It was only forty minutes but it felt like hours and hours. Then I was shown into a small office. Office! Well that's a bit of an understatement. It was a grand little room with expensive-looking art work on the walls and rather elegant drapes round the windows. All the same, it made me feel sick, waiting there, and it spelt out that this is a really important thing I'm about to do.

Then the door opened and I thought thank goodness at last someone is coming. But I had the shock of my life. It wasn't Klaus or one of his colleagues. It was none other than Herr Hitler himself. Yes, Herr Hitler came into the same little room that I had been shown into.

I don't know who was more surprised, me or him. He's smaller than you'd think actually. In fact, he looked like a scared rabbit. He mumbled something that sounded like an apology and then raised his arm and said "Heil!" or at least that's what I suppose he said. I had the presence of mind to raise my arm back but in all my confusion I didn't say anything though I'm sure I would have said "Heil Edler!" I don't think he noticed, though. Hans always says nobody notices. Perhaps he's right.

It was only after he'd scuttled out that I remembered what I had in my handbag. Yes, Mutti, you may be shocked to hear it, but I always carry a small pistol with me these days. I wish to God I'd thought to use it. The man was on his own. I could have shot him before anybody got to him. I might even have been able to escape. Even if I didn't get away with it and we all had to suffer because of it, it would have been a good thing don't you think? It might have saved a lot of other people a lot of misery.

Hans certainly curses me for not thinking quickly enough. I didn't, though, but I have taken a few steps to get me and Renate out of the country. I'll ask you one more time, Mutti. Will you please consider coming? Klaus will help you too.

Of course, Hans is forbidden to move.

I'll give you more news when we have it.

Your loving daughter,

Käthe.

Clara's hands trembled as she folded the letter and put it back in the envelope. Oh God! It was true then. Her other child was planning to leave the country as well. And taking her only grandchild. They'd had a conversation the other week. Käthe had visited her in a hurry and she'd given them her blessing. It had been all right in theory but now it was a reality.

Her daughter was carrying a pistol in her handbag? She could have shot Hitler? Hitler, for goodness' sake. If anyone dared to do it it would be Käthe. And she hadn't thought of it. But she'd copied Hans and almost said "Heil Edler". That was something at least. She tittered.

"Clara, what is it. You're as white as a sheet? But you're laughing," said Karl.

"Käthe almost shot Hitler and she's going to England."

"And that's funny?"

"She was so flustered she almost said 'Heil Edler'. Like Hans does."

Karl smiled. "But Clara, don't you think you should try to get out too?"

"No way. I wouldn't let that horrible little man win. I need to stay here in case I get the chance to shoot him myself. Besides, you and the children need me. Now, not another word."

She made her way up to her office. She thought she might do her accounts. That always made her feel calmer.

22 December 1938, Stuttgart: Christmas?

It was getting dark. Where were they? They should have been here hours ago. She hoped nothing had happened to the train. But if they didn't get here soon they might not get here at all: it was snowing heavily. Of course, Renate loved the snow and she would be staying with her friend, Hani, for a few days. No doubt the two young girls would really enjoy some cross-country skiing and some rambles in the snowy woods. It would take their minds off all this nonsense for a few days.

If they ever got here.

She could make out a figure struggling through the snow. The telegram boy! Of course, he wouldn't attempt to ride his bike in this weather. It must be taking him a lot longer than normal to deliver his messages.

And yes, he was coming towards the house. Oh, she did hope it wasn't bad news.

"Can I get you a warm drink before you carry on?" she asked the young man, even though she was anxious to open the message.

"No, it's fine, Frau Lehrs. Walking in this is quite hard work. It keeps me warm and I must get on."

Clara took out her purse and looked for a few coins. "Well, here's a little something for your trouble."

"Frau Lehrs, I'm not allowed to…"

"Nonsense. It's Christmas. I won't tell if you don't." She looked at him in a way she knew would mean he would not be able to resist. *One trick I've learnt by my age.* She smiled to herself as the boy put the money into his pocket.

"Merry Christmas to you too, Frau Lehrs."

As soon as she had closed the door she tore open the envelope.

TAKING LATER TRAIN STOP WILL ARRIVE MAIN STATION AT 1650 STOP WILL TAKE TAXI FROM STATION STOP DON'T WORRY STOP

Thank goodness that was all. They may have tried to telephone but the lines, she knew, had not been working very well over the last few days.

She looked at the clock. Ten to four. They'd be arriving at the station in an hour. Maybe it would take them another half hour to get to the house – by the time they'd found a taxi. If the taxi managed to get there. Or perhaps she could get Christoph to walk into town and help them up the hill with their luggage. He could take the sled.

She decided to bake some biscuits. That would take her mind off things and keep her occupied until they arrived.

As she was taking the biscuits out of the oven, the doorbell rang. She rushed to open it. A taxi's engine growled. It had managed to negotiate the hill. Christoph was already helping her visitors to get the cases out of the car. Thank goodness they had got there safely.

"Get off home, Christoph," she called.

"Thank you, Frau Lehrs. Good evening to you all." He pulled on his coat and set off.

Renate, sure footed as ever, ran up to her grandmother and hugged her. Then she burst into tears.

"Whatever is the matter?" said Clara.

"I can't go to Hani's because she's got chicken pox. And I can't go to your school."

Clara looked at Käthe who shook her head. Clara could tell that this was a conversation that would have to wait until later.

"She knows," said Käthe after Renate had gone into the house. "She knows she's a Mischling."

"Let's get inside," said Clara quietly.

She was unable to coax Renate to try any of the biscuits. Nor did she eat much at supper later. And she hardly said a word all evening. She made no protest, either, when her mother told her she looked tired and she ought to go to bed early.

Clara offered to tuck her in, if she didn't think she was too old for that. Renate agreed with a nod of her head. "But Oma, you don't need to tell me a story," she said later when they were in her bedroom. "Just tuck me in. The stories are lovely but now I really know they're not true." She turned her head to the wall.

Clara wanted to stay. She wanted to tell her granddaughter that everything would soon be all right. That the nonsense would soon stop. But she had the feeling that the girl wouldn't believe her.

"Now then," said Clara, when she got back downstairs, "you'd better let me know what you've been planning."

"We've found out about a scheme organised by the English. They're transporting Jewish and Mischling children to Britain," said Hans. "They have to be sponsored."

"Sponsored?"

"£50. As you can imagine that isn't a problem for us."

"And Ernst has found a family she can stay with and he has obtained a place for her at the Steiner School in London." Käthe looked at Hans. He nodded. She took a deep breath. "They've also found a job for me but I won't be able to go out until March. It will take longer to process the paperwork."

What my children are planning behind my back, thought Clara. "And what was this about her not being able to come to my school? There was never a question of that, since the school was closing. What was she talking about?"

"We'd told her that so that she could give her school friends a reason for her moving away. She thought she was coming to live here and going to go to the Waldorf School."

"But you decided to tell her the truth today?"

Käthe nodded. "She was getting so wound up about this class letter. With the Wilhelm Löhe closing as well, the girls have decided to keep in touch. They're writing it all in an exercise book and as you can imagine she went a bit mad with illustrating her contribution. She was so excited, Mutti, and I knew that it was going to end in disappointment. I'm afraid I just came out with it. Then, as you can imagine, there were several dramas and we were delayed."

"Well it's shame she can't go and stay with Hani. It would have taken her mind off it."

Käthe and Hans exchanged another look.

"We thought it best that she didn't go. It's better for her and Hani that Hani doesn't know what's happened. So we also sent a telegram to the Göddes saying that she had chickenpox."

"Oh dear, oh dear," said Clara. "All this conniving. The poor child. What a shock for her. Hani must be disappointed as well."

Käthe nodded. "I don't think it's going to be a very good Christmas."

The next morning Clara managed to coax Renate to help her to make an Apfelstrudel.

"We have to stretch the pastry so thin," she said as she pulled the dough they'd made together it across the kitchen table, "that you can read a newspaper through it."

"I don't think I ever want to read a newspaper," said Renate. "Don't they say that Jews are a disgrace and doesn't that mean you and me?"

Clara stood up straight. "Look at me." She placed her hands on the girl's shoulders. Two serious brown eyes looked back at her. "Listen to me. Two things: one – Jews are not a disgrace. I expect you know lots of them as well. Like the ones who own the bakery near to the synagogue. They're not a disgrace are they?"

Renate shook her head.

"And secondly: you are not Jewish anyway. Even those idiots in the government only design you as a Mischling, not as a Jew. You are German through and through really. And you can believe what you like. Are you a Christian? Do you believe in God?"

Renate shrugged.

"You see. You are simply a young German girl. Who is learning how to make Apfelstrudel like she ought to."

Renate took one of the edges of the dough and started pulling it gently. "Is it because of Mutti being Jewish that she kept cancelling visits to the opera? And is that why she wouldn't let me go on the school trip to Mostviel in the summer?"

"She wouldn't let you go on the school trip?"

"She said I hadn't got over my cold properly. Well, I had had a cold but it was only a little one and I don't think it should have stopped me going to Mostviel."

"I don't know," said Clara. Käthe had been that scared?

"And how can Hani have had chickenpox? We both had it before. Don't you remember, Oma? When I came here for the summer when we were seven?"

"Mmm. Come on, this looks ready. We'd better get the filling into it and get it into the oven if it is to be ready for this afternoon."

"I can't speak English, either."

"I expect you'll soon learn."

Later, while Renate was out with Hans and Christoph who had brought his toboggan round, Clara said to Käthe, "You know, when you lie to children you should be very careful what you say. You of all people I would have thought would have known that you can only have chickenpox once."

Käthe gasped.

28 January 1939, Stuttgart: alone

The children had all gone home except the ones whose parents were going to fetch them later; they were having a nap. Clara glanced at the clock. It was almost two. Perhaps Renate would already be out of Germany. She hoped so. She hoped there had been no problems at the German border. She hoped this family – Smith, wasn't that the name? This Smith family would be kind to her.

Goodness, all of her family would be in England soon.

Clara realised she was lonely.

Then she thought of Kurt and his angels. She hadn't thought about him for some time. She could almost hear his voice. "But you are doing angel work Frau Lehrs. You're doing it for the angels."

Those angels asleep downstairs, she supposed. And the ones who had gone home. Yes, it was sad that all of her family would soon be in England. But she was meant to be here. She was sure of that.

28 February 1939, Stuttgart: a visitor

The doorbell rang. Everyone stopped what they were doing. All of the children knew that if anyone came to the house they must be absolutely silent and pretend that they were not there. Clara, Karl and Christoph all looked at each other. Karl nodded to Christoph. Christoph set off up the stairs.

Clara heard him open the door. It sounded as if he was talking to a young girl. She couldn't make out what they were saying but she thought the girl sounded like Hani. Goodness, she hoped she hadn't come asking about Renate. She didn't want to have to tell any more lies.

Christoph came galloping down the stairs. "It's Renate's friend. She's got a puncture in her bike-tyre. I've said I'll help her mend it. That's all right, isn't it?"

"Of course," said Clara.

"Right," said Karl, turning back to the children, "we can carry on but still be very quiet."

"Oh, Hani wouldn't tell a soul. You can be sure of that," said Clara. "Her parents know all about us after all."

"Yes, but we don't to put her in an awkward position. It's really better if she doesn't know anything. Yes, help her but try and be as quick as you can."

Christoph nodded and ran back upstairs.

Clara and Karl were able to carry on the lesson. Clara tried to keep the children as calm as she could. Liesel, she noticed, was distracted and her eyes glazed over. Poor child. She must be tired.

A few minutes later Christoph reappeared. "It's useless," he said. "It needs a new inner tube. I've said I'll get one and put it in. And, Frau Lehrs, may I borrow the car to take her home? I think she's frightened she's going to be late for BDM."

"Of course, that's fine." It wouldn't do for the girl to be late for BDM – from what she'd heard it was all very strict.

Karl frowned. "Yes, we'll get her out of the way more quickly. Do try not to encourage her to come again, though."

Clara was about to reply that she thought he was being a bit harsh, when Liesel fell to the floor and started shaking. She'd managed to wedge herself awkwardly in the doorway and her head was bumping into the frame.

"Help me move her," said Karl, "but try not to constrain her." He looked up to Clara. "Don't worry, it's happened before. We don't need to do anything else. She'll come out of it of her own accord."

Clara had never seen anything like this. Her heart was beating fast. The poor, poor child. It didn't bother the other children, though. They must be used to it too.

After a few minutes the shaking stopped. The girl opened her eyes and she looked a bit bewildered.

"It all right Liesel," said Karl. "We're here."

At that precise moment the door opened. The children stopped talking immediately.

"Ah, Hani Gödde," said Karl.

"Sorry I left you so long," said Christoph. "Liesel had a seizure and they needed my help."

"How nice to see you, my dear," said Clara. "And yes, of course, Christoph will take you home in the car."

"It's all right. I'll walk," said Hani. She blushed.

"No. No question of it. And I'm sorry I've not been in touch," said Clara. "But you can probably see why. We've been busy."

"How's Renate?" said Hani. "Is she better from the chicken pox?"

"Ah," said Clara. That damned stupid lie again.

"It's only me," called another voice.

Oh dear. Hani's mother. This was going to be awkward.

"Shall I come down?"

Hani's eyes and mouth were wide open for a few seconds. Then she put her hand over mouth. Of course. Clara knew the Göddes had forbidden her to come and ask anything about Renate.

Clara grinned at Hani. "Don't worry. It'll be all right," she whispered.

"Only I've managed to get a good supply of pencils and paper from that new printer in town. They'll deliver it tomorrow," called Helga as she came down the stairs. She opened the door. The colour drained from her face and she gasped as she saw Hani.

"Don't worry, Helga," said Clara quickly. "She only came because she had a puncture. Christoph is going to mend it for her."

"You really don't have to worry about anything," said Helga, after Christoph had taken Hani home. "She won't say anything to anyone. She knows already that Ralf and I have some meetings that we have to keep quiet about. She also knows that we don't quite agree with everything that's going on but that we must never show that in public."

"Yes, she's a reliable enough girl. But it's wrong of us to involve her in this too much," said Karl. "It's not fair to expect someone of her age to keep such a big secret."

"Is it a secret, though?" said Clara. "No one has actually ever said you couldn't run the school here, have they?"

"No, but they haven't said that we could. I think that it's more that they've forgotten about us." Karl sighed. "And I also think that someone somewhere is turning a blind eye. There are some good people about. But we still need to remain inconspicuous."

"Yes, agreed," said Clara. "But enough of telling young people lies. Hani has seen some of this and she needs to understand exactly what's going on."

Helga sighed. "You are so right, Clara. Leave it to me. I'll talk to her. I'll make her understand. And about how important it is to keep quiet."

Clara nodded. "Thank you," she whispered. Karl was right. There were some good people around. And Helga Gödde was one of them.

1 March 1939, Stuttgart: new help?

"I explained it all to her last night," said Helga as the three of them sipped a well-earned cup of tea after the last of the children had gone home and all of the preparations had been made for the next day. "She understands why the school exists."

"Yes, but does she understand how important it is to keep quiet about what goes on here?" said Karl.

"Yes, yes, she does. Though at first she thought she could help and it could be one of the charitable acts the BDM encourages her to do. That was difficult."

"That's precisely the problem. And she must never mention what we do to the other BDM girls. Goodness knows how committed some of their parents are to the party."

Hmm, thought Clara. And have to ask the young people themselves to tell lies.

"But she really is keen to help," said Helga. "And I, er, I said she could."

Karl sighed.

Clara clapped. "What a wonderful idea. It will be so good for her. She's a fine young girl, we all know that. But this will give her more confidence and some real life experience. What do you say, Karl?"

He grimaced.

"It would only be a few hours after school or in the evening when she's not needed by the BDM."

Karl shook his head. "It's too dangerous. We can't risk her telling someone else."

Helga flushed bright red. "She wouldn't. She just wouldn't. She's a good girl."

Karl sighed. "I know she's a good girl. One of the best. But we've no idea what she would do under pressure. She's still very young. We shouldn't expect too much of her."

Clara signalled to Helga that she should see her out.

"He'll come round," she said as she held the door open for Helga. "I'll work on him."

"She'll be really disappointed if she won't be allowed to come after everything."

"It won't come to that. Trust me." Clara rubbed the younger woman's arm. "I'll see to it that he changes his mind." She began to form a plan.

7 March 1939, Stuttgart: the other half of truth

The doorbell rang. Clara glanced at the clock. Good, the girl was right on time. She hoped this would work. She hadn't told her much about what she was planning. Better that way. This would really test her – and if she actually failed – though Clara didn't think for a moment she would – well so be it. Maybe Karl was right and she was wrong. But she didn't actually think so. She was sure young Hani would pass the text.

She hurried to the door and opened it straight away. Yes. Exactly what she'd wanted. Hani, still in her BDM uniform. And my goodness, didn't' she look smart? It really suited her. She looked quite the young woman. That navy blue skirt made her look slim. Her shirt was a dazzling white. Helga and Wilma were really looking after her, then. Though Clara did notice the shirt was not tucked into the skirt all the way round. Still, she expected they had been busy. And anyway, the little flying jacket fitted neatly over it all and more or less held everything in place.

"So nice to see you," said Clara ushering the young girl into the lounge. "Thank you for coming."

"Thank you for inviting me."

"Make yourself at home while I go and get some biscuits and coffee – or would you prefer lemonade?"

"Just water, thank you, Frau Lehrs," said Hani. "The BDM meetings really make you thirsty."

"I'm sure they do."

Clara quickly went to the kitchen and put a few of the biscuits she'd made on to a plate. She poured two glasses of Sprudel. She was glad the girl had only asked for water. Timing was important. Karl would be home any minute. Making tea or coffee would have taken longer.

By the time she got back to the lounge she was pleased to see that Hani had tucked her shirt back in and generally made herself more presentable. Goodness, she was growing up.

She thought of Renate. What was happening to her in England? Was she growing up quickly, too?

239

Hani stood up as she came into the room.

Clara shook her head. "No need for that my dear. You've been working hard – school, BDM – make yourself comfortable. You deserve a rest." She set the drinks down on the small table in front of the sofa. "Right. Tell me all about what you've been up to with the BDM. Do you enjoy it?"

"Mm." Hani waved her head from side to side. "It's all right, I suppose." Her eyes lit up and she smoothed down her skirt. "I do like the uniform, though. Except it's not all that practical for some of the things we have to do." She rolled her eyes. "My shirt keeps coming untucked and one of the girls there is always telling me I look scruffy."

"Well I think you look very smart."

"Thank you."

"So what is it you don't like about it?"

"They keep saying that only German people are good and God loves only them but I don't quite get that."

"Do you ever talk to any of the other girls about that?"

"No, I keep those thoughts to myself. I talk to Mutti and Vati sometimes, though."

"And what do they say?"

"That I should join in all of the things that the BDM girls ask me to do – except if they ask me to do something that I know is wrong."

"And have they ever asked you to do anything you thought was wrong?"

"Not really, no."

"You know that your Mutti and Vati are doing some important work don't you? And that it's top-secret?"

Hani nodded. "I don't know very much about it. They say it's better that way. But Mutti comes to help you here, doesn't she? And that's part of her secret work, isn't it?"

"And you want to come as well?"

Hani nodded. "But Doctor Schubert doesn't want me to, does he?"

"It's not really that he doesn't want you to. In fact, he thinks you'd be very good. He worries about what might happen if the other BDM girls found out you were coming here. That's all."

"Well, they wouldn't would they? I wouldn't tell them." Hani looked alarmed. "It's not that I tell lies. It's another form of the truth. Today, for instance, I told them I had to dash off because I wanted to go and help those less fortunate than ourselves. They actually cheered me for it."

Clara smiled to herself. That was exactly what she wanted to hear.

And right on cue she heard Karl coming back from his training session. Everything was coming together perfectly.

"Karl, come in here," Clara called.

The lounge door opened and Karl's eyes widened as he saw Hani sitting there.

The girl was up on her feet in no time and held out her hand to shake Karl's. "Good evening, Doctor Schubert. Frau Lehrs invited me to come and have coffee with her after my BDM meeting."

Karl turned towards Clara and raised one eyebrow.

"I'll make you some tea. Go and change into something more respectable, then Hani can tell you all about what we've been discussing."

She pushed him back into the hallway. "You really can trust that girl. You'll see. Now, come and join us in the lounge as quickly as you can and hear what she has to say."

A few moments later, there were more biscuits on the table and all three of them were sipping cups of black tea.

"Tell Doctor Schubert what you told me about the BDM and about what your parents have been doing." Clara nodded encouragingly to Hani.

Hani repeated what she had said earlier. "But I don't tell lies," she said. "Just other forms of truth."

Clara noticed a smile playing at the corners of Karl's mouth. Was the girl winning him over?

"So, what do you think?" asked Clara later as she returned from letting Hani out. She deliberately started stacking the tea things so that she didn't need to look at him.

"Clara, Clara, I know what you're doing."

Clara placed the last plate on to the tray and looked Karl squarely in the eye. "You really don't think you can trust that girl?"

"Of course we can trust her. But can we trust them?"

"We probably can't. Neither can we be sure exactly what we'd do if they got to us either. And she's coping with those BDM girls all right. That can't be easy. Without even telling as many lies as some adults feel they have to."

Karl shook his head. "Okay, okay, Clara, you win." He pushed his fingers through his hair and shrugged. "In fact, I guess the girl will even be an asset."

"Of course she'll be an asset. An absolute gem, I'm sure."

Clara gathered up the tray of dirty crockery and made her way to the kitchen. She smiled to herself as she washed up. First thing tomorrow she would be able to tell Helga Gödde the good news. She'd already arranged for her to come in early.

10 March 1939, Stuttgart: the new help settles in

Clara heard the squeak of the bike wheels and then the rattle as Hani propped the bike against the back wall. Good. Let's see if today would go better. As she'd promised, the girl had popped by every day on the way home from school and spent a couple of hours helping them before setting off for her BDM meeting. Except that so far she'd actually been more of a hindrance than a help. Goodness. It wasn't her fault. She was so self-conscious and Karl was still a bit sceptical. Yet day after day, she'd turned up and she'd been cheerful about it. And here she was again.

The back door clicked open. "I'm here, Frau Lehrs." Hani stumbled in. Her cheeks were bright red. Clara could see she had been exerting herself to get here as quickly as possible. Her sweater was slung over her shoulders. Her blouse had come untucked and her hair had come loose from her plaits.

"Nice to see you!" Clara was already pouring her a glass of water. "Now get your breath back and then I'll tell you what Doctor Schubert wants us to do."

Clara smiled to herself as the girl drank the water thirstily. It was quite clear that she was really enthusiastic. The Sprudel was gone in seconds. "More?" Clara held up the bottle.

Hani nodded.

"We'll have tea and biscuits later," said Clara. "But first we're to cut up some paper for tomorrow's art lesson and mix up some paints ready. We can put them in the classroom once they're done. They won't dry out overnight."

Hani sighed. "I don't suppose he'll let me loose on anything more important."

There was no keeping anything from this girl. Karl's words had actually been: "At least she can't do any harm with that – expect perhaps making the sheets too small or the paint too thin."

Clara smiled at Hani. "Don't worry," she said. "We all have to start with the simpler things."

She watched as Hani started cutting the paper. Actually the girl was being really careful – slow maybe but that didn't actually matter. There was plenty of time and it was better that it was done properly rather than rushed.

"I'm looking forward to seeing what they paint tomorrow," said Hani.

There. The girl was really interested in the children. But when Karl was around he flustered her. She sensed Karl's lack of enthusiasm about these arrangements.

"I think that will be enough, Hani. Shall we get on with mixing the paints?"

"How much de we need of each?"

"Two pots of red, yellow and blue, and one each of white, green, brown and black. They can mix other colours themselves. In fact I think that is what Doctor Schubert wants to work on tomorrow."

As they were finishing Karl burst into the room.

"Are the paints not ready yet? I'd really like to have everything sorted out before you have to leave."

"We're just finishing. Hani's been a real help."

The girl blushed bright red.

"You'd have got it down quicker if you'd done it on your own," Karl muttered.

Clara shook her head and frowned. It was too late, though. It was clear that Hani had heard every word. Her face went an even deeper shade of red. She turned back to the sink and began washing the spoon she had used for the powder paint.

"Come on, Karl," said Clara. "I'll help you carry these down and set them up."

She would come back and sort Hani out later.

"I really don't know that it's such a good idea." Karl and Clara started putting the pots of paint and the paper out on the tables. "The girl gets in the way more than anything else. She holds us up all the time."

"Give her time, Karl. She's young and a bit self-conscious."

Karl sighed. "I suppose so."

They worked in silence for a few minutes.

Clara neatened the materials on the last of the tables. "There. All done. I expect you'll get them to do some lovely pictures tomorrow. You might get her to help."

Karl grimaced and shook his head. "I don't know about that."

Then they heard someone scream. It sounded as if it was coming from the front garden.

They rushed upstairs but Hani already had the front door open. "Come on bring him through," Clara heard Hani say.

It was Frau Becker and Thomas. Thomas was alternately yelling and sobbing.

"I'm so sorry about this. But he'd left Doggles and he insisted on coming back for him. Then when he caught his foot on the side of the path…"

"It's all right. We'll soon get him sorted." Hani showed them through to the kitchen.

Karl went to rush forward but Clara held up her hand. "Just watch," she said.

They could see all that was going on through the open kitchen door.

"You sit there and I'll get a cloth so that we can clean that sore knee of yours." Hani pointed to one of the kitchen chairs. Frau Becker helped her son on to the chair. "It might sting a bit. But you'll be a brave boy, won't you?"

The child had calmed down. He was still hiccoughing gently, his thumb in his mouth and his head buried in his mother's skirt.

"Good boy. Good boy." Mrs Becker stroked his head.

The boy's legs stiffened as Hani bathed the wound. She grinned at him. "There. You are being brave. Now I'm going to put some of my magic potion on it. You'll have to be brave again. This will sting even more but then we can put some nice clean lint on it and some plasters."

Thomas winced as Hani smoothed the disinfectant across his knee. Then he relaxed as she covered the cut with some lint and fastened it in place with some plaster. "And I'm going to tie a nice clean bandage round it to hold it all in place." She worked away at the little boy's knee for a few more minutes. "There. All done.

You'll have to limp for a while I think. I'll go and see if I can find Doggles."

Clara stuck her elbow in Karl's ribs. "Go and get the toy!" she whispered.

Karl turned on his heels and made his way back downstairs.

Clara went into the kitchen. "Frau Becker, will you and young Thomas stay and have a little snack with us? I was about to make some tea. And we have biscuits and I'm sure I can find this young man some lemonade."

"You're so kind, Frau Lehrs and…" She turned towards Hani.

"Hani Gödde. Our new unpaid help." Clara bustled over to the sink and filled the kettle with water.

"I want to sit on Hani's lap," said Thomas.

"Then you shall." Hani sat down on one of the chairs and opened her arms to him.

He crept up on to her lap, snuggled into her shoulder, closed his eyes and put his thumb in his mouth.

A few seconds later Karl appeared in the kitchen carrying the rather battered Doggles, an apology for a toy dog with its missing ear and eye. He held it out to Thomas. "Here you are young man."

Thomas stretched out his arm without opening his eyes and grabbed the toy. He wasn't as keen on it as he had before. "Want to stay on Hani's lap," he muttered.

"There you are you see," Clara whispered to Karl.

"I give in. I can see you're right."

"It was always a matter of time. She needed to find her stride. And I think she's just found it."

All would be well, Clara was sure of that.

13 April 1939, Stuttgart: some truths

Clara was busy scrubbing out paint pots at the sink in the basement when she heard the backdoor shut. That was odd. Christoph was in the classroom repairing one of the shelves. Karl was preparing some lessons and Helga and Hani weren't due until this afternoon. Perhaps Helga had popped round with something early or wanted to pick up something from the house.

She wiped her hands on her apron and made her way upstairs. She opened the kitchen door and yes, there was Helga. She looked terrible, though. She was pale and there were dark circles round her eyes.

"What on earth is the matter, my dear," she said, pulling out a chair for her and nodding that she should sit down.

Helga took a deep breath. "I don't think Hani should come anymore."

"Oh dear. Why ever not? What's happened?"

"Some of the BDM girls got to her yesterday. They'd come back from a camp and the one in charge – she's a bit of a so-and-so – decided that they had to have a class about racial purity before they were allowed home."

"Goodness me!"

"It gets worse."

"Go on."

Helga sighed. "One of the girls saw her coming here. They know you're Jewish."

"Oh dear."

"And so, of course, she worked it all out about Renate. I had to tell her. I didn't really want to – I don't want her knowing too much. It made her sick, Clara. She actually vomited. She was such a mess when I picked her up. They'd worked her hard at camp and then all of this poisonous stuff about blood-lines. Ralf and I thought it might be better if she didn't come here anymore."

"I understand. I do understand, Helga. It's a pity, though. She's such a help."

Helga nodded.

At that moment Karl came into the kitchen. "I thought there might be a chance of a cup of coffee? Good morning, Helga."

"Helga's got some bad news," said Clara. "We don't think Hani should come anymore."

"Oh?"

While she made the coffee Clara explained all about what had happened.

"The poor girl," said Karl. "And what a way for her to find out about her friend. But perhaps it's for the best. If something did happen, while she was here…"

"That's what Ralf and I thought, too," said Helga.

"She helped us so much, though, and she was so good with the children." Clara remembered how well she'd amused them as some of them waited for their parents to collect them in the afternoons. She and Karl were exhausted by that time.

She brought the coffee pot over to the table and poured out three cups.

"We'll manage," said Karl. "Anyway, as it's the school holidays we have a bit of slack. We can work out a new routine. It'll be fine."

"I can come more often. I can help out in the afternoons like she's been doing. Ralf would be happy for me to do something like that. He can easily find someone else to do his paperwork."

"That's very kind of you, Helga. Are you sure?" Would Helga have the patience that Hani had with the younger children? Clara somehow doubted it. That girl was a natural teacher if ever she'd seen one. "If you could help with some of the preparations and the cooking, perhaps I can help Karl more with the children?"

"Anything. Anything at all." Helga finished her coffee and stood up. "Look. I'd better go. I'll go and discuss this all with Ralf. I'm sure it will be fine."

"Don't you worry about a thing, Helga." Karl stood up and put a hand on Helga's arm. "It'll all work out."

As soon as Helga had gone, Karl rinsed his and Helga's cups out and made his way down to the cellar. Clara guessed he was going to see how the shelf was coming along. She stared at her own cup of coffee. She'd hardly taken a sip and it had gone cold.

That poor girl. She would miss her for sure. What a way to find out about her friend! Surely if they'd told her the truth she would have been able to deal with what had happened yesterday more calmly?

She heard Christoph clattering up the stairs. "Is that right what Doctor Schubert said, Frau Lehrs? That Hani can't come anymore?"

"I'm afraid so, Christoph."

"Why not?"

So, Karl hadn't explained. Clara suddenly felt weary and didn't want to go into the whole story. "We'll tell you properly over lunch," she said. "For the moment let's say that she knows a bit too much for her own good." *But there will be no more telling young people lies. Not if I can help it.*

"Will the lunch be long? I'm starving."

"It will be a while yet, I'm afraid. But take a bread roll to keep you going. I hope you like Frau Gödde's cooking. She'll be doing a lot more soon."

"I expect I will. I don't mind what I eat when I'm hungry and I'm nearly always hungry."

Clara smiled. That at least sounded healthy and natural.

7 May 1939, Stuttgart: Christoph has an idea

"Frau Lehrs! Frau Lehrs!"

Goodness, who was that calling her from the street. Clara looked up from the flowerbed she was weeding. It was Christoph. What was he doing here on a Sunday? She rarely asked him to come on a Sunday. Oh, he was more than willing, but she didn't like to abuse that good will. Only very rarely did she ask him to come and do something – and she did always ask and she did always say it was perfectly all right if he didn't want to – he must have some free time and she respected that.

Christoph ran up the path. "I met Hani at the tennis courts and we've come up with a brilliant plan." Then his eyes grew round in horror and he clapped his hand over his mouth. "Sorry," he whispered.

"Come on." Clara picked up her basket of tools, walked round towards the back of the house and signalled that Christoph should follow her. "I need a break anyway. Let's go inside and see what we can find. Then you can tell me all about it nice and calmly."

They both washed their hands. Clara poured some apple juice and set out a plate of biscuits. "So, tell me. You saw Hani, and?"

"Yes, she was watching some other people playing tennis so I went and spoke to her. And then I had this idea. Goodness knows where it came from. But she said she was missing working here and I said we were missing her. We are aren't we?"

Clara nodded. "Indeed yes."

"Well, it's simple. She could disguise herself as a boy and she could come back. Nobody would recognise her."

Clara almost choked on her apple juice. "How on earth would she do that? How could we make it look convincing?"

"She's quite tall and she's quite strong."

That was true. And she was a lot more slender than she used to be. As she was growing taller and possibly because of the exercise she was getting with the BDM and the longer journey to school.

"And I can borrow some clothes from my brother. If she

scrapes her hair up into her cap it will be convincing enough to anyone outside. She could still be Hani indoors."

"She's getting a bust on her. She'll have to flatten that." Clara put her hand in front of her mouth and tittered when she realised what she'd said and she saw Christoph's face go bright red. "Sorry but it's true."

Christoph looked down at the floor. "Perhaps it wasn't such a good idea."

"No. No, I think it's worth a try." Then she had a really wicked thought. "Maybe we can get her just to do it. We won't tell Frau Gödde or Doctor Schubert yet. Let's make it a surprise. We can even see if she can convince the children – they'll see through it before the adults if anyone is going to. We can call her Hans."

"So, do you think we should go ahead?"

"I do indeed. How soon can you get the clothes to her?"

"I've said I'll give them to her next Sunday."

"Good, then tell her – rather – him – to report for duty a week on Monday. Ha ha – the others are in for a surprise!" She raised her glass to clink it with Christoph's. "To Hans Gödde."

"Hans Gödde."

They heard Karl come down the stairs. "Who are you talking to, Clara?" he called.

"Not a word." Clara winked at Christoph.

15 May 1939, Stuttgart: Hans

"I've something to tell you," said Helga as she and Clara were cutting onions in the kitchen.

"Oh." More dramas. Clara was feeling tense already about what they'd planned for later. What if it all went wrong? What if Helga and Karl got angry and the children saw through it straight away? What if they laughed?

"We've decided to let Hani come back. If you and Karl don't mind of course."

"Good." Except it was almost disappointing. She had been quite looking forward to their little trick.

Helga stopped chopping. "Except."

"Ah. There are conditions?"

"Well, we want to disguise her as a boy."

Oh. They knew.

"It was Christoph's idea, apparently. I caught her yesterday trying on some clothes that he'd borrowed from his younger brother. It was really convincing, Clara. Especially if we gather her hair up under a cap and well, flatten her breasts a little – you know '20's style."

So, it sounded as if Hani hadn't said that Clara already knew. Good for her. That girl had a healthy sense of humour. "This sounds like an exciting idea. But you know what? Let's not tell Karl. Nor the children of course. That will be the test."

"But what shall we tell them when she turns up?"

"He. When he turns up."

"All right. He."

"We'll get Christoph to say that a cousin is calling round to see if he can do any work for us."

Helga giggled. "You are good at working these things out."

"We have to have some fun, don't we? It would be rather dull if we didn't laugh a little wouldn't it? Especially these days."

Helga nodded.

*　　*　　*

252

Lunch time came and went. Some of the children had gone home and Christoph was amusing those who were still waiting for parents to arrive. Karl was upstairs in his study preparing lessons for the next day. The doorbell rang. Clara, Christoph and Helga exchanged a glance. Clara was finding it difficult not to giggle.

"I expect that's your cousin, Christoph," Karl called down the stairs. "Show him in, will you."

"I'll keep an eye on them." Helga waved her hand towards the children who were still playing in the garden.

Very nice, leaving it all to us, thought Clara. But perhaps it was for the best. She would only make Hani nervous.

Christoph answered the door. Clara almost gasped when she saw Hani standing there. She really did look more like Hans. The shirt hung loosely on her but otherwise you really could not tell she was a girl. What would happen when she spoke, though?

"Doctor Schubert, may I present my cousin, Hans Tellermann."

Clara held her breath as Hans Tellermann shook hands with Karl Schubert.

"Well, Hans, how old are you?"

Was this going to be it? Would she give herself away now?

"I'm fourteen, sir. I'll be fifteen next month," said Hani in a surprisingly deep voice.

"Do you know anything about working with children?"

"I have lots of brothers and sisters, sir."

"Well I tell you what. You go outside and help Frau Gödde with those children playing in the garden. Let's see how you get on. And you do know we can't afford to pay you much?"

"No problem, sir. When Christoph told me what he did I wanted to help."

"Go on then. We'll see."

Clara and Christoph watched though the window with Karl. It was clear that Hans was getting on really well with the children. But did they realise it was really Hani?

Oh dear, what was she doing? She was always saying that they shouldn't deceive young people and here she was deceiving a dear colleague and that group of young people outside and encouraging two other young people and another adult to tell lies. It wasn't right. "Karl, there's something you should know," she blurted out.

Karl turned to her and smiled. "That Hans is really Hani Gödde? And that you, Christoph and Helga knew all along?"

Clara felt her cheeks burning. "Karl, I'm so sorry. It was a terrible thing to do."

"Don't worry, Clara. It's a very good idea. The disguise is superb. The only thing that gave you all away was your nervousness. And in the end this way we can get more help without having to tell any more people about what we're doing."

He shouted through the open window. "Hans, Helga, children, come on in. Hans, yes, we'll be hiring you."

They all trooped indoors. Gilbert, one of the little boys, was staring at Hani. "You look just like Hani," he said. He pulled at her cap and Hani's hair came tumbling down. "But I like you even better as Hans, actually."

"I think it will do. It will do very well indeed," said Karl. "As long as we're all careful."

Clara giggled and Hani grinned. Christoph and Helga exchanged a smile.

1 June 1939, Stuttgart: unwelcome news

That would do. The flowers would make a lovely display on the dining table. There were enough there. She didn't want to deplete the garden too much. Just a few more leaves. They needed a touch of greenery and at least she could take as much as she wanted of that. All of the shrubs needed a good cut back anyway.

She heard the squeaky wheels of Herr Janke's bicycle. It was always such a comforting sound, an indication that the rest of the world was still there and had something to say. He'd started calling here every day at about this time and usually stopped to chat for a few minutes. He always came to their house first as there was often so much correspondence for them. He would leave his bike propped up against their wall and would then walk to the other houses.

But today he was doing no such thing. He actually started stuffing the envelopes into the mailbox.

"In a hurry today, Herr Janke?" Clara called.

"Oh, Frau Lehrs, I didn't see you there." He blushed bright red and carried on pushing the envelopes into the box.

What did he mean? Usually, if she wasn't in the garden he would ring the doorbell and hand her the post personally. Sometimes she would offer him coffee and even if he didn't have time for that, he would stay and chat for a few moments.

Not today, though, evidently.

"You're in a hurry today?"

He nodded. "My wife and I have an appointment this afternoon. I need to be home early." He turned away from her, got on his bike and pedalled hastily away. She wondered what had happened to the rest of the mail for the street. Perhaps there was none.

She put the flowers down on the step and took the mailbox key out of her pocket and opened the box.

Her heart almost stopped when she saw the fat white envelope with the Reich's crest on it. So, that's why, she thought.

She gathered up the envelopes and walked slowly back into the house, ignoring the flowers. She put the rest of the mail on the small table in the hallway and held on to the big envelope.

It was made of expensive paper. It was white and stiff. She rubbed her finger over the embossed Reich's emblem. How could anything so elegantly presented bring bad news? Why would they go to all this trouble and expense if they were going to tell her something she didn't want to know? To make it important, perhaps?

She didn't want to open it, but she knew she must. She walked slowly up the stairs still staring at the envelope.

They've spelt my name wrong, she thought and wondered why she hadn't noticed straight away.

Klara Lehrs, it said. No "Frau".

I'm Clara, not Klara.

She made her way into her room and sat on chair in front of her bureau. Her hands were trembling.

She stared at the envelope for a few more minutes. Then she took a deep breath, took the letter-knife and slit across the flap.

The paper inside was less elegant, though was still quite thick. It wasn't a letter, anyway, more a sort of command.

Klara Sarah Lehrs, Jewess of the first order, and therefore of non-Aryan race, you are hereby commanded to sell at a reasonable price the property 20 Schellberg Street, with immediate effect, to an Aryan person.

We expect and await your complete cooperation in this matter and trust that on receipt of this instruction you will immediately commence actions that will facilitate the swift sale of the property.

We offer assistance in rehousing should you not be able to make arrangements for your accommodation.

We can also offer help with the sale. You property is very fine and will be of immense interest to German families.

We forward this request in the name of the German people.

Heil Hitler.

Well, at least they said it was a very fine property. But who was this Klara Sarah Lehrs supposed to be? Nobody she knew. All this nonsense about Aryans and Jews. She, Clara Lehrs was German, a citizen of this planet, a woman of this world and let that be an end to it.

She stood up and walked over to the window. She looked out at the garden and beyond that to the street. The gardens all looked so lovely. All of the flowers were out and the grassed areas were green and well-tended. This was a happy street and her house was a happy home.

So much had happened to get her here. Ernst's death, Ernst Junior's interest in Rudolf Steiner, her time at the Lauenstein and then finally selling her pearls, borrowing from Doctor Kühn and her brother and building this house.

She thought about some of the children who had lived here. There had been so many happy times. Some hard work as well, and occasionally there had been tears. But it had mainly been happy. She'd hardly ever had to raise her voice.

She heard some laughter coming from the cellar. It was good that those children could still laugh. There must always be laughter.

What would happen to the Hilfsklasse if she sold the house? Where would those children go? Whatever she did, she must make sure that that could carry on. She must sell it to someone who would understand. There was only one possible person.

"30.000 Mark will be absolutely fine. That more than covers all the bills I need to pay to the authorities. Then with what's left I can rent somewhere to live. I have my pension still."

There was a pause. He didn't seem to want to say anymore. Should she ask him about the Hilfsklasse?

Then he cleared his throat. "You don't need to look for a room. You will of course carry on living there as before."

That was a relief and it was what she had hoped.

"And the Hilfsklasse?"

"Let's talk about it tomorrow. I'm sure we can sort it all out sensibly."

There was another pause. Well, he said they could sort it out tomorrow. Better in person, quite probably. "I'll see you tomorrow then. I'm so grateful."

He sighed. "I'm so sorry it can only be 30,000 Mark."

"Don't be sorry. And thank you so much."

He hands were still shaking as she put the receiver down. It looked as if the Hilfsklasse might be all right. Perhaps.

2 June 1939, Stuttgart: news with cheesecake

"Look, I'm going to write a note to Hans. I don't want him to overhear our conversation. I'll be back in a couple of minutes. It's so good of you to agree to this, Doctor Kühn."

"For goodness sake, call me Emil. It's about time."

He sat down on one of the chairs.

"As you please. And you must call me Clara." She took a piece of paper from the writing desk and thought for a few seconds. Then she wrote:

Dear Hans,

Can you please wash out the paint tubs and see if the pictures are dry? It will be nice if they can take them home today. I'm sorry I can't greet you personally. I'm having a meeting with Dr Kühn this afternoon. I hope we'll be finished before the children go home.

Clara Lehrs

"I'll pop this in the kitchen," said Clara. "That should do the trick, I think."

She shivered as she thought about the other letter, the one that had ordered her she to sell her house to an Aryan German but by the time she was back in the study she was simply glad that that particular German was going to be Emil Kühn.

"You know I insist that you stay in the house. I shall rent a room out to you but you must carry on considering this to be your home. You must carry on as if nothing has changed."

"Thank you, Emil. Will you move in?"

"I think it would be wise, don't you?"

"Well, there's plenty of room." Clara waved her arms around.

"Look, here are the papers," said Emil. "I think it's all quite clear."

Clara sat down and read through the documents.

"If we go along to Wallbergs we can sign the papers and it will all be completed."

"And it's 30,000 Mark – that's right, isn't it? Plenty if you promise to keep the rent low."

Emil nodded. "I'm glad we've been able to settle this so quickly. We can get the money into your bank account in about three weeks and then the house will be mine. No need for you to worry anymore. I'm sorry that I can offer you so little." He stood up, ready to go.

Clara opened the study door. "Oh, it's not a problem. You're doing what has to be done. And better that you have Haus Lehrs than it goes to a complete stranger."

As they turned to go out of the room, they came face to face with Hani. Definitely Hani – her hair was loose. She stood with her mouth and her eyes wide open. She gasped and dropped a pile of paintings she had been holding.

Emil turned towards the door. "Ah, my dear Fräulein Gödde, let me help you." He came out into the hallway and started to help her pick up the paintings. "Frau Lehrs has told me all about the good works you've been doing here. Splendid. Splendid. But maybe I shouldn't call you Fräulein Gödde. Hans, isn't it? Well done that man. Good. Good. Do give my regards to your parents."

He handed Hani the paintings and reached for his hat and coat from the stand. "And ladies, I wish you good day."

"Thank you so much. For everything," said Clara, as she let him out of the front door.

Goodness, the poor girl looked like a ghost. This wouldn't do. "Leave the paintings on the hall table, my dear," said Frau Lehrs. "You've had a shock. Go and sit in the lounge and I'll bring you a glass of lemonade. That cheesecake should be ready as well. I'll get Christoph to deal with the pictures."

Clara made sure the girl was comfortable and then busied herself in the kitchen cutting a piece of the cheesecake and pouring some lemonade. She found Christoph and told him to sort the paintings out.

Then she returned to the lounge with a tray holding two glasses of lemonade and two slices of cheesecake.

"Here we are." She placed the tray on the small table in front of the sofa. "Do tuck in. This cheesecake is rather splendid, even though I say so myself and I shouldn't."

Hani took a sip of her drink. It was clear though that she could hardly swallow it.

"I really didn't want you to hear that," said Clara. "We'd meant to keep it a secret from everyone." She took a bite of her cake and then frowned. "Though I suppose eventually everyone will find out. Your parents know, of course. Perhaps I should tell Christoph after all. Hmm."

"But what's going to happen to the special class?" asked Hani.

Clara laughed. "Of course," she said. "You think I'm moving. No, no. Not at all. Everything will carry on as normal. I'm renting a room from Doctor Kühn. But I shall live here as I've always done and the class will carry on as normal. You won't know the difference. I promise."

The girl was able to swallow again and began to look as if she might start eating her cake properly.

"In fact," Clara continued, "with the money I get for the house I'll be able to spend a little more on the class. Yes, it's all to the good. Anyway, that will get them off my back for a while. They have what they want. Haus Lehrs will belong to a proper Aryan German. And I'm sure things are going to get easier. The worst is over."

Hani had stopped eating again and was staring hard at Clara.

"Oh, but you're not eating your cake," said Clara. Then she had an idea. Should she do it? Yes, she should. She sighed. "I know what will cheer you up. I'll pop and get something from my study."

She returned to her study and quickly found the letter she wanted to show Hani. She read it again to make sure.

Sunday, 14 May 1939

Dear Oma,

You'll probably be pleased to hear that my English is getting better and better. I can now follow all of the lessons really well. I don't mind any more that I'm working in a class for children a year younger than me. Because the work is easy it helps me to understand the actual language. I can

261

understand what the teacher is saying now and I can answer questions. I can even write quite well, though it's still a bit difficult to follow what the other children are saying when we're out in the yard. They speak so fast!

I've met a super new teacher called Mrs Cohen. She came to teach us when our regular teacher, Miss Thompson, was called away because her father was ill. She managed to explain to the rest of the class that I'm German and Jewish at the same time. She also helped me to understand that I'm not peculiar because I feel so mixed up about who I am. It's the same for her because she's more English than Jewish. She's really nice.

You'll never believe it. I'm actually going to play in the cricket team! My class mates can't believe how well I understand that English game. Thank goodness for cousin Gottfried. I'm so glad he spent all those weeks last summer teaching me what he'd learnt in England. And of course, I can run.

The girls in my class are getting really friendly, and I'm regularly invited to tea by one or other of them. The other day Mutti made a wonderful Apfelstrudel. My friend and her family really enjoyed it.

Mutti is quite happy because we have found a little delicatessen not far from the flat. It was the Polish people who live in the ground floor flat who told us about it. Of course, it is Polish, not German, but all the same we can get some things we miss: salami, black bread (yes, we actually miss that. Who'd have thought it?) and cheesecake. Of course, Mutti makes an excellent cheesecake, almost as good as yours, but you can't buy Quark in England. And the people at the Polish delicatessen do get Quark, but they use it all up in the cheesecake. The nearest you can get to it is a sort of cream cheese, but it's not the same. So we have to buy the cheesecake.

Mutti is well and sends her love. I expect she will write to you again herself soon. Have you seen anything of Hani?

*Does she know what has happened to me? I'd love to write
to her but Mutti says it's best not to.*

I'll write again soon,
Your loving granddaughter,
Renate

Yes, everything was fine there. She shouldn't really have kept it. But she had, and it was a good job too.

She went back into the lounge. "This is Renate's latest letter," she said. "I've not got round to burning it yet. And I promise from now on I'll let you read every single one before I turn it into boiler fodder. You know, she would love it if you would write to her but I think it's best not to, though. I promise that I'll give her some news about you every time I write."

She placed the letter on the table. The poor girl looked as if she couldn't believe her eyes. "There," said Clara. "I'll leave you to read in peace. The parents will be coming for the children any minute now and I want to make sure they all take their paintings home. And do eat up your cake. Don't take this trying to look like a boy too seriously. You're getting terribly thin, my dear."

She noticed the girl's hands were trembling as she opened the letter. Clara closed the door and left her to it.

She pottered about for twenty minutes in the kitchen and then went back to see how Christoph was getting on.

"It's nearly all done, Frau Lehrs," he said.

"Good. There is something I want to tell you."

"Oh? I'm worried, Frau Lehrs. You look very serious."

"Well it is serious but nothing really to worry about too much." Clara took a deep breath. "I have to sell the house to Doctor Kühn."

"Why?" Christoph's eyes were round with surprise.

"Oh, one of those silly new laws." She paused and looked him straight in the eyes. "You see, I am Jewish really."

Christoph flinched.

Well, she should have expected that. "Nothing will change, though. Not as far as you will be able to tell. I shall still carry on living here and the Hilfsklasse will continue as before."

Christoph looked up at her. "You don't look Jewish."

263

"No? Well there you are then. Now, I must get back to Hani." She noticed he was staring at her as she turned away.

When she got to the lounge, it was clear that the girl had finished reading the letter and she was drinking the last of her lemonade. "Good," said Clara. "You've finished. I hope you liked the letter. And I see you liked the cheesecake in the end. Could you put those things in the kitchen? And then come and help get the children ready to go home? Oh, and you'd better put the letter in the furnace when you come down."

Clara made her way down to the basement. Would Hani do as she'd asked and burn the letter? She wouldn't insist. It was entirely up to her, Clara decided. She hoped she would though.

The children were getting excited about going home. "Hans will give you your pictures," she said. "Be patient."

A few moments later she heard the clatter of the furnace door being shut and Hans came into the classroom. Hani's hair was once more pushed under the cap. He grinned at Clara.

"Frau Lehrs," said Christoph as they made their way upstairs, "is it true that you gave Hans a piece of cheesecake? Is there any for me?"

"Of course there is."

10 July 1939, Stuttgart: Isabella Kühn

Clara couldn't quite put her finger on it what it was, but something was making her uneasy about today. Something was going to happen, she felt sure of that. Was it all this talk of war that was bothering her?

The classroom was buzzing. All four of them were in there with the children. It was always a bit exciting like this at the end of the school year anyway. It wasn't something pleasant that was going to happen, this time though. She was sure of that. She had this dark feeling of dread.

Christoph and Hans were talking quite earnestly. She couldn't make out what they were saying. Perhaps they were worried as well about there being another war. Oh dear. Would Christoph be called up? Would they expect him to be a soldier? He looked so young. And if he went how would they manage to lift some of the older children who needed help? Hans – Hani – was quite strong for a girl but it wasn't the same. Karl couldn't manage on his own these days. What would they do?

And Hani? Would she be expected to go on one of these work schemes they were getting up for young girls? Quite probably. Oh dear.

Then the doorbell rang.

Hani looked at her. Clara took a deep breath. "Children, quiet now," she whispered.

The children sat as still as statues.

Doctor Schubert nodded to Christoph who had gone white and seemed glued to the ground.

"Go on," mouthed Dr Schubert. "Go and see what they want. Now!"

Christoph's face went bright red. Then he sprinted up the stairs.

They heard him open the front door.

"Good afternoon," they heard a voice say. "SS Obersturmführer Poll. I understand that this is the residence of Dr Emil Kühn. Is Doctor Kühn at home today?"

"I'm afraid he's at the office," said Hans.

"Well, may I come in and wait for him?" said the officer. He didn't give Christoph any choice. He barged right into the house.

"If you'd like to wait here, sir," said Christoph. "I'll let you know as soon as Doctor Kühn arrives."

Christoph then came back down the stairs.

"I've shown him into the lounge. I didn't know what else to do," he said.

"Leave this to me," said Clara.

"Clara, you shouldn't," whispered Karl.

"It'll be fine. Trust me. Hans, you go out the front and warn off any of the parents until I've got rid of him. Wait until I'm in the lounge, though."

Clara made her way up the stairs.

"Ah, Obersturmführer Poll," she said. "Isabella Kühn. I'm afraid my son is away at his office at the moment. He will be here soon. May I offer some refreshment whilst you wait?"

"No thank you, madam. I'm fine."

Clara's heart was beating fast.

"Then please make yourself comfortable. May I ask what business you have with my son?"

"It's to do with the purchase of this house. I'm afraid my comments are for him alone."

"I see. Well, I'm sure he won't be long."

Obersturmführer Poll stared at her. He looked as if he could read her thoughts. She must keep calm. She really must.

"It's lovely weather we're having, isn't it?" she said.

"It's of no consequence with the work that must be done."

"I suppose not."

The officer's face softened. "It can't be easy for Doctor Kühn taking over a house like this."

"No, he found it quite harsh having to buy it off the Jewish lady."

"I don't think 'lady' is the right word."

"Maybe not."

Clara heard three taps on the front door. Then she heard Liesel call "Mutti." This could be a disaster. She couldn't deny it was happening. She'd better pretend this was all supposed to be.

She opened the lounge door. "Ah, Hilde," she said to Liesel's mother whom Hani had just let in. She looked at Liesel and smiled. "She's been such a good girl. I'm sorry I can't ask you to stay for some tea but I have company at the moment. Do give my regards to your mother."

Obersturmführer Poll was standing behind her. Hans showed Liesel and her mother out. Clara could see she was trying to keep her face turned away from the SS officer.

"Isn't that one of the children from the old special class at the Waldorf School?" asked Obersturmführer Poll.

"It is indeed. It's so difficult for the parents now that they have no school to go to. Liesel's grandmother is a dear friend of mine. I was helping her daughter out for a few hours."

"Will your son be long?" said the SS officer.

She turned to Hani. "Hans, dear, will you ask your cousin to cycle round to Dr Kühn's office. I'm afraid the telephone isn't working. And then carry on with what you were doing before."

Hani nodded, still keeping her back to the two of them.

"That boy is so sullen," said Clara as she closed the lounge door. "I don't know why my son keeps him on. But I suppose until he is settled in…"

"If you don't mind, Frau Kühn, I'd like to get on with some paperwork whilst I wait."

"Very well."

At least he hadn't suspected anything. She left him in the lounge and made her way to the basement. As she opened the door to the classroom, several of the children looked at her. Karl raised an eyebrow. She shook her head, closed her eyes and leaned against the wall. She could hear her heart thumping. They all seemed to wait for hours.

Then she heard Christoph's bike squeak. She rushed back up to the lounge. "I think my son is here."

As she glanced at the hall clock she realised that Christoph had in fact only been five minutes.

The officer looked up and put his papers away. "Good."

The lounge door opened and in walked Emil. "Ah there you are," said Clara. "Obersturmführer Poll is here to see you."

The officer stood up. "Heil Hitler!" he said.

"Heil Hitler!" replied Emil.

Clara couldn't help herself. She mumbled "Heil Edler!" Then she wished she hadn't.

The officer didn't flinch, though. "I have come to ascertain that the sale to yourself from the Jewish woman has indeed gone through today."

"Yes, it certainly has. Here are the papers." Emil Kühn pulled a bundle of documents out from his briefcase.

Officer Poll spent a few minutes looking at them. He nodded. "Now, if you don't mind I would like to take a look at the house." He went to leave the lounge, but paused in the doorway. "And the Jewess is still living here?" He started shuffling some papers. "Klara – with a 'K' Sarah Lehrs?"

"Klara with a 'K', Sarah Lehrs?" whispered Clara.

"Yes, we insist on German spelling," said the officer, "and all Jews who have no Jewish name are assigned the name Sarah or Israel. For convenience."

"I see," said Clara. "Very sensible."

"Clara with a 'C' Lehrs is renting a room from me for the time being," said Dr Kühn. "She's out shopping at the moment. You know that it can be difficult. She'll probably be some time."

"That is satisfactory," said the officer. "Can we proceed on the tour?"

Obersturmführer Poll looked carefully at pieces of furniture and the decoration as they went from room to room.

"And all of the furnishings are your own?" he asked.

"Oh, no, no, no," replied Emil. "I arranged with Frau Lehrs to keep them."

"The woman obviously has excellent taste," said Clara.

"Especially for a Jew," said Obersturmführer Poll. "I hope you got it all for a fair price."

"Extremely fair, I would say," said Clara.

The officer started to go down the cellar steps.

"Anyway, as you can see, all there is down here is a boiler room," said Emil Kühn as their visitor arrived at the bottom.

"What about this door?" asked the officer, rattling the handle of the classroom.

"Oh, Frau Lehrs couldn't find the key," said Emil. "She's not used this room for years. She thinks it's full of old junk. We're going to get a locksmith to come and open it. You do appreciate; we couldn't really start doing anything until today."

"Very well," said Obersturmführer Poll. "All seems to be in order. You do realise this can only be a temporary arrangement for the Jewess. I'll leave you in peace. Thank you for your time. I can see myself out." He clicked his heels. "Heil Hitler!"

"Heil Hitler," mumbled Emil.

The officer ran up the stairs and out of the front door, slamming it behind him.

Clara followed Christoph, who rushed down the stairs and unlocked the door to the classroom.

"You can breathe easy, now, children," said Clara.

Hani was red-faced and frowning. "Oh bugger old fury-chops," she said. "I'll give him 'Heil'!"

All of the children stared at her. Christoph's mouth was open.

What had the girl said? Clara tittered "Old fury-chops?" She giggled again. What a good name for the horrid little man.

One or two of the children began to snigger. Within seconds everybody was laughing loudly.

Hani's face became again. "Oh, I told Frau Schröder we would let her know when it was safe to come back."

"I suppose I'd better go and telephone her," said Clara, though she wasn't sure she would be able to keep her face straight long enough to make the call. She was still giggling as she made her way into the hall.

27 September 1939, Stuttgart: war

Clara found it hard to believe that they had been at war for almost a month. She was at war with her children. They were all in England and England had declared war on Germany. It didn't really feel like war though. Everything was carrying on as normal. The sun was shining, too. And everybody said it would all be over by Christmas.

Of course, though, they all had their ration cards. She looked at Christoph's. He had left it on the kitchen table. He got a little extra – just 62.5 grams of cheese in two weeks, 125 grams of butter and three eggs. There wouldn't be any more cheesecake any time soon, then. But he had told her something about being able to get some supplies from his uncle's farm.

Oh, she wished they would all come to their senses, these self-important men who thought they knew what was best for the world.

She could hear Christoph and Hani talking as they were tidying up some pieces of pottery that the special class children had made. One or two bits needed tweaking to make them stand upright, but Clara thought they were good on the whole. The two young people were quite animated as they talked. Clara guessed it wasn't the pots that worried them.

Oh dear. She expected Christoph might be called up soon. Why did they want to make these young men into soldiers? Why did they want to teach them to kill? Hopefully it wouldn't come to that. But it must be worrying for them.

The doorbell rang. Clara felt herself stiffen. For several seconds she couldn't move. The she took a deep breath and set off towards the front door. Hani and Christoph had stopped what they were doing. She raised her eyebrows at them and tried to smile. She hoped she'd been reassuring.

She felt as if she was moving in slow motion as she made her way towards the front door. Hani and Christoph followed her on tiptoe. Her hands trembled as she manipulated the latch.

It was the telegram boy. A weight flew from her chest.

"Telegram for Lehrs," he said.

"Thank you." Her relief was only fleeting. What could this contain? She started trembling and fumbled with the envelope. Then she smiled. It wasn't really a telegram at all. The writing was familiar. It was a Red Cross post card. From Renate.

"School now at Minehead. In a nice old house. Family has twin boys. Have to help with little ones. Help on farm too. People nice. English good now. Renate."

She handed the post card to Hani. "She's having plenty of adventures, then," she said. There was something she needed to do, though. She hated it. "But I'm going to tell her not to write any more. I don't want to make it difficult for her. We'd only be worried anyway, if we didn't hear and there'd probably actually be nothing wrong."

A shadow passed over Hani's face. I know, she thought. It's horrible. But we've got to do it. She tried to sound cheerful. "Anyway, this silly war will all be over by Christmas and that idiot man – what did you call him – old fury-chops? Maybe he will leave us alone as well." She giggled.

The girl smiled faintly. Oh dear, she was still worried. Well, they were worrying times but Clara knew it was best to keep cheerful.

Someone tapped three times lightly on the door. "Ah, here we go," said Clara. "Are you ready, Christoph?"

Christoph nodded.

She opened the door. It was Peter Schröder's mother. She was always so helpful and cheerful but today she looked worried. "Ah, Frau Schröder," said Clara. "Do come in."

Hani turned to go down the stairs. She could manage Peter by herself, Clara knew. He was able to walk very well on his own. She nodded to Hani.

But then Frau Schröder began to sob.

"My goodness, what is the matter, Frau Schröder?" said Clara. She had been right. Frau Schröder had been worried about something. "Come and sit down a while." She started to steer Frau Schröder towards the lounge. "Hans, would you go and fetch Frau Schröder a glass of water. Christoph, you're on door duty."

Hani brought the glass of water to Frau Schröder.

"Thank you," she said. "I'm sorry to make such a fuss. But you know, every day when I come here I'm quite surprised to find Peter still here. One day they will come to get him. One day they will take him away. It's not only the Jews, you know. It's everybody who is defective. And my little boy's not whole."

"But he's so precious," said Clara. "And we shall continue to look after him well. You know that, don't you?" The boy was a treasure. How could anybody think he wasn't worth the effort just because he took a little more looking after than a normal boy?

Frau Schröder nodded.

"We are blessed," said Clara. "Someone, somewhere is looking after us." Kurt's angels, maybe? What that boy used to say had seemed so exaggerated at the time but now it really did seem as if someone was looking after them.

There was the sound of two sets of footsteps on the stairs coming up from the cellar.

"Where's Mutti?" they heard Peter say.

"You can go into the lounge," said Christoph. "Your mother's in there."

Clara squeezed Frau Schröder's hand.

The lounge door opened and in ran Peter. "Mutti, why have you been crying?"

Frau Schröder laughed. "Because I am so happy that Frau Lehrs and Hans and Christoph, and Doctor Schubert of course, have been looking after you so well. And I know they're going to carry on doing that."

I hope so, thought Clara.

"Can we go home, Mutti?" said Peter.

Clara thought for a long time about what had happened that afternoon. In fact, Karl found her sitting in the dark just before supper, her afternoon tea cold and untouched.

"Clara, is there something wrong?" he asked.

Clara shook her head. "No. Not at all. Karl, do you believe in angels?"

"Yes. Yes, I do. But I don't think we really understand exactly what they are."

"No, probably not. Kurt did, though didn't he? I wonder whether he still does."

"I should think so." Karl laughed. "He wouldn't let a little thing like a war or a spot of persecution put him off, would he?"

"No, he most certainly wouldn't. Sensible young man. Do you think someone is looking after us? Someone human, I mean, not angelic?"

Karl shrugged. "I don't know. They did send that SS man."

"Oh yes. Obersturmführer Poll." She smiled when she remembered their conversation. "So perhaps it's the angels after all."

Her eyes met Karl's. She could tell that he was as aware as she was that they were in the middle of something big, very big indeed but neither of them could give it a name.

She stood up. "Right," she said trying to make her voice sound as bright as possible. "I'd better make a start on some supper."

22 April 1940, Stuttgart: new housekeeper

"So, she's really happy to do that for Doctor Kühn?"

"Yes. She says she doesn't care about not being able to study. She prefers housework."

"It's a shame. She's still a young girl. She should be enjoying herself at her age."

"Ah well. Chance would be a fine thing." Helga scrubbed the potato hard. She gritted her teeth as she did it. Then she stopped and laughed. "There's one thing about it, though. It saves the problem of – you know." Helga gestured to her chest.

Clara tittered. Yes, it was getting difficult to carry on calling Hani Hans. She was really becoming a young woman.

"And another thing. At least she won't have to go away from home to do her RAD. It's quite cruel. I think, how they take these young women go away from home to do this hard domestic work. Much better that she's amongst people she knows."

"No, that's good. You'd miss her." Clara finished scrubbing the last of her potatoes and started to chop them. She wasn't sure she thought it was right, anyway, sending these young girls out to work in unfamiliar homes. It wasn't natural. "Of course, I'll carry on looking after the house as usual. Karl will want her to work with the class more than anything."

"It's a disgrace, Clara, that Emil isn't allowed to pay you for your work here."

Clara shrugged. "I have all I need. So, when will Fräulein Gödde start? Goodness, doesn't it sound funny calling her that?"

"As soon as school's finished. As long as all the paperwork's come through."

"I'll finish these off. You go and see how they're getting on."

She chopped the rest of the potatoes making her knife as noisy as she could on the board. They were mad if they thought she wouldn't work. As if she could be idle. The money didn't matter. It didn't matter at all. There was just the work. Work was everything.

14 January 1941, Stuttgart: more visitors

"Why do you always have to go and do cooking?" asked Peter. "And why do you always have to wear an apron like an old Hausfrau?"

"Well, you know it's because I'm Doctor Kühn's housekeeper," replied Hani.

"But you're not," complained Peter. "Frau Lehrs is."

"Frau Lehrs is getting a bit too old to work all the time," said Hani.

Am I? thought Clara. We'll see about that.

"No, she isn't," said Peter. "She still plays with us and she still makes us nice cake."

I do my best with what we've got, thought Clara.

Hani sighed. Well, it was her turn to get the lunch. Clara guessed she'd rather stay down there with the children. But the girl was turning out to be quite a good cook. She didn't need to sigh, really.

"I liked it better when you were Hans," said Peter. "Why can't you stay and play with us?"

Clara hoped that Hani had remembered there was a pot of water about to boil waiting for her in the kitchen. She must get the Spätzle on so that they were ready at the same time as the stew. It was always tricky getting it exactly right: cook them for too long and they would stick to the pan and if you didn't cook them long enough they were chewy. It wasn't as easy as with the dried Italian pasta.

"I look too much like a girl these days to pretend to be Hans," said Hani.

Clara smiled to herself. Hani was rather good. She managed to tell the children enough to stop them being curious but not so much that they might give themselves away if questioned. "Come, on, Peter," said Clara. "Let me read you a story until lunch is ready."

Hani made her way up to the kitchen. She'd be back down soon with the tray of meals for the children and the parents would be here soon for the others. Clara was relieved though that she had bothered to push the big cupboard in front of the door. It really helped to make it look as if the basement only held the boiler room. After the last visit from the SS, Christoph, Karl and Emil had rearranged the garden, exactly the same as Herr Ehrlichmann had done to his, so that you could see nothing of the extended basement from the outside of the house. It meant there was no natural light going into the classroom but it did make it safer.

They were all always covered in bruises from pushing the heavy piece of furniture backwards and forwards. Clara heard the familiar scraping across the floor and knew that they were safe. For the time being at least.

"Right," she said settling Peter on her lap. "Which story would you like? The one about the little girl with the lovely red cloak or the one about the beautiful princess who sleeps for a hundred years?"

"Neither," said Peter. "I'd really like one about pirates and robbers."

"Oh, that's not so nice," said Clara.

"Something a bit quieter, Peter," said Karl.

The little boy jumped down and wandered over to the book case and chose a book that had a picture of moths on the front.

"That's fine," said Clara softly. "We can read a book about nature study if you like."

Peter clambered back on to Clara's lap and stuck his thumb in his mouth.

Clara opened the first page of the book. "Oh, look," she whispered. "Doesn't it have splendid wings?"

Then the doorbell rang.

Why did people always have to turn up just before the parents were due to arrive?

Clara put her finger to her lips.

"Hush, children. Quiet now," said Karl.

They heard Hani go along the hallway and then the front door opened.

"Heil Hitler!" said a mature man's voice.

They heard Hani mumble a reply.

"My, my, young Sturmmann Fink," said the voice.

There were two of them then?

"I think you're in with a chance there. The young lady is quite taken with you. It looks as if she already has the desired Hausfrau skills. Pity she's working in a house where a Jew has lived – still lives in fact – and a pity her hair is so dark. But I expect nevertheless she's a good Aryan specimen or she wouldn't be allowed to do this job." He laughed. "Is the Jew at home?" he said more soberly. "We have some paperwork for her."

"I- I- I'm a-a-fraid she's out," stammered Hani. "She keeps out of our way most of the time."

"Well, will you give her this?" said the officer. There was a pause. "You won't mind, will you," said the officer, "if we take a look around? We want to make sure that she is not hiding any of her friends here."

At that moment Emil arrived. "It's all right, Fräulein Gödde," he said. "I can take it from here. I trust this won't take long," he said. "I'm expecting some guests for a working lunch. I'm sure you'll excuse my housekeeper if she gets back to the kitchen."

They couldn't make out what was being said after that. The children carried on with their activities but seemed to know they must keep quiet. Clara and Peter looked at the pictures in the book, trying to turn the pages without making a sound.

Then they heard footsteps coming down to the basement. Clara and Karl didn't have to tell the children what to do. They sat absolutely still and didn't make a sound at all.

"You see," said Emil. "The cellar only extends this far."

"Hmm," said the officer. "So what's with this cupboard? You know, people have been known to hide Jews behind cupboards. Sturmmann Fink, will you please take a look."

Clara's heart was going so fast and thumping so hard that she was sure everyone could hear it smashing into her rib cage.

Then they heard the three quiet taps on the front door. One of the parents was arriving. Clara and Karl exchanged a glance. This was awful. They were going to be found out and then what would happen?

Clara held her breath as she heard Hani open the door.

"Good afternoon, Herr Becker," she heard Hani say. "I'm afraid the lunch will be a little delayed. We've had some unexpected visitors."

Was she speaking so loudly for the officer to hear or so that they could? Despite everything Clara couldn't help smiling. Poor Herr Becker would probably be totally bewildered and wouldn't be able to work out why he was being invited to lunch. Oh, she hoped he understood what Hani was trying to do.

But then somebody was prodding and pushing at the cupboard.

"There can't be anything behind here," she heard the younger man say. There was something oddly familiar about his voice now that he was so close to them. "It's screwed to the wall. Anyway, nobody could move that in a hurry."

You'd be surprised, thought Clara. But who was this young man? What did he mean, the cupboard was screwed to the wall?

"Gentlemen, can we hurry this up?" she heard Doctor Kühn say. "I believe another of my guests has arrived."

Then there were another three taps on the front door. Clara listened hard and recognised Frau Schröder's voice. Another lunch guest, then?

Clara smiled again and Peter put his hand in front of his mouth and pretended to laugh.

Clara put a warning finger on her lips.

The footsteps went back up the staircase.

"Thank you, and good day to you," the officer said. "At least you won't have to put up with the Jew for much longer. Heil Hitler!"

Clara winced as she thought of him saluting and Emil and Hani returning the salute. The door banged. She was pleased that neither Emil nor Hani had said goodbye.

It was chaotic after that for the next hour and a half. They had to get the children who were staying fed and they had to get the ones who were going home out safely and explain to the parents who came to collect them that there had been another visit and that they'd got to take even more care in future. The children

278

themselves, who had been really good while it was all going on, were now quite excited. Then there was the meal itself and the clearing up afterwards.

Hani was rather quiet, Clara realised. "Are you all right?" she said to the girl when she had a moment.

Hani nodded. "It was such a shock seeing Wilhelm like that."

"Wilhelm?"

Hani nodded again. "He used to work for us before he got called up."

"Yes, of course. I remember him. No wonder his voice had been so familiar then. And good of him to make out that the cupboard was screwed to the wall."

Soon it was time for all the children who were going home to go, and then those who were staying were hidden safely behind the cupboard, having their nap. All of the dishes that were waiting to be washed up were in the kitchen.

Hani was still quiet and she was pale as well.

"There is something else, isn't there, my dear?" said Clara.

Hani sighed. "They left you this." She took an envelope out of her apron pocket and handed it to Clara.

Clara's hands shook as she took it. The great swastika and the picture of the eagle jumped at her. The ink was blacker than she'd ever seen before. It was even more threatening than the other letter she'd had.

She thought she knew what it contained. "Ah! I think I'll take this up to my room and read it quietly. I have a feeling it may take some digesting."

An hour later Clara was still sitting staring at the letter. It had been short and to the point. She was no longer allowed to live in the house on Schellberg Street. She had to go and live in one of the ghettos. She, Klara Sarah – Klara Sarah, indeed – was no longer allowed to live with proper Aryan Germans. Almost immediately.

One of the places they'd mentioned was Rexingen. She had some cousins there, didn't she? If they were still alive, of course. She would see if she they would have her.

The noises of washing up had stopped. It was quiet downstairs. Perhaps Hani had gone home or maybe they were all working in the cellar. She'd better go and see.

She could hear Karl and Hani talking as she got nearer.

"I should get you to do this more often," said Karl. "You're really good at it."

Hani laughed. "I would have quite liked to have been a teacher if it wasn't for all of the studying."

"You should be ashamed of yourself, Hani Gödde," said Clara. "You should always follow your dream, no matter what it costs. Am I to presume you are still here because you are so nosy? You want to know what was in that letter."

"Well it might be an idea if you told us," said Karl, "in case it's something we can help with."

"You can't," said Frau Lehrs. "There's nothing we need worry about yet. Now, who would like some tea? And there are some vanilla biscuits I baked last night."

7 January 1942, Stuttgart: leaving and arriving

"You're sure you don't want me to drive you there? Or Karl can go with you on the train?" said Emil.

"No, not at all. I don't want to get any of you into trouble."

"Clara, it is no trouble you know that."

"It's fine," she said. "I don't have much to carry."

All three of them looked down at the small suitcase and basket she had packed. Emil had given her a thick travelling rug. "For the journey," he'd said. "It will keep out the cold. You may need it afterwards, Clara. To keep out the cold." Was she imagining it? Was there something sinister in what he was saying? Why had he said it twice? She knew, though, he wasn't talking about the winter.

"Let us at least bring you to the station," said Karl.

"No. I want to be on my own and have time to think a bit."

Karl shook his head. "Clara, really."

"Well, you can help me as far as the tram stop. It's still slippery." She'd never ever been so grateful for snow. It had delayed this journey by five days.

No one said anything for a few minutes.

"Well," said Clara. "I suppose I'd better get going."

The three of them had to concentrate quite hard as they walked to the tram. It had started to snow again. Despite everything, Clara now hoped that there would be no delays. If she was going live in Rexingen, she wanted to get there as soon as possible.

A couple of times she almost slipped. She was glad that these two younger, strong men were carrying her luggage for her.

There wasn't actually much opportunity for conversation.

Almost as soon as they got to the stop, a tram arrived. It took a couple of minutes to get Clara and her luggage on board and the driver was anxious to get going. It was mid-morning and there were only a few other passengers. None of them were too interested in her. Most of them gazed out of the windows, lost in their own thoughts. Clara was glad there was no time for any protracted goodbyes. It was better this way. It was as if she was going on a normal journey.

I wonder whether they know, thought Clara. They probably didn't. She was an ordinary German – yes German – elderly housewife off to visit friends for an extended holiday. Yes, she must think of it that way.

But also, she must make the most of this journey. This town had been her home for many years. Goodness knows when she'd be back... if at all... at her age.

The tram trundled gently down into the centre. The snow was stopping and a watery sun was shining on the other six hills. This was so different from the other tram rides. When she took Leo, then Käthe and eventually even Rudi all over Berlin. You didn't get views like this from those trams.

Too soon they arrived at the main station. Oddly Clara began to feel excited. She'd told Hani and Christoph that she was going on holiday. She really felt as if she was, now. A kind gentleman helped her with her luggage to the right platform. Did he know? He didn't look as if he did. And she loved stations. She always had. All that hissing steam and those loud toots. Then the chug-chug as the trains set off. All going to exciting destinations.

Rexingen? Was that place exciting? Well, it wasn't that far away but it was on the edge of the Black Forest. The Black Forest was a lovely place for walking holidays. She was going to get to know some new people. Yes, all of this was exciting, actually.

Her train chuffed into the station. She was travelling third class. But that didn't matter. It was still an adventure.

A few minutes later she was settled in a seat next to the window. Of course, this wasn't quite what she was used to. She'd always travelled first class before. It wasn't going to be a long journey, though. She could put up with the hard bench for that short time. And it didn't smell. Were the rest of the people in the carriage like her, having to go and live in a certain place because of the families they came from? Anyway, it certainly wasn't like the first time she went on the tram in Berlin.

It soon became crowded and it was quite warm by the time the train set off. At first it was engulfed in its own steam but then that cleared and Clara could see Stuttgart out of the window.

This is not the last time, she thought. I shall be back. Yes, she would be back and she would take her house back. Sometime in the future. Now, though, she would try to enjoy Rexingen. There would be fresh air. Walks in the sunshine. Berries to be collected and eaten later in the year. Perhaps there would be a garden. They could grow vegetables.

They were soon out of the town. Clara wiped the mist from the window so that she could see the snow-covered countryside. It was beautiful even in the winter. She should count herself lucky. Yes, she was going to a ghetto. But at least it wasn't a squalid part of some town. She would be able to breathe in Rexingen.

They raced past the fields and the woods. The landscape became hillier. The sun was getting low in the sky and she worried that it might start snowing again or would become so cloudy that it would got dark early.

The train stopped.

"Excuse me," she said as she tried to get to the door with her luggage.

A young man dressed in dark clothes took her suitcase and basket. "Make way for the lady," he called to the fellow passengers.

Seconds later, Clara was standing on the platform, a mist of steam from the engine swirling around her. As it cleared, she caught a glimpse of the surrounding countryside and a few lonely looking buildings.

So, she thought. This is to be my home. So be it.

Where should she go now? They'd told her the house was 6 Gaisgasse, but where was that? Maybe she would ask directions. She hoped it wouldn't be too far. Her case and her basket were light but they would soon become heavier if she started to walk.

A young man stood on the platform. He looked thin and cold. His clothes were totally inadequate. He wore the little black skull-cap her brothers had only worn occasionally. But seeing him dressed like that reminded her of all those years ago when they all lived in the big house in Mecklenburg.

"Are you Frau Lehrs?" the young man asked.

"Yes, I am."

"I am Shmuel. I am the grandson of your cousin Jakob."

Clara nodded.

"I'm to take you to the big house first. Then my mother will show you your room. I have Adiv and the sleigh here."

"Adiv?"

"He's our horse. He's strong but thin. I don't think you will be too heavy, Frau Lehrs. Nor your luggage."

It was beginning to get dark as Shmuel helped Clara on to the sleigh and stacked her luggage safely. They made slow progress up the winding lane. The horse was not in a good condition. She could have walked beside the boy but she thought she might offend him if she suggested it.

They moved in silence. Shmuel wasn't inclined to make conversation. Besides, the sleigh creaked quite noisily and the runners screeched as they slid across the snow.

Soon, though, they arrived in what Clara presumed must be the middle of the village. There was light coming out of several windows.

"Come," said Shmuel. "We all meet in the big house in the evening. We light a big fire and we keep warm. My mother makes soup for everyone from what my father, my uncles and my brothers have caught in the woods." He started to unload her luggage. "By the way," he said, waving his hand at a dark alley. "That's Gaisgasse. Your room is in number six, at the other end."

"Can we go there? I'd like to see where I'm going to stay."

"If we are quick. My mother is anxious to meet you."

"We'll take my things up there and then we'll hurry back."

Shmuel nodded.

He took Clara's luggage and started marching up the alleyway. It was quite dark but a thin light shone through one window. They arrived at the last house. Shmuel pushed the front door open. "I'm afraid it sticks, and it doesn't shut properly but at least you will live on the second floor. You won't feel the draught. I'm sorry – the light doesn't work here."

Clara made her way carefully up the stairs. At least the light worked on the first floor but it only served to show her how threadbare the carpets were. The walls had dirty marks on them and the paint was flaking off in several places. There was a damp, musty smell about the place.

Clara followed Shmuel along the corridor. He stopped by the third room on the right and opened it. He flicked on the light switch.

Clara's heart sank when she saw the room. It was so shabby and neglected. "My mother didn't want you to see it like this. She wanted to meet you first and then she was going to come back with you and help you to make it more comfortable."

"Oh we can soon do that," said Clara. "I can put this lovely blanket over the chair. And I have some scarves in my suitcase."

"There's a small paraffin stove and we have plenty of paraffin. You can use that to keep you warm during the day. It smells a bit, though." Shmuel wrinkled up his nose.

"Yes, we can certainly make this cosy." It would be quite a challenge, Clara knew. Still, there was always something you could do. She didn't believe in giving into despair.

"May I take you to the big house, Frau Lehrs?"

"Yes. Yes. Let's go and meet your mother."

Shmuel led Clara back down the alley and round the corner to where the bigger houses were. She could see that several people including some family groups were making their way into one of the houses.

"Come," said Shmuel.

She followed him thought the front door, and into a large sitting room where a log fire blazed. There was a delicious smell of hot soup. How do they do it? Shmuel had said that they went hunting, hadn't he? They must be quite skilled then.

One of the men tapped another young man on his shoulder. The young man got up immediately and gave his seat to Clara. A few moments later, someone offered her a bowl of soup and a chunk of coarse brown bread. She hadn't realised how hungry she was. It tasted delicious though she couldn't tell exactly what was in it. Perhaps it was better not to know.

A woman about the same age as Helga Gödde came and sat next to her. Her clothes were shabby and she looked tired. Yet as soon as she saw Clara her eyes lit up.

"Frau Lehrs?" she asked.

"Yes. Are you Shmuel's mother?"

"Yes. Your cousin Jakob's daughter-in-law. Esther."

"Please call me Clara. Is Jakob here?" Clara held out her hand to Esther.

"He's in the barn looking after Adiv."

"Is there something wrong with the horse?"

"No, no, except that he's hungry. But we try to look after him as well as we can."

It was beginning to get so warm in the room that Clara had to remove the woollen cardigan she was wearing over her blouse. She noticed that although everyone looked tired they were beginning to chat and laugh as the fire warmed them.

"This is a very good idea," said Clara. "Gathering everyone together in the evening."

Esther smiled. "We think so. It saves on fuel and makes people less anxious." She rubbed Clara's arm. "I'm sorry about your room. I didn't want Shmuel to show it to you until I could explain. I'm afraid it's all we've got. But I will help you to make it more comfortable."

"I'm sure we'll work well together."

Clara looked at the people around her. They weren't such strangers really. She'd always kept her Jewish friends and she remembered lots of the people she'd known when she was a young girl. This was her home. And she would make the best of it.

22 January 1942, Rexingen: new friends

Clara was used to the smell of the paraffin stove. It didn't bother her anymore. And it did keep her room quite cosy though it was always cold when she woke up in the mornings. The trick was to sleep in as many clothes as possible. The trouble with that, though, was that you couldn't move much in your sleep and you woke up stiff. Never mind. The days were getting longer and it would soon warm up. In fact it was sunny today.

She looked around her room. It was quite cosy. Esther had given her a pretty cloth to cover the old rickety table and she had photos of the family on show. She and Esther had worked hard in the first couple of days to get rid of all of the dust and to make the windows shine. After that she'd been able to keep it nice and clean.

It hadn't taken her long to realise that her clothes were too bright. All the older women here wore mainly black. So, she'd given her brighter things to the clothes store. She hoped some younger woman would be happy to wear them. And she'd selected some darker ones for herself. Not all of them black, though. And though she'd not really liked the thought of wearing second-hand clothes, she'd had to admit that these one had been well laundered. At least she looked like the other women her age.

Everyone had been so friendly and she'd actually begun to look forward to the evenings by the fire in the big house.

"You must let me help with some of the work," she'd said to Esther.

"We wouldn't dream of it," Esther said. "An old lady like you should be getting some rest at your time in life."

Clara wasn't so sure about that. She knew Esther had not meant it unkindly. But she was also missing the Hilfsklasse. She must find something to do, something to make herself useful.

She looked out of the window. It certainly was a fine day. She would wrap up warm, go out and see who she could get talking to.

She was already wearing two shawls and managed to pull her thick overcoat over those. She pulled one of the shawls up to cover her head. A real Jewish woman, she thought as she made her way outside. Even if she was really wearing these clothes to keep warm, at least she would look quite normal walking through the streets of the little town.

It was so cold outside that she could see her breath. But she didn't feel too cold as the air was still and even the weak winter sun had some warmth in it. In fact, as she walked along she began to feel almost too warm and soon had to discard one of the shawls. Everyone was busy and she really didn't want to disturb them at their work. Some of the children were at Schul and she would have loved to help but she probably wasn't Jewish enough.

It was hard work for everyone, just to survive. She could see that. The men who weren't out looking for rabbits or birds to kill were mending things though they hadn't got the right material or equipment. The women were busy looking after the children, making meals with unusual ingredients, cleaning and mending clothes and trying to make the poor living places as cheerful as possible.

One or two people greeted her as she went along but no one had time to chat for longer. She saw Shmuel harnessing Adiv to the sleigh.

"No Schul today?" she asked.

"No, it's my turn to do the mid-week wood collection. We older boys take it in turns."

"That's a shame. You're missing out on your education."

Shmuel shrugged. "I don't mind. I like doing the men's work."

Clara smiled. He was certainly grown-up for his fourteen years.

"What's the matter, Frau Lehrs? Is there a problem?"

"No, no, Shmuel. It's fine." Clara smiled. It wasn't fine, though. The boy shouldn't be working like that. And he shouldn't be so thin.

She watched as he and Adiv set off. There was nothing she could do to help.

They were brave, both of them.

She turned back towards the village. A young woman was sitting on a log. She was bending and her hand was in front of her mouth. She leant forward and vomited.

The poor girl. She remembered how sick she had been when she had been expecting Käthe. Leo had been so small at that time. Yes, it was a strange how Leo had reacted to the crucifix but that had not made her feel nauseous. There had been such a definite physical cause for that. She was expecting a baby. And that was exactly what was the matter with that young woman. The woman leant forward and vomited again.

She needed some help. Clara was sure of that. She started making her way over to her. "Can I help, my dear?" she said as she got closer. The woman got up from the log, tears in her eyes. She shook her head and ran away.

"It's tragic," said a voice.

Clara turned round to see Esther standing next to her.

"Her husband died four weeks ago. Influenza. There was nothing anyone could do. A child is on the way. And there is the other little one too."

Clara nodded. It was such a sad world to bring a child into. And so this woman already had another to look after. The poor woman must be worn out.

"Is there anything we can do to help?"

Esther shook her head. "She's too proud. She needs good nourishment but as you know that isn't always possible here."

"There must be something, though," said Clara.

Esther shrugged. "We've tried everything." She turned and went back towards the big house.

"What's her name?" called Clara.

"Selda."

Selda. Could she help Selda?

She didn't have long to think about that. A tiny girl, not more than three or four years old, appeared from nowhere and rushed past. "Mutti! Mutti!" she cried, running in the direction that Selda had gone. The young woman didn't appear to hear her. And then the child tripped and fell right in front of Clara.

The little girl started to howl.

"Oh dear, oh dear," said Clara. She bent down and helped the child up. Her legs had not been protected by any stockings and her

289

knee was bleeding quite spectacularly. It would need cleaning and probably covering for a while. Not so easy with cold water and a lack of medical supplies. Clara knew she should do something. She didn't want to take her away from her mother but in fact she couldn't see the girl's mother at all.

Esther had seen it all and came rushing up to Clara. "Kyla, are you hurt."

"I want my Mutti," said the little girl. Her chin wobbled and she was surely going to start crying again.

Esther shook her head. "I told Selda to go and get some rest and that I'd keep an eye on Kyla but there is so much to do and of course, she's too little to understand that her mother needs some time to herself."

Clara had already taken the little girl's hand and the child had a thumb in her mouth, though silent tears were crawling down her cheeks.

"I could take her to my room and bathe her knee. I think I can find an old scarf to wrap round it. And then maybe I could tell her some stories and we could sing some songs." She put an arm around the girl and then bent down so that their faces were level. "Would you like that, Kyla? Then by the time we've done all of that your knee will feel better and we can go back to your house and Mutti will have had a rest as well? Perhaps she'll feel better, too. Would that be a good idea?"

The little girl nodded. Her dark brown eyes looked deep into Clara's and then she smiled.

"Frau Lehrs, you are a miracle worker. How do you do it?" Esther shook her head and smiled.

"I'm used to children," said Clara.

"Thank you so much!"

A few moments later they were both in Clara's room.

"Sit there like a good girl while I go and get some water for your knee," said Clara. "I really won't be long at all."

Kyla nodded.

The water in the tap was cold, of course but it would have to do. She still had a scrap of soap left. That at least might clean the

290

wound. She found a piece of grey towel that had once been white. At least it was clean. She took that all back to her room.

Soon she was bathing the little girl's knee. Kyla squirmed.

"Does it sting?" said Clara.

"Tickles!" Kyla giggled.

"Well, that's a good sign."

The knee had stopped bleeding but Clara knew it needed to be covered and kept clean. She had kept back one favourite scarf, a chiffon one with wild flowers printed on it. She took it out of the drawer and wrapped it carefully round the girl's knee. "There now. Is that better?"

Kyla nodded.

"Shall we have a story?"

"Yes, please."

"Do you have a favourite one?"

"The one about the princess who pricks her finger and sleeps for a hundred years."

"Then that is what we shall have."

Clara sat down on her old lumpy armchair and pulled Kyla on to her lap. The little girl snuggled up to her and between them they managed to tell the story.

"Can I go and find my Mutti?" said Kyla when they had finished.

"I think we can do that," said Clara. "We'll go together, shall we?"

Kyla nodded. "What shall I call you?"

"What about Mutti Lehrs? That's what some other children I looked after used to call me."

"Mutti Lehrs," said Kyla slipping her hand into Clara's.

So, I have something to do, thought Clara.

15 February 1942: old friends

It was quiet. Too quiet. Maybe it was that extra blanket of snow. It covered the ground and softened the sounds all around. None of the children had come to see Clara today. That was unusual for a Sunday. Yes, Saturday was their day of worship and a little work was sometimes done on a Sunday. There was no Schul, so the younger children had come to see her for the last couple of weeks whilst their parents got on with some of their chores. And it was official: they'd all started calling her Mutti Lehrs. But today there could be little work done because of the snow and she guessed everyone was having some extra family time.

She gazed over at the pictures of her own family. How different it all was. Ernst was dead and the rest of them were in England. Germany was throwing bombs at England and England was throwing them at Germany. Madness. Goodness knows if they were even alive.

Oh, such gloomy thoughts. They wouldn't lead anywhere. She had some work to do here and she was making herself useful. Just not today.

She heard a soft neighing outside. Adiv. She got up out of her chair and wandered over to the window. Yes, sure enough Shmuel was harnessing the horse to the sleigh. The animal and the boy looked as thin as each other. But Shmuel was still enthusiastic and the horse didn't complain. Good for them.

Shmuel noticed her watching, grinned and waved. Yes, she had friends here. She must be grateful for that. She mustn't mope.

She decided she would write to her family. Of course, she wouldn't be able to send the letter for some time, not until the war ended and goodness knows where she would send it but she should tell them about her experiences here. She would address the letter to all of them but hoped she would find Ernst junior at some point and then she could send it to him with instructions to pass on her news to the others. This was a good plan. And it would stop her feeling sorry for herself.

She took her pen and some paper out of the little rickety cupboard and sat down at her table to write. She soon became really absorbed in what she was doing and although she heard Shmuel and Adiv come back with the sleigh she didn't get up from her table straight away to go and look through the window. She thought she'd heard voices she didn't recognise but when she looked outside there was no sign of anyone except Shmuel and his father, his uncle and his brother who were unloading the wood from the sleigh.

I'm imagining things, she thought. Age, I expect.

She felt quite sleepy and as soon as she'd finished off her letter and put it and her writing materials back in the cupboard she sat down again in her armchair and closed her eyes.

She woke with a start when the door was pushed gently open. Someone was coming into the room. What did they want with her?

Then she realised. She should have recognised those voices earlier. Of course she should have. Hani and Helga! Hani and Helga were here. Unbelievable! How had they known where to find her? Would they get into trouble for coming here?

She got up out of her seat. "How nice to see you. Come in. So kind of you to come and see me."

Helga was holding a huge basket full of groceries. She heaved it up on to the table. "We've brought you a few things."

A few things? Enough supplies for the rest of the winter, Clara thought as she looked at the basket on the table and the smaller one Hani was carrying along with some bags.

"Oh, that is so generous of you," said Clara. "I'm afraid I have nothing to offer you. But come and get warm."

She noticed Hani wrinkle up her nose. "I'm sorry about the smell," Clara said. "You do get used to it after a while. They won't let us buy any fuel for the central heating. But there was a good supply of paraffin on one of the farms. And then every evening we gather in the big living room of the house next door and sit round a log fire."

"That's what Shmuel had been collecting the logs for," said Hani.

"Yes, he's a good boy," said Clara. "He and his brother. Now let me see what you've brought me. I'll have to give some to the family next door."

"But we brought it all for you," said Helga. "It's so kind of you. You really shouldn't. We've already given him a loaf of bread."

"Oh, but the young people need the extra food more than I do," said Clara.

"How are, you, really?" said Helga, helping her to unpack the bags and the basket. There was more bread, some apples, some large overstuffed Maultaschen, Spätzle, two cabbages, some sugar, a dark Pumpernickel loaf and some peppermint tea.

"Oh, I'll do," said Clara. "We have just about enough. They're letting us keep everything from the farms at the moment, though soon there won't be any eggs. We're having to kill off the chickens one by one."

It was foolish, she'd thought, killing off the chickens. Much better, really, to carry on enjoying their eggs. But people were so desperate for food, for meat in particular.

"How are you getting on with everybody?" asked Helga. "Is it strange for you, being with so many practising Jews?"

But they're such lovely people, thought Clara. "Everybody is really kind. They don't mind at all that I've become a Christian. And I do go to the synagogue with them on a Saturday now. It's the same god, after all. But you know, everybody here is a bit afraid, despite their faith. So, can I make you a cup of tea? I've only peppermint tea, I'm afraid."

"No, no, Clara," said Helga. "I've told you, these supplies are for you."

But the whole point of having food was to be able to share it, wasn't it? Never mind. They wanted to be kind and she ought to allow them to do just that. "Very well," she said. "Let's sit down and make ourselves cosy." She turned to Hani. "And you can tell me all about what's been happening with the special class. No more unexpected visits, I hope. I guess it's easier now that I'm out of the way."

The girls looked anxious. So perhaps things weren't going so well on Schellberg Street. Hani opened her mouth, though, to start telling her something when the door burst open and in ran Kyla. She was well dressed for the cold, but her jumper and leggings had great big holes in them. Her nose was running.

"'Mutti, Lehrs, Mutti Lehrs, tell me a story," said the little girl.

"But where is your own Mutti, Kyla?" asked Frau Lehrs.

Selda ran into the room. Her clothes were worn as well. She looked tired. Her dark hair was plaited and wound into coils over her ears, but many strands were escaping, and some were getting in her eyes. "I am so sorry, Frau Lehrs," she said.

Clara was aware that both Hani and Helga were staring at the young woman. They'd probably not realised how bad things were here.

"It's all right, Selda," Clara answered. "You can leave her with us. You should go and get some rest. But let me introduce you to my good friends Helga Gödde and her daughter, Hani. They have been so helpful to me."

"Any friend of Frau Lehrs is a friend of mine," said Selda. She shivered and swayed. She wasn't really getting any better, then.

"Go and lie down," Clara commanded. "We'll amuse Kyla."

"Thank you, Frau Lehrs. You are so kind."

"Remember," said Clara. "It will get better. You're almost through the worst stage. Spring is on its way." But it was taking a long time, Clara thought. She really should be better by now. Still, she mustn't let the young woman see how worried she was.

Selda nodded and smiled.

She turned to Helga and Hani. "The poor girl. She is in the first stage of a new pregnancy." She told them all about what had happened to Selda's husband. "And this child has so much energy. The poor woman is exhausted. I shall have to see what I can give her from what you've brought."

"But it's for you!" protested Helga again.

"She needs it more than I do," said Clara. "Come on. Let's see if we can sing some songs and tell some stories with this young lady." She looked over the child's head. "Don't say anything about the special class in front of any of the people here," she mouthed.

"What they don't know can't hurt them."

Hani looked as if she enjoyed playing with the little girl. She knew most of the songs that Kyla sang. She'd sung them herself as a child. Kyla knew a few more as well in Yiddish that Clara half knew.

"A long time since I've sung any of those," she said.

Kyla gobbled up the stories too. Little Red Riding Hood, Sleeping Beauty and Cinderella. Then Noah and his Arc, Moses in the Bulrushes, and Abraham and Isaac.

"Tell me the one about the tower falling down," said the little girl.

"Oh, that's not such a nice one," said Clara.

A pink glow burst into the room and lit it up.

"Will you look at that?" said Clara, picking up the little girl and holding her up to the window.

The grey clouds had rolled away leaving a few white ones against a pale blue sky. It faded to pink where the sun hung low. The snow-covered hills, no longer hidden by the mist, reflected the setting sun.

"See," said Clara. "The greyness always goes eventually."

The door opened gently. It was Selda.

"They'll be getting the fire ready in the big room next door," she said. "Are you going to come along, Frau Lehrs?"

"Well you look better, my dear," said Clara. "You know it is fine for you to leave this little one with me any time you like. She is such a good girl."

"Will you come with us?" said Selda to Hani and Helga.

"We ought to get back, really," said Helga. "We'll come again in two weeks' time. Is there anything particular you'd like us to bring you?"

"You might look out some clothing for this poor young woman and her child, if you have the chance," said Clara.

Selda blushed and looked at the floor.

Hani nodded thoughtfully.

"I think we could walk back to the station," said Helga. "It's a shame to disturb Shmuel and make that poor horse work again. It'll be easier now that the bags are empty."

"He'll be offended," said Clara.

Clara, Selda and Kyla waved though the window to Helga and Hani as they stepped out of the front door. Shmuel spotted them leaving straight away and Clara could see that he was insisting that her two friends should climb into the empty sleigh.

Water was dripping from the trees, Clara realised. She turned to Selda. "I think they'll be back and the next time they're here it will be spring. Adiv will soon be able to eat the fresh grass again."

Selda nodded.

"You see," said Clara. "We must always have hope."

Kyla was jumping up and down. "Mutti Lehrs, do you think they'll let me sing some of the songs I've practised? Tonight while we're by the big fire?"

Clara stoked the girl's hair. "I should think they will. And that will be splendid indeed."

Selda smiled and for the first time ever Clara thought she saw some light in the young woman's eyes.

14 May 1942, Rexingen: the keys of the kingdom

Clara had begun to feel more and more like the Pied Piper. She and Kyla and been going for a walk through the village and Amos and Ben had joined them. They were not much older than Kyla. Daniel and Eli had been helping their father repair an old cart but as the four of them had walked past Eli had cried "Where are you going, Mutti Lehrs? Can we come with you?"

"Doesn't your Vati need your help?" Clara had replied.

"It's all right. You can go," the boy's father had said. "They're actually more hindrance than help," he'd whispered to Clara. "I can get on much better without them."

So, then six of them had trooped on out of the village. Liah and Naomi had joined them because their mother was in a good mood and thought that on this fine day she could manage the big bake without them – having more people in the kitchen made it too hot. Clara knew, though, that really she was glad to send the girls away because they were rapidly running out of flour. Soon there would be no more bread at all. The girls were growing and were hungry all of the time. The good mood had been for show, then.

"Where are we going, Mutti Lehrs?" Eli asked.

"To look at nature and see how the flowers in the fields are clothed so beautifully yet they don't spin or weave," she'd replied.

The boy had looked puzzled but he'd carried on walking happily enough.

And here they were, sitting in the meadow, surrounded by poppies and cornflowers. The red and blue flowers were glorious and the grass was a lush green. The yellow bees were bright in the sunlight as they danced and buzzed.

Somewhere there will be honey, thought Clara. If only she knew how to keep bees. That was something else she must learn if she ever got the chance. "You see?" she said. All right, the bees are as busy as we are when we work. But look how happy they are. Look how they dance."

If only they weren't all so hungry. But soon there would be berries. And the vegetables they had planted were growing well. All they needed was sunshine and rain and there'd been plenty of both. You couldn't buy that. It was given freely.

You could live without bread or meat.

Clara noticed someone dressed all in black walking slowly across the meadow. Was it one of the older women, perhaps? She smiled at herself for thinking that: she was one of the older women herself, wasn't she? But she didn't feel like it at the moment surrounded by all these youngsters.

As the person got nearer she realised that it wasn't one of the women at all. It was Rabbi Freymiller. He wasn't a practising rabbi any more. He never led any of the meetings in the synagogue. Clara rather suspected that the new race laws and this war had made him lose his faith. Yet he still wore the black robes even when it wasn't the Sabbath. So, there must be something left. He was always kind anyway and she enjoyed his company.

Rabbi Freymiller was rather out of breath when he met them. "Not so young as I used to be," he complained.

"Come and sit with us," said Clara. "We're enjoying the flowers and the sunshine."

"I think if I sit down I may not be able to get up again," said the rabbi.

"Oh, we'll help you," said Ben.

"Yes we will," Amos added.

"Very well then." With a lot of effort and a considerable amount of groaning the old man sat down on the grass. "You are right to enjoy all of this." He waved his arm over the field. "It is God-given and priceless. No one can take this away from us. Not the Allies with their bombs, nor the Nazis with their Blutschutz laws."

Ah. So maybe he hadn't lost his faith after all. Or maybe it was changing. It was becoming more like her own.

"Has there been more news about the bombings?"

The rabbi nodded. "It's quite relentless. But the Germans are giving as good as they're getting." He shook his head. "The foolishness of men and war."

Clara's stomach flipped. What if her children and her grandchild were in London and the Germans were throwing bombs at them? He stomach flipped again when she realised that both she and the rabbi had referred to the Germans as if they were something different from themselves.

Rabbi Freymiller sighed. "I wish more had gone when all the young people went."

"The young people?"

"1938. They went to Israel. That's why there was room for people like your good self and why we needed more of our own to keep our little community alive."

Of course. She had heard a little about this. But there was nothing they could do except wait and hope.

A bee buzzed as it passed her ear. She could hear others in the background. The heads of the flowers bobbed in the gentle breeze. Then she realised. There was something she could do. Of course there was. What she did best.

"Come on," she said, getting up on to her feet. "Amos, Ben, help Rabbi Freymiller. Then, when you're back at the village go and tell all the grown-ups to meet an hour early at the big house and bring any food they have to share. And poems and stories they'd like to recite or read out loud. And musical instruments if they play them. Liah and Naomi, go and tell your mother and her helpers to meet me in an hour's time at the big house."

The children scrambled to their feet and with a bit of effort Amos and Ben managed to help the rabbi up.

"Boys," he said. "I will help you with your message. I don't know what Frau Lehrs is up to but whatever it is, it will be good. And we don't say no to Frau Lehrs, do we, eh?"

Clara laughed. She took Kyla by the hand. "You and I are going to pick a few flowers."

"There," said Clara, as they arranged the flowers in the chipped white jug on the little table at the front of the room. "Don't they look pretty? And remember; never pick too many wild flowers. They don't keep long and really they're best left for everyone to

300

enjoy outside. But today is important and we want to make the table look nice."

Kyla looked at her with those dark serious eyes.

Clara smiled. "These have lasted though. Because we dampened my scarf in the brook and wrapped them in that. If you do pick wild flowers you should always wrap them in some damp paper or a damp cloth so that they keep until you can put them into a jar of water."

Yes, the meeting room looked good. The sun was shining outside. The windows were open and it was pleasantly cool inside. Liah and Naomi's mother and the women who helped her with the cooking were laying out the little extras that everyone had brought along. Clara herself had donated the peppermint tea and the biscuits that Helga and Hani had brought along last Sunday. And someone had found some honey and they'd dissolved it in warm water to make a sweet drink for the children.

"Why did you want to start earlier?" asked Esther.

"Because I think we have something to be thankful for."

Esther raised her eyebrows. "Well we're all glad to stop working earlier, I guess."

Clara shrugged but looked towards her flower arrangement. Esther's eyes followed her gaze. She nodded and smiled.

The last of the group had come into the room. All eyes looked towards Clara and everyone stopped talking. It was time.

"This is the key of the kingdom," she started reciting. She had used this little poem so much with the Waldorf School children. It was good for her new friends too.

"In that kingdom there is a city.
In that city there is a town.
In that town there is a street.
In that street there is a lane.
In that lane there is a yard.
In that yard there is a house.
In that house there is a room.
In that room there is a bed.
On that bed there is a basket.

In that basket there are some flowers.
Flowers in a basket,
Basket on the bed,
Bed in the room,
Room in the house,
House in the yard,
Yard in the lane,
Lane in the street,
Street in the town,
Town in the city,
City in the kingdom.
Of that kingdom this is the key."

This was her contribution. This was what she could offer. She held her breath as she finished. What would they all make of that?

There was a few seconds' silence and then everyone started clapping.

22 August 1942, Rexingen: leaving

So, it had happened. What they'd all been dreading. The soldiers had arrived early that morning. They'd come quite calmly. They'd not made a big fuss. They'd told everyone to assemble in the big house.

"If anyone is caught hiding or if anyone tries to run away, there will be severe punishments," a big man in a fine uniform had said. "If you cooperate everything will be better for you. We are transporting you to a place where you can live more comfortably with your own kind. Please pack a small suitcase and report to the main house. Make sure you have any money handy. We need to charge you for your transport."

No one had argued. Everyone had done as they were told.

"Can I come with you?" Kyla had asked.

"I think you must stay and look after Mutti." It could be that they would take her somewhere different from the rest of the people. Perhaps an old people's home? She hoped Selda would be all right. She was enormous. Would she survive a journey? It looked as if the baby was due any second.

The soldiers weren't rough. They weren't friendly, either. Just ordinary men doing their jobs. Their eyes were cold though and nobody dared look at them or do anything other than what they'd been told to do.

Now they were waiting. Some people were sitting but most were standing. One by one they were called forward to talk to the officer in charge. Once the conversation was over, they were marched out to the trucks waiting outside and as these filled up, they set off.

The older children, Clara noticed, were being separated from their parents and the boys were being kept separate from the girls. Were they perhaps being taken to boarding school?

At last her name was called.

Clara pulled herself up out of her seat and shuffled over to the desk where the officer sat. She felt all of her seventy years. She was moving like other people her age did, not with her usual bounce and enthusiasm. What was happening to her?

"Frau Klara Sarah Lehrs?" said the officer.

Clara looked carefully at his face trying to see if there was any expression on it. He looked through and beyond her.

He's only doing his job, she thought. "It's just Clara Lehrs. Clara with a 'C,'" she said.

The man shook his head. "All Jews must germanise their names and if their name isn't Jewish, they must add a Jewish name. You know this, surely? So, Frau Klara Sarah Lehrs, how much money do you have?"

"Six thousand two hundred and sixty-four marks."

"That will do. It won't quite cover the cost of the transport and a few years in the old people's home. But it will be enough for now. Please give me the money."

Old people's home? So, she was right. But she didn't want to spend her time just with old people.

"Frau Lehrs?"

Clara nodded and opened her suitcase. She took out the envelope containing the rest of her money and handed it to the officer. He clicked his fingers and a young soldier came over and took the envelope. "Six thousand two hundred and sixty-four," she says. "Count it and see that it is all there." He turned back to Clara. "If there is a shortfall, and anyway if you live more than four years, we might find something to sell. Or find some work for you to do."

Four years? They were giving her four more years to live? She couldn't decide whether to she should celebrate that or worry about it.

The officer wrote something on a label and handed it to a young woman dressed in army uniform.

"Let me pin this to you," said the woman. "There will be a lot of people on the transports and this will help the operators to get you into the right place."

Clara stood up while the woman pinned the label on to her. She was able to read what it said. It was just a number: 811.

So, I'm a number now, she thought. She couldn't decide whether that was better or worse than being known by the wrong name. "Where am I going?" she said.

"To a lovely place called Terezin. Now hurry on out. You have a long journey ahead of you. My colleague will show you which truck to get into."

Clara picked up her suitcase and made her way out. Her steps were quicker again. It wasn't that she felt less old. She was old. They'd made that quite clear. It was more that she wanted to get this over with – whatever this was.

Three big army trucks stood outside. A soldier was standing near the door. "Over there," he said. He pointed to the truck on the left.

Clara walked over to it. Even the small case was getting heavy. Another soldier stood near to the truck. He snatched the case from her and threw it to the back of the vehicle. Then he hauled her up into the truck. He really held her arm quite tight.

Thank you. I'll have a very nice bruise there, she thought.

"Hurry up and sit down," called the soldier. "We want to get this transport moving."

Clara looked into his eyes. He's so young, she thought. He can't be more than about seventeen. What are they teaching them these days?

The young man read her thoughts. He blushed deep red and looked away. "Ready!" he called as he fastened the back doors. All the bright sunshine was gone at once.

The truck-driver revved the engine and slowly they pulled away.

Clara's eyes gradually got used to the dark and she could see the other people in the truck. Quite a few of the older folk, certainly. No one was saying anything. But then also there was a small child lying with its head on a younger woman's lap. As she looked around she noticed one or two other small children. And their mothers. And all of the mothers had rounded bellies. So, was it perhaps old people and those who would soon give birth? Were they going to the same place?

"Frau Lehrs," said a voice. Selda. Was Selda also going to the same place as her?

"Mutti Lehrs!" said another voice. The next minute Kyla was sitting next to her.

"Do you know where we're going?" asked Selda.

"A place called Terezin," replied Clara.

"Will we go all the way in this truck?"

"I don't think so. I should think we'll get on a train at some point. That's why they've given us these labels. So that they know how to direct us at the station."

"We could have walked to the station."

"I think they'll probably take us to Stuttgart."

It went quiet again. The truck carried on rumbling along the road. It wasn't at all comfortable. Every time it went over a bump she shook so much Clara was convinced she would fall apart. But she was sure she was right. They'd already gone too far to be going to the local station. Yet it was clear that this truck would not get much further than Stuttgart.

"I guess they'll take us to the Nordbahnhof," said a man Clara only knew vaguely. "I've heard that they took a lot of people there last year. After all, anyway, that's the place they use for transporting goods. And that's what we are now." He flicked his label.

Was he being harsh?. If they were being taken to an old people's home and a home for nursing mothers, and they'd taken all of their money, surely they were going to be looked after properly? So, some Germans didn't like Jews. Well, this way they didn't have to live with them, but they'd probably look after them better than they could look after themselves. "We'll have to see," she said.

There was not much more conversation after that. Then Clara got the impression that they had arrived in the town as the truck slowed down and made more stops and starts and turns. Eventually the engine stopped. Someone opened the doors and shouted, "Everyone out. Leave your belongings. They will be loaded on to the trains separately."

A few seconds later they were out in the bright sunlight. It was hot and there was no shade. There were thousands of people there, many of them old, but a few woman and children as well. And all wearing these labels as if they were parcels waiting to be posted. What looked like hundreds of trucks stood there, suitcases and bags still piled up untidily.

What would happen next and when? How long would they have to wait in this unbearable heat?

She could now see Selda's label. 809. Very close to hers. Perhaps that meant they were going to the same place and they would be travelling together. "That's good at least," said Clara, pointing to the labels.

Selda smiled but Clara could still see the fear in her eyes.

The two women sat on the floor and tried to keep themselves and Kyla cool. Clara took off her headscarf and she and Selda took it in turns to hold it up over the three of them to make a bit of a sunshade. It didn't take long each time, though, until their arms began to ache. Selda looked pale and Clara was quite worried. I hope all of this won't stress the baby too much, she thought.

Then Clara's heart missed a beat. Hani Gödde was standing a few feet from her. What was she doing here? What if she saw her? Clara's heart pounded.

It would be terrible for the girl to see her like this. On the other hand, at least she would be able to let the Gödde know what had happened to her. It would have been such a shock for Helga and Hani if they'd turned up next week and found the village deserted.

"Hani!" she called. Hani looked round frantically. Then when Clara made eye contact with her she frowned.

She doesn't recognise me, thought Clara. It had only been three weeks since the girl and her mother had visited but she knew she'd lost weight in that time. And she probably didn't look her best at the moment, what with the heat and worrying about Selda.

"Hani, it's me. I'm so glad I've seen you."

The girl's eyes grew rounder. "Frau Lehrs! What's happening?"

It was clear that she was alarmed but was trying her best to hide it. She'd better try and reassure her.

"They're taking us away to an old people's home in the east," she said. "I've had to give them the last of my money. But there will be plenty of food, and fuel for heating, and even entertainment. They have some splendid concerts, apparently. They have promised to look after us well. The worst is over."

Was she convinced? Clara couldn't tell. Hani was still frowning and screwing her face up against the sun.

A soldier started moving the group.

"Oh, here we go," said Clara. "We're off to get the train from the Nordbahnhof. Give my love to your mother."

"Yes," murmured Hani. She was staring at the label pinned to Clara's coat.

I wish she hadn't seen that, thought Clara.

"Nice one," murmured a man behind her as they were marched towards the platform. "Concerts, you say. I wish I'd brought my fiddle."

So do I, thought Clara, wondering whether he was being sarcastic or could indeed play the violin. Why couldn't people stay positive? It was important.

She noticed that the truck she had come in was still there. Would they load their entire luggage on to the train directly? At least it saved them having to carry it. It was a good 500 metres to the station.

Everyone shuffled forwards slowly. No one spoke. There were quite a few young people, she noticed, not only older folk like herself. So perhaps she wouldn't be stuck in an old people's home. Or, at least if she was, perhaps Selda and Kyla would be able to visit. Would they be permitted to come and go? Then perhaps she could go and see them.

She tried to look more closely at the people around her. But everyone was just staring ahead. The only person who gave her any eye contact was Kyla. The little girl smiled at her and held out her hand. Clara took the hand. Selda pulled the child back towards her and Kyla let go.

The 500 metres were interminable. The nearer they got to the station the slower everyone walked. Several of the soldiers barked at them to hurry. When they did get there, they were marched to the far end and then along a platform that went on forever. Soldiers holding clipboards were looking carefully at their labels and were shouting out numbers. Signs on the sides of carriages also contained numbers.

"How long will it take us to Terezin?" Clara asked one of the officials.

He shook his head and shrugged. "On a good day, eight hours. But there aren't many good days."

Oh dear. That would be demanding. Claro noticed none of the carriages had corridors. Would they stop for food or for the toilet?

The train stretched on and on, carriage after carriage.

"Old lady! In here," shouted one of the soldiers. He pointed to an open door. Clara went to climb up into the carriage. She obviously wasn't quick enough. The soldier pushed her quite roughly up the steep step. She fell to the floor and banged her knee.

Another bruise, I guess then, she thought.

Selda and Kyla followed.

The carriage was almost full. It had seats but only the hard wooden ones. One of the windows was cracked and had a small hole in it. Even so, there was no breeze and it was stifling. The body odour was strong this time. Worse than that first time on the tram. There were no seats left and there was no room to sit on the floor. A man and a boy stood up to let her and Selda sit down.

"Thank you," said Clara. "We must take it in turns."

"We'll see," said the man.

No one spoke and everybody avoided everybody else's eyes. Even Selda and Kyla appeared reluctant to talk, though Kyla stared at Clara. Clara smiled but Kyla only stared back.

At last the engine let off steam and Clara could feel the wheels rumbling beneath her. They were on their way.

22-23 August 1942; train journey

The wheels rolled on and on. Clara couldn't see out of the window. There were too many people between her and it. There was light coming through the top of it and occasionally she saw steam billow past. She couldn't tell where they were going but the sun wasn't shining directly into the carriage. The light suggested it was behind them. Yes, they were going east for sure.

One of the men tried to open the window. It was jammed shut. Only the faintest of breezes came through the tiny hole in the glass. It wasn't enough to cool the carriage down. The heat and the stench were beginning to make Clara feel queasy. She was normally such a good traveller. These circumstances were exceptional, though. Goodness knows how poor Selda felt, and other people who didn't travel so well.

"I think the only thing I can do is break it," said the man. "Cover her head and look the other way," he said to Selda. Kyla was sitting on her lap. She had fallen asleep and her head was on her mother's shoulder.

The man took off his shoe and started hammering at the window around the part where the hole was. The glass was quite tough and it took him several goes before it finally splintered and then most of the window fell out with a crash.

Kyla woke with a start and began to cry. Selda pulled the girl's head back down to her shoulder.

The man started throwing the broken glass out of the window. His arm caught on one of the jagged pieces still stuck in the frame. It started to bleed quite badly.

"Here, let me," said Clara, taking out a handkerchief. She bound his arm up as best she could. It stopped bleeding but she was worried as it was quite a long cut. "I'm sure they'll sort you our properly when we get there."

"I doubt it," said the man. "And I expect I'll be in even more trouble about this broken window."

"Well, me and you both," said another man who was finishing off the job for him.

At last, all of the glass was out of the top window. Everyone cheered.

"We'll tell them it fell out," said the second man. "You'd better keep that wound hidden, though."

"It's not as if they can do any more to punish us than they are already," said a woman.

A pleasant breeze came into the carriage. It still wasn't all that comfortable because so many people were in there but at least it was a bit better. And people were beginning to talk.

"Frau Lehrs," Selda called across the carriage. "Give me your hand."

Clara didn't move at first. What did Selda want?

"Come on. Please. Give me your hand."

Clara got up out of her seat and took two steps so that she could put her hand into Selda's outstretched one. Selda placed Clara's hand on her swollen belly.

Something kicked, then kicked again.

"Can you feel him? He's still alive." Tears were running down Selda's cheeks.

"Mummy, why are you crying?" said Kyla, looking alarmed.

Selda stroked her daughter's hair. "I'm crying because I'm happy that your baby brother is so strong." She looked at Clara. "I hadn't felt him kick since the men arrived this morning. I thought the shock had killed him," she whispered.

So that was it. That was why Selda had been so quiet. Clara laughed. "You're sure it's a boy?"

"Absolutely."

Kyla was still looking bemused. A ghost of a frown creased her forehead.

"Don't look like that," said Clara. "If the wind blows, you'll stick like it. Put your hand on your Mutti's tummy and say hello to your baby brother."

Kyla stretched out her hand and tentatively put it on to her mother's bump. Her eyes grew round. "It tickles," she said.

Clara smiled and stepped back towards her seat.

"Poor little mite," said a woman that Clara guessed was the same age as her. "A funny old world he's coming into."

Clara was glad the stranger didn't say exactly what she was thinking. That it would be better if this child was not born at all. "We must keep hopeful," she said.

The woman tutted and looked away.

The broken window and the announcement that Selda's baby was still alive had broken the ice. People began to talk. But it was still stifling in the carriage and the chatter made Clara feel drowsy. She was aware she was thirsty. So thirsty, in fact, that she was beginning to feel dizzy. And she needed the toilet. There was an ache in her kidneys. It didn't do to hold back at her age. But she must.

Despite the discomfort she couldn't stop her eyelids drooping.

She woke up with a start. The train had stopped and there was the sound of doors being opened and soldiers shouting. Then there were voices outside. It was dark. She wondered how late it was. Her watch had stopped.

Kyla was shaking her mother's arm. "Mutti, I need to wee-wee."

Don't we all, thought Clara. Gosh, she hoped they were being let off to relieve themselves. She would have to wet herself soon for sure.

"It's all right," said Selda. "I think they're getting us off the train to go to the toilet."

But it was too late. Urine trickled down the little girl's legs and a puddle formed on the floor.

"Now the place is going to stink," said one of the men.

Kyla began to cry.

"She can't help it," said Clara. "She's only a very little girl."

She didn't know how much longer she could hold on herself. How was Selda managing? The size of her belly suggested that the baby would be bobbing about on her bladder. She remembered that only too well though it was a long time ago.

A soldier let them out of the carriage. "Come on scum," he

cried. "Go and relieve yourselves in the woods. But anyone who goes in more than ten metres will be shot."

The old man who was sitting in the corner of the carriage didn't stir. He was fast asleep. Clara went over and shook him. He opened one eye.

"Don't you want to come outside and get some air?" Clara asked him. He shook his head then shut his eyes again.

Clara followed the others. Desperate as she was, she couldn't work out what to do. A young soldier stared at her and Selda. It was easier for the men. They could point their penises at a convenient tree. Selda somehow managed to remove her drawers under her skirt, spread her legs out and urinated on the ground. Clara couldn't quite manage to do that.

"Come, Frau Lehrs, I will help you," said Selda. She spread her skirts out wide. "I will hide you from that rude man's stare." She glared at the soldier who scowled back at her but then, Clara was glad to note, turned his back on them and walked away.

She stooped, pulled her drawers down and scooped her dress up behind her. She found it hard to release the contents of her bladder. This didn't feel right. Yet the pressure was agony.

"You musssst let go Frau Lehrssss. You musst," whispered Selda. "Now." Selda rubbed her gently in the lower abdomen.

The "sss" sound and Selda's massage did the trick. The warm liquid came away from her. Thank goodness. The dull pain in her back eased straight away and the pressure dissolved.

"Better?" said Selda, as she helped her up.

"You had a long wee-wee," said Kyla.

"I did, didn't I?" said Clara as she straightened her skirts and stood up again. "I feel much better, thank you."

"I wish they'd give us something to drink," said Selda. "Except then I suppose we'd need to pee again."

"We still ought to drink. Shh!"

"What's the matter?"

"Over there. Let's go and look."

"What is it?" Selda looked to where Clara was pointing.

"I think I can hear water."

"They said we shouldn't go more than ten metres into the forest."

"Well, they're not looking at the moment. And I don't think I care if we get left behind, do you?"

Selda shook her head, grabbed Kyla's hand and followed Clara through the trees.

The sound of running water grew louder and Clara was pleased to find that she had been right. There was a stream nearby. "Can we reach, do you think?" she asked Selda.

"Let's try," said Selda, helping both Kyla and Clara down the steep bank.

"Thank you my dear," said Clara. "But mind you don't slip."

The three of them were able to scoop up handfuls of water from the stream. It was cool and fresh.

"That's better. So much better," said Selda.

Clara washed her face and hands and then helped Kyla to do the same.

Selda looked around. "We could slip away," she whispered. "No one is watching."

Clara followed Selda's gaze. It was true. The soldiers were all looking the other way, And even if they had been looking, perhaps they would ignore an old lady, a pregnant woman and a little girl. But where were they? Would they be welcome here? They must have been travelling at least eight hours already.

Then she remembered the old man on the train. She was a bit worried about him. And they had no money and nothing to trade. Perhaps it was better after all if they stayed with the others.

There was a rustling in the bushes.

"Ah ladies," said a man's voice.

Clara looked up to see a soldier grinning at them. "Feeling modest were we? You needn't have worried. What's to see in an old dried-up Jew or a pregnant whore? Now the little one's pretty." He patted Kyla's head. She turned away and pushed her face into her mother's skirt. "But of course, she's too young. Now then ladies. That's it then. Back on to the train."

"That's settled that then," said Clara. It was most likely just as well, she thought. It would be hard to get by without money. They probably couldn't speak the language of wherever they were. And there was the old man.

They joined the others getting on to the train. Doors slammed. A few moments later the wheels started turning and they were on their way.

The silence had returned and the other passengers were staring ahead again.

Best to sleep, thought Clara. She felt more comfortable, after relieving herself and drinking the water. Goodness knows what was waiting for them at the other end. Best to get some rest while she could. She closed her eyes and soon the motion of the train made her drift into a dreamless sleep.

It was getting light when she woke up. The others apart from Selda were still asleep and because they had slumped forwards or slid down into their seats and the ones who had been standing were lying, piled up, one on top of the other, she could see through the windows. Sun was peeping through a fine mist. There were trees and grass, but no sign of any farmland. They must be right in the countryside. It could have easily been in Germany, though it was flatter than Clara was used to. Like the north of Germany. It's a new day, she thought. And we'll soon see our new home.

The train was slowing down. Selda was awake. "It looks like we're here," she whispered. Other people around them began to stir. Still few people spoke.

The train stopped completely.

They could hear the soldiers shouting. Doors started banging. Then they could hear the men more clearly. "Out. Everyone out and line up on the platform." Their own carriage door was flung open.

Kyla jumped.

"Come on, we must go," whispered Selda.

People got to their feet and started moving. Clara noticed that the old gentleman in the corner was still fast asleep. She pushed her way through the others to get to him. She shook him gently. "Come on, we must get out."

There was no response, though. Then she realised. His lips were blue and his hands were ice cold. He would never wake up again.

She and the old man were the only people left in the carriage.

"Come on old woman, hurry along," called one of the soldiers who had climbed up into the carriage. "We haven't got all day."

Clara turned to face him. "I think this man has died."

The soldier's eyes flinched and his shoulders stiffened. For a moment Clara thought he looked concerned. Then he shrugged and frowned. "Well, we'll deal with the body later. You must go and line up with the others."

"I hope we'll be able to give him a decent funeral?"

The soldier laughed.

23 August, Theresienstadt: new home

Gradually they were herded along the platform and started to leave the station.

"They're treating us like cattle," said Selda.

Clara shrugged. "I suppose we've got to get to wherever we're going somehow. I don't suppose they could put taxis on for us. I expect it won't be far."

"I hope not," said Selda. "I don't think she'll be able to walk for much longer."

Everyone was walking slowly. That made it worse. It made your feet ache more.

Selda was right. It wasn't long before Kyla needed carrying. The young woman hoisted her little daughter up on to her hip.

She shouldn't be carrying her like that, not in her condition, thought Clara. "Let me take her," she said.

"I couldn't, Frau Lehrs. She would be too heavy for you. I'll be fine."

Clara hoped so. Perhaps Selda was right. Perhaps she wouldn't be able to carry the child far.

Occasionally one of the soldiers would shout at them. "Come on, scum. Move along."

But no one walked any faster.

There's so many of us, thought Clara. We could push them out of the way.

Then, though, she found herself walking quite closely to one of the soldiers and in the next instant was looking into his cold blue eyes. It was easy to see why no one dared disobey.

Yet she could hear birds singing. There was the smell of freshly cut grass, and the sun still shone even in this unwelcoming place.

They turned a corner. In front of them stood a large building.

"That must be it," muttered Selda.

Clara nodded.

It was grim-looking place. It could have been quite a pleasant building. If the door and window-frames had had a lick of paint and if there had been some sign of life beyond the dull windows. Nothing said home about this place.

They were led through an archway over the top of which was the inscription "ARBEIT MACHT FREI." It did, did it? Work made you free. Perhaps they were right. It could be that doing some work made you feel as if you had a purpose in life. She'd rather work than be left idle, most certainly.

The people who were already there stared at them as they were led into an inner court-yard. No one offered them a smile or a greeting but Clara supposed that was because the soldiers were keeping a strict eye on them.

"Women here!" barked an official. "Men over there."

Clara and Selda shuffled over to where he had indicated. Kyla held on to Selda's skirt.

"Children over six here." He pointed to the third side of the courtyard. Kyla clung even more tightly to her mother.

"It's all right," said Selda, stroking her daughter's head. "I think they're going to let me and you and Frau Lehrs stay together."

"Line up!" called the guard. "Straight lines. Stand up straight."

Clara thought they were already standing in straight lines and they were standing as straight as they could. What else did they expect from a seventy-one-year-old woman, a heavily pregnant young woman and a little girl?

"I don't think he's German," whispered Selda.

"Oh?" said Clara.

"I think he's Jewish."

Since when did being Jewish mean you couldn't also be German? Oh, yes, of course; the race laws.

"I think he's one of us." Selda nodded. "Look at him."

Clara stared at him. How could Selda tell he was Jewish? He did have darker skin. He was rather thin. He certainly wasn't a blue-eyed, blond-haired wonder. But not all Germans were anyway. He was coming over towards them.

"Stop talking," he said quietly when he was level with them. "You will get into trouble. And you will get me into trouble as well."

"You're one of us, aren't you?" said Selda. "You're Jewish, aren't you?"

"So what if I am? I have to survive, don't I?" His deep brown eyes looked from Clara to Selda and back again. "It's really important to do as you are told. It really, really is."

He stepped back. Another official, a woman this time and definitely German, started counting them off. "… twenty-eight, twenty-nine, thirty. Follow me."

They found themselves being led into a room full of three-tiered bunk beds.

"Find yourselves a bed," said the woman. "And put an item of clothing on it to indicate it's yours. Then come back outside so that you can be assigned your duties."

"Duties?" said Selda. "How can they expect you and Kyla to do duties?"

"I expect I can. Kyla certainly shouldn't have to work though. She's such a little girl. She should be learning and playing. And you should be resting. What are they thinking?"

"Kyla can sleep with me," said Selda.

"Then you take the bottom bunk and I'll take the middle one. We can use the top one to store some of our things – once we get them, of course."

"Are you sure you can climb up there, Frau Lehrs?"

"Of course I can." What was the woman thinking?

It didn't take long to sort that out. Clara took a good look around the room. It was dull but relatively clean though there was a smell of unwashed bodies. She touched the mattress on the bed. It was thin, and stuffed with straw. But it would do. A light, rather moth-eaten blanket covered it. That would be fine now, but it might not be warm enough in the winter. Perhaps they wouldn't be here in the winter. This must only be temporary, surely? They wouldn't be expected to live like this for long, would they? The other twenty-seven women and children wandered back out to the courtyard. Clara, Selda and Kyla followed them.

It was getting hot. The women tried to shade the children from the fierce sun.

"You will be given your work details," shouted a man in a grey military uniform. "Remember, Arbeit macht frei! Those who refuse to work or who work badly will be moved on to another camp. One that is not nearly so liberated as this one. Your Ghettowache will instruct you where you are to work."

"Ghetto?" whispered Clara. "They told me 'old people's home'."

"Arbeit macht frei! Huh! This isn't a ghetto. It's a labour camp."

The young man they had seen earlier came over to them. "Don't worry," he said. "I'll find some easy work for the three of you. But please, ladies, try to look as if you are cooperating."

"You're seriously expecting this little one to work?" Clara pointed to Kyla.

"She'd better look as if she's being useful or..." He looked away.

"Or what?"

He looked back at Clara. "Or she'll have to go to another camp. A much harsher one."

Clara nodded. "What's your name?"

"Benjamin Schulzer. Not that it matters."

"Why do you do this, Benjamin Schulzer?"

Benjamin's eyes didn't blink as he looked back at Clara. He shrugged. "To keep my mother and father and my younger brothers safe. While I do this work for the camp commandos and as long as my family does their work they can remain here and be reasonably well looked after."

"Are they all as thin as you?" He was thin but not as much as Shmuel and the other young lads in Rexingen had been.

"Thinner. I get better rations because I'm working for them."

Clara couldn't think what to say. Surely, though, if he'd refused, if they'd all refused, they wouldn't be able to organise work camps like this.

Benjamin was looking at the ground. His face was bright red. "I don't even know if I'll be any good at this. But they told me if I didn't do it they'd kill my family."

320

Selda gasped, then retched and vomited. Her legs gave way under her and she ended up sitting in her vomit.

"Oh no," said Clara. Her own heart was thudding and she felt light-headed. She couldn't really believe what Benjamin had told them.

One of the military guards came over. "Is there a problem here?" he asked.

"No, everything's fine," said Benjamin as he and Clara helped Selda up.

The other guard moved away.

"When shall we get our things?" asked Clara.

Benjamin shook his head. "Not for two or three days, if at all."

"What? But we're filthy and we need to change our clothes. Selda especially."

Selda looked as if she was about to cry.

"Mutti." Kyla was whimpering.

"I'll see what I can do after I've taken you and the others to the coffin workshop."

Had she heard right. Coffin workshop? Goodness.

"Follow me," said Benjamin, speaking to all of the women, not just them. "No dawdling." Clara could tell he was trying to make himself sound stern. He was not really succeeding. Even so, all the women followed him silently. Their faces had glazed over again.

"Good," said Clara as Kyla held on to the edge of the coarse green material. "Now, I'll snip here." She made a fine cut on one edge, "and then another here." Again she opened the rather blunt scissors and made another little cut. It wasn't easy, but the material finally gave.

"And then we tear!" cried Kyla, clapping her hands.

Clare tore the cloth and handed it to Kyla who spread it out on the table ready for Selda to cover it in glue. Then the three of them would place it carefully on the inside of the coffin before they then went on to prepare more cloth for the lid.

Other women nailed the pieces of wood together to build the coffins. Clara guessed that some of the men had cut the wood; they were brought into the workshop already the right shape. All the coffins were different in size.

"Made to measure," one woman said.

"They must expect a lot of people to die around here," said another.

"You don't suppose they'd bother with coffins for us, do you?" a third added.

"Huh! Even Aryans have to die!" said someone else.

Clara wondered what had happened to the man on the train. There was no sign of anyone preparing a funeral. Perhaps she'd ask Benjamin when – if – they saw him again.

"This glue makes me feel sick," said Selda.

If Clara was honest she didn't notice it anymore. The camp was full of smells, none of them pleasant. But already, after one afternoon, she was used to it. It didn't bother her now. Would she notice the difference if it went away? Poor Selda. It must be her pregnancy. Oh dear. What a place to be pregnant in. Would they look after her here? And the baby, when it came?

The door swung open. Benjamin came in carrying a bundle of clothing.

"Listen," he said looking straight into Clara's eyes. "Look as if we're talking about work and don't mention this to the other women. They might get jealous. But there are a few clothes there for the little girl and for you two. And one or two things for when the baby comes, if it survives." He turned to Selda. "You will get a uniform once the baby has been delivered. Until then you'll be allowed to wear your own things or whatever you can find."

"You couldn't find our suitcases, then?" asked Clara.

Benjamin shrugged and looked away.

"We're not going to get them back, are we?" said Clara.

Benjamin shook his head.

"And will I get a uniform, too?"

He shook his head again.

Selda touched Clara's arm.

"The privilege of old age?" said Clara.

Benjamin shrugged again and then looked straight at Clara. She tried to read his face and work out what he was thinking or feeling but she couldn't. "So where did you get these from?"

"Don't ask," he said. "It's better that you don't know." He turned to the others. "In five minutes time you are to line up for soup and bread. Make your way out into the courtyard."

Clara opened the bundle wide enough to be able to see the clothes. She could see some fine silk. Black. But expensive-looking. Who had that belonged to and where were they now?

"Hurry along," called Benjamin.

Clara tucked the bundle under her arm and followed the others out.

11 September 1942, Theresienstadt: a special roll-call

Something had woken Clara. She couldn't figure out what. No one else was awake in their dormitory.

She was exhausted. They worked hard and had little rest. At least that meant even these crude beds provided a sanctuary. No one could take away the pleasure of nestling down at night or of waking before it was time to get up and relishing lying there. She would use those early morning moments and nights when she couldn't sleep despite the weariness to do something that was like praying – after her own clumsy fashion. It was about being grateful and finding hope. Yes, even here there was something to be grateful for. The friendship of the other women. The fact that they were still alive. The sun that still shone. And yes there was hope, always there was hope. This could all end. At any moment. Normal life she'd taken so much for granted before was now something to hope for.

But today she didn't know whether she would be able to move even if someone came and shouted that they were all free. What would the Ghettowachen do to her if she refused to move – because she couldn't? They'd have to drag her out of bed.

The sun was streaming in through the window. Could that have woken her up? Surely not. It did that every day.

And she could move, actually, because she found herself leaning over the edge of her bunk so that she could look down at Selda and Kyla. Had the little girl been having a nightmare again? It wasn't Selda's labour starting, was it? She must be overdue, mustn't she?

Mother and daughter were both sleeping peacefully. Kyla's arm was hanging out of the bed. Clara shuddered as she saw the number tattooed on that small arm. How could they do that to a little child?

How the poor girl had cried when she came back. It must have been even worse while they were doing it.

"It really did hurt," said Selda. "Not even having Kyla was so painful."

Several of the women had got infections in their tattoos. One woman had become seriously ill with a fever but was recovering.

But Clara didn't have a tattoo.

"Your skin's too wrinkly. They won't be able to do it," Benjamin had said. Another privilege of old age then.

And there was the hair. Selda and Kyla had had their heads shaved.

"It's to stop the spread of lice," one of the women who'd been there longer had told her. It had made poor little Kyla look even more tiny and vulnerable. Clara noticed that a fine down was growing back. How long before they would shave their heads again? And would their hair ever grow back the way it had been? They say that it never does.

Clara touched her own hair. It was still thick. There was still a lot of it, but it had become white and brittle. And again, she seemed to be exempt from this. *Old people don't get head lice, then?* Another blessing.

Kyla stirred a little in her sleep. Then she opened her eyes and saw Clara looking at her. "Mutti Lehrs," she said and smiled.

There was always room for a smile.

Clara then became aware of voices outside in the courtyard. She turned to look out of the window. Already many of the men were being marshalled into lines and some women were making their way out of some of the other dormitory buildings. Roll-call. But why so early?

Other women in her dormitory were beginning to stir.

"What's going on?" asked one woman.

"I don't know," said Clara.

This was something new and a sliver of fear gave Clara some strength. She slid her legs over the side of the bed and got herself down to the floor. She would get up and be ready for whatever was going to happen next.

Another woman had already taken the slops and had come back with the wash bucket. Clara was soon splashing her face with the cold water. As she finished when the door was flung open and a

Ghettowache she'd never seen before came bursting in. She was a hard-faced woman with cold blue eyes.

"Everyone is to line up in the courtyard."

Clara realised she wasn't German. Perhaps a local woman – a Jewess maybe – who like Benjamin was saving her family by working here.

"What's happening?" Clara stared into the young woman's eyes looking for some sign of humanity.

The woman's stare remained cold. "We're having roll-call early," she said. Could she detect a little softening in her tone? Had she understood that Clara knew why she was doing this? "You're all to line up and be counted more carefully than normal." The guard turned to the other women. "Come on, all of you. Get out of bed. In two minutes you must be lined up outside." The harshness was definitely back in her voice.

Selda had hardly moved. "I'm sorry. We must go," Clara said to her.

Selda groaned and rubbed her back.

Clara's heart started thudding. "It's not...?"

Selda shook her head. "No I think I lay funny."

That was probably true. It must be cramped with Selda the size she was sharing a bunk with Kyla – even if it still seemed the best thing to do. And thank goodness it wasn't the baby coming. Clara wasn't sure exactly why this special roll-call was being made, but she had a feeling that a woman giving birth in the middle of it may not be considered exactly convenient.

They were ushered outside and lined up. Clara found herself standing next to a woman from one of the other dormitories. It was someone she recognised from the coffin workshop. She didn't know her name, though and she hadn't spoken to her before.

"I hope you know some poetry or some plays off by heart," said the woman. "It gets tedious if we have a special like this. And I hope you're strong. If you faint they take you away and people don't normally come back. Stay strong, old woman."

Clara looked at Selda who was to her right. She was standing

326

stiffly, staring at nothing in particular. She looked all right. And Kyla, bless her, was keeping still, and hardly fidgeting at all.

The woman was right. It was tedious. Normally roll-call was quite straightforward but today they were taking more care. And it did help reciting poetry. She went through some of the pieces that she and Ernst had liked so much. And especially that verse he had read to her when she had been so ill. She could almost hear his voice reading it.

Four times the guards, this time accompanied by soldiers, started over. Had someone escaped? Had they found a broken fence or something?

They were standing towards the back. Clara's back was beginning to ache and her feet were sore. She hoped that the numbers would tally this time. As soon as a soldier had walked past and counted them, Selda gasped and there was the sound of fluid splashing on the ground.

The woman on the other side of Clara nudged her. "Don't let them know," she said. "They'll take her off to the medical centre and you'll never see her again. When this is over get her back to her dormitory. I'll cover for you in the workshop."

The numbers did tally, this time, and they were ordered to line up for the thin watery breakfast gruel.

"Go on," whispered the woman. "Take the little girl. I'll cause a distraction." She pushed the woman on the other side of her. "Oi. You big fat cow. Wait your turn."

The woman looked at her, surprised but then caught the other woman's eye. "Who are you calling fat? You're the greedy beggar round here."

"Get back there," whispered the first woman to Clara. "And once the baby's here, keep it hidden until the morning. Say it arrived in the middle of the night. They probably still won't let her keep it but it's the best chance she has."

A guard and a soldier made their way over to the two women who were fighting. Clara saw their opportunity and got Selda, Kyla and herself back to the dormitory as fast as they could go. It wasn't easy. Selda's pains were obviously coming quite quickly now.

Every few steps she had to stop and hold her breath. It was less than fifty metres to the dormitory but it took forever. Clara was so afraid they would be seen.

They managed to get back unseen, though. For a few seconds she felt relieved. Then she couldn't work out whether she would be glad if the baby came quickly and she could know that mother and child were safe and as well as they could be in a place like this or whether she would prefer it to come slowly so that they didn't have to hide it for so long.

Then she had another alarming thought. Was she going to have to oversee this birth on her own? Sure, she'd had three children herself and she'd been present at Renate's birth. But all that was quite a long time ago.

"What's the matter with Mutti?" Kyla's eyes were filling with tears.

Come on woman, get a grip, Clara told herself. These two needed her to be strong. "You're soon going to have a baby brother or sister."

Kyla's eyes grew round.

"Brother," muttered Selda. "Definitely a brother."

"If you say so." Now, she must do something sensible. She got Selda on to the bed. "Take your drawers off. Don't you think?"

Selda smiled weakly. "They're soaking wet anyway."

"Quite." She timed Selda's contractions by counting. Every two minutes, she reckoned. So, the little one was well on its way. She ought to put something under her to preserve the bed a bit.

There was a spare bed in the dormitory. One of the women had died two nights ago. That would do. She fetched the things from that bunk and tried to put them under Selda. But it made her head too near the next bunk.

"Perhaps it would be better if you were on the floor." Clara pulled the two mattresses and the rest of the bedding off the bunk and set them out on the hard stone.

Selda nodded and in between the pains managed to get herself down on to the makeshift bed.

It seemed all right. She was helping Selda through her pains.

328

When should she start pushing, though? How would Clara know? What if she got a strong urge to push and she wasn't quite ready? She knew that could do a lot of damage. She would have to hope.

Then there was a tap at the door. Clara's mouth went dry but before she could react the door was gently pushed open and a young woman about the same age as Selda came in.

"I'm Susannah," she said. "Benjamin sent me. I'm a midwife."

Thank goodness.

Susannah knelt down next to Selda, pushed up her skirts, made her bend her knees and thrust some rags under her back so that she was tilting up towards her and she could see what was happening. She felt Selda's abdomen and then thrust her fingers into the opening between Selda's legs.

Selda winced.

"Sorry," said Susannah. Then she grinned. "It's time to start pushing. Your baby will soon be here."

Selda's face scrunched up.

"Push now." Susannah put her hand on her shoulder.

Selda screeched. "Why did you have to leave me? Why did you have to do this to me?" She was looking from side to side as if she had lost someone or something.

"But I'm here," said Clara, taking her hand. "And Kyla too."

"I think she's talking to her husband," said Susannah. "Is he here at the camp?"

Clara shook her head. "He died not long after she became pregnant."

"Ah." Susannah pursed her lips. "It's not unusual for women to curse their husbands when it gets to this stage. But at least it's a sign this is nearly over." She smiled at Kyla. "It would really help if you held your Mutti's other hand every time she has a pain."

The little girl took Selda's hand and started patting her arm.

Selda had three more powerful pains and the three others encouraged her to push really hard. Her eyes rolled in their sockets.

Susannah frowned. "She's getting exhausted. The head keeps presenting then going back. I think there may be a problem with the baby." She took Selda's hand from Kyla. "With the next pain don't push but pant to hold him back."

The next pain came, and Selda did as Susannah had asked her.

"I'm sorry, this will hurt." Susannah had her fingers up inside of Selda. "Yes, she muttered. "As I thought. He's got the cord around his neck." She frowned. "Keep on panting."

Selda panted, her face screwed up in pain. As the contraction softened she whimpered.

Then Susannah grinned. "That's it. He's free. With the next pain, push really hard and he will be here."

The pain came. Clara and Kyla allowed Selda to grasp their arms really tightly.

"The head's here," cried Susannah. "Push, push, push."

A lump of flesh that may have had a head, arms and legs but didn't quite look like a baby slid on to the mattress.

Susannah wiped some of the blood and fluid away and laughed. "You have a baby boy."

"I told you," said Selda. But then she frowned. "He's not crying. Why isn't he crying?"

"Shh," said Susannah. She put her ear to the baby's chest. "His heart's strong." She looked at Clara. "Clean his eyes and mouth. Wash his face in cold water and rub his tummy. I'm going to cut the cord."

Clara busied herself with the water but looked out of the corner of her eye, amazed as she saw Susannah bite through the cord.

"Spit!" Susannah held out her hand to Selda. Selda did as she was asked and Susannah rubbed the fluid over the end of the cord. "This is the best way to clean the cut. And carry on pushing with the pains. We have to deliver the after-birth." She looked at Clara, her eyebrows raised.

Clara shook her head. Please let this baby live, she said in her head. Please.

Seconds later a bloodied sack-like mass with the bluey-red cord still attached slid on to the floor.

At that precise second the baby cried.

Selda laughed. "We'll call him Nathaniel. His name is Nathaniel. Give him to me."

Susannah nodded. Then she looked at Clara. "You and the little one should go to the workshop. If anyone stops you on the way say you came back to the dormitory to change your clothing."

Clara handed Nathaniel over to Selda and watched as Susannah helped the young mother to put the baby to her breast." Come on," she whispered to Kyla. "We must go."

"I'll look after them until you get back," said Susannah. "Oh, and on your way, take this and give it to the men at the vegetable garden. They won't ask any questions. It's good for the plants." She wrapped Selda's after-birth in a rag and handed it to Clara.

The rest of the day passed slowly in the workshop. Clara longed to get back and see how Selda and Nathaniel were doing. Kyla was anxious too to see her mother again. And it wasn't so easy to keep up with the work with only Kyla to help. It was too much for the small child to lift up the heavy pieces of baize. And she wasn't concentrating.

A bit frightening for one so young to watch her mother give birth.

Fortunately it was Benjamin on duty in the workshop. He'd said nothing when they came in, but nodded briskly. The two women who helped earlier had raised their eyebrows but didn't say a word.

I suppose we don't really know who we can trust, thought Clara. She hoped Kyla wouldn't say anything but thought warning her might scare the child. The little girl had picked up that she needed to keep quiet, though. Children could be so beautifully sensitive about these things. She remembered her Hilfsklasse children who had always been so good whenever they'd had unexpected visitors.

The men at the kitchen garden had been careful as well. It wasn't unusual for kitchen waste to be taken for composting and the man in charge had just nodded as he'd taken the after-birth from Clara. Fortunately two of the guards had been too busy chatting to take much notice of her and Kyla.

There was a brief moment, though, when one of the women delivered a coffin lid and looked at Clara meaningfully. "Well," she whispered. "Is everything okay?"

"A boy. Nathaniel."

The woman rubbed Clara's arm. "I hope you can keep him safe."

I hope so, too, thought Clara.

At last the afternoon ended and the bell went to signal that it was time to go and line up for the thin soup and hard bread. She would save most of hers for Selda. She would take only a couple of mouthfuls for herself.

She and Kyla made their way out into the courtyard with the others.

"Your friend will need more food," one of the women said on the way out. "We'd offer to help but we're allowed no food this evening as a punishment for the fight earlier."

"I'm so sorry," said Clara.

"Don't be," said the woman. "We did what we had to."

"Thank you." People were being so helpful.

"Hey, old woman and little girl," Benjamin shouted as if he didn't know them. "Come and join this line." He pointed to a queue of men which was actually longer than the one they'd been standing in.

He was up to something. They'd better do as he said. Clara took Kyla's hand and joined the back of the queue.

They had only been standing there a few minutes when someone tapped her on the shoulder. She turned to find herself facing a man she had never met before.

"The baby will be allowed to live," he said. "We've made sure of it."

"How do you know about the baby and how can you be so sure he'll live?"

"News gets around. It's best not to ask how. What you don't know can't hurt you. That's why I won't tell you my name either. But I can tell you this: I'm still running a business from the inside here and I'm providing them with cheap tools. It allows space for a little bribery. They wouldn't be without my goods. It gives me a bit of say-so – though of course I can't use it too often. But the little one will be safe."

"Oh. That is so," she struggled for a word "– brave."

The man shrugged. Then he gestured with his head to the serving station. "Go to the front. No one will mind."

Clara looked round to see if any of the guards were watching. Only Benjamin, and he gave the slightest nod.

"One for you. One for the little girl. And one for the nursing mother," said the man who was serving. He handed her three metal cups and a bag of bread cubes. "All of the men have agreed to give a drop of broth and a mouthful of bread. Can you carry them all right?"

"You'll be able to help, won't you sweetheart? It's for your Mutti and your baby brother?" Clara turned to Kyla.

Kyla nodded. Her dark eyes were round.

When they got back to the dormitory Selda was sitting up in her bunk, Nathaniel on her breast again. She handed him to Susannah who burped him and changed the rags she was using as a nappy for some fresh ones. "You'll have to get into a routine with washing these," she said.

Selda ate the soup and the bread hungrily. Would they ever be able to get her enough to eat? Then Selda's face collapsed and tears started to run down her cheeks.

"What if they take my baby tomorrow? I won't be able to bear that."

"They're not going to take your baby." Clara told her all about the encounter with the man who had bribed the officials and how the other men had all supplied food for her.

Nathaniel was here to stay and she would do her best to help keep him safe. She knew she could count on others as well.

Later that night Clara couldn't sleep. The day had been too eventful. The women had come back as soon as she'd finished telling Selda all the good things that people had done for them. They'd all fussed and cooed over the baby.

"A child's a blessing, even in a place like this."

"Let one of them try and lay a finger on him."

"He has his sister's eyes." Kyla had giggled with delight.

Oh, and much more had been said. She couldn't remember it all. People had been so kind though – and they'd taken risks. Even if she didn't sleep tonight she knew she would get through tomorrow on that kindness alone. It was that good thought that eventually allowed her to sleep.

29 September 1942, Theresienstadt: the final journey

The door to the workshop was open. It was warm for late September. A gentle breeze made a few fallen leaves rustle in the doorway. It was good like that. It got rid of the smell of the glue. It still amazed Clara how nature carried on as if nothing had happened. As if there were no terrible places like this one and as if there was no war going on. The trees were still remembering to go golden and drop their leaves in the autumn.

Selda had stopped for a few minutes to feed Nathaniel. Despite everything the baby was thriving. He was putting on weight, they thought. He'd at least regained his birth weight. In such a short amount of time, too. Selda was looking healthy also. She'd regained some energy. The baby was sleeping well and they hadn't had many disturbed nights.

It's just me who doesn't sleep, thought Clara. Perhaps it's because I'm getting older. Perhaps I don't need as much sleep as the youngsters. She really didn't feel too bad on it, though.

Kyla looked pale. The child wasn't able to play and she wasn't getting enough fresh air. She was staying up late every night with the women and she was trying so hard to be helpful to her mother and her baby brother.

Now, here she was as well, becoming expert at handling the lining cloth.

I hope they'll be as kind to her as they've been to her mother and brother, Clara thought. People had carried on being helpful, finding extra portions of food and water for Selda and making or finding bits of clothing for Nathaniel.

"You're quiet today, Frau Lehrs," said Selda. "Is something the matter?"

"Yes, you're dreaming, Mutti Lehrs."

"Am I?" She supposed she was. She became aware that Kyla was holding out a piece of cloth to her. She took it from the child and laid it on the table. She then covered it with glue and Kyla helped her to ease it into the coffin. Clara pressed it down firmly. There! That was a nice neat job. She was getting better and faster at doing this. She hoped people weren't dying faster, though, but of course with a war on – well, it was to be expected.

Selda had finished feeding the baby and was about to burp him.

"Oh, let me," said Clara.

"There, go to Mutti Lehrs." Selda handed her the baby.

Clara took the little one in her arms. He gurgled quietly. It was so lovely to hold this little bit of new life. She nuzzled the top of his head. Why did babies always smell so lovely? Yes, even here. Well, apart from when they needed changing. Better make the most of this, she thought. I'm not sure how much longer this is going to last.

Where had that silly thought come from?

Nathaniel burped loudly and began to grizzle.

"I'll take him now, shall I?" said Selda.

Clara passed her the child and Selda secured him into the sling she'd made that held him close to her chest. This was such a practical arrangement. Little Nathaniel was perfectly content that way and Selda could get on with her work. Why didn't all mothers do that? It made for happier babies. And sure enough a few seconds later he stopped crying.

They'd found a box for him to sleep in, but most of the time he stayed in the sling, close to Selda.

I wonder how big he'll be before she'll have to stop doing that? Then Clara knew she wouldn't be there to find out.

What were these thoughts that she kept having? But she was absolutely certain. Certain that something was going to happen today. Something that would take her away from this camp, from the workshop and from these good people.

"Are you all right, Frau Lehrs? You look pale." Selda was staring at her.

She really must snap out of this. "I'm fine my dear. It's age I guess." She laughed. "And this wonderful glue." She turned her nose up and her lips down.

Selda laughed. "You take care, Frau Lehrs."

Yes, she must. She must take care that they didn't find out what strange thoughts she was having.

Oddly, she was beginning to feel – well – excited.

The feeling wouldn't go away. Something was going to change, she knew it. It was like when Ernst came home. Was this nonsense going to end then, at last?

The morning passed and it was soon time to go and queue for the thin soup. When it was her turn she caught the eye of the woman serving. It was the pleasant young one who worked in the kitchen. She nodded at Clara and filled her cup to the brim. More for Selda, then. Clara had the oddest feeling that this was the last time she would hold a cup out like that here.

She felt the urge to talk to as many people as possible. She made her way around as many of her friends as she could.

Kyla skipped over and slipped her hand into Clara's. "You're talking to everyone today, Mutti Lehrs. Don't you want to be with me and Nathaniel and Mutti?"

"Of course I do." She stroked Kyla's hair. Of course she wanted to be with them. They were her family now. She sat down next to Selda and handed her the cup of the unappetizing liquid.

"You should have some yourself," said Selda.

"I've taken a couple of sips. You need it more than me. Keep your strength up for Nathaniel and Kyla."

Selda frowned then smiled. She touched Clara's arm. "You're so kind. You're like a mother to me."

"That's all right then."

The feeling would not go away. The moment was getting nearer all the time.

The bell rang and they all started making their way back to the workshops. Clara noticed though that some of the older folk, the ones the same age as her and older, were being held back. They were being lined up as if for a special roll-call. Would they want her to do that as well?

She wasn't entirely surprised, then, when Benjamin came over to her and touched her arm lightly. "Not you Clara. Not today." Then he looked down on the ground, his face bright red. He looked back up and made eye contact for a split second. "You're to line up with them over there." He turned round and hurried away from her.

So, it's beginning, thought Clara.

She made her way over to the others.

"Do you think they're taking us to that old people's home at last?" she asked the man she ended up standing next to.

He shrugged.

"Don't talk," snarled one of the guards.

They stood around for about an hour. They were inspected, prodded and poked, and counted three times over.

"Very well," said one them at last." We're transporting you further east. You may collect enough for the journey from your dormitories. You won't need anything else. Everything will be provided once you're there. You are then to come and stand in line to get your transit number. Take no more than ten minutes. If anyone fails to turn up all of you will be punished."

So, another journey. She looked again at the people around her. All of them old – most of them even older than her. The promised old people's home, then, surely?

Back in the dormitory Clara found a couple of shawls and some handkerchiefs. She put the rest of the things on Selda's bed. She didn't know whether she'd be allowed to use them. She had to wear the same striped uniform as the other women now. But maybe she could make them into something for Kyla or Nathaniel. Or perhaps this would all be over soon and they'd be able to go back home.

Home! This had been her home for the past few weeks. "Goodbye," she whispered as she pulled the door softly behind her.

The queue was already quite long when she joined it. Slowly they shuffled forward. They were all staring again, not looking at each other, as they had at the beginning of the journey here.

Thoughts and memories tumbled through Clara's head. She was day-dreaming again, she knew, but it didn't matter. No one wanted to talk. Soon, then, she found herself face to face with the official who was issuing the transit slips.

"Name?" said the young man.

Goodness. He couldn't be more than about nineteen. He looked quite pale and actually a bit scared. And so thin. Almost as thin as one of them. Why were they getting such young people to do this sort of work? Still, she guessed that it was better than them fighting in a war. One mother at least would be relieved.

"Name?" he said again.

"Lehrs. Clara Lehrs."

The young man looked at the list in front of him. "Klara Sarah Lehrs? Geisgasse 6?"

Clara looked at where he was pointing. "Actually, it's just Clara Lehrs. And Clara with 'C'. But yes, that's me."

The young man frowned. He sighed and then grunted. Then he too daydreamed for a few seconds. At last he picked up his pen and wrote "Clara Lehrs" on the slip.

"Thank you," said Clara.

He stared at her for a few seconds. "You'd better follow the others." Then he signalled for the next one to come forward.

"You'll get your reward in heaven, young man," Clara whispered. At least she had her own name back.

She followed the others who were shuffling, with shoulders stooped, through the main entrance and along the street. She could no longer read the words over the arch for she had her back to them. She could have turned round and looked but she didn't need to. She knew what they said. "Arbeit macht frei." Did it? Was that it? She had done her stint, had she? She had worked hard throughout this final stage of her life. Now she was free.

They were obviously heading for the station. Another train journey, then? Soon she would feel the wheels under her feet again. How many hours – or even days – would it be this time? She looked sideways at the people who were walking next to her. Oh, she would have her work cut out here. One woman was sobbing quietly and another was frowning. Didn't they know that whatever happened they were free inside?

She remembered Kurt and his angels. She could almost hear his voice. "The angels are watching and waiting to work with us. There is angel work to be done." Was that what that young man had been doing? Angel work. That small act of kindness, spelling her name right? It wasn't much but it felt important. Was he one of the angels, then?

A beam of sunlight peeped out between the grey clouds and illuminated the trees. There was no doubt about it; the autumn colours were glorious this year. That was certainly something to be grateful for. And now she had hope as well.

She straightened her back and looked forward. She could see the steam coming from the train. They were nearly there. They would soon be speeding on their way to the next place she would call home.

22 August 1956 Rexingen: Kyla and Nathaniel

"There's not a lot left from that time," said Herr Grünbaum, the man who had shown them round. "People really want to put it behind them. There's been some new building. Some streets have changed their names. And most of the belongings of the people who lived here have gone. Do you recognise anything?"

Kyla shook her head. "Not really. Well, maybe some things look a bit familiar. Some of the buildings, perhaps. And that big meadow outside the village. We played there sometimes. Mutti Lehrs used to take us there. But it was a long time ago."

"Indeed. We tried to keep a few things as they were. But people wanted to change everything. They wanted to forget."

Nathaniel wobbled her arm. "Who was Mutti Lehrs again?"

Why couldn't he pretend to be interested? They were doing this for Mutti after all.

"She was a really nice old lady who looked after Mutti and me. She was there when you were born. She used to tell the loveliest stories."

"Oh."

"And you think this lady was taken to a death camp?"

"Auschwitz. Yes we're sure it was Auschwitz."

Herr Grünbaum shook his head. "If you can bear it, can you write this all down for me? I'm trying to put together a picture of what life was like then."

"Of course. We'll be pleased to." It was odd. She could remember so little about this village yet everything about Theresienstadt was so clear – even about the time Mutti Lehrs had still been there and when Nathaniel had been born. Later as well when they'd started the football team and the orchestra, and the week when they'd spruced it all up and made it look like a holiday resort just before the man from the Red Cross came. Then another memory surfaced and made her shudder. That day when they'd installed the gas chamber. Everyone had known what it was for and had feared that they would be the ones to have to use it – or worse still to have to operate it.

The tattoo on her arm began to feel sore. It always did when she had a bad memory of the camp.

"Well, at least you two survived. You must really try to put that all behind you and look to the future. You have your whole lives ahead of you." Herr Grünbaum smiled then frowned and clapped his hand in front of his mouth. "I'm so sorry. I wasn't thinking. Your poor mother."

"Well, at least she spent a few years of normal life outside the camp. But the doctor said the depression was too deeply seated before she got out."

"Quite so. Quite so."

Nathaniel had turned his back on them. Kyla knew he was trying not to cry. All she wanted to do was put her arms round him and sob with him. But she knew he would hate that and he would hate her if she showed any sign of weakness.

Something bubbled up inside her. It made her so angry, what they'd done to them at that place. "I actually think it was the camp that stopped her wanting to live. She gave up fighting it. If only Mutti Lehrs could have stayed with us. She would have kept Mutti going."

"I am so sorry." Herr Grünbaum shuffled from foot to foot. "There are a few things… they're not much and mainly broken and neglected. But perhaps you would like to see them?"

"Yes, that would be nice." Perhaps there would be something. Something that would make her remember more of the time she spent here. Of when her mother had been happy. Mutti had always said she was happiest in Rexingen. Even though that was where Vati had died.

Nathaniel turned back to them and grimaced.

They followed Herr Grünbaum up the lane towards his house. He was a nice man really. She ought to be friendlier towards him but she was still finding it hard to keep control of her feelings. She had to be strong for Nathaniel.

Herr Grünbaum was trying to keep a record of all the Jewish

people who had lived in the village. He didn't want people to forget. He thought every single one of the Jews had who lived here should be remembered. Oh, she wished Nathaniel wouldn't be so sullen. And she wished she could be a more cheerful herself. But she had to concentrate so hard not to cry.

"I have kept a few things I found in some of the apartments here." Herr Grünbaum had shown them into a large garage at the side of his house. "You can spend as long as you like looking. Then come on into the house and have some coffee and cake. I'll show you what else I've found out."

"Thank you," whispered Kyla.

And at least Nathaniel had the manners to nod, but as soon as Herr Grünbaum had disappeared into the house he screwed up his face again. "It's all really old stuff."

"Well of course it is. It was old then." Kyla looked at everything. She didn't really recognise anything though in some ways everything was familiar. Battered and broken like most things she'd seen throughout her life.

"Did you really live with stuff like this even before the camp?" asked Nathaniel.

He was getting to be such a snob. Did he not remember how bad it had been there? He'd been spoilt since they'd got out. She decided to ignore him.

Then something caught her eye. A little cupboard with a metal clasp. She made her way over to it and touched it. Then she remembered something about a white tablecloth and some photos of a girl who was a little younger than Nathaniel was now.

The clasp was rusty. She pulled at it but couldn't get it open.

"Let me try." Nathaniel pushed her out of the way and grabbed the clasp from her hands, twisting it violently. "Oh!" he was holding half of the fastener in his hand.

"What have you done?" Typical. He was always breaking things these days. He didn't know his own strength.

"Look, there's something in there." He fished into the cupboard and pulled out a sheaf of papers. "It looks like a letter or something."

"Let me see."

Nathaniel handed Selda what he'd found.

"It is a letter. It's one that Mutti Lehrs wrote."

Kyla's hands trembled a little and she couldn't bring herself to look at the writing at first. What if it revealed some secret she'd rather not know? Plus it would be disrespectful of Frau Lehrs's privacy.

"Well, then, are you going to read it or not? If you don't it's a waste of a broken lock."

He was right, she supposed. Maybe Mutti Lehrs would want her to see what she'd written anyway. She took a deep breath and began to read.

Rexingen, 15 February 1942

Dear Ernst, Käthe, Rudi and Renate,

I've no idea if, when or how you will ever get this letter but I hope that one day one of you will read it, and pass it on to the others. I hope you are all still in touch.

I would like to assure you that I am well and content here in Rexingen. The people are very kind, even though we are poor and I have had to become Jewish again. There is a lot of warmth and everyone shares what little they have. There is a lot of love and spirits for the most part remain undaunted. It is so clear to me that in fact we believe in the same god, whatever he – or she – actually is. We're not clever enough yet to understand these things fully.

I've taken on the role again of being Mutti Lehrs. I've befriended one young woman particularly who lost her husband just after she became pregnant with her second child. Her little daughter, Kyla, is delightful and comes to me when her Mutti needs a rest. And somehow that set everything in motion and all of the younger children in the village began to regard me as their second grandmother. So Renate, if you ever come here, you will have a lot of new cousins to get to know. It seems I have found a purpose again.

We all gather in the evenings to share a meal and sit

344

round the log fire. We're often hungry but at least here we are better off than those who live in ghettos in the towns. We grow a few vegetables and make use of what grows naturally. Occasionally we hunt.

You may wonder why I hesitated and hesitated about leaving and didn't in the end join you all in England. Well, I just could not leave the Hilfsklasse to survive on its own. You may argue that I've had to anyway. This is true. But even here there is something of a miracle: by the time I was ordered to leave everything there was in good hands. Karl Shubert was comfortable in my house and Helga Gödde and Hani were really helping. Renate, you should be so proud of your friend. She will make an excellent teacher one day. Hopefully all of this nonsense will soon come to an end and people will be able to resume their normal lives.

Today is a pretty day. The countryside is covered in snow. I'm sure the sun will shine later. That's the thing. All of this human silliness and nature takes not one bit of notice. The seasons come and go. The sun still feeds this planet. Oh boys and Käthe, what you and Professor Einstein could tell me all about that! And Hans too.

Ernst, I want to thank you for taking such good care of our family. I'm sorry your old stubborn mother would not comply, but Herr Hitler, of course, didn't know what he was taking on when he challenged CLARA Lehrs. No doubt you are doing a deal of good furthering the work of the Waldorf schools in England.

Rudi, did you ever get to Canada? I hope you are still enjoying playing with your numbers and I hope you are taking good care of that chest of yours. Have either of you two met a nice young lady yet? I'd like a few more grandchildren, thank you, even though I have Renate and all the fine youngsters here.

Käthe I'm so sorry that you and Hans have to live apart. Given the nature of his work it's understandable. But at least you are with your child in England. Some families I know have to be split up. To think that Hans is involved in designing some of the very weapons that are being used on you in England. Gruesome. I don't condemn him for it. It is just the way things have worked out. Be courageous my dear.

Renate, I hope it's not too confusing for you. Perhaps you wonder whether you are German or English, Jewish or Christian but actually you are all of those things but more than anything else you are Renate, who is stronger because of everything that has happened to her. Remember, home is where you are and what you make of it.

Well, I'm feeling my age and I'm actually very sleepy. I hope that I can get this letter to you soon and that soon after that we can all meet again,

Your loving Mutti and Oma,
Clara Lehrs.

Then Kyla remembered. Singing with Mutti Lehrs and hearing her tell stories. Then that one particular afternoon when Mutti Lehrs had visitors –it snowed that day – was that the day when she wrote the letter? They'd been nice, the visitors and they'd helped Frau Lehrs tell her stories and they'd sung with her. Oh, and she remembered Mutti singing while she worked. The other children – she remembered playing with the other children. And Vati; she remembered Vati. He was such a nice Vati – full of laughter but strict and kind at the same time. Then he became so ill. Why did he have to become ill and leave them?

She couldn't stop them. The tears raced down her cheeks, yet as they did she began to feel lighter. As if someone had taken away the heavy luggage she'd been carrying.

"What's the matter? What did that letter say?" Nathaniel's eyes darted about as if he was looking for an answer to that question somewhere in the garage.

Kyla couldn't speak. She handed him the letter. As she watched him read she took her handkerchief out of her bag and tried to wipe away her tears but they still kept on coming.

Nathaniel shuffled from foot to foot as he read and kept running his hand through his hair. Finally he looked up at Kyla. "She must have been a really interesting lady, Mutti Lehrs." He sounded as if he had a lump of butter in his throat.

Kyla could only nod. The tears started coming faster again. Then Nathaniel was hugging her and she was hugging him back and she could tell as she held him that he was sobbing too. Her grown-up, manly little brother who had already had his Bar Mitzvah, who broke things by touching them, was sobbing about Mutti Lehrs, about their own Mutti and about the goodness and the badness of human beings.

Someone coughed. Kyla and Nathaniel broke apart. Nathaniel turned to face the wall.

Kyla could see that his shoulders were still going up and down. She turned to see who was there.

Herr Grünbaum was looking at them. "Have you found something of interest?"

She fumbled for her hanky again.

"I see you have." He pointed to the letter which was now lying on the floor. "Bring it into the house and I'll show you what else I've got. I've made the coffee."

Nathaniel turned round and nodded. His eyes were red.

Kyla wanted to speak but couldn't. All the effort of keeping control was making her throat sore.

Herr Grünbaum touched her arm and Nathaniel's back. He smiled. "Don't hide those tears on my account. There has to be tears. Tears are good."

They followed him, arms linked, into the house.

Glossary

Arbeit macht frei
Work makes you free. These words were displayed over the entrance to many of the concentration camps.

BDM
Bund Deutscher Mädel the girl's equivalent of the Hitler youth. It was compulsory for girls aged 14-18.

Blutschutz(gestez)
Blood protection (law). This aimed to protect Germans from contamination by Jewish blood

Dachfest
When the roof goes on to a new house a party is held in celebration.

Hilfsklasse
Special class. This was originally housed in the Waldorf School in Stuttgart but became independent even before the school was forced to close. Clara Lehrs agreed to host it in her home on Schellberg Street. It stayed there until it moved to bigger premises in the 1960s.

Ghettowache
A guard at the camp. Often these would be other Jews. There would also be military guards.

Goetheanum
The world centre for the anthroposophist movement. It is a very distinctive building as was the original. It is named after the German playwright Goethe.

Kaffetrinken
Drinking coffee in the afternoon. This is usually accompanied by delicious pastries.

Lebkuchen
A type of gingerbread, often covered with a thin layer of icing. A much harder version of this, **Printen,** exists around Cologne and Aachen.

Maultaschen
Large squares of stuffed pasta

Mischling
A child who has two Jewish grandparents. Renate Edler was a Mischling of the first order as she had two Jewish grandparents.

Nordbahnhof
The north station. Several transports left from this station in Stuttgart. It has now been shut down and a memorial has been built.

Oberleutnant
First Lieutenant

Oberst
A high military rank, similar to group captain or colonel

Obersturmführer
Lieutenant

Pumpernickel
Very dark rye bread

RAD
Short for Reichsarbeitsdienst – compulsory work experience for young men and women.

Romanisches Café
A well-known Berlin café, frequented by artists and writers. It had simple furniture and food. It had to shut down during the Nazi era. A Romanisches Café still exists in Berlin today though it is nothing like the one that Clara and her friends used to visit.

Shomer
A shomer would attend a Jewish wake and help watch over the corpse. The shomer's job is to protect the Jewish faith in all sorts of circumstances. Oddly, although Clara Lehrs had been Christian for some time she employed some of the Jewish rituals at her husband's funeral.

Schul
Within the Jewish community in Rexingen this was a mixture of

...essons and religious instruction.

...parkling dry white wine made by the champagne method

Spätzle
A think pasta made with egg

Sprudel / Sprudelwasser
Sparkling water

Stollen
A type of Christmas cake. It is a sweet bread, often moistened with alcohol, containing dried fruit and sometimes marzipan.

Sturmmann
A low rank in the SS. There is no equivalent in our army.

Tiergarten
Literally "animal garden". This is the name of the zoo in Berlin. It was designed in the 1830s and was in Berlin before many of the other green places in the city.

Wiener Kipferln
Small crescent-shaped vanilla-flavoured biscuits. These are usually eaten at Christmas.

Fact and Fiction in Clara's Story

We know very little about Clara's life. We have a few facts and figures about her birth and her family. Her son, Ernst Lehrs tells us something of her personality in his autobiography. No photos remain. The house on Schellberg Street still exists and a plaque outside it still says "Haus Lehrs". There is a "Stolperstein" in front of it. Stolpersteine – literally stumbling stones – stop you in your tracks and tell you you are near a Holocaust victim's house.

We know that she lived in Rexingen for a while and was transported to Theresienstadt and then Treblinka. For many years her immediate family thought she had been killed in Auschwitz. In researching for this book, we have been able to establish exactly where she lived in Rexingen and that on her transport paper from Theresienstadt to Treblinka they actually reverted to her correct name – Clara Lehrs instead of Klara Sarah Lehrs.

She did work at the Lauenstein. She did know Kurt and his carer, Sister Greta, and we have a few hints in Ernst's autobiography that this young man had an obsession with angels.

The house on Schellberg Street was built to accommodate students of the Waldorf School who needed to board. She raised some money towards it by selling her pearls. All of this is true. Some of the scenes from the Waldorf School are based on Deitrich Esterl's *Die Erste Waldrofschule* (Waldorf Press: 2006). (The first Waldorf School.)

We know that she offered her home to the Hilfsklasse (special class) after the Waldorf School was forced to close. It had already become independent from the Waldorf School. What happened there we can't be sure about but we do know that the school carried on without hesitating throughout World War II and after and that this is some sort of miracle. Children like those in the Hilfsklasse were as unwanted as the Jews. There is a certain irony in Clara hiding them.

Ernst Lehrs hints at her stubbornness and her bright sense of humour. An acquaintance relates that she was an optimistic person

...ouraged others. I have built on that extensively with that ...al writer's tool: the imagination. Clara has been an incredibly ...ce person to invent.

Selda, Kyla and Nathaniel are completely invented. Yet we know that Clara was Mutti Lehrs to all of the Waldorf School children who lodged with her. It's highly likely that she acquired this name again both in Rexingen and in the concentration camp.

The blurb for this book asks if her story is a tragedy. Had she been less optimistic and more selfish she may have left Germany in time. Are her unwavering faith in the goodness of human beings and her keen sense of humour then fatal flaws or are they in fact qualities that enhanced her life and helped her to encourage many others?